TORO!

AN ALLIE PARSONS NOVEL

Chris — I hope you enjoy Toro! ... Thanks so much for reading it. All the best

Frank C. Schwalbe

ISBN: 1500249394
ISBN 13: 9781500249397
Library of Congress Control Number: 2014911341
CreateSpace Independent Publishing Platform
North Charleston, South Carolina

CHAPTER ONE
NINE YEARS AGO

Allie Parsons couldn't have known.

That hot summer night, he strode confidently into the *Inferno*, the seedy Tampa strip club that Allie currently called home. Each step coincided perfectly with the beat of the strobe so that this swaggering behemoth appeared to glide, rather than walk like the other intoxicated and lumbering mortal men who were clearly his inferiors. Dressed in European cut designer clothes, with his thick black beard and with enough discretionary time to spend hours at the gym- all the girls dancing for their livelihood that night knew a guy like this could change their lives.

Drunk men disappeared into the shadows of the dark club as he passed but he didn't register their existence. His eyes fixed on Allie.

And she took notice.

The regulars with their foul beer breath and bad teeth would whistle, slur catcalls, or tuck puny tips into her g-string. But his eyes stared into her soul and called to her, conjuring images of power, strength and awe.

Between each boom of the bass and with every sweep of the spotlight, Allie searched for him. The raucous crowd cheered and clamored for her attention as she twisted and glided across the beer stained stage in her nude stilettos.

As usual, she had smoked pot and took a couple of shots of tequila before going on stage, so she couldn't think straight. But in those days, Allie was high more often than sober.

She knew so many creeps. But this guy, this man, dressed well and exuded confidence. His amazing muscular build looked powerful on his impressive tall frame. He towered above the other men. He wore distressed jeans with a tight, white, cotton shirt and brown leather boots that appeared made for him. And every time Allie saw him, his eyes followed her.

That is, when Allie could find him in the crowd.

The 'Toro Task Force' showed great interest in her description. After all, she remained the only living eyewitness of this brutal and powerful killer.

At that point, as Allie told an incredulous Officer Festoon of the Tampa PD, she felt she had nothing to fear. How could someone with eyes that glowed blue like Christmas lights under that thick black hair, be a monster?

But when she finished her shift, he had vanished. Allie faced another night alone.

At 1:30 AM Allie pushed aside the curtains and walked back to the dressing room. After tying her boot laces, she checked her makeup in the mirror. Her tan face looked tired and she worried about the wrinkles forming around her eyes and lips. She remembered her mother telling her that too much smoking would ruin her looks. I do look 30 instead of 24.

Leaning towards the mirror, Allie smoothed her long black hair that draped across her shoulder.

Out of nowhere, he appeared next to her neck, smiling and caressing her hair with a gentle touch. Allie jumped and gasped, drawing in his alluring musky scent.

She recognized him at once and turned towards him, too wasted to detect the danger.

"I could take you away from all this. Release your soul." His low voice resonated as he leaned against her shoulder, stroking her hair. "If you're not free, I'll see you some other time, Beautiful."

Allie picked up the joint she'd just rolled and took a long hit. She stared at him in the mirror. She found him seductive. He had all his teeth and his clothes were impeccable. He must be a man of the world, not like most of these local losers! She was so high.

And those eyes.

"First…" She pulled the joint away from her lips and held up her right pointer finger. "I gotta know your name."

"Call me Bull." He chuckled. "Just Bull. 'Cause I strong like bull." He spoke in a convincing Russian accent and drummed his chest.

"Bull." Allie giggled. "Bull. I like it. It's different."

But it couldn't be his place, she knew. Not on the first date with a guy from this club.

Going back to her place would be alright. Miss Mable would have the kids in bed and she knew she had an emergency plan in case this guy turned out to be some weirdo. She came from a good family and she knew she was smart, unlike the other stupid girls.

"Yeah, sure. But we go to my place. Follow me. What ya' got to party with?"

"More than you can handle." He winked and smiled.

They always underestimate me. She winked and smiled back then led him to the parking lot.

By the time she reached her apartment, a couple of shots of bourbon from the bottle beneath the driver's seat of her Honda and the rest of the joint had her pretty well lit. Bull parked next to her and grinned from his new Lexus sports car.

As they climbed the stairs to the second floor of the old brick Ybor City building, he gently touched her shoulder and smiled.

He smiles a lot. Allie smiled back again. Bull's a nice guy.

Allie unlocked the door quietly and let him in.

"What've you got?" She turned and closed the door.

Bull backhanded her across her cheek and knocked her into the flimsy kitchen table. Allie fell to the floor and smashed into the cabinets beneath the sink. Several glasses came crashing down onto her scalp.

"I've got you!" Bull's voice bellowed.

As Allie fought to clear her head, she stared up at the figure towering over her. The smile was long gone and his face was one menacing sneer with glowing, ice-cold, blue eyes.

"So beautiful." He sounded almost tender.

"Mommy?"

For a split second Bull turned his head to look back towards the tiny voice, but failed to locate its source.

Allie spotted her opening. With a lightning-like reflex, she kicked with all her might and caught him square across his knee with her boot heel.

Bull roared in pain and Allie commando-crawled across the linoleum to the carpet. She sprang to her feet and dashed to a 10' tall bookshelf.

With an athletic leap and reach, she knocked the tattered Hawthorne, Hardy, and Miller paperbacks off the top shelf, sending them tumbling to the floor. She gripped the Smith and Wesson .38 snub nose revolver that had lain hidden by her favorite authors and whipped it around just as she landed back on her feet. Her finger found the trigger and she swung the gun to chest level.

Bull was waiting for her.

Allie saw only the silver streak of the hunting knife as the sharp, serrated blade cut across her cheek and cleaved it to the bone. Fat, blood and bone tissue tore from her face and splattered across the far wall.

Allie felt a searing pain in her left eye and suddenly couldn't see the right side of his twisted face. He caught the wrist that held her gun hand and squeezed it tightly.

Bull smiled and his lips formed a cruel smirk.

"I absolutely love the devil tattoo on your neck, Allie Parsons." Bull's hot, humid breath expanded deeply and descended down her ear canal, filling it with a tight, putrid pressure. "You are my little priestess."

Allie strained against him and gasped for breath, sucking in his animal scent.

"You've read about zombies and vampires, they're nothing compared to what's coming for man. We are as old as Methuselah."

"Aagh!" Allie kicked and spat and fought and pushed and gouged with every bit of strength she possessed. Bull slashed with the hunting knife and squeezed her right arm like a vice. Allie caught the sharp blade with her small hand and bare fingers as it flashed past her face, just before it sank into her chest.

"Mommy!" The plaintive cry emerged from a darkened doorway.

"What? You have a child?" He spat in Allie's face.

Allie drove her knee into his chest and knock him off-balance.

Bull's eyes grew wide. The veins in his head and neck bulged. He shoved her arm with the pistol into the wall. Her fingers tightened and the trigger slid back. Two shots erupted with a deafening bang and Allie smelled gunpowder.

The bulldog from Miss Mable's apartment next door howled.

Bull shoved Allie violently against the wall as he backed towards her door.

"Mommy!" It was her daughter.

Allie's head smashed against a sturdy stud in the cheap wall and she felt a jolt of pain. "Chrystal! Get Luke! Run!"

Her own words sounded far away and Bull's face faded as she lost consciousness.

"Remember me." She heard him speak as her eyes closed. His voice rumbled like thunder. "I'll return. Druden demands your death. I'm Toro."

CHAPTER TWO
PRESENT DAY

Allie's elation spread from her heart to her head. She felt a warm rush of energy and happiness, more exhilarating than any drug she'd ever taken. Making the moment even better was that her AM radio received a strong signal. With her windows down and a hot wind billowing in her hair, Allie sang at the top of her lungs and hummed to 60's music as she whipped around the retirees in their shiny, new Cadillacs.

She dodged the last remnants of rush hour traffic and veered off a familiar I-75 exit ramp. A ways off, but within striking distance of the Honda, she saw the spire of her church.

Awesome! Even if the engine gave out here, I'd coast down the ramp and could walk. Allie knew this for certain because the engine quit working six months and a transmission ago at this exact spot and by hoofing it in her cheap but comfortable flat shoes, she made it to the doors only 20 minutes late for the service.

But today the pistons continued to hammer and the old tires turned. The check engine light flickered as she pulled into the church parking lot.

I thought that thing was burned out. Allie killed the engine and it knocked a couple of times before dying with a terminal groan and a puff of smoke.

She peered through the dirty windshield and searched the parking lot for her daughter, as the pinging and dinging of her car faded.

Where is she? Allie huffed and scanned her surroundings.

In her excitement, all Allie wanted was to hug Chrystal. Oh, come on, Chrystal. I'm not that late. Where are you?

Several preteen girls trickled from the brick building and found their parents in their shiny SUV's. The after school youth group had adjourned, from the looks of things.

Allie grabbed her phone and texted her daughter, "I'm here. Love."

Chrystal texted back, "Lot by the gym."

Allie sighed. She'd forgotten Chrystal asked to be picked up in the rear of the church in a parking lot seldom used.

She turned the key and gnashed her teeth as the Honda went through its usual shimmying, shaking and popping. Allie relaxed her lips and smiled. After 200,000 miles, she could excuse the old car as long as it started.

Allie strained her biceps and forced the steering wheel around. The car limped across the bumpy lot and towards the back of the church.

She caught sight of her daughter's thin frame towering over Pastor Virgil. His rusted Saturn sat in the handicapped spot. The cracks in the pavement were filled with tall grass and several seasons of stray pine straw lay scattered across the faded yellow stripes.

Allie decided to let the engine run, because the loud start-ups embarrassed Chrystal. She stopped next to Virgil's car and waved.

"Chrystal, Pastor Virgil, I did it! I finished my last day of med school!" Allie beamed as she yelled through her open window.

Her door flew open with a shriek. Allie leaped out of the old car and scooped Chrystal up, turning circles in the parking lot.

"I know! 'Bout time. How long did it take ya'?" Virgil's raspy voice cracked. He smiled as he watched Allie and Chrystal embrace. Despite his recent weight loss, his cheeks still appeared plump and rosy. Bright white hair poked out of either side of his bald head. "Ten years or something?"

"No, Virgil. Four, like everybody else." She laughed then released Chrystal and squeezed Virgil's stiff shoulders before giving him a quick kiss on his forehead. His face turned beet red and he massaged his scalp where she'd delivered the kiss. "And I graduated before the world ended."

"Tease me if you will, but the apocalypse is not far off. We are circling downward. 'When the Lamb opened the second seal,'" Virgil raised his index finger towards the sky, "'I heard the second living creature say, Come and see! Then another horse came out, a fiery red one. Its rider was given power to take peace from the earth and to make men slay each other. To him was given a large sword.'" Virgil's lips broke into a rare, spontaneous smile. He returned Allie's hug, though it was as awkward and hasty as his grin. "Revelation 6:3-4. But good for you, Sweetheart. I'm proud of you,"

"Way to go, Mom! That's awesome!" Chrystal gave Allie an energetic fist-bump.

"When do you start your new job?" Virgil's smile faded and his face returned to its regular stern countenance.

"I start with the medical examiner, Dr. Mann, in the morgue tomorrow. He wants me on the job early, so I'm ready to go." Allie looked down and kicked a small rock.

"That's great, Honey, but no break?"

"No, Virgil." Allie shook her head. "No break. But you know, I'd rather just jump in. I'm really nervous, but I think it would be worse having to wait."

"Who'd you say you're workin' with?" Virgil furrowed his eyebrows and squinted.

"Dr. Mann. In the morgue."

"Leopold Mann?"

"Yeah." Allie crossed her arms and tilted her head. "Don't tell me you've heard of him?"

Virgil narrowed his eyes until they were slits and pursed his lips. "Sure have. Ran across him years ago when all this Toro business was so bad. What an arrogant ass! Sorry, Chrystal."

"I'm okay." Chrystal blushed and looked down at her shoes.

He shook his head in disgust. "I tried to get some information from him about those murders, because so many of our congregation wanted to know. But he sat behind his desk like it was a throne, and he preached to me about the sanctity of the law. Listen, Honey, as a preacher, I know when I'm being preached to. I just had to tell him that there are evil forces at work in this world and it may end soon--"

"I've heard stories about him from people at school."

Virgil opened his mouth. "The world—"

"Dr. Mann is famous, but everybody says he's a real pill. I've been studying my tail off to impress him."

Virgil stood with his jaw squared and his hands planted on the waist of his baggy khakis. Allie had become familiar with the patches of failing fabric in the cuffs and pockets. Long ago, she became convinced he only owned one pair of pants.

"The world is coming to an end! Don't let that man get to you, Allie! Stand up to him and be strong. You will defeat evil, whereas he is sure to fail."

"Virgil--"

"I don't think 'Judgment Day' will be kind to that arrogant--"

"Virgil!" Allie glanced towards Chrystal.

"'Judgment Day' will not be kind to him." Virgil nodded, having said his piece.

"Actually, I'm sort of sick to my stomach, Virgil, so I really do want to go ahead and start so I can deal with him. I need this."

"Mom's worried she's going to pass out when she sees her first body in the morgue!" Chrystal teased, the bright red of her cheeks now fading.

"Chrystal, I'm not!" Allie suppressed a smile and shook her head.

"Yes, you are, Mom. You said so."

"Fine. Maybe a little. Maybe. It would be humiliating."

"You almost fainted in Anatomy."

"Okay. I confess. It's hard for me. But I'll be fine."

"Of course, you will." Virgil patted Allie on the shoulder. "You're tough and strong, Allie. Keep your faith. People foretold you'd drop out of medical school and you finished despite them. Didn't you?"

Allie nodded and sighed.

"Honey, you just show any doubters that they're wrong again."

"Hey, I'm up for another fight." Allie smiled and held her fists up in her best boxer stance.

"Oh, dear Lord!" Virgil shook his bald head. "Please don't knock anyone out! There's been so many."

"I'll be fine. I can do this...So, are the treatments still going okay?" Allie relaxed and changed the subject.

"I'm doing well. Chemo ain't easy, but I do what I gotta' do. Have you heard from your Mama? Didn't know if she'd call you on this special day or not."

Allie crossed her arms and looked down at the cracked asphalt. "She'll call me if she wants to know. To be honest, I don't think she cares." She sighed and for a second no one spoke. "But you know, it's fine. I've moved on. Everyone has to make choices."

"She's a hard, difficult woman." Virgil shook his head. "Don't worry, you know she never liked me neither and she's one of the main reasons I ain't the primary preacher in this church no more. People think I'm crazy...But anyway, this is your blessed day. Bask in it. Enjoy the moment."

"I will, Pastor. I feel free. For the first time in a long time, I feel free."

CHAPTER THREE
NINE YEARS AGO

"Luke's dead!"

Allie's head throbbed as she fought through her drug-induced fog. She opened her eyes and could barely make out the frail form of her mother. A flimsy nylon curtain acted as a door in the tiny room. She heard repetitive, plaintive cries for 'help', the jangle of a stretcher being rolled and someone yelling, "Get vitals on the seizing guy in room one!"

The high-pitched beeping from above grew faster as her vision cleared. Allie glanced down and saw a thin, crisp, white sheet covering her from collarbones to ankles. It felt cool and coarse against her legs.

Allie raised her arm to scratch her eye, still lost in a haze. She decided she couldn't find her face in her stunned state and dropped her arms by her sides. The stretcher squeaked.

"I'm in a hospital." She groaned and tried to open her eyes.

"Luke's dead! Why is he dead, Allie?"

Her mother's voice? How? Why?

"My head is killing me." Allie moaned and rubbed the back of her neck.

"Listen, you little slut!" Her mother shrieked. She stood up suddenly and grabbed Allie by the collar of the hospital gown. "My grandson is dead and you owe me some answers!"

Allie felt her mother's hands clamp on her shoulders, shaking her like a dirty rug. "Who killed him? Did you kill him? Was it you?"

Through her blurry vision, Allie could tell her mother's black hair was tussled and she wasn't wearing makeup. Allie couldn't remember ever seeing her without makeup.

Her mother retreated and pulled her purse close to her thin body. Despite her stupor, Allie saw drops of fresh red blood on her mother's otherwise pristine white sleeve.

Allie lifted her trembling hand to her cheek until her palm slid through a warm, thick liquid. Her fingers probed beneath the saturated gauze covering her eye socket. As she rotated her arm, a flap of skin lifted from her cheek.

Allie touched bone.

Instantly, she felt agonizing pain. She jerked her hand away.

"That will scar! It will at least be a physical scar you will remember. Your eye is gone. You will remember that, at least!" Her mother's voice trembled and her eyes moistened.

"Luke's dead?"

"Yes! He was shot in the head! Shot in the head! They found a gun in your hand. Do you hear me? Are you listening? Your son is dead!"

"Dead?" Allie's world spun out of control. This must be a nightmare; a really bad trip, like her friends talked about.

"Yes!" Her mother hissed. "Look at you. You don't even care!"

"No, no, no! Where is Chrystal? Is she safe?"

"I've taken her. She's going to live with me. I'm her mother now! She's my daughter now! Allie Florence, the only thing you deserve is jail. And this time I won't hire a lawyer for you and you'll stay there."

Allie wanted out of this nightmare. Her head pounded and she longed to close her eyes and curl up under a warm blanket with her two beautiful children, instead of shivering beneath this cold, thin sheet.

She heard the tinny sound of curtain rings sliding across the rod.

"Knock, knock." A tired, young, female voice interrupted them.

"I'm Dr. Martin. Good, she's awake." Her words came in rapid-fire succession as Dr. Martin jotted on her clipboard. "Anyway, Mrs. Parsons, Allie's CT showed a small subdural bleed. Meaning, she's bled inside her skull, but outside the base of her brain, because of the blow she took when the assailant assaulted her. She has a substantial concussion. She'll need a few days before the police question her. These concussions can be tricky. Let's let the brain heal. Allie, the ophthalmologist will be here soon and try to save your eye."

Beatrice Parsons lowered her head and pursed her thin lips. "Let them question her now. She's fine."

"Good, then..." Dr. Martin hesitated, closed her mouth and tilted her head. "I'm sorry. You want them to question her now?"

"Yes. She's ready. Get some answers. Please, get some answers about how this happened. She needs to tell them what happened to my grandchildren. Luke is dead!"

The doctor folded her arms and closed her white lab coat across her wrinkled, green scrubs. "I understand you're upset, Mrs. Parsons. But really, Allie needs rest."

"She's awake. Look at her. She's awake. Ask her anything you need to." Her mother sniffed and Allie could tell she was crying. "There's no concussion. She's stoned again."

"Yes, Allie is awake, but she's far from okay, Ma'am. She needs to get in the OR very soon and then she's going to the ICU."

"I don't give you permission to repair that cut nor permission to fix her eye. She's had this coming for years!" Her mother sputtered and wiped her eyes. "I refuse. Send that eye doctor away."

"But we have to bring her in. She's an excellent eye surgeon." The doctor raised her hands and her mouth fell open in disbelief. "She's going to try and save Allie's eye. Don't you understand how serious this is?"

"Then clean it out and bandage it. Put some tape on it until she talks! Do you hear me?"

Bea snatched her purse and stood up. She threw another glance towards Allie and whipped the curtain to the side. Allie could hear her mother's heels clicking down the hall.

CHAPTER FOUR
PRESENT DAY

Chrystal wrinkled her nose and squinted as Allie and Virgil spoke. She was already taller than Allie and thin as a rail, with pale skin and blonde hair. Because of her gaunt appearance, she could have walked the runways in Paris.

"Okay. What's wrong, Chrystal? I'm guessing it's the car."

"Mom, please turn it off. You're going to make me nauseated with all that exhaust." As she spoke, Chrystal covered her nose with the sleeve of her pink Lacoste shirt. "It stinks really bad."

"Alright, but it will backfire and smell when I turn it on again. That makes you gag. Which would you prefer?"

"That we buy a new car."

"Not happening."

"Carly's mom bought a new car and she said it was really inexpensive. And you've got this great job now." As she spoke, Chrystal lowered her arm from her nose. Too much makeup for a 12 year-old, but Allie decided not to start that argument again.

"It couldn't be as inexpensive as nothing. And nothing is exactly what my monthly payments are right now."

Virgil tussled Chrystal's hair. "What's in a car anyway, Miss Chrystal? Just supposed to get you from one place to another. Look at mine. It's about to fall apart, but it's all I need. And there's not a lot of time left for this world of ours anyway. Revelation says *Look, I'm coming soon! My reward is with me, and I'll give to everyone according to what they have done."*

"Pastor Virgil, did you know some cars have leather seats and air conditioning. Imagine that! Air conditioning is this amazing invention that cools air. And it doesn't use ice cubes from a fast food drink." Chrystal stomped her foot and crossed her arms.

Allie couldn't help but laugh.

"We don't have air conditioning." Chrystal threw her arms in the air. "Really! We live in Tampa, Florida where it's hot 500 days a year! Carly's car even has a TV. Some cars have satellite radio, but I'm listening to Sports Talk Radio on AM. Why, Pastor Virgil?"

"Tell me. Why do you listen to sports talk radio, Chrystal?"

"Not because I'm a Bucs fan! I listen to sports talk radio, because-get this- because it's the only station that broadcasts words we can understand."

"She's embarrassed because her friends tease her." Allie chuckled and rolled her eyes. "But I've got a great station going now."

"Is it in English?"

"Get in the car, you ungrateful knucklehead."

"Mom, I'm being so serious." Chrystal slumped her shoulders and shook her head. "Please, don't laugh at me!"

"My laughing stops now." Allie watched her daughter hoist her oversized backpack from beside Virgil's rusty car. "I won't laugh anymore."

"Thank you, for being such a kind, caring mother. I'm not being sarcastic, so don't yell at me."

"Say goodbye to Pastor Virgil."

"Bye, Pastor Virgil. See you next week," Chrystal heaved her full backpack over her shoulder and lugged it to the Honda.

"Bye, Honey. Thanks for coming today. Congratulations, Allie."

Chrystal opened the squeaky door and threw her backpack in the rear seat where it landed with a solid 'thump'. Allie sat behind the wheel and slammed her door.

"This is so not fair." Chrystal pouted as she sat in the front passenger seat and shut the door. "So not fair."

"But you're funny."

"Please, don't tease me, Mom."

Virgil waved as Allie drove the noisy car from the parking lot.

"Thanks, Virgil! Okay, Chrystal, what is not fair?"

"Where should I start?" She sat turned away from Allie with her arms crossed.

"Start at the beginning, a very good place to start."

"Mom, no cliché's!"

"So, I shouldn't say, fair is a place you go to get cotton candy?"

"No."

"I'm sorry. I know I've promised not to do that. No clichés. No puns. So. How should we discuss this then?"

"Let's not!"

"How about a different approach? What's the first thing that comes to mind when you think 'not fair'." Allie attempted to honk at a black Mercedes that cut her off, but her horn was still out of commission.

"Okay..." Chrystal fished a small paperback book from her backpack. "Well, for one thing, we're going to our house which is a dorm. It is a one bedroom, one bathroom dorm with a living area that doubles as a dining room and kitchen." She zipped the backpack. "Why can't we live in a real house that has a real yard and some rooms? I want my own bedroom. I don't like the shared bedroom. Now that you have an awesome new job, can we please move?"

"It's loud in this car, Honey." Allie yelled over the turbulent wind blowing into the lowered windows. "Please, speak up."

"Fine!" Chrystal gritted her teeth and turned her head slightly towards Allie. "It is...it is a one bedroom...really, can we please move?"

"Well, since I'll be a new medical resident at the university and we still have no money, we have to make do with what the university offers." Allie continued to shout as she turned the wheel and flew past another slow car. "You do have a bedroom."

"We share it! Just because you sleep on the couch doesn't mean it's my bedroom."

Allie jerked the Honda into the middle lane. "No. Well, anyway it's not a dorm. It's graduate student housing which is completely different. Honey, is there anyone to your right?"

Chrystal peeked over her shoulder. "No. But Mom, it's a dorm for people who are like 20 or 30. Please. I live in a dorm and I'm only 12 years old. And to make it that much worse, I live in a boring dorm with people who are actually serious about studying."

"Thanks. That's a blind spot. But that's good, because you apply yourself and get good grades." Allie slipped into the right lane.

"I get good grades so I'll be able to go to a great college and get out of this place!"

"I'm okay with the fact that you want to better yourself and leave me. Maybe it's not fair that you live in a dorm. There are worse places that people live. When I get out of residency we'll live in a nice apartment or home. What about a condo at the beach?"

"How long?"

"Five or six years. And then, out of university housing and living at the beach."

"Hopefully, I'll be in college and in a different dorm. That means, I'll have spent all my life that I can remember in a dorm. It doesn't sound like a good thing to me."

"Okay, Chrystal. Listen. Roll up your window so I don't have to yell."

"But it gets so hot."

"Just for a second, please."

Chrystal rolled her eyes, huffed and rolled up her window. Although the old car still rattled, at least Allie could hear.

"Dr. Mann said he could see me presenting lectures overseas." Allie lowered her voice. "He's given speeches in London and Paris.

It's a great opportunity. He said he could arrange for you to be there, too. That's something nice to think about. It could be the two of us... in Europe."

"That would be great, Mom." Chrystal sighed. She opened her mouth and then closed it. She turned towards Allie. "I'm glad you finished medical school and got this job. I'm very proud of you."

"Thank you. I appreciate that." Allie smiled and tightened her grip on the steering wheel. "See. We're working through this. What's the next thing that's not fair?"

"Can we just be quiet for a while? I don't want to talk about it."

"I understand, but you have to."

"Why, Mom? I don't want to say anything hurtful."

"Because I'm your mother and it'll break my heart if we don't talk about this. I promise we'll only cover two things that are unfair tonight. I won't ask you about anything more until next week."

"I really don't want to talk about it."

"Does it have to do with a boy?"

"No!"

"Good, because there are no boys good enough for you."

"Mom, that's stupid."

"It's true, though."

"I just want to read my book." Chrystal opened the tattered book at a folded down page and started to read.

"What are you reading?"

"*The Scarlet Letter*. It's by Nathaniel Hawthorne".

"Where did you get it?"

"Mrs. Blake gave it to me. It's extra credit for English."

"I doubt she gave you that. She would never offer that book to a 12 year old student."

"Yes, she did." Chrystal's voice faltered and she stared down at the small paperback she held. "No, sorry. She didn't. But I really love it."

"You're very young to be reading that book."

"I know, but I really like it, Mom."

"Chrystal, you're very smart and very mature. But you have to promise me, if I let you read that, we need to discuss it. Let's talk about what it means and what it meant to his readers when he wrote it."

"Okay. I didn't know you'd heard of it."

"Yeah, well, I have bright spots in my past, too."

Except for the occasional pops from under the Honda's hood, they rode the next five miles towards the university in utter silence.

"Mom, I don't have a place to have my birthday party!" Chrystal closed the book with a loud snap.

"I thought we were going to have it at the university pool?"

"No." Chrystal groaned and slumped in her seat. "Nobody will come. I mean, oh, *my God.*"

"Don't use that language."

"Sorry. I mean, this is so embarrassing. I'm turning 13 and nobody is going to come to a birthday party at that pool." Her eyes started to tear and her voice quivered.

"It's nice."

"It's a hideous place. It's dirty and messy and so crowded. I have it there every year, Mom! It's like something little kids do." Chrystal cringed and swung her book towards her nose so that the sketch of Nathaniel Hawthorne on the back cover hid her face.

"Chrystal, Honey, we don't have a lot of money."

"Mom, please."

"How about at the park? We can cut out decorations and play--"

"No." Chrystal threw the book into her lap.

"A park at the beach."

"No."

Allie sighed. "Church?"

"No."

"Where would you like to have it, then?"

"The Tampa Country Club would work." Chrystal looked towards Allie with her eyes wide open and eyebrows raised.

"Where Carly had hers?" Allie's voice rose and she squinted as she glanced at Chrystal.

"Yeah."

"Only...they're members and we're not."

"Can't we become members?"

"No. We cannot become members."

"Why, Mom?"

"Because you don't just become members of a country club. It's very complicated, and expensive."

"Grandmother will pay for it, if I ask."

"That's not going to happen! *End of story.*" Allie punched the steering wheel.

"Fine. Then, I won't have a party."

"Chrystal, you should have a party."

"Why?"

"Because it's your 13th birthday and you should do something with your friends."

"I really don't want one. I'd rather just forget it."

"Okay, we'll drop the subject now and come back to it later."

"We can do that." Chrystal pulled her book close to her face. "I won't talk about it then either. I'm not having a party. *End of story.*" Chrystal punched the dashboard, blushed and looked away.

"Okay."

"Fine, then."

They rode along in silence.

"Chrystal..."

"I really want to read, Mom."

"Okay."

Allie looked out the window and changed radio stations. The static of a special tune caught her ear. She turned up the volume and softly hummed along with a disco song from the 70's. As the song grew louder, Allie tapped the wheel with her hands and sang a couple of lyrics.

"Come on, Chrystal. You love this one. Honestly, we may be out of range in a few seconds so it's now or never. Please, help me out. We have awesome harmony."

"Mom, that's stupid."

"Really, Honey. It's my last day of med school. There's a good station on the radio. And you love this dorky song. Please. For your nervous mother who's about to start being a doctor. We make an incredible team, just the two of us."

At first, Chrystal moved her head closer to her book. After a second, she looked up. "Don't worry, Mom. You won't faint. You'll do great for that mean guy."

"Thanks, Sweetie. I love you. Thanks for being behind me all these years. I know it hasn't been easy."

"Sure. No problem." Chrystal looked in Allie's eyes and touched her hand on the steering wheel.

Allie smiled then bobbed her head, looked around the highway and sang a few more lines.

Chrystal's lips began to move. Slowly, the volume of her voice rose, and after a few seconds, they had a nice duet going. Allie sang her lungs out with the red and orange sunset in the rear view mirror.

All of a sudden, Allie fell silent and stretched her neck to look in the rearview mirror again. The sun was hidden behind a cloud, so she could see the traffic behind her.

"What's wrong, Mom? You love this part."

"That black Mercedes has been following us a long time. He cut me off earlier...never mind." She narrowed her eyes, raised her chin and surveyed the scene again. "It's gone. Alright, Chrystal... *big finish!*"

A few minutes later, they pulled into the crowded, asphalt parking lot of their dorm. Allie managed to find a parking space near the squat, white, two story, cinder block building. A fine example of 60's Brutalism, it had the look of an old roadside hotel that needed painting.

Allie turned off the car and the engine sputtered a few knocks and pings before quitting. Chrystal unbuckled her seatbelt and reached for her backpack. "Mom, why does Pastor Virgil keep talking about the end of the world? Everyone thinks he's crazy."

Allie sighed and pushed hard on her car door. "He started that about nine years ago, Honey. He's always been kind to us and he's an honest man. Maybe he's eccentric. Anyway, I love him even if other people don't."

"I'm glad they let him stay around."

"Yeah, me too, Sweetie. He literally built that church."

"Yeah. He showed me."

Chrystal lugged her heavy backpack up the stairs as Allie struggled to juggle her books and keys. Out of the corner of her eye, Allie thought she saw a large black sedan turn the corner.

Allie turned to look. "Is that the same car...."

There was no large black sedan in the parking lot.

"It must have been my imagination."

CHAPTER FIVE
PRESENT DAY

Despite the sauna-like Tampa summer outside, the cold, dry air inside the modern, concrete morgue tickled the hairs on Allie's arm and the pervasive smell of formaldehyde flourished in the sterile corridors.

Allie walked quickly down the vault-like halls, with the white-haired Dr. Leopold Mann. They seemed oblivious to the chemical odor as he continued to quiz Allie.

"And, uhm, of course there are Café au lait spots." Allie toyed with the buttons on her lab coat and cleared her throat.

"You're correct." Dr. Mann stroked his salt and pepper beard and picked up his already brisk pace. "You've studied since our interview. Few residents give me all the diagnostic criteria of Neurofibromatosis. Apparently, you've applied yourself. I'm glad to see it."

Allie opened her mouth to speak.

"But you need to answer faster! I expect much more from my residents."

Despite his thick German accent, Allie had no trouble understanding him.

"I really want to do well. I try to keep up with my reading, Sir, although my grades could have been better." Allie blinked and her right eye closed completely, but her left eyelid did not cover her artificial eye.

"Then improve. I'm always eager to be impressed."

"I'll try."

"Not good enough!" Mann paused at a pair of swinging doors labeled 'AUTHORIZED ENTRY ONLY'. Allie noticed a hand written sign above the doorway. In large red, block letters it read, 'Abandon Hope, All Ye Who Enter Here'.

Allie sighed. This is my final hope. "I'm sorry, Doctor Mann, I don't follow you."

"This isn't kindergarten, Doctor. We no longer do our best and then pat ourselves on the back." He paused and looked down at her. "We succeed."

"I'll try... I'll succeed, Sir."

"You'll succeed or you'll not be here long." He held the doors open for her, but she stopped short of crossing the threshold. "Of course, that's one of the main reasons I chose you out of all the resident applicants. I'm not exaggerating when I say that there were more excellent candidates this year than ever. Molly, who was number one in your class, really coveted this spot."

"I feel I can do well in this assignment. But I'm not at the top of my class."

"But you work hard and adapt, I'll grant you. If you excel in my program, then you will be very successful. By successful, I mean presenting lectures in Las Vegas, New York, London and Paris. All places I've been in the last year. Do you see the importance of all this?"

"I do, Dr. Mann." Allie slid both hands into her lab coat pockets.

"Are you sure?" Mann narrowed his eyes and stared at her. "Because, I need to be assured that you are driven."

Allie swallowed and cleared her throat. "I am."

"There's no turning back." Mann nodded and his white hair bounced. "No turning back. Just move through this passage and you will embark on a most important journey."

Allie exhaled and took a tentative step forward. She looked up, eyed the threshold and felt as if she was drifting on a boat as she passed beyond the secure doors.

Mann released the doors and they swung solidly shut behind him.

"You'll need to prove your worth, Dr. Parsons. You're now a member of a select group."

"I'll try…" Allie gnashed her teeth and shook her head, "I mean, I'll do it, Sir."

"Listen carefully. I'm going to a conference in London tonight, which will put Byron in charge of the morgue. I realize I'm leaving soon after you start, but you'll be expected to respond to the challenge. Make sure all the autopsy reports are completed and ready for my signature. Do you understand?"

"Yes."

"I expect perfection." Mann marched down the hall with Allie trailing. "Now, be forewarned. The body before us is very decomposed. I hope you won't faint." He nodded his head and smiled as if talking to a child. "You see, this happens with some inexperienced residents."

Allie paused.

Mann continued a few feet beyond her, then stiffened. He stopped and looked back. "Are you quite alright?"

"Yes." Allie shoved her hands further into her pockets. "I'm a doctor."

"Of course."

Allie took a deep breath and moved towards him. After a few strides, she was by his side.

"Now, here is the second part of my instructions." He jabbed his finger towards Allie. "Realize that, although, we study specimens under microscopes, we are under microscopes ourselves. You are not to go to a crime scene until I'm back. Do you understand?"

"Yes. I'll be ready," Allie gulped as she gazed at the ceiling and austere walls. "I promise. I'll do all that is expected of me. This position means a lot."

"I have to warn you, Doctor. This is an especially challenging assignment. You will be expected to understand my instructions quickly and contribute immediately. We're a busy department with enormous accountability. If you can't keep up, you'll be replaced."

"Thank you...We both thank you." Allie looked down at her feet and shuffled.

"We?"

"Oh. My daughter, Chrystal, and I thank you."

"Well then, make sure neither of you do anything to lose it."

As they passed into the next room, the rapping of their heels on the shiny, waxed floor echoed off the walls and down the long empty hall.

Mann paused in front of two more heavy metal doors. A corkboard to the left was plastered with multicolored flyers that advertised apartments for rent or 'cats free to a good home'. There was one dog missing.

"I'm told you have a passion, and someone told me you're as smart as the devil."

"Well." Allie shrugged and raised her dark eyebrows. "Uhm. Thank God for that, I guess." She turned her gaze back towards him and smiled.

"Thank God? No. I think you are responsible." Mann swung the door open. "Yes, you're responsible, Dr. Parsons. God has no role here. Science, facts and results are our trinity."

"After what I've been through, I can't take credit for being here."

"Interesting. Explain."

Allie raised her eyebrows and opened her mouth. "Uhm..." She tilted her head and stood up straight. "I have to give God the credit."

"And yet, you have a demon tattooed on your neck?"

"It's a long story." Without thinking, she ran a finger along her scarred cheek. "Really, nobody wants to hear it."

"Perhaps the short version?"

"Maybe some other time. I'm eager for you to show me what's behind those doors."

Mann paused and scratched his bearded chin. He rested his index finger on the clean-shaven skin beneath his nose and looked at her face.

"Doctor. You're an enigma. Over the years, I've developed a talent at assembling small details into a large picture. You have multiple old piercings throughout the cartilage of your ears."

He raised his chin and extended his index finger to touch her lobes. "Yet, today you wear two simple pearls."

Allie flinched. Mann pulled his hand away, but continued to study her.

"You have a heavily scarred face and an artificial eye. Multiple tattoos. One of which is a demon. Your clothes are from a discount rack. You act and speak as if you're 50 years old, but I know you're 33. You're unlike any resident I've worked with before."

Allie squared her jaw and nodded. She tilted her head. "I have a history."

Mann paused, then smiled as he waved off Allie's statement. "No matter." He shook his head. "Alright, then. Our first case is waiting for us. Let's go in and you tell me what you think. You'll like this. You can put all your recent hours of reading to good use."

"Finding the cause of death?" Allie exhaled and relaxed her shoulders.

"No. That's pretty clear, Dr. Parsons. It's finding the killer. Byron... He's my assistant...Byron, we're ready!"

Dr. Mann flung open the final door and motioned with his head for Allie to follow him. As she stepped into the refrigerated room, Allie felt chilled to her core.

The formaldehyde smell in the dissection room was overwhelming. It stung her nose and condensed at the base of her tongue to produce a dull, sour taste. Her eye oozed warm tears as she endured the sting of the cold air and aerosolized preservatives.

In front of her stood a sturdy, shiny, stainless steel table, about the height of a pool table. The flat surface slanted gradually towards a drain at one end. Once the autopsy was complete, Allie knew that hosing the table down would send rivulets of water, blood, tissue and other fluids off the sleek surface and down the pipes.

A cadaver lay on top of the table. The victim had pale skin and appeared short and stout, the significant fat of his belly leaned slightly to the left. Allie couldn't really guess his age because the front of his head was missing. What should have been his face, resembled raw hamburger. The remainder of his head was hairless.

The corpse exhibited extensive decomposition. Skin peeled and hung from his hands like black and violet tinged tissue paper and a minute amount remained attached to the fat on his abdomen. The entire scene reminded Allie of a macabre Halloween display.

"It's easy to see the cause of death."

"If you say so." Allie gulped and turned pale.

"Yes, of course. Shotgun blast to the head." Dr. Mann stepped towards the corpse, turning his back to Allie. "But what we really want to discover is who is responsible for his death...who shot this victim."

Allie's heart raced and her head spun. I'm responsible. Luke's dead! It should have been me on that steel table.

CHAPTER SIX
NINE YEARS AGO

After fitful nightmares filled with serrated, jagged blades and bullets that flew randomly and killed innocent children without remorse, she would awake in the ICU to his wrinkled face, bald head and sparkling blue eyes.

During her time in the hospital, Virgil didn't talk much. He simply asked if she needed anything then called the nurse for ice chips. Virgil tenderly brushed the hair away from the still unclosed wound on her face. The laceration remained raw, bloody, and ragged. Like a canyon, it cut deep.

In her delirium, she heard him saying, "Oh, Allie. What is His plan? Why does this concern you? I don't understand."

She opened her eyes in a sudden rush of panic.

Except for the beeping, and red and green lights of the monitor, she was alone.

The next day he held her hand and she knew he was there again.

"Luke?" It all had to be a bad dream. She needed to hold her son.

Virgil lowered his head and spoke in a soft, gravelly voice. "He's gone, Child. He's with God. An innocent victim. It's not your fault, Sweetheart."

"Gone?" Allie couldn't catch her breath. She broke into a cold sweat and her entire body shook. "No. Virgil, please tell me he's okay! I'm dreaming. Tell me it was a bad trip, please!"

Virgil leaned over and held her trembling hand. "You need to let Luke go. He's with God, now. Let's go say goodbye."

Virgil pushed Allie in a wheelchair down to the hospital morgue.

There, as her son lay on a cold steel table covered in a coarse, thin, white sheet, she said 'goodbye'. Virgil held her hand as she cried.

She stroked Luke's blonde hair, touched her finger to his cold cheek and shivered uncontrollably. Allie sobbed for hours and didn't know how her heart could continue to beat against the pain and pressure in her chest.

It was all a blur.

The next Sunday, Virgil missed the church service to sit with her and talked about how nice it would be at Clearwater Beach. The aqua Gulf of Mexico was still smooth even though fall was approaching.

Allie lay in silence. For long stretches, she wanted to shrink into the smallest dot possible and then blink out of existence.

At times, they sat in the room and said nothing. Virgil was very comfortable with the silence. As Allie's brain healed from the injury, she alternated between sleeping and crying. Frequently, after waking from a bad dream, Virgil would help her face her real nightmare.

Several weeks after Luke's death, her mother delivered a thick stack of legal papers. As Allie attempted to read through the legal lingo, Beatrice, in a stern voice, explained that she intended to acquire permanent custody of Chrystal. Chrystal was with her now. Chrystal was happy. Allie could continue living the lifestyle she'd chosen.

It appeared to Allie that she would lose her daughter, as well as Luke. When Virgil stopped by for a visit, he noticed the papers.

"What are these?" He flipped through the stack. "It doesn't look like light reading."

"Mom is going to take legal custody of Chrystal." Allie began to sob. The anger, fear and sadness that she had locked deep inside her heart, erupted. "There's nothing I can do about it. I'm going to lose her, too!"

"Child, hush!" Virgil clenched his quivering jaw. "That's the way these people work. They want to kick me out of our church, too. The one I helped build with my bare hands."

"Why?"

"Because I'm telling them of a horrible evil that's coming. But listen to me carefully."

"Yes."

"Do you want to keep Chrystal?"

"Yes. I need her with me." Allie wiped her eye.

"Why?"

"Because."

"You're going to have to be more convincing than that, Allie."

She closed her eye and laid her head back on the thin hospital pillow. "Because I love her more than anything and I would die for her. I should have died instead of Luke. I can't lose both of my children. I can't."

Virgil nodded. "In all the years I've known you, that's the first time I've heard you talk with such passion about loving another person. You've had some passion about punching people, but never about loving them."

"I do love her, Virgil, with my whole heart. I can't live without her. Nothing will matter to me if she's gone."

"Then you will get her back."

"But I'm a terrible mother. I'm a terrible person. I shot Luke. It was my fault. They're not going to leave her with me! I'm horrible!" Tears rolled down her face and soaked the dressing taped across her cheek.

"Allie, listen to me. I've watched you since you were old enough to toddle around the nursery. You're one of the most intelligent and kindest people I've ever seen. Your mother told me you scored in the genius range on those IQ tests."

"So I've been told." She wiped her nose again. "But, they also said I have antisocial personality traits."

"Well, you're headstrong and stubborn like a herd bull. You have a smoldering anger that just never cools. Your mother even put you in those special classes for the smart kids."

"And I got into fights, there."

"Why?"

"Because some boy picked on me and I lost my temper. I hurt him pretty bad."

"You're so much like your father. After he left you and your mother, you never recovered. But you have to know that God loves you. And God forgives you. Now you must forgive yourself. You must seek him. *Therefore if any man be in Christ...*" Virgil closed his eyes as he spoke. *"He is a new creature: old things are passed away; behold, all things are become new."*

"But Virgil, I've got no job. I can't afford my rent. I can't afford food." She looked around at the tubes and pumps and large flat screen TV. "How the hell am I going to afford this?"

"Well, here's what you're going to do." He wagged his finger at her. "First of all, you're going to stop those drugs you've been using. Second of all, you're going back to school so you can put that brilliant brain of yours to good use. Third, you're going to clean up your language and change the type of people you're spending time with. Fourth, you're going to learn how to control your temper. You are going to do this because you love your daughter and your daughter needs you!"

"I don't have a dime!"

"You must trust in God."

"Pastor—"

"Allie! Don't be defeated before you even start. I know of a part time job. There are student loans once you're back in school. You can live in student housing. There are so many ways to get back on your feet. You're building your house stone by stone on solid rock, but you've got to start building. You're going to do this for your daughter and God."

"Virgil--"

"Allie Parsons, you listen to me."

"But--"

"Listen!"

"Virgil--"

"There is a battle coming. And you are so desperately needed."

"What do you mean?" Allie squinted. "A battle? You mean physically fighting?"

"I feel it in my gut. *I looked, and there before me was a pale horse! Its rider was named Death, and Hades was following close behind him. They were given power over a fourth of the earth to kill by sword, famine and plague, and by the wild beasts of the earth.* That's Revelation 6:8. We all have to face our demons and our greatest fears. But Allie, you have to be ready. Pull your life together or you will lose. We will all lose."

Allie lay back and stared at the ceiling. Though she didn't understand Virgil's reasons, she knew he was right. She had to change. And for the first time, she felt a glimmer of hope.

CHAPTER SEVEN
PRESENT DAY

"**A**re you quite alright, Dr. Parsons?" While studying her face, Dr. Mann lifted his chin and scratched his beard.

Without warning, Allie's knees buckled and she slumped to the floor. Mann seized her upper arm just above the elbow and caught her. His biceps and triceps tensed trying to support her full weight. She stopped just before hitting the linoleum.

"You had a vagal reaction. You almost passed out."

"Aagh. Sorry. I'm fine." Allie struggled to her feet. The overwhelming feeling of nausea began to subside.

"Perhaps, we should end this and reevaluate in the morning." Mann turned and started to walk away from the body on the table.

"I'm fine, Dr. Mann. It's just a shock."

"The first time you see remains such as this, it can really throw you."

"No. I've seen it before."

Dr. Mann stiffened. "This victim? You've seen him? How could you even recognize him?"

"What? Him? No... not him. I have no idea who he is. It's hard to explain."

Mann sighed and relaxed his shoulders, but his grip on Allie tightened as she dipped to her right. She smoothed her hair, swallowed and steadied herself.

"Can you continue, Dr. Parsons?"

She eased herself back down to the shiny, waxed floor and covered her face with both hands. "Just a lot of memories. Give me a second. It surprised me."

"You look sheet-white. Your lips are gray."

She took several deep breaths and ducked her head between her knees. "I'm sorry. I hate to fall out like that." She wiped a tear from her right eye and sniffed through her stuffy nose.

"I'll admit, he is decomposed more than most. But I can get another to assist me if you can't continue."

"I'm fine. I'll be okay." Allie raised her head. Tiny beads of sweat dotted her upper lip.

"How much time do you need, Doctor?"

"I'm getting there. I'm feeling better." Allie gritted her teeth and worked her jaw back and forth.

"So, you've seen a homicide victim in a morgue before? Hmm?"

"One." Allie sighed and rubbed her eyes.

"Anything interesting?"

Allie sat up straight. She smoothed the wrinkles out of her plain blue skirt and white blouse. "I'm better now."

"You look improved. You've got color back in your face. Now, the corpse you saw before, what can you tell me about it?" Mann leaned forward and offered his hand to Allie.

She sighed and extended her arm. There was so much to say.

"Tell me, Parsons." Mann bent over and grasped her elbow. "Let's see how much you learned from your experience. We'll turn this from something emotional into logical. Describe it in excruciating detail. Then maybe you won't have the same reaction when you're here next."

"There was nothing logical about any of it, Dr. Mann. What's logical about the killing of an innocent boy?" Allie removed her elbow from Dr. Mann's grip and pulled herself up. "Pastor Virgil Paul has helped me come to terms with it, but there is no logic in it. But, thank God, I have my daughter."

"Virgil Paul..." Dr. Mann stroked his bearded chin. "Surely you're not referring to that crazy old vicar who marched in front of the courthouse carrying signs proclaiming the end of the world is near. His parishioners defrocked him."

Allie cleared her throat and swallowed. "He's eccentric. Old school."

"He had the audacity to lecture to me about releasing confidential information to the public. Interesting individual."

"Yeah, of course. You're right. That describes him."

There was a short silence and then Mann spoke. "Anyway..." he scratched the back of his neck. "What memories are you hiding in that neophyte mind of yours?"

CHAPTER EIGHT
EIGHT YEARS AGO

After the sutures were removed from Allie's face and the skin edges had mended, a series of gold scabs formed along the margins of fresh scar. Her doctors told her that the rosy-pink, meaty areas that had emerged in the healing wound were called 'proud flesh.' A black patch covered her empty left eye socket.

As she listened to the testimony in the modern, fluorescent-lit courtroom, Allie picked at the scabs. Tiny golden flakes of hard amber serum fell from her face.

Allie's mother sat at the table to her right, stiff and erect. Allie guessed that if they were on speaking terms, her mother would command her to leave her wound alone. However, except for messages conveyed through attorneys, they hadn't communicated in a week.

The judge sat before them, flanked by a court reporter and an empty witness stand.

Most importantly, the future of her relationship with her daughter faced them all.

"I understand and appreciate the issues raised by you as the grandmother, Mrs. Parsons." The judge, hovering over a small stack of papers with her hands folded together, leaned towards the plaintiff. "Clearly, Allie's lifestyle has been an issue. But the testimony of Virgil Paul, her minister, and the change in her conduct and outlook as documented by her social worker have convinced me that custody of the child, Chrystal Parsons, should remain with her mother, Allie Florence Parsons." She spoke with a soft voice and nodded after each point.

With a pound of her gavel, the judge adjourned the court.

Miraculously, Allie was once again the legal guardian of her daughter.

She heaved a huge sigh of relief, slumped back into her simple wood chair and rubbed her face. Her lawyer offered a quick 'congratulations' and hurried out of courtroom B to locate his next client. By the time she glanced in her mother's direction, Beatrice had left the courtroom.

Allie sighed again, swung her head around and glanced over her right shoulder. Pastor Virgil, dressed in a worn brown sport coat, plaid shirt and clashing teal tie, sat alone in a stiff chair. He smiled after catching Allie's glance and the many wrinkles framing his grin seemed to meet somewhere in the middle of his bald scalp. He turned both thumbs up and continued to smile.

"Thank you!" She mouthed the words and nodded. She wiped a tear from her eye.

It was the beginning to a fresh start.

CHAPTER NINE
PRESENT DAY

"I'm sorry I passed out. I really can't discuss this with people I don't know very well. Let's just keep going." Allie straightened her lab coat.

"Apologies do not help, Dr. Parsons. Go into the specifics of the victim's wounds, so that you can learn." Mann spoke in a gruff tone. "You have to get beyond all this."

"Oh, my..." Allie tilted her head back and ran her sweaty palm through her hair.

"Go ahead and spit it out, Dr. Parsons. Tell me about it."

Allie knew of Dr. Mann's legendary impatience with subordinates. She prepared herself for a small dose.

"It's really difficult to talk about it."

"For Godsakes, it's about the science, Parsons! What was the cause of death? It's about the medicine. It has to be removed from your emotions. If you want to be a physician, you have to approach patients objectively and let go of the personal feelings. I can't spend much time on these sorts of matters."

"It was my son, Dr. Mann." Allie's voice softened. She spoke as she looked down and smoothed her lab coat. "My son, Luke, was in the morgue."

Dr. Mann paused and rubbed his chin. His jaw tightened and then relaxed. "Oh. I see. I didn't think about that."

"I guess this whole thing was like when I viewed Luke's body. It's still a struggle for me."

"I'm sure it was traumatic. If I'd known you'd be so emotional, I wouldn't have asked you about it."

"It's not your fault. It's okay."

They stood silently for a few seconds. Dr. Mann stared at the ceiling as Allie rubbed her temples with the tips of her fingers.

Finally, Dr. Mann cleared his throat and placed his arms behind his back again. "I didn't anticipate that you'd be incapable of proceeding. Here's what we'll do." Mann raised his nose slightly and scrunched his lips. "You...will go back to the office. Then, I'll return and start this case. You can join me tomorrow, if you're prepared. If you're not, then we'll have to consider the alternatives."

"I shot him. My son, Luke..." Allie's confession spilled out in rapid fire. "I accidently killed him."

"We don't need to do this. Let's move on."

"No. I don't want you to think I need or deserve any pity. I don't want to be coddled."

"I never coddle. But this information is not pertinent."

"No. We're going to talk about this now!" Allie took a deep breath and raised her voice. "Everyone who finds out wants to know. If I don't explain, it will affect how you act towards me. I know how this goes. It happened all through school. People stare....whisper...treat me like I'm a freak..."

She raised her chin towards the ceiling and shook her head. "You have to realize, this is an important appointment for me. I have worked very hard to be here. There is no back up plan. I have a teenage daughter depending on this. This time, I'll not let her down."

"I don't wish to pursue this topic further."

Allie squared her shoulders. "Usually, when people ask me how I lost my eye, or got this scar, or say, 'Allie Parsons, you're that girl,' I just walk out. But I have to tell you, because I have to keep this job!"

"Stop." Mann held up his hand.

"A serial killer attacked me. He followed me home..." She swallowed hard and took a deep breath. "He followed me home *after I asked him to*. After I opened the door for him...he attacked. I grabbed my gun and as we were fighting, it went off and a bullet went through the wall—"

"Stop!"

"And I killed my son..." Her last words trailed off into a whisper.

"Are you quite finished?"

Allie nodded.

"Don't presume to enlighten me on a case I know so well. I was the medical examiner investigating those murders." Mann knitted his brow and stared blankly past Allie at the bare wall. "You were the only one to survive? Yes? You gave a description? Yes?" Mann stopped and rubbed his head. "Of course, now it all makes sense."

"That's me. Guilty. I know you were the medical examiner. I read your reports. Pastor Virgil remembered your name."

"I've been here a long time." He eyed her scar while sliding an index finger along his own cheek. "That would have come from the hunting knife he liked to use. And your *eye*... It's inconceivable you could survive an attack by such a strong, cunning individual."

"I'm a survivor."

"Those were bad times for Tampa. As you probably know, we did eventually identify 'Toro'. It's unfortunate he was shot by the police before he could be tried in court."

Mann cleared his throat and squinted. He turned his head towards Allie. "What happened to your son was a tragic accident. The fact you were able to thwart a titan like that is difficult to fathom. He was massive."

Allie spoke haltingly, her voice nearly a whisper. "Like they wrote in all the newspapers and reported on TV... I was stoned. I brought him back to my apartment...I exposed my children to him...Luke died when I pulled the trigger. I have to live with that. Nine years have helped..." But I'm not sure 1000 would be enough.

Mann lowered his gray head and stared at the thick white socks visible beneath his brown leather sandals. "Well, now you're a doctor, so I expect you'll act like one and not a...." Mann blushed.

"A stripper."

"Yes, that."

"I didn't do that for long. I really needed the money."

"You're in no condition to be effective today, go—"

"No! Let's get started now. I want to do this autopsy."

"I won't permit you to slow me down. Are you certain you're ready?"

"One hundred percent."

Allie stood unblinking as Mann stared into her eyes. He looked away and nodded. "Let's begin, then. The detectives are anxiously awaiting answers."

CHAPTER TEN
PRESENT DAY

Allie followed Mann towards the autopsy table.

"This is going to be a high profile case, so pay close attention. Meet Mr. Franz S. Bergman. If you're a person of faith, as you claim to be, this was Franz Bergman. His soul has left and all that remains is dust in some fancy form. For our purposes, this is still Franz Bergman, but the metabolic and electrical processes that animated his cells have ceased to function."

"Too bad there's no lightning."

"What?" Mann, squinted and turned towards Allie.

"That might save us the investigative trouble. If we could reanimate him, he could tell us what happened." Allie grimaced.

Mann glanced down at her and wrinkled his brow. "Well, since I don't have access to large voltage and there are no storms in the forecast, we'll have to rely on our powers of deduction to tell the story."

"You're right. There's only one resurrection I really care about anyway."

"Be that as it may, our task is to bring his story to life. Now tell me what you observe about him. Besides the fact that his face is gone, of course."

Allie paused and steadied herself again.

"Can we continue?"

"Yeah. Of course. Poor guy." She placed a hand on her hip. A bead of sweat formed on her forehead, but Allie still managed to force a smile. "I feel bad for him and his family. We do need to find his murderer. Uhm..first... I'm thinking...uhm...Where was he found? Under what circumstances?"

Mann nodded, folded his hairy arms behind his back and turned towards the body. "He's described by his medical records as a short and heavy, but healthy man." Mann stooped slightly and his gray hair bobbed up and down as he paced beside the table. "He was reported missing by his wife. The police found him floating near his dock. His wife positively identified the corpse."

Allie nodded, using the period of discussion to steel herself for the upcoming examination.

Mann recited the patient's history. "38 years old, white male. He grew wealthy in Germany manufacturing optics. Retired to Florida 10 years ago. Now, tell me what you see. First, glance through his medical records on the table behind you. Use that clipboard to fill out the autopsy forms. Pay attention to every detail."

"Alright." Allie hesitated and looked for the documents.

"Doctor, I suggest you begin."

"I am. I will." Finally, Allie spotted Bergman's chart. "Got it." She made her way towards the records and over the next five minutes, examined the dictations in great detail. After turning the last page, she picked up the clipboard, hesitated and then approached the autopsy table.

Her gaze never left Bergman's body. She took a deep breath and eased closer. Her lips drew tight and she rubbed the back of her teeth with her tongue as she circled the cadaver and jotted careful observations.

"I'm waiting." Mann hovered over Allie, with his hands behind his back.

Allie ignored him and continued to examine the body closely. After nearly 30 minutes, she stopped, lowered her clipboard and stared at Dr. Mann.

"Well?" Mann glowered.

"There's a lot of decomposition, but here's my best shot." Allie took a deep breath, then dove in. "He's 5'-4", 250 pounds. Multiple stab wounds. I count 12 across both sides of his chest. One coming from below his sternum, probably entered the right ventricle of his heart. That would have killed him pretty quickly. He would have bled out...uh...exsanguinated in his chest after a few contractions." Allie looked towards Dr. Mann and raised her eyebrows.

Dr. Mann nodded while stroking his gray beard, a signal for Allie to continue.

She swallowed and licked her lips. "And...the shotgun wound to the face appears superfluous. He was probably already dead. The muscles didn't contract. No arterial bleeders." Allie raised her shoulders and wrinkled her brow.

Dr. Mann gave a single nod.

"Looks like the assailant removed his ears with a knife. The two wounds in his abdomen are consistent with a big blade. I don't see defensive wounds on either hand." She bent over to study his hands then looked at her own scarred palm.

Dr. Mann offered no commentary.

She forged on. "But it's hard to tell, because... I think... the bacteria and fish of Tampa Bay got to him. The water washed away a lot of blood and skin and trace evidence." Allie stood still and quiet, looking up at her mentor.

Mann rocked up and down in his sandals, so at his tallest, he towered nearly a foot above her. He placed an index finger over his closed lips, but didn't speak.

Allie held her ground and leaned slightly towards him.

After a moment, he broke the silence. "Tell me, Dr. Parsons. What does this suggest?"

Allie leaned back and took a deep breath. "Well, that's the question, isn't it?" She cleared her throat. "It's a passion killing. Someone hated him and did a big overkill. Anyone of several stab wounds could have finished him. Obviously, the shotgun blast would have done it, but I feel certain that came after the stab wound to the heart. Then, some of it looks like intentional mutilation."

"I believe you're right."

Allie cocked her head. "Really?"

Dr. Mann looked at Allie without blinking his piercing blue eyes. "Can you start to hypothesize on a motive or suspects?"

Allie cleared her throat. "You rule out the spouse first. His wife was with his son in New York?"

"Supposedly. The police are verifying that. They're operating on the theory that it was a robbery. A window was broken in the Florida room."

"You left that out."

"It doesn't change your observations. What about time of death?"

"Rigor mortis is absent, but with the heat and being in the water, I don't have a guess."

"It's hard to determine in this sub-tropical heat and with the water. Your textbook won't cover the specific environmental conditions we deal with in this climate. When the police reached his body this morning, he was at the water temperature."

"And there's early to moderate putrefaction." Allie pinched her nose.

"Lividity, this splotchy purple discoloration, is at it's maximum, but the pattern isn't specific enough to clarify any details of his death."

Allie leaned in for a closer look at the discoloration.

"I believe he was murdered about 72 hours before being found, based on all these details and when his wife last spoke to him. What else can you find? Birth marks, piercings, tattoos, scars, needle marks?"

Allie circled the table again, then stopped and shook her head. "Nothing else of significance."

"I agree. I turned him over earlier and examined his back. Nothing of note there. Byron photographed him." Mann stamped his foot. "You have one hour to complete the external exam. Leave the abdomen, chest and brain until the detectives arrive. They'll want to cover the internal exam with us. Byron will complete the photographs at that time. Any questions?"

"No. I'm good to go!" Allie hoped she sounded more confident than she felt.

CHAPTER ELEVEN
PRESENT DAY

Dr. Mann and Byron entered the autopsy suite exactly one hour later, as Allie was finishing up her notes. Both were clad from head to toe in operating room attire, with facemasks hanging around their necks. Dr. Mann didn't acknowledge Allie, but busied himself with setting up the recording equipment.

Byron handed Allie a yellow surgical gown, blue mask, hair cover and shoe covers, all in a neat pile. "You're going to need these, Sugar. They'll protect you from the hazards of the job, Hon." He placed two similar stacks of gear on a stainless steel cabinet that held shelves filled with medical instruments.

Allie smiled. "Thanks, Byron. You know—"

"You better get suited up, Sweetie. We're already behind and Dr. Mann doesn't like to run late." Byron turned from Allie towards the stainless steel cabinet and began to assemble a tray of instruments.

Allie rolled her eyes and donned the gear Byron had given her. She struggled with the facemask and its attached plastic shield as two men entered the autopsy suite.

The short, stocky, white guy had close cut blonde hair and a boisterous laugh. The other man- African-American, tall and lanky- appeared more reserved. Both wore collared dress shirts rolled up at the sleeves and sported worn dark ties that appeared fuzzy against their crisp, white shirts. Detective's badges were pinned to their belt loops.

Allie froze when she saw the loud, cocky man leading the pair. *Why do these things have to happen to me?* She secured her face-mask over her nose and mouth. *God must have some strange sense of humor.*

Her first day was turning into a disaster.

"Byron, my buddy, I love the smell of a new autopsy!" The portly policeman spoke in an enthusiastic, high-pitched voice and had an exaggerated southern drawl. He pinched his nose dramatically and waved his other hand. "This one is pret-ty rank! But it's a bigwig who was done in, so I gotta be here."

Allie groaned. It was Pug Festoon!

Byron suffered a hearty slap on the back that knocked him forward. He grimaced, rubbed his cheeks, then scratched his graying, curly black hair. "Good to see you, Officer...I mean, Detective." Byron retrieved the masks and gowns and distributed them to the detectives.

"Detective Festoon, we're ready to make the incision." Mann tightened his lips.

"Awesome! On the ball as..." Festoon turned on his heels to face Allie. "Who have we here? New blood in the coroner's office? No pun intended. But let's admit, it was a pretty good one." Festoon smiled and raised his eyebrows.

The Detective sidled over to Allie and stuck his hand out. "Detective Robbie Festoon, Tampa PD." He opened his eyes wide. They sparkled a bright green which matched the intensity of the artificial glow from his brilliant, white teeth. "My friends call me Pug. I hope you'll be my friend, Sweetheart. This here is detective Hector Westbrook." Festoon placed the blue mask over his face and secured the elastic bands behind his ears. He threw the yellow gown into the red trashcan marked 'Biohazard.'

"Good to meet you." Westbrook spoke in a deep baritone as he shook Allie's hand. He placed the facemask over his nose and mouth and tucked the gown under his arm.

"I'm Dr. Parsons. I'm the medical resident working in the coroner's office." Allie pressed her mask still more firmly across her face.

"I assure you, the quality of this investigation will not suffer." Dr. Mann looked at Festoon and motioned towards Allie with his right hand.

"Parsons." Festoon rubbed his thick chin with his chubby fingers. "Hmm. Have we met?"

Allie took a deep breath. "I think you pulled me over for speeding."

Festoon smirked and studied her more intensely. "Funny. No, it was somewhere else. I'm sure we've met."

"While you're working on that mystery, Detective Festoon, let's get started on this one. Dr. Parsons, tell the detectives what conclusions we've drawn before we make the Y incision."

Allie cleared her throat and began reviewing the initial exam. The detectives stood rapt with their arms across their chests and heads lowered. Periodically, Allie could feel Pug eying her. His gaze felt like heat on her cheek; out of reflex, she lowered her head and turned away.

"We checked out the wife's alibi. Her name is Jez or Jess Bergman." Westbrook placed his folded gown on the table. "It's solid. She was in New York when her husband was killed. She was there for a week. That doesn't mean she didn't have something to do with it, though."

"What about the overkill part?" Byron pulled his mask away from his face. "It seems like somebody had it out for this guy. Stabbed him repeatedly and shot his face off. It would have taken some time to do all that." He let go and the mask popped into place.

"I agree." Westbrook looked curiously at Pug, who was still staring at Allie. "The two main reasons we see overkill is to hide an identity or because of deep hatred. But, we know the identity."

"Yes, we certainly do!" Mann squeezed his hands into a pair of tight blue nitrile gloves.

Westbrook stole another inquiring glance at Pug. "We only found a pretty meaningless vase missing. There was a minute amount of blood by the door facing the pool. Bergman and the perpetrator may have had an altercation there. We found a few traces of blood on the dock. Really not much at all. The culprit cleaned up very well. We're not even sure where the murder took place. The alarm didn't sound. No one reported hearing a gunshot."

"What about employees?" Mann crossed his arms.

"We're trying to contact them. We've reached two who worked in the house, but they can't tell us much. They never saw Mr. Bergman. Mrs. Bergman dealt with the staff. Other than providing alibis, they were of no help."

"Is there anyone else you're investigating?" Mann handed Allie a pair of gloves.

"There's a pool guy. We're still looking for him." Westbrook raised his eyebrows. "Mrs. Bergman says the he and her husband recently had a serious argument. His name is James Smith."

"Unless there is some corroborating evidence, I would eliminate him as a suspect." Mann nodded and picked up a scalpel.

"Why, Dr. Mann?" Westbrook pull his mask down and looked over the plastic shield.

"The overkill. The murderer probably had a turbulent history with Bergman. Unless the victim and the pool man had an emotional relationship, James Smith wouldn't be too high on my list."

"We'll keep an open mind." Westbrook tilted his head and stared incredulously at Mann.

"You were in on the Grave Digger autopsies!" Festoon wagged a finger at Allie.

"What? No!" She pulled her gloves on with a loud snap.

Westbrook coughed and glared at Festoon. "Anyway, the perpetrator chained the victim to an anchor. But the chain was too long. At low tide Bergman's head bobbed on the surface. Two hours after Jess Bergman called in a missing person report, we found him."

Allie scratched the scar beneath her surgical mask and cleared her throat. "Where did I leave off?"

"Time of death." Westbrook gave a reassuring nod.

"Thank you. Our best estimate is 72 hours prior to discovery. Any...," Out of the corner of her eye, Allie saw Festoon staring intently at her. Quickly, she turned away. "Anymore questions?"

Festoon rose on his tiptoes and shifted his gaze between Westbrook and Mann. "Hector, Dr. Mann? Let's cut! Looks like Bergman was a bigger fan of grits than me." He chuckled, patting his soft belly with both hands. "He's what I like to call 'porkulent'."

"If you'll start with the initial incision, Dr. Parsons." Mann turned towards Allie, handing her the scalpel.

"Right." Allie drew a nervous breath. She gently gripped the scalpel between her thumb and middle finger and placed her index finger softly on top of the handle. She sliced a large 'Y' shaped incision across Bergman's chest, then continued deeper through the rectus abdominus muscles. She penetrated the peritoneum and opened the abdomen. Bergman's skin and fat parted as if she were cutting through a soft baked potato.

A sour smell oozed into the room as the coils of his small bowel wiggled between the parted dome of muscle and slid out with a slick, wet sound. The unpleasant odor rapidly degenerated into a horrendous stench.

For the first time, Allie was happy that formaldehyde and disinfectant inundated the autopsy suite. Though the preservative stung her eyes and painted the fiber of her clothes with an invisible film, it did constrain the rotten smell that rose from Bergman's belly.

"The smell indicates there has been a significant amount of decomposition. Would anyone like some menthol paste for their mask?" Mann held out a small canister to Byron.

Allie gasped. "I'll take some!"

"Just a smear beneath your nose." Byron dipped a finger into the container and it came out covered in thick green paste. He passed it to Allie. "Right above your upper lip, Sugar."

"You can use that stuff, Doc, but then you get the smell of menthol scented poop, which ain't a lot better than plain poop, in my opinion."

"I'll take my chances." Allie lowered her mask enough to smear a thin green film under her nose.

"Thanks." She pulled her mask back over her nose.

"Dr. Parsons, get the bone cutters, and incise the sternum to enter the chest."

"Bone cutters…" Allie looked around. "They would be…where?"

"Right behind you on the table." Mann pointed over her shoulder. "Hand them to Dr. Parsons, Byron."

"Here you go, Allie." Byron handed her the instrument.

Festoon slapped his thigh and crooned. "Well, if it ain't Allie Florence Parsons!" Mystery solved.

CHAPTER TWELVE
PRESENT DAY

"That's me!" Allie's heart raced and hot blood flooded her brain. "Now, I remember. Let me take a look." Festoon lowered her mask with his stubby fingers. "Yep. Scar never did heal right, did it? You're not wearing a patch. Got a fake eye, too?"

"Do you mind, Detective?" Allie reached up and pressed her mask back tightly against her face.

"I wonder..." Festoon reached behind her and lifted the hair off her neck. "Is ole' Hades still there?"

"Take your hands off me!" Allie's eyes flared, and she slapped his hand away with a surprisingly fast flick of her forearm.

"That's the Allie I remember!" Festoon's beer belly shook as he laughed. "Fast as lightening and mean as a badger. Just look at you, all doctored up and everything." He took two steps back and swung his gaze from her head to her toes. "You've still got it, Girl."

"Stop! This is my department and you will cease harassing Dr. Parsons. Parsons, continue with the autopsy." Mann's face glowed red above his mask.

"This is the girl from our 'Toro' task force."

"Congratulations on your keen powers of observation, Detective Festoon. However, at the moment we are focusing on this exam."

"But, Doc!" Festoon ignored Mann's barb. "This woman is infamous! I think I arrested her three times before... Anyway, she survived 'The Bull'. Allie is the girl he couldn't kill."

"You got me, Pug. Let's move on." Allie grabbed the bone cutters out of Byron's hand and swiveled back towards Bergman's body.

"Did you know she's been arrested for possession of marijuana and narcotics, Doc? How did you get into medical school with that kind of record?"

"I assure you, if Dr. Parsons' performance is not up to the standards I've set, she will be replaced." Mann's veins bulged along the sides of his head.

"With all due respect, we're hip deep in a murder investigation and it's being conducted, in part, by a convicted felon."

"Never convicted." Allie whispered with her head lowered.

"What's that?" He stepped close to her. "I'm sorry, my hearing must be going because of all that loud music from that club you danced in. 'The Inferno' or 'The Cave' or something like that."

"I was never convicted." Allie turned towards him and met his gaze with her defiant eyes. "Never guilty in a court of law, Detective Pug."

Festoon turned away, shaking his index finger. "Actually, Miss Parsons. Your mother always had that famous attorney, Duncan Maxwell. Charges dropped. Charges sealed and, I'm guessing, expunged."

"Detective! Dr. Parsons! That's enough!" Mann slammed his fist on the autopsy table. "There will be no unprofessional behavior in this department!"

"I heard you found religion. Left the bars, nightclubs, dens of inequality."

"You mean iniquity? I have! And now, I have work to finish, as do you."

"As long as the Doctor here," he gave a tilt of his head towards Mann, "is comfortable with how this might look when it goes to court. Remember OJ? Crime lab loses samples? We've got a convicted felon here. How's that going to look in a State of Florida court?"

Allie stiffened and opened her mouth.

Pug cut her off. "My bad!" Festoon held both hands up in feigned surrender. "We should have called you Torodor since you were the one who fought the bull and lived."

"It's Toreador, Pug."

"Detective! Are you going to be able to continue?" Mann leaned towards Festoon.

"If this case gets thrown out, I'm not going down with this ship, because I warned you." Festoon shook his head.

"Dr. Mann, I'll step aside." Allie angrily ripped off her mask while backing away from the body.

"Dr. Parsons!" As he spoke, spit flew from Mann's mouth. "Dr. Parsons, this is my morgue and you will stay! I'll not have my authority undermined by either of you!" Mann turned his stern glare in Festoon's direction.

"Fair enough, Doctor." Festoon held up his hands again.

"Proceed, Parsons." Mann's color returned to normal, but sweat beaded above his brow.

Allie wiped her eyes and relaxed her clenched jaw. She replaced her mask and attempted to hide her shaking hands by tightening the muscles in her thin forearms as she placed the blades of the bone cutters on either side of the sternum and squeezed tightly. There was a moment of intense pressure in her hands and fingers before Bergman's sternum gave way and the bones separated with a loud 'crack'. Allie cringed.

"How's your daughter, Allie." Festoon whispered over her shoulder.

Using the sleeve of her yellow gown and a strong puff of air through her tense lips, Allie blew a strand of black hair away from her eyes. "She's fine."

"I guess you got custody back from your mama. Family court always goes with the mother. Even if that may not be the obvious choice."

Allie's grip on the bone cutters grew tighter and she ripped through the remaining ribs as if they were thin chicken bones.

A huge hole in Bergman's heart had allowed four liters of blood to escape into his chest where it had clotted. As Allie had suspected, the stab wound would have killed him instantly. The remainder of the autopsy turned up nothing unusual.

There was a nagging detail about the autopsy that bothered Allie, but fury clouded her thinking.

Yes, you jerk! I did get my daughter back!

CHAPTER THIRTEEN
EIGHT YEARS AGO

Soon after the custody hearing, Allie's lawyer arranged for transfer of Chrystal to Allie. Despite the bitter battle, the court eventually forced Beatrice Parsons to relinquish custody of Chrystal.

Allie told her lawyer she would meet Bea and Chrystal alone. There would be no attorneys present.

While Allie waited in the parking lot of the small strip mall, she adjusted the hood of her rain jacket and tucked her cold hands into the pockets, trying to keep them dry. One of Florida's sudden, brutal afternoon storms had skimmed over and unleashed its impossibly chilly rain from its low-lying, thick, green clouds. Allie knew the storm would be gone in minutes; crickets and birds would begin chirping, and steam would rise from the new puddles formed on the hot pavement.

The steam would make a perfect entrance for her mother's car. In recent years, whenever Bea and Allie talked, their relationship was reduced to smoldering ruin.

They were supposed to meet and exchange Chrystal at 3:00 PM. Allie arrived at 2:00 PM on the dot, just to make sure she was there first. She knew her mother would be pulling in at 2:30 and if Allie arrived after, she would act as if Allie were late.

As Allie sat in her car, she considered how they had decided to meet here. Originally, Bea wanted to meet in a bail bondsman office across from a club called the 'Bleu Honey,' where Allie was once arrested. Allie knew her mother was making an overt dig at her qualifications as a mother.

Allie had suggested her church.

Bea said it was too far. The police station would do, nicely.

"I'm not sure how to get there, Mother. Pastor Virgil's place is near you."

"I'm taking Chrystal to the park before we come over and that's all the way across town from that crazy fool's house. And you know very well how to get to the police station. You've been there enough."

On and on it went, until they settled on the surf shop in this strip mall. Not the nicest area of town, but Allie had no ties here. She was sure, though, that her mother made some vague connection, between surfers, people who went to raunchy bars and Allie's former life.

At precisely 2:30, a yellow cab pulled into the parking lot and stopped several spaces away from Allie's Honda. As if from a movie script, steam from the asphalt rose around Allie's mother as she emerged from the rear door.

Bea helped Chrystal hop out of the car and bent down to give her a hug. She whispered in Chrystal's ear and the child nodded obediently.

Then Bea stood, held Chrystal's hand and walked towards Allie.

Bea wore a designer skirt and blouse with red-soled high heels, and, as usual, was carrying her vintage Gucci purse. Little Chrystal was wearing a flowered Lilly Pulitzer dress and black patent leather shoes.

As she drew closer, Allie could see her mother crying and her mascara began to run. Bea dabbed her face with a linen handkerchief.

"I see you're on time for once."

"I'm early, actually, Mother."

"Better late than never."

"I'm early, not late."

"But you're late in learning to be early."

"I see." Allie frowned. "I should have known."

"Should have known what?"

"That no matter what time I arrived, it would be the wrong time in your eyes."

"That's a role you play very well. Martyr. I'm not impressed that you're on time for once, after years of disappearing for weeks on end. Or coming to my dinner party high with your trashy friend. Pardon me, if I'm not proud of this new Allie."

"Mother, I love you." Allie bit her lip. "I'm sorry it's come to this, but I want you to know, I apologize for all of that. I have no excuses. I wish you'd forgive me."

Bea dabbed her eyes again. "You're also a little late in that speech, Allie. Maybe three years ago... But I decided for my own health, I had to let you go. You had to live your own life, and I mine, and they could never meet. Otherwise, I would go insane."

Allie pursed her lips and felt her own tears mingle with the now warm rainwater on her face. "I'm sorry to hear you say that."

"Yes, well. We all choose our paths. Well, here is dear Chrystal. My angel. Please, for the love of God, take good care of her. Protect her." As Bea spoke, she fought back tears and bit her lower lip. "This, I must say, is the hardest thing I've ever had to do."

Bea turned towards the cab and signaled the driver. He hopped out, grabbed a small pink suitcase and carried it over.

"Did you buy all this for her?" Allie motioned to the dress and the suitcase.

"Yes, I did."

"It's all beautiful. Thank you. Come here, Chrystal. Give me a hug."

Chrystal looked up at her grandmother, who nodded. Slowly she walked over to Allie and hugged her thigh.

"I missed you." Allie embraced her daughter.

"No need for long goodbyes." Bea managed to fight her frown into a smile. "I'm going now."

"What's with the cab?"

"I'm moving to New York. I was offered a position there with a magazine as a fashion editor. It's through a dear friend, and I turned it down, initially. But I think now is the time."

"So you're leaving?"

"I'm going from here to the airport."

"Wow. That's sudden."

"Yes, well. That's the way it is sometimes. You know, I lost you long ago. I lost Luke. And now I've lost Chrystal. I have to separate myself from here and heal."

"You can see her anytime you want, you know."

"I'll talk to her when she's ready. But it will be only with her."

"Whatever you want."

"I can see you're finally thinking of others."

"Mother!" Once again, Allie caught herself and took a deep breath. "Whatever you want."

"Okay, then. That's it. Take good care of her, Allie Florence. That's the last thing I'll ask of you." Bea turned and strode across the wet pavement towards the cab. After several steps, she paused and then turned back towards Allie.

"Allie, I know when your father left, it was hard on you. You were only five and loved him so dearly. And perhaps in my grief I was distant. I know I can be demanding. I'm sorry if that's caused you pain."

"That's all in the past, Mother."

"Allie, please keep a close eye on her. Use your underworld connections to help you if you can."

"Underworld connections?"

"Yes, your acquaintances. That man that attacked you...Bull... Toro. Whatever. Personally, I don't think they ever caught him. You're the only one who's seen him and lived."

"So."

"You're the only one who could identify him."

"I'll be fine, Mother. I can take care of myself."

"That you can. That's one thing you've learned over the years. But be smart. And most of all, take care of Chrystal."

Bea slipped into the cab and shut the door. It pulled out of the parking lot, and with steam enveloping the doors and tires, disappeared down the street.

CHAPTER FOURTEEN
PRESENT DAY

The gray-green clouds that dotted the horizon and blacked out the sun earlier in the afternoon dumped their steamy water and departed before Allie's workday in the morgue ended. When she stepped through the doorway and onto the sidewalk, the asphalt was smoking with a sauna-like fog mingled with a cool, cloud-borne breeze that tickled her cheek. The green palms and the shorter palmettos shimmied in the turbulence created by the competing humid and cool forces, and the smell of ozone hung heavy in the air.

Although she completed the autopsy on Bergman, Allie had yet to dictate it. She had five more dictations pending and the work never ended, because as Byron told her, 'death never sleeps'.

But for some reason, she couldn't finish the Bergman case. Something just didn't click, though Allie couldn't identify what bothered her.

It would be easy to dictate something- anything- and then sign off.

Yet, she hesitated.

Allie knew she could work it out. It would just take some extra time to determine what detail she overlooked; what inconsistency gnawed at her.

That's understandable. It's my first dictation and my first big case.

Dr. Mann would have to be patient, though that didn't seem to be part of his personality. Mann planned to leave that evening for his conference in London and just before he caught his cab to the airport, he had called Allie into his office for a meeting.

Mann started barking orders before Allie had a chance to sit. "First, I expect that when I return, you will have that dictation ready for me to sign so that I can certify your completed work and my findings will be official public record. Is this understood?" Mann did not look up from the papers on his desk as he spoke to her.

"Yes, Sir." She slid into her seat.

"Second. You are never to embarrass or reflect badly on this department again. Your interaction with Detective Festoon was unprofessional and inexcusable. I'll let you go without hesitation if I feel you are a detriment to our reputation. Is that understood?"

"Yes, Sir, but Pug, I mean Detective Festoon was…"

"Is that understood, Dr. Parsons!" Mann still did not look up from his papers.

"Understood, Sir."

"And believe me, young lady, I'll hold you to that. Before I depart, I may leave you a note or two with some tasks for you to finish. You must complete whatever tasks I assign. You'll find I'm not a big fan of email."

"Dr. Mann—"

Mann laid his pen down, but still did not look up. "That's all. You may leave now."

At first Allie hesitated but then stood and rotated on her heels towards the door. After a step, she stopped. "I hope you have a nice trip."

"Thank you." He turned his chair away from her and towards the window.

Allie left the office determined to wrap up the Bergman case with the best dictation Mann had ever read. She simply had to do it.

Fine. No problem. I'll finish it tomorrow.

Allie made her way outside, and felt happy to be away from the morgue and done with her first day. She enjoyed the tickle on her lips brought by a thin current of surprisingly chilly air. Even in the worst Tampa heat, an anomalous wisp of cool wind could find you and give a second of relief. Yet always, the heat followed.

As she stepped from the curb onto the pavement, she spotted the squat Detective Festoon weaving through the parked cars and pulling the hood of his department issued rain jacket away from his box-shaped head.

Allie clenched her teeth. Pug and Westbrook must be here to review the findings on the Bergman case.

Allie was stuck out in the open...too late to turn around and retreat into the building. She had to face Pug.

Allie planned a path past the detective that kept them from coming face to face.

Her worn and rough high heels provided more grip than when she first bought them, but Allie worried she'd slip on the slick asphalt in front of the two policemen.

She could not to let that happen. She stepped carefully and allowed her feet to land safely before taking another step towards Festoon.

"Detective." Allie approached the detectives.

"Ms. Parsons." He nodded and glanced across the hood of a blue hatchback.

The click-clack of their heels echoed through the parking lot as Allie made a beeline for her car.

"You have to admit, it's hot and steamy. Just the way you like it."

Festoon snickered and punched the taller Westbrook in the shoulder.

Allie turned and tilted her head. "Detective Westbrook, how can you work with a cop like this?"

Westbrook raised his hands and shrugged his lanky shoulders. "No one said being a cop was easy, Dr. Parsons."

"You still got it going on, Girl." Festoon turned to towards Westbrook and whispered, "If you didn't see her face."

Based on the pressure building behind her eyes and ears, she knew these immature taunts still got to her.

Allie remembered in the sixth grade, a boy in her class for gifted students teased her about her figure. She demanded he stop, but the boy responded by teasing her more. In a fit of rage, Allie broke his tibia and his nose; he landed in the hospital for two days. If it weren't for Virgil's intervention and phone calls, Allie would have spent significant time in a juvenile facility.

She opened her mouth, but then closed it. Shaking her head in frustration, Allie turned and continued to her car.

A few steps later she reached her Honda. As she fumbled for the keys, she spotted a neatly folded note stuck under the windshield wiper.

Allie paused, cocked her head and stared at it. A chill ran up the back of her neck.   The keys tumbled from her hands and bounced under the tire.

Crap!

She kneeled and chased them with her hands. Finally, her fingers found the keys, and she stood up quickly.

She whacked the back of her head on the mirror.

A sudden jolt of pain filled her skull and Allie saw swirling bright lights that buzzed like bees.

Jeez! When she opened her eyes, she spotted the note again and ripped it from beneath the rough rubber of the wiper. Still grimacing in pain, Allie nervously unfolded it and read.

"Glad to see you have recovered from our first meeting. Looking forward to our next encounter. I'll be in touch. Bully for you. Take care of our friend Franz."

Written in a very neat cursive, it looked as if someone had spent much longer than necessary to simply make the note legible.

Despite the humidity, the hairs on Allie's arms stood erect, as if static-charged on a dry, wintry day. Her heart skipped a beat.

In the distance she heard Pug chuckle.

She turned towards Festoon who was just steps from entering the building. "Hey, Pug! This is not funny."

Festoon rotated and crossed his arms. "How's your head? I saw you hit it pretty hard."

She waved the note in the air like a small flag. "Bully for you? Like in 'Bull', 'Toro'? Really, even for an upstanding officer of the Tampa PD, this is bad."

"I have no idea what you are talking about, Allie. Really, I don't."

"It's a sick joke and it's not funny at all! He's dead. He can't write anymore of these notes from where he is now."

Westbrook shrugged. "I don't know what she's talking about."

"This note on my car. 'Bully for you. Take care of our friend, Franz.' Sound familiar?"

"I didn't write no note! I'm tellin' you!"

"You were coming from this direction."

"I'm parked 20 feet from you."

"Westbrook, are you part of this?" Allie raised the note and shook it again.

"I didn't write anything, Dr. Parsons."

Allie crumpled the paper and shook her head. "Somebody around here has a sick sense of humor."

"Allie, Darlin'..." Pug rolled his eyes. "Honey, I bet it was Dr. Mann. Don't Europeans say things like 'bully for you'? "

"He's not the warm and fuzzy type." Allie glanced back down at the message. "Though, he did say he might leave a note." She unfolded the wrinkled paper and read it again. Maybe I'm over reacting. Maybe he's trying to be a little more human.

The writer used such elegant cursive...it had to be meant as an intimate note. Perhaps German's communicate better through writing.

She opened her car door and tossed the note in the front seat. "I'll ask him. You're not trying to punk me, Pug?"

"I had nothing to do with no note! I've written enough reports on you, that you ought to know my writing by now."

"Westbrook?"

"Promise, Dr. Parsons. Not guilty."

"Alright." Allie plopped into the driver's seat and huffed.

She slid her sunglasses over her eyes. Dr. Mann must have written the note.

It's really weird that he would do that especially after blasting me in his office, but that must be the explanation.

As Allie backed away from the parked cars, she saw Pug and Westbrook watching her from the morgue's front door.

Although she was already late getting home to Chrystal, she braked and hesitated in the parking lot. Her stomach tightened into a painful knot as she watched the two men turn and enter the building. She had accomplished so much over the last nine years. So much fear had been left behind.

This note revived the anxiety and trepidation of those terrible days of Bull. Bully for you. Was it a clue, a veiled reference?

After all these years...

There was no way Toro could be back.

CHAPTER FIFTEEN
THREE YEARS AGO

Allie would never change her tattoos.

An ornate green cross, drawn in the old Celtic style, found its center at her umbilicus. When a bemused Pastor Virgil spotted the ink, he simply shook his bald head. "Who can argue with a cross?" He gulped red punch and tea from a clear plastic cup.

The other tattoo was difficult for Virgil to accept. He and Allie frequently argued over what it meant.

"Allie, he has nested on your neck, Sugar."

A demon with bat wings, small horns and a sinewy tail and hooves lay claim to the back of her neck, just under her long black hair. Reds, purples and greens flashed through the clouds near its pitchfork, highlighting its wicked sneer.

To Allie, the first tattoo represented the direction she wished to go. The demon clawing the nape of her neck reminded her of where she had been. And it warned her she could descend again, if she strayed.

"Mom! Your tattoos!" Nine year-old Chrystal ran off in her cute little, yellow bikini to play with the popular kids by the edge of the lake. After Virgil left to find more tea and punch, only the whispers and secret stares of the other women kept Allie company.

She ignored them and turned her attention to the Pathology text that she held. She ranked in the middle of her medical school class, but didn't want to fall any lower. She slid on her dark sunglasses so they covered her remaining eye and partially covered the patch protecting her left socket. She sunk lower in her seat and pulled a simple white t-shirt over her tattoos and black bikini top.

All her transgressions were now safely hidden.

As she immersed herself in the basic anatomy of the esophagus, the small talk from the ladies faded away.

At first, Allie studied the textbook and gained ground in the first chapters of the Pathology section. But then her thoughts wandered.

One of the last memories of her father took place at this lake. Allie had stood in the water, very near where Chrystal played now. Allie loved her father. Yet for some reason, he left her when she was five, and never returned.

For many years, Allie and her mother didn't recover. Their relationship would never be the same.

Without anyone to guide her, Allie descended from there.

Then Toro tried to kill her, and she hit rock bottom.

"How's the studying, Allie?" She looked up to see Virgil staring over her shoulder at her textbook.

"Doing well, Virgil. I have an exam tomorrow. I'll be up all night."

"That looks awful." He scowled at the picture.

"There's worse. You look horrified."

"No." He waved his hand. "It's not the picture. Honey, I've delivered calves and then made them steers, so I've seen a lot of blood and guts. I've just got this pain when I swallow. I have to force it down."

"Is that why you're drinking all that weird tea?"

"It does go down easy."

"I'm studying GI diseases. That picture is of an ulcerated squamous cell carcinoma of the esophagus."

"Is it curable?"

"Probably not at that stage. Maybe you should see a doctor about your swallowing. Get a check up."

"I'm fine. Listen, I've just heard big news. It's not a 'check up' but I received another check."

"Another check?" Allie cleared her throat. "And..."

"Your tuition is all funded."

"Are you serious? That's so wonderful!" Allie fell back on the grass with a big smile on her face. "Medical school is all paid for." She stood up and hugged Virgil. "Thank you so much."

"Don't thank me, Honey. Give thanks to the Lord and whoever is sending these checks to me. *And my God will supply all your needs according to His riches in glory in Christ Jesus.*"

"Amen. You still don't have any idea who it is?"

"Not a clue. Checks from a Cayman Island account come with instructions that they are to pay for your tuition and expenses in medical school. That's all I know. So, that's what I've been doing. They've kept coming and now you're covered for all four years."

Allie sighed. "I'm dying to know who's doing this. One day, Virgil, I'll try to track down whoever it is and make it up to them. But right now, it is such a relief to have the money taken care of."

"If they want to remain anonymous, then I say honor their wishes and let them stay that way."

"I'm not going to argue!" She took a deep breath. "But what I need to do right now is keep studying and plugging away."

"You'll be fine."

"Yeah. It's all down hill from here."

CHAPTER SIXTEEN
PRESENT DAY

The melodic ring from her phone wrenched Allie back to reality. The nervous knot in her stomach tightened as Pug and Westbrook disappeared inside the building. She picked up her phone and saw the familiar background photo of Chrystal imitating a nun from the 'Sound of Music'.

"Hey, Honey." Allie started the Honda.

"How's it going?"

"Good! I finished my first day." She produced the most cheerful voice she could muster. As Allie spoke to Chrystal, she pulled out of the morgue parking lot into the rush hour traffic.

"Great! Tell me what happened."

"It was...eventful. I ran into people I hadn't seen in years. Dr. Mann is quite the jokester. He's loads of laughs."

"That sounds like fun."

"I'm glad it does. But it's new to me and it'll get easier. Here's the good news... If I can pull this off, Dr. Mann said we could be visiting Europe."

"Good job. So, you didn't pass out?"

"Not completely."

"Mom!"

"I felt a little faint. But I recovered and I'm back to normal now! What are you doing?"

"I'm in the shared bedroom finishing my homework. What are we having for supper?"

"I was thinking spaghetti."

"Sounds good. I love you."

"I--"

A familiar beep-beep rang in her ear. Allie pulled the phone away and stared down at the caller ID.

Are you serious? After all these years? What could he want?

The loud blare of a horn ripped her from her thoughts. She steered the Honda off the yellow line and veered it back into her lane.

"Mom, are you okay?"

"I'm fine. I'll see you at home in a little bit. I've got to stop and talk to somebody."

"Who?"

"An old friend. I need her to set me straight. I'll see you in an hour."

Allie hung up, set her phone on the passenger seat and gripped the steering wheel firmly with both hands. As she waited, Allie pressed the gas pedal lower and whipped past the slower cars, glancing intermittently at her phone. It lay infuriatingly dormant on the seat.

With an abrupt beep, her voicemail alert sounded and Allie pressed her head back against the seat and groaned. Why now?

With a roar of the engine, the Honda shot ahead and Allie careened off the first exit. After a rapid right turn at the light, she screeched to a stop in a gas station parking lot.

Allie accessed her voicemail, pulled the phone to her ear, and listened.

"Hey, Allie. It's Duncan Maxwell. I was reading the 'Hires and Flyers' of the 'Tampa Business Magazine' and saw that you were honored with the assignment to the Medical Examiner's Office. I'd love to meet you for lunch or dinner. Give me a call, Allie Cat."

Then... silence. It was him. After all these years. His confident, soothing voice sounded the same.

It was the same voice that had seduced her years ago, when he was her mother's 'lawyer with benefits'

Of course, Duncan would call now. Years after their last conversation and just when things were beginning to straighten out, he calls. As desperately as she wanted to smoke a cigarette, she also wanted to call Duncan.

She knew both were bad for her.

That's why she needed to visit her old friend. Allie had to see Francesca.

CHAPTER SEVENTEEN
PRESENT DAY

Black shadows and yellow lights covered the walls, floors and ceiling along the hall where Allie nervously made her way. Even through the thumping music beat and the loud rambunctious crowd, Allie could hear the failing wood of the old building squeak under her feet.

At the end of the dimly lit hall, she saw a battered door with jaundiced light streaming from its borders and falling to the floor like a highlighter in Chrystal's homework. Allie had been in that dressing room many times before, but now gratefully, she felt like a stranger.

It had been another life, both in years and behavior.

Allie pushed open the door and squinted as she peered at the mirror bordered by bright light bulbs. It used to be her mirror.

Toro first talked to her in that spot.

The door eased open and Allie realized little had changed. Except now a beautiful blonde, garbed in a white silk dressing robe that cascaded across her thin shoulders, leaned towards the mirror and carefully applied her dark eyeliner.

"You have two seconds to leave or I'll call Pablo and that means you'll die because he was with the Cuban Army in Angola and trained by the KGB and CIA. He carries a knife the size of Kansas." The blonde slid the eyeliner across her lower lid.

"You forget he's ticklish." Allie wiggled all 10 fingers and smiled.

The blonde turned towards the door and stared at Allie, her eye-liner pencil still poised below her left eye. "No, it's not!" Her voice rose two octaves. "Oh-shut-up!"

"Back from the dead, Francesca." Allie shook her head.

A huge smile blossomed and her eyes sparkled. "Allie Parsons! Come here!"

Allie stepped forward and embraced Francesca.

"I can't believe it, Allie! You look great! How long has it been? Eight years? Nine? You packed up and moved on. Wow, you look good!"

"Thanks." Allie took a step back and looked around the room. "You, too. You haven't changed a bit."

"Thanks, Sweetie. I know the cigarettes are getting to me, but I can't live without 'em. Grab a seat while I finish my makeup. Tell me everything!"

Allie sat down beside Francesca as she began to apply the eyeliner.

"Chrystal doing okay?"

"Yep. She's getting A's in school."

"And you're in college?"

"Just finished medical school."

"So, you're a doctor?"

"Hard to believe, but I am."

"You were always so smart. If anyone could make it out of here, it would be you. Could you hand me my cigarettes from my bag, Hon."

Allie fished a pack out of the canvas blue bag near her feet and handed them to Francesca. "Well, I'm poorer now than I was when I worked here."

"I'm not complaining about the money, Honey. It's still good." She put her eyeliner down and pulled a cigarette to her lips. Francesca raised her lighter and, after two puffs, sat back in her seat. "The prob-lem is everything that comes with the job." She held the cigarette in her right hand and crossed her thin thighs. "Smoke, Hon?"

"I'll..., thanks." Allie sighed. She pulled one from the pack and lit it off Francesca's. "It's been a while since I had one of these. I've almost quit."

"I'll tell you what's been a while, Missy. It's been a while since we had a girls' night."

"We had some wild times."

"Oh, my gosh! Remember when we showed up stoned out of our minds to that bash your mother threw. She was so pissed." Francesca leaned back and laughed. "We thought it was hilarious!"

"Mom still reminds me of that. That is, when she talks to me. I lived with you for six days then stayed at Duncan's until she calmed down."

"Actually, Allie, what happened was your mother called the cops, she thought you'd gone missing."

"Oh, yeah. You're right. I think Pug found me."

"I still see him around. He's as much a jerk as ever, but fatter."

"So I've heard."

"Remember the worst mess we were in?" Francesca puffed on her cigarette. "Remember that short, little, fat guy we met at the club? He pulled a gun on us in his apartment and before he could do anything, you kicked it out of his hand and knocked him cold. I can't believe we did that. I wasn't afraid to do anything as long as you were with me. Ain't no one tougher than Allie Parsons."

Allie coughed. "I'm trying to make wiser choices."

"You're not here so, now I've got Pablo to protect me."

Allie nodded. "Those were...those were crazy days."

Francesca bit her lip, rubbed her neck and then stared intently at Allie. Her angular cheekbones curved below her warm brown eyes and stood out even more in the shadows cast by her cigarette. "It's not my birthday for another six months and I'm guessing..." Francesca took a long draw off her cigarette, "I'm guessin' you're here because he called."

Allie bit her thumb and let her cigarette dangle from her fingers. "He did. Just a few minutes ago."

Francesca nodded. "That also explains the smoke. But you did good. You came by to seek my wisdom, like I told you to do after the twins were born."

"I remembered. When he left me with the kids, I had nothing. No father, essentially no mother, no money...But I had you."

"And what did I tell you, Hon?"

"You said 'if Duncan ever calls again, do not talk to him! Call Francesca. I have to remind you of all the scummy things he did.'"

"It was something like that. Your memory is a lot better than mine. So, this is the first time he's called you in almost 13 years?"

"Yes. He read about me in the newspaper. Don't worry. I didn't speak to him. He left a voice mail."

"Aah, Duncan Maxwell." Francesca tucked her legs beneath her and leaned back in the chair. "What girl hasn't fallen for a handsome bad boy? Born with a trust fund from his grandfather's cigar empire and adding to his wealth with his lawyer dealings."

Allie closed her eyes and leaned back.

Francesca continued. "I still have goose bumps when I think about that luscious silky blonde hair. That cocky grin and his perfect white teeth. Even after all the trouble he caused me...Although it wasn't half of the mess he left you in. His green eyes sparkle when he talks to you, and you feel you're the most important person in the whole world." Francesca took a deep breath. "I don't know why he's not Governor."

Allie opened her eyes and sat up. "You're right. He's Mr. Charisma."

"Duncan would party with us at night and the next day, we'd see him on TV doing an interview about a famous case he'd won. Remember that?"

"Of course, I remember that. You're supposed to be reminding me of why I should never see him again."

"Oh, yeah." Francesca sat up and crushed the cigarette on her makeup stand. "Sorry, I still get caught up in him sometimes. Alright, remember this, Miss Allie. Duncan seduced you when you were 17. He was your mother's lawyer and sometimes your lawyer.

Somehow, he made you agree to not say anything to his wife or your mother."

"I was so young and scared. I couldn't fight my way out of that."

Francesca looked in the mirror and applied bright red lipstick. "He took advantage of that. Has he ever paid child support?"

"Nope." Allie bit her lower lip and gazed at the floor.

"There's another reason to stay away from him. What decent guy would haul teenage girls around, buy us dope, party with us and then dump us while he went to work? We just couldn't hang with him. He should have known better. We were just babies. He was a man!" Francesca ran her fingers through her hair. "And it wasn't like that was a one time mistake, Girlfriend. He strung us along for years."

"Thanks, Francesca." Allie crushed out her cigarette in an overflowing ashtray. She stood up and stared blankly at the peeling paint on the wall. "I think I've got it from here."

"Good. You're pissed off enough to stay away from the jerk?"

"Definitely. I'm not going to call him. I'm done with him."

"Perfect. Are you going to hang out for my show? A lot of hot guys out there."

"I've really got to get back to Chrystal. I told her I'd make spaghetti for dinner."

"Listen to you! You're living the American dream!"

Allie opened her mouth to speak and then paused. "I'm working on it."

"So, you never asked for any child support, nothing?"

"No. And it's worked out well. Duncan has no claim to Chrystal. He's never seen her. I doubt he knows her name. I want to keep my past separate."

Francesca nodded. "Speaking of Chrystal and all, it's been so long since I've seen the little thing. Bring her by sometime. I'd love to reunite with the doll." She stood and gave her heavy make-up a final check in the mirror.

"Here? I'm sorry, Francesca. Not here!" Allie shook her head.

Francesca pulled her robe tightly around her shoulders and stepped away from the mirror. "Yeah. Of course, I didn't mean in this sad place. I run by the university area sometimes. I know some guys over there. I'll swing by your apartment and the three of us can hang out."

"Yeah." Allie ran her fingers through her hair. "Definitely. We'll meet up. I've been so busy with my new job. Give me a call when you're in the area. When I have the time, we'll hang out."

Francesca scratched her head then gave Allie an awkward hug. "Sure, Babe. Thanks for stopping by. But, you know, work calls."

Francesca took two steps towards the door then turned back towards Allie. "Sweetie, he carved your face up real bad. But it healed good. I like the fake eye. Nice touch." She smiled. "Keep a look out with your eye that works. Everyone knows the cops didn't kill Toro. You're a real toreador, but I'm sure he's still around."

Allie's jaw dropped and she stiffened.

Francesca continued towards the door, but paused again. "I don't think you could cut it as an entertainer here anymore. It's a good thing you got educated."

Allie's eyes narrowed and she pressed her lips tightly together. Her lower jaw jutted and her breathing grew slow and deep. Control your temper, Allie.

"I've seen that look before, Allie. Careful, Hon. You don't want to lose it after you've gotten so high and mighty. You were crazy back then, but you ain't the same girl, now."

Francesca wrenched open the door and the thumping bass of the club's music exploded into the dressing room. She vanished into the dark hall.

Allie rubbed the scars on her face and felt her artificial eye. She mussed her hair as the concussion of the music rippled through it. Her heart rate slowed and the blood that filled her red cheeks began to cool.

She had managed to control her temper- a huge accomplishment. Now, she needed to get home to Chrystal.

CHAPTER EIGHTEEN
PRESENT DAY

Allie couldn't sleep for several reasons. The most obvious was that she and Chrystal had purchased an incredibly uncomfortable couch at an estate sale two weeks ago. Though a bargain buy at $100, the couch warped her back, twisted her vertebrae and sent her muscles into spasms.

Also, she was tormented by thoughts of Duncan's call and the awkward conversation with Francesca. Hours of tossing and turning on that horrible couch, did nothing to exorcise the worry from her mind.

And finally, there was the note left on her car.

Allie hoped to speak with Dr. Mann by phone first thing in the morning. As soon as she arrived in the office, she tossed her thick textbooks onto her cluttered desk and headed to Byron's office to ask for Mann's phone number.

"Is this about an M.E. case, Sugar?" He sipped coffee and perused the sports page of the Tampa Tribune.

"Not exactly."

"Then I've got bad news." Byron folded the paper, cupped his hands behind his curly black hair and lifted his feet onto the desk. "He's not available, unless it's an emergency. The State owns that phone, and the frugal State of Florida looks at every perk really carefully."

"So....so, I can't call him?"

"Allie, you gotta' understand, he's in London. That's in Europe, Sugar. Out of network calls are very expensive."

"I know where London is. No exceptions?"

"Emergencies only. When you deal with death all day, there's not much else that seems quite as important."

Allie sighed and stretched her back.

"But, if you feel this is an emergency, Allie, a real honest-to-goodness, no-holds-barred, old-fashioned emergency, then I'll call him, Hon."

She hesitated and mulled over Byron's offer.

"It has to be an emergency?"

"Yes, indeed."

Allie paused. "Well...no, never mind. I don't want to nag him." She sighed. "It can wait. Did Dr. Mann say anything about leaving me a note?"

"Nope." Byron shook his head and shrugged. "He leaves me notes now and again, but he didn't say anything about leaving you one."

"Alright." Allie rolled her eyes and turned. "I'll finish the dictations."

"Good. I'll get things going on the autopsies. They'll keep us busy all day." Byron lowered his feet to the floor and placed his hands on his knees. "Allie, Dr. Mann told me to remind you to finish Bergman's dictation. I would get on it. He does not accept excuses."

"I understand." She yawned. "I'll finish it and the others, and meet you in a couple hours."

"Good choice, Hon. I'll see you in a little bit." Byron smiled and unfolded the sports page.

Allie raised her mug of coffee, as if in a toast, took the last sour sip, and headed to her desk.

Immerse yourself in work. Soon Mann will be back and this whole thing will be settled.

She glanced at the pile of files and charts on her desk. After only one day, there was already a backlog of work.

Allie sat her empty mug on a file cabinet and grabbed the top folder from the stack of papers. She raised the microphone from her dictation device. Where to start?

She continued to stare at the handle in her hand as if it were an alien. I'm telling a story. That's all. Tell the true story, Allie.

Allie took a deep breath and pulled the microphone to her lips.

At first, Allie spoke quietly into the dictation device. A few sentences later, her voice grew bold and confident. An hour later, she smiled and stretched. She'd finished the first five reports.

Then, Allie reached Bergman's chart. She hit a brick wall.

Allie felt restless. She shifted in her seat and swung her legs. She took a short break and ran tepid tap water into her coffee mug.

Allie still couldn't shake the feeling that she must be missing an important detail in her dictation. Her misgivings drove her crazy. She gulped some water, which tasted bitter from the coffee.

Maybe the physical pain caused her anxiety. While dictating Bergman's report, Allie couldn't escape the agony of her lower back. She stretched her aching shoulders, rotated her narrow hips, and grimaced.

I used to be fit. Chrystal has to start running with me. It'll do her good, too. I'm too young to be this old.

Byron stuck his head inside the doorway of the tiny office and interrupted her in mid-grimace. "You have a call."

"A call?" Allie pushed 'pause' on the Dictaphone and straightened her back.

"Line four." He held up 4 fingers.

"Is it because Dr. Mann's not here?"

"No. She wanted to talk with you."

"It's not my daughter's school is it?"

Byron laughed. "Nah. Some lady who said she knows you." He paused and raised his chin.

"Who is it?"

"She wouldn't say. She said it was urgent."

"That sounds important. My first official call. "

"Congratulations. But don't take too long. We can't allow long personal calls during working hours."

"I won't be long."

"See you in a few, then." Byron disappeared through the door.

Allie punched the flashing button on her phone. "This is Allie, I mean Dr. Parsons,"

"Is this Allie Florence?" The caller spoke with a cultured British accent.

"Yes. I'm Dr. Parsons."

"Allie, It's Jess. You might remember me as Jess Howell."

"I'm sorry. I don't remember you." Allie rubbed her sore back. "How can I help you?"

"I worked with your mother several years ago when she was still in Tampa. Now I'm Jess Bergman."

"I see." Allie pulled her fingers away from her back. "Interesting." She forgot her back pain and reached for the pencil and pad of paper on her desk. "I don't remember my mother speaking of you." Allie cleared her throat and tensed her hand to write. Did I hear you correctly? Bergman... is that the name...."

"That's right."

Allie shifted in her seat. "Are you calling in reference to an autopsy?"

"Yes, my husband's."

Allie tapped the pencil on the desk. She heard the caller take a deep breath.

"So, how have you been? Chrystal must be in her teens."

"She'll be 13 next week."

"I can't believe it, Allie. *Tempus fugit*, yes? Bea used to talk about her all the time. She's doing well?"

"Very well. Time does fly. How about you?"

"I suppose I'm doing well, under the circumstances."

"Oh. That was a stupid question." Allie closed her eyes. "I know this must be hard for you. It's a small world. I'm working on your husband's case and you knew my mother. I had no idea. I'm sorry about your loss.

"It's been difficult dealing with your police department. This is a stretch for me, Allie. I'm reaching out to a friend's daughter who doesn't even remember me. But I'm in pain and I need answers. My husband was brutally murdered in our home. I need some help from someone who knows what's going on. Detective Festoon said you were doing the autopsy."

"You're correct." Allie scribbled the time and date on her notepad. It seemed like a good start in documenting a conversation.

"Thank you. It's hard to believe. I mean... Well, you know. I feel like I've been limping through life these last few days."

"I hope your son is okay." Allie lifted the pencil away from the notepad. "It can be difficult explaining these things to kids. I know."

"You're right. After a fright, Isaac seems to be doing alright. Franz traveled quite a bit on business. He's used to his father not being around. Both of us are doing the best we can."

"Honestly, I've been there, myself." Allie brushed the hair away from the scar on her forehead. "I'm finishing the dictation to this case, just now."

"Detective Festoon told me this morning that you're new. 'Really raw', I think he said. I was ignoring him like I've learned to do, and then I heard your name in all those words he was saying. I wondered, could that be the Allie Florence I know?"

"I don't remember mother speaking of you. But, we haven't been close over the last few years."

"She talked a lot about you, Allie."

"I'm sure she did."

"She missed you when you were gone for so long. She admired your independent side and I always thought that, in some ways, she was a little proud that no one could rein you in. Bea talked all the time about how smart you were. She knew one day you would turn your life around. She told me that."

"My mother said those things? My mother?"

"Bea could be difficult, I know."

"That sounds more like my mother."

"Bea was very demanding of her employees and, I guess, of you, as well."

"Yes, she was."

"I was sorry she went to New York, but I know it was a great opportunity."

"From what people tell me, it was a good move for her. Like I said before, I'm sorry about what happened to your husband."

"Thank you, for all the time you're putting into solving his, his... well, his horrible murder."

"We're all doing our best. We're going to find this guy."

"That's the reason I called." Allie heard only silence, then Jess drew a loud breath. "My husband knew Toro's identity...and that's why he's dead."

CHAPTER NINETEEN
PRESENT DAY

"I'm sorry, Mrs. Bergman, but I can't talk about this. Please take any information concerning a possible suspect to the police. Thank you for calling. Goodbye."

"Wait! Just hear me out! Don't hang up, Allie. Franz believed Toro to be an employee of ours. He's a very disturbed man who developed much of our optics equipment. But most recently, he was attending to our pool. His name is James Smith. He is extremely charming and a genius. Franz was so convinced James had something to do with Toro, he felt obligated to keep him close by. Let me tell about the evidence we have. Franz saw--"

"Obviously, you've told the police about this guy, so bring it up with them again."

"We did. This led the police to investigate him, but they eliminated him as a suspect. If you read the report of the Toro commission, you'll find he's mentioned."

"I can't remember all the details of that report, Mrs. Bergman, but I accept the commission's opinion that the police caught and killed the real Toro when he resisted arrest."

"Allie, Dear, you know they're wrong, don't you. You suffered through a very brutal attack and they didn't come up with the right answer. Did they? And now my Franz is dead!"

Allie sighed and bit the pencil so forcefully that her teeth pierced the wood. "Mrs. Bergman, Dr. Mann headed that commission and I trust him. He's an excellent pathologist and investigator and really there's no reason I shouldn't think that they came to the correct conclusions."

Allie pulled the phone from her ear and began to drop it towards the receiver.

"Allie! Please listen. I think you'll find Dr. Mann wasn't as...he wasn't as precise as he should have been!"

Allie heard Jess' distant tinny voice through the phone.

"Allie! Fine. Ignore my danger. This is for your own good. And Chrystal's! Please listen!"

Allie held the phone suspended in the air.

"Allie, please."

With a sigh, Allie pulled the phone back to her ear. "Why do you say that?"

"Have you read the commission's report closely?"

"I've looked through it a few times."

"When Franz and I first started to worry about James Smith, we read it carefully. Franz was not physical. He may have been short and stocky, but he was also very smart. He read through it one time and memorized it."

"That's impressive, because that report is organized into chapters."

"Dear, there are gaps. Dr. Mann left a few important things out. Look at it yourself."

"Gaps? Like what?"

"DNA from the crime scene. Where did it go?"

"There was no DNA."

"Read it again, Allie."

"Thanks for your advice, Mrs. Bergman, but I'll stick by Dr. Mann."

"Something happened on that committee to find Toro, Allie. I don't understand it. I bet if you mention James Smith to Dr. Mann, he'll tell you the fellow had nothing to do with the killings. You believe Dr. Mann is good, Allie, and I understand, but there is something underhanded going on."

"Well, there's nothing I can do."

"There is, actually. I got this crazy idea. Franz never thought of this. I have a picture of James, and I want you to look at it."

"You have a picture of him?"

"Yes, I have a few from our security system. They're not very good, but I want you to look at them and tell me what you think. Does he look like the mad man that attacked you? Allie you're the only one who knows what Toro looks like and I believe he matches the description you gave. I think he looks like all the artists' renderings."

"Why didn't your husband just tell the police?"

"He wanted to wait until he had some evidence that would change their opinion. But it never came."

Allie leaned back in the chair and ran her hand through her hair. She sighed. "I'll talk to Detective Fest...Westbrook. The police will contact you and take your statement, Mrs. Bergman."

"Allie,"

"Yes?"

"I really need you to come over so I can show you and see if our fear is legitimate."

"Come over?"

"Please, I want you...no. I implore you to look at these pictures of Smith. Was Franz on to something? Just come over and see. I want my husband's killer found and I want you to be safe."

"I can't. I have to pick up my daughter."

"I understand, but if he killed my husband, attacked you and brutally murdered those other girls, then we need to catch this man. Your daughter is not safe. My son is not safe. And Allie..."

"What?"

"I don't think you can take the risk of not coming over. Be responsible for your safety and Chrystal's. Do this for yourself and all the citizens of Tampa. If we have a chance to catch this guy, we can't walk away."

"Mrs. Bergman, I just can't. I'll be happy to forward you a copy of the pathology report when I finish. "

"Before you try to foolishly forget your past, before you discard all my opinions as rubbish, read the commission's report again."

"I'll think about it, Mrs. Bergman."

"When James drove off in that black Mercedes sedan that Franz had given him, he left the most hateful, heinous note. That's why I'm so worried."

"Left a note?" Allie sat up with a jerk despite the pain in her back.

"Franz destroyed it, unfortunately. I'll give you my number if you want to talk."

"A black Mercedes was around..."

"What?"

"Never mind. I'll think about it, Mrs. Bergman."

"Please don't let him finish what he started. Take my phone number."

She jotted her number down and before Jess could speak again, Allie hung up.

She leaned back in her chair and stared at the ceiling.

Allie would do anything to keep Chrystal safe.

CHAPTER TWENTY
PRESENT DAY

Allie wrestled with Jess Bergman's suspicions as she headed to Byron's office. She found him leaning back in his chair, listening to music.

"Hey, Byron." She gave a half-hearted wave and tried to smile. "How's it going?"

Byron straightened, pushed back in his chair and removed his earbuds. "Fine, Allie. I was waiting for you so we could get started."

"I really need to call Dr. Mann. It's kind of... actually it's an emergency."

"What?"

"Possibly, an emergency, that is."

Byron looked askance. "What's up?"

"It's about something he might have written, and I've got some questions." She fidgeted with her pencil. "I need answers." Allie kept her eyes locked on his.

Byron placed the earbuds on his desk. "If you say so." He shrugged, pulled a sheet of paper towards him and scribbled a number. "I doubt he'll fire you." He handed her the paper.

"That's good to know." Allie took the number from him.

"He won't want to waste the minutes. I think you may be looking at strike two, Allie." He gave a sly grin and made a batter's swing.

Allie winced. "I get three, don't I?"

"Probably. But he throws a lot of strikes and they come very fast."

"Thanks for all you help, Byron."

Byron replaced his earbuds. "Anytime, Hon. When you finish your call, let's get to work."

"I'm on it."

Allie wore an exaggerated grin until she rounded the corner. She walked back to her desk and plopped down in the chair. She sighed and eyed her phone.

Her first three attempts to dial the number ended when she punched the wrong digits. On the fourth attempt, she got it right.

Allie heard a single ring and felt hopeful. She held her breath, but the call went straight to voice mail. "No!" She groaned. Allie hung up and hit redial, but once again she instantly reached Mann's voice mail.

"Uh, Dr. Mann, this is Allie. I have to ask you an urgent question about a note left on my car. Call me when you get a chance. Bye." She grimaced and pulled her hand away and stared at the phone, as if it were toxic.

Allie Parsons, please. You wasted his minutes and what a freakin', horrible voice mail. Now he really will fire you when he gets back.

There was always email, but Dr. Mann had told her he didn't like them. Couldn't hurt and it might work. She typed a quick note asking about the letter and hit send.

Time to get moving.

Allie found Byron and they started on the autopsies. For seven hours they studied, photographed, documented and carved specimens from the dead that rolled through the morgue. After Byron called it quits, Allie remained and worked another hour.

At 6:00 PM she heard Byron collecting his belongings. Her work was done and there was nothing to do but go home and see if Mann would respond. Allie scrubbed her hands in the cold water and dried them with a paper towel.

She checked her email again, but found no new messages.

By the time Allie turned out the light, Byron was gone. She hesitated in the dark hall and stared at the floor.

The Toro Commission's report was online. She should read through it, as Jess had suggested. In the past, she'd dove into the hundreds of pages. She'd hoped for reassurance that Toro was dead. But after being overwhelmed by endless charts, diagrams, transcripts, summaries and, most of all- memories- Allie would quit and not look at it again for two or three years.

It was too painful to read. The grief was too raw.

Allie would be late picking Chrystal up, but by now that was a familiar theme.

CHAPTER TWENTY ONE
THREE YEARS AGO

Medical school had become a challenge. Late nights in the library turned into later pickups at daycare. Allie checked her watch, rolled her eyes and groaned. She swept her books and papers from the cubicle, hurried towards the door and sprinted to the parking lot. Loose papers went sailing in the warm air behind her.

'Easy-Breezy Child Care' would close in 15 minutes. If she hit the lights right, Allie should arrive just as they locked the doors.

As she reached her car, a familiar female voice called out from behind her. "Hey, Allie. We're going to grab a couple of beers. Why don't you come?" It was the confident and cheerful voice of Molly Pritchard.

Allie stopped a few feet from her Honda, grimaced and turned around. By the time she faced Molly and her entourage, Allie had managed to maneuver her lips so that they resembled a smile.

Molly was in her mid-twenties, several inches taller than Allie, and classically pretty with shiny black hair. She possessed high, angular cheekbones and an athletically thin build.

Ranked number one in their medical school class, Molly's astonishing ability to gather students into social groups surpassed even her incredible intellect.

As a result of her many talents and inexhaustible enthusiasm, Molly was elected class president. The unmistakable message to everyone: give up competing for Dr. Mann's Pathology spot; it belongs to Molly.

"I'm really sorry, Molly." Allie shook her head. "I've got to pick my daughter up at after school care and then check on a friend. I appreciate the offer."

"No problem." Molly smiled and nodded. "We're all terribly busy. I've got a ton of studying and then there's the student government business."

"Crazy times. I know." Allie backed towards her Honda and gave an awkward laugh. She ended up sounding more maniacal than amused.

"Maybe next time. Our beer nights are open to every student."

"I'll keep that in mind. But honestly, they charge an extra $10/hour if I'm late getting Chrystal, so I gotta' go."

"Ciao! Health care for all!" Molly turned and with the rest of her group, began their trek towards the bar.

"Ciao." Allie waved as they walked away. Child care for all would be more helpful.

Allie jumped in the old Honda, turned the key and squealed away. Fifteen minutes later, just as the staff was locking the door, she pulled into the daycare parking lot. Allie ran to the door where Chrystal greeted her with arms crossed and a pouty face.

After making her apologies and arguing with Chrystal about the necessity of the car seat, they began their drive to visit Pastor Virgil.

"I need new shoes, Mommy."

"Why, Sweetie?" Allie glanced back at Chrystal as she maneuvered through heavy traffic along Dale Mabry Highway

"They aren't shiny. I think Grandmother wants me to have shiny, black shoes."

"She'll think your shoes are fine. She's going to be happy to have you in New York."

"Is New York big?"

"You know it is, Sweetheart. You ask that every day. It's huge with lots of stores and lights. You'll love it."

"I'll love it." Chrystal held a *Magic Tree House* book in her lap. "Where are we going now?"

"We're going to check on Pastor Virgil. He isn't feeling well." Allie pulled into the drive-thru of a fast food restaurant and rolled down her window. "I'll have the chicken combo with a strawberry milkshake, please."

"Yay! I can put his puzzles together."

A few minutes later they parked in front of Virgil's arts and crafts style home in Old Hyde Park. It had begun to decay after 50 years under the canopy of oak and pine trees. Rotting wood in the fences and cracked concrete on the steps and sidewalks were becoming more common, as the houses and their occupants aged. Allie released Chrystal from her booster seat and they walked hand in hand and rang Virgil's doorbell.

"Come in!" His gravelly voice emerged from the dark interior.

"Pastor Virgil!" Chrystal bounded through the front door.

"Hey, Honey! What are you up to?"

"I'm going to New York City in one week. Can I play with your puzzles?"

"Good for you! Of course, you can play with the puzzles. I have them stacked up waiting. See if you can finish that horse one. He reminds me of an ol' plow horse I had when I was a boy, farming around here."

"Thank you." Chrystal dashed off into the den.

"Virgil, how are you?" Allie bent over his bald head to hug his thin shoulders.

"Oh, in some ways I'm doing very well, Allie. I'm so glad you two are here. Look at you. You brought food. Take it on into the kitchen. I just cleared the table off. I was going to have me some broth."

"I brought a strawberry milkshake and fried chicken. I was hoping you'd feel well enough to eat them."

"I'll take the milkshake. Thank you so much."

They ambled into the kitchen and sat down at an old oak table covered with dents and scratches.

He took a sip of the milkshake. "Ah, that's good. Goes down easy."

"So, did you go to the doctor?"

"I did."

"And?"

"Well..." He took another sip of milkshake and looked her in the eyes. "Thanks for making me see a doctor. They tell me I have cancer. Isn't that the darndest?"

Allie narrowed her eyes. "What?"

"I've got cancer. I can't swallow my food."

"How?"

"You were right when you said something was wrong with me. I have cancer of my esophagus, just like in your book. That's why I haven't been able to eat. They saw it on the cat scan and showed me the pictures. It looks like it's spread." He took another sip.

Allie felt her eyes welling up. "I didn't think it was anything to worry about. What's going to happen?" Her voice shook.

"Radiation, chemotherapy and maybe surgery. My doctor thinks I've got some time left. Maybe years. Maybe not. Doctors don't like to make those predictions. I'm not sure what your book says, but it doesn't matter anyway."

Allie's sniffed. "I'll help you anyway I can."

"I know you will. Have some chicken, Honey. It's getting cold."

"No, thanks. I'm not hungry."

Allie looked at the ceiling. "Virgil, I want you to know, you've been like my father for so long now." She wiped her nose. "Please, let me help you."

"Allie, don't worry about me. If it's my time to go, I'll go. I've been without Sylvia 15 years now, and maybe this is God's way of getting us back together. I'm okay with that."

"I know, but it's really hard for me." Allie wiped the tears from her cheek.

Virgil placed his hands on hers. "If you really want to help me, finish your schooling and all the training to be a doctor. I'm so proud of you. Sylvia and I never were able to have kids, but I feel God sent you to me. I have never seen anyone pull her life together like you. So promise me, you won't quit. Allie, you inspire me."

"Oh, my gosh, Virgil. Those guys in my class are so smart and so driven. School is their talent. They're like elite professional athletes and I'm some rec league hack yelling 'Hey fella's, throw me the ball!'"

Virgil laughed and squeezed her hands tighter.

"I work hard, but I'm really terrible at this. Sometimes I do want to quit."

Virgil raised his eyebrows and took another sip of milkshake. "You asked what you could do. You could drop out, but you'd be throwing away a second chance. A second chance you've been given to help you and Chrystal."

"This is so hard."

"I believe this is a challenge for you. You've got many more to come and there are going to be difficult battles along the way. But you've got to be prepared to win them all. There may not be much longer for any of us."

Allie was familiar with Virgil's 'end of the world' speeches. She looked at his gaunt face and twinkling eyes and simply nodded. "Okay. You're right. I'll do it. I'll stick it out. I promise I'll finish med school and medical training."

"No matter how hard it is?"

"No matter how hard. I know I have to do it for Chrystal and it means a lot to you, too. I won't promise what my class rank will be, though."

"You know what they call the person who graduates last in his medical school class?"

"What?"

Virgil grinned and patted Allie's hands. "Doctor!"

CHAPTER TWENTY TWO
PRESENT DAY

Allie reminded herself that in high school, she had qualified for the state meet in pole vault and was competitive in the 100, 200, 400 and mile and placed in most meets without really trying. Those memories provided her some comfort, because three miles into their impromptu run, she realized she'd underestimated Chrystal's athletic ability.

As Allie chased her daughter, her heart pounded and her lungs greedily grabbed any oxygen that filtered through the dense, wet air.

"Pace yourself, Sweetheart. This is a long run. Save something for the finish."

"We're almost done, Mom. We'll sprint back to our dorm." Chrystal bolted ahead.

When Allie arrived at their dorm and collapsed on the rough sidewalk, Chrystal was sitting on the steps checking her phone messages. "I get the shower first. I'm sweaty."

"Sure. Give me a chance to rest. I'm a little sweaty, too."

"Good run. You're right. That was fun. Did you burn off your anxiety? How's your back? I don't know if I can do this tomorrow. I'm kind of tired." Chrystal jabbered and texted simultaneously.

"My back is better. Wait... I got a note yesterday..." Allie gulped and pursed her lips. "Have you seen anyone unusual around here? Someone in a black Mercedes?"

"I've seen a lot of weird people. They're everywhere. What are you talking about? Who?"

"I don't know." Allie struggled to sit up. "Maybe a bearded--"

Her phone rang and as Allie slumped onto the ground, it tumbled from her sweaty hand and landed at Chrystal's feet.

"Are you going to get that, Mom?"

"Not sure. See who it is, will you?"

Chrystal rolled her eyes, but reached over and retrieved Allie's phone from the sidewalk. "Mom's phone. Yeah, she's right here."

"Who is it?" Allie pushed up on her elbows and took the phone out of Chrystal's hand.

Chrystal shrugged her shoulders and sat back on the steps. "Some man."

Allie glanced at her caller ID, and her worry became reality. It was Duncan. Her weary body collapsed onto the sidewalk and she stared at the ominous clouds growing bloated and dark with rain. Ugh!

Still too exhausted to do anything except hold her phone and breathe, Allie stared at his name, glowing brilliant white at the top of her screen.

Her thumb, spontaneously, drifted towards the 'end call' button.

"Allie?" Duncan's voice sounded commanding and confident even through the small speaker.

"Are you okay, Mom?" Chrystal looked down at Allie.

"I'm fine." Allie sat up and spoke into the phone. "Duncan. Hey. I'm running with my daughter. I don't really have time to talk."

"I'll be quick, Allie. Please, don't hang up on me. I know you don't owe me anything, but I would very much like to sit down and talk. I need this."

"Duncan, I'm very busy with my new job and my daughter."

"I understand, but if you could just spare a few hours one evening. I need some closure. We never had any. There are things I need to discuss."

"Duncan--"

"Let's make it dinner. It'll be brief. Nothing fancy. We'll talk in a public place then you can be on your way."

"Short conversation? Quick supper?"

"Then I'll disappear. I promise. No strings attached. Please?"

Allie took a deep breath. She felt drained and had no strength to oppose Duncan. "Okay, as usual you talked me in to it. Where and when?"

"How about Berns, Thursday?"

"I thought you said nothing fancy?"

"The Columbia, then."

"So 'casual' is off the table."

"Not at all. They know me there. It will be casual, I promise. People even wear shorts now."

"What time?"

"Eight."

"Okay. I'll see you there at eight. Bye."

"Allie--"

She hung up, stared at her screen and placed her phone in her shorts pocket.

"What was all that about, Mom?"

"Just an old friend. Hey, thanks for the run. I haven't been distanced like that since I ran against an Olympic qualifier in the State Games."

"You're so weird." Chrystal wrinkled her nose and smiled.

Allie pulled her phone back out and scrolled through her contact list.

"Who are you calling now?"

"Another old buddy. Her name is Francesca...Menendez. There she is." She pushed 'dial', thought better of it, then hung up. "Forget it."

"Changed your mind?"

Allie shook her head and grunted. "That's water under the bridge. I'll handle this and be done with it forever." Allie reminded herself to keep moving forward and not to be led into temptation.

CHAPTER TWENTY THREE
PRESENT DAY

After Allie showered and changed into clean cotton shorts and a t-shirt, she slid her laptop computer from the old backpack her mother had given her for Christmas when she was 16. She felt exhausted but relieved to be clean and dry.

A sudden storm rumbled over the Bay and the setting sun was hidden behind clouds. The only thing that frightened Allie more than fireworks was being outside during lightning.

Through the thick cinder block walls of her graduate student apartment, Allie could hear the deep rumble of thunder and felt the windows vibrate so intensely it seemed they would shatter.

Allie sat on the old couch with her elbows propped on her knees and her hands covering her face. She was deep in thought and scarcely noticed as the room grew darker and rain pelted the windows. Both table lamps were off, and as the ominous thunderheads obscured the sun, the soft glow from her computer grew brighter in the darkening room.

As Allie sat in the twilight created by storm and electronic light, her mind wandered back to her college years and the five-year anniversary of the attacks. She thought about the Tampa Tribune's series of articles describing in vivid detail 'Toro's Time Line of Terror'.

One article had made her particularly angry, because it attempted to provide an in-depth profile of Allie. It was headlined, 'The

Toreador!' Despite the newspaper's best efforts, Allie had refused to be interviewed. Allie scoffed, if you want to drive me away, all you have to do is mention the murders.

Allie thought about Phillip Spears, a classmate with black hair and the most adorable dimples. She smiled. He had asked her out three times. At first she declined, but on his fourth try, he sent a hilarious card with cartoon trolls and heart shaped candy.

Allie remembered being suckered in when she saw the trolls. The next day, Phillip had phoned and they met on campus at the 'Bull Ring Café', a favorite of students wanting a fast meal.

However, when Phillip had asked about Toro for a second time, the meal of microwaved pizza and Budweiser, ended abruptly. Looking back now, she appreciated that one of the trolls had looked like Phillip.

Ever since the attack, Allie realized, she had built a reputation of being awkward and antisocial.

How strange. I went from party girl to hermit.

Allie closed the lid on her computer and roughly rubbed her already tussled hair. She peered across the dark room, looking for an old, brown shoebox. A corner of the box was barely visible behind a stack of dusty VHS movies.

Why?

She uncrossed her legs and walked stiffly over to the shelf. She squatted and gently wiggled the box from behind the bulky tapes.

It was a box that once held a very small pair of white Adidas tennis shoes. Shoes that would delight a three year-old boy.

They were now buried with Luke.

Allie pried the dusty top off the box. She raised her eyebrows and pursed her lips to fight back the tears.

Inside, she found a tiny gold crucifix, a small orange and blue football, three muscular action figures, and a pacifier.

Allie started to silently cry. Chrystal's birthday was a few days away. But so was Luke's.

If there was any chance Toro was back, she had to know. If Jess Bergman was right, she couldn't let her children down. Not this time.

Allie wiped her tears away. She picked up the crucifix and kissed it tenderly before laying it beside the football. She replaced the lid and slid the box behind the tapes. Her hand lingered on the box before she returned to the couch and opened her laptop.

As she'd done many times in the past, Allie typed the web address to the Toro commission's report and clicked the links until she found it. Reading the report was agonizing, but tonight she would see it through.

Allie found the compilation consisted of 412 pages of reports and testimony, a table of contents and several dozen appendices that included multiple diagrams and photos. The website indicated that Florida's 'Sunshine Law' made all the evidence public record.

Allie clicked until she found victim number one, Sara Larson. Pages 14-92 dealt with Sara.

According to the reports, Sara had dark hair like Allie's, but paler skin. Though a young and pretty gymnast, she still possessed a small layer of baby fat under her skin. These findings had been meticulously documented by Dr. Mann on page 14.

According to her parents who had had lunch with her hours before she was murdered, Sara smiled as easily the day she died as when she giggled while reaching for the colorful mobile that dangled above her crib. Their statements were documented on page 30.

Despite her door being bolted and chained, Toro had apparently rocked it off its hinges, though the exact mechanism could not be determined. Loud music from a neighbor drowned out any sounds of the assault. A copy of the police report included these details on page 35.

Allie looked at the timeline of Toro's murders. Sara had been stabbed to death three weeks before Allie's attack. She lived in Bradenton, several miles south of Allie, and was last seen in a bar two blocks from her apartment. The next day, Sara's landlord discovered the grisly crime scene when he entered her apartment in an attempt to collect the delinquent rent.

According to the description of the evidence, skin-like material found under Sara's fingernails may have come from the killer.

Allie clicked on the appendix in the report and stared at the Sara's senior high school picture. "Why her?" She sighed.

Allie left that page and skipped to the summary of evidence presented to the commission. The committee concluded that, based on Dr. Mann's testimony, there was no DNA and the material under Sara's fingernails was not flesh, but an organic substance of an unknown nature, possibly dough from baking. All the blood present at the crime scene was from Sara.

Microfibers from a textile not present in the apartment were collected at the scene. The killer may have transported the fibers to her apartment, per the report.

She skipped victim number two, Allie Parsons. She couldn't bear to read it.

Pages 204-289 recapped victim number three. Renee Rowan had been beaten and stabbed to death four weeks after Allie was assaulted. The murder had taken place north of the Tampa/St. Petersburg area, in Renee's mobile home near Crystal River. Allie once met Renee. She was a prostitute and made the money that supported her heroin addiction by bringing men back to her trailer. She remembered Renee being stoned but sweet. As Allie also recalled, Renee was fascinated by garden gnomes, but this was not in the report.

The file photos showed a rusty, single-wide mobile home with mold and moss growing on the outside walls, parked in an isolated clearing off a long dirt road on 20 acres of scrub land owned by her daddy.

Someone had ripped the siding off her trailer and slipped through the gap. Dr. Mann had concluded Toro must be incredibly strong.

Next, Allie read the statement from Renee's drunk boyfriend. He described finding her body. He managed to thoroughly contaminate the crime scene before calling the police. When the police arrived at the trailer, they found her boyfriend sobbing, with stained clots of Renee's blood covering his clothing.

His name was immediately released to the press as the primary person of interest in Renee's killing.

The boyfriend's alibi of being in the Dixie County Jail at the time of the murder held up, and the police were forced to look elsewhere for a suspect.

As with victim number one, it initially appeared Renee scraped her killer's skin with her fingernails. However, in a later report Dr. Mann determined the material to be caulk and the entirety of the copious quantity of blood coating the greasy floor, dirty walls and dilapidated ceiling, belonged to Renee. In addition, Dr. Mann testified that Renee had probably been too intoxicated to fight.

Victim number four, discussed in pages 290-322, lay for days until discovered by hunters on flat, shrub-covered low-land in a hammock of palm and pine trees near I-75, around Plant City. Two hunters had just killed a hog rooting near the body. After no one claimed her corpse, the mutilated remains were cremated at the county's expense and the State officially changed her name to Jane Doe.

Her face had been surgically removed by the assailant and no DNA profile could be found. No fingerprints matched and, because the killer thoroughly scrubbed her with bleach, no evidence, other than hog and coyote saliva, remained.

The last paragraph on page 326 concluded that Toro had evolved into a skilled serial killer. One of the best.

However, Allie realized, the report lacked the essence of what Tampa had endured.

As she read back over the descriptions of the victims, Allie relived the stress.

Allie remembered years ago, while in the hospital recovering from Toro's attack, she would use the narcotic pain medicines to calm the fear. She wouldn't allow herself to head down that path again.

She wiped her forehead and massaged her scalp. Then Allie turned back to the computer screen and clicked on the tab labeled 'suspects'.

A search through nearly 100 names led her to James Smith, a cousin of Sara Larson, the first victim, and the man Jess Bergman felt killed her husband. James Smith went by several assumed names and since fifth grade, had been diagnosed with anti-social personality disorder. He possessed an amazing ability in math as demonstrated by his perfect SAT score. Over the years, he accumulated arrests for various assaults on women, though never with a deadly weapon. He also served short jail stints for minor misdemeanors. Allie noted the report didn't mention his employment.

Even though James didn't provide a single corroborated alibi for any of the nights there was a killing, the commission did not consider him a strong suspect. No physical evidence existed to link him with a crime scene.

As Allie read further she found that after being interrogated, Smith disappeared and remained lost to follow up. Apparently, he stayed clean and accumulated no further arrests on his rap sheet.

Allie shook her head and clicked on the next tab. Great! He's been in Tampa this whole time and no one knew it.

According to the commission report, the suspect most likely to be Toro was Stan 'Bull' Kozlowski. Despite being in 10 line-ups, Allie never picked him out. He did own a carpet made of fibers identical to those found in Sara Larson's apartment. In addition, he frequented the bars where Allie worked, and because of his hulking figure, several of his buddies called him 'Bull'. Another friend said he and Kozlowski had recently driven the long dirt road down to Renee Rowan's trailer.

Most importantly, after a few drinks he reportedly bragged to friends that he was the 'dude who killed those girls'. Although the report included those details, he vehemently denied them when questioned by authorities and he volunteered to take a lie detector test. There was no explanation of why the police didn't give him one.

Eventually, Tampa Police shot Stan when he created a violent scene at the foot of the Sunshine Skyway Bridge. According to official reports, he threatened officers by waving a handgun at them. During her interrogation, his girlfriend screamed that he'd cracked because of the endless police pressure. She added after calming down, Kozlowski had been drinking tequila for two days.

The Tampa Police finally concluded that Kozlowski committed 'suicide by cop' because he'd recognized there 'was no way out of the situation he had perpetrated on the public.'

Allie sighed and sat back on the sofa. She really needed a cigarette.

CHAPTER TWENTY FOUR
PRESENT DAY

At least she needed to smell a cigarette. These 'moments of requirement', as she called them, were becoming more infrequent. But occasionally when she was stressed, Allie longed to lay on her back in the cool grass, stare at the stars and feel soothing tobacco smoke warm her chest.

An old crumpled pack of cigarettes was stashed in the lowest drawer in her desk. Silently, she pulled the pack with matches from beneath the pile of papers as she stared intently at Chrystal's closed door.

Allie slipped the pack into the pocket of her cotton shorts. "I'll be outside getting some air. Text if you need me."

"Okay, Mom. I'll be here in the shared bedroom."

Allie slipped out and slunk down the sturdy metal stairs into the cooler, humid air. The storm had passed from the Gulf towards Lake Okeechobee. The thunder sounded like a distant rumble seconds after each flicker on the horizon. Allie made her way to the parking lot near the community green and lifted a cigarette to her lips.

Her fingers fumbled as she tried to strike the match against the coarse and frayed edge of the box.

Something brushed her shoulder.

Allie whipped around and in a split second had her fingers tightly around her assailant's neck. "What gives?"

"It's me, Allie! Andrew Wong. You're choking me!"

"Sorry, Andrew." She backed away with the unlit cigarette still clenched in her teeth. "You scared the crap out of me!"

"Apparently." He coughed, held his throat and bent over. "Wow! You're fast!"

"You shouldn't sneak up on me."

"No one in my Tae Kwon Do class can take me out that fast. Where did you learn to do that?"

"I don't know. It's all reaction and reflex. Are you okay?"

He straightened and noticed the cigarette sagging between her lips and the matches she'd dropped near her ankles.

"I'll be alright. I didn't know you smoked. I'm learning so much about you."

"Oh." Allie looked sheepish and pulled the cigarette away from her mouth, shoving it, along with the matches, into her pocket. "I don't really. I got this craving for one, but I don't really. I'll... just throw it away."

Wong wiped his neck and then rubbed the front of his jeans. "Those things will kill you over time. But, you just about killed me instantly."

"I know, Andrew. I'm sorry about the hand to the throat thing. It just happens." Allie shook her head.

"I guess I mostly see you at the pool and I wave first. I'll remember that. 'Hello' can save your life."

"I'm impulsive."

Andrew was six inches taller than Allie, and looked about the same age with a thin, athletic build. His long, black hair was parted down the middle and nearly reached his shoulders.

"Hey, actually, what I wanted to know was... before you tried to kill me, is what would Chrystal like for her birthday? Being a lab nerd, I'm not real good at picking gifts for teenage girls. I don't think she'd be interested in thermonuclear theory, which is what I'm working on right now. After all, I'm--"

"A rocket scientist." Allie finished his sentence and smiled.

"Almost done. One more year."

"You're a rocket scientist-in-training." Allie tapped his shoulder with the back of her hand. "You don't need to get her anything, Andrew. But, thank you. It's very thoughtful."

"Yeah, but her party's here at the pool, so I really want to bring something."

"Actually, there's been a change of plans. Apparently. It's not at the university pool anymore."

"Oh, in your apartment, or the beach?"

"Neither. I actually have no idea where it's going to be."

"She can't decide?"

"It's more complicated than that. It involves the horribly intricate mind of a teenage girl high on hormones."

"Hormones! That's why I stick to the simple subjects like aeronautical engineering."

"Good decision."

"So, what would Chrystal like?"

"Don't worry about it, Andrew. She's really tough to shop for."

"I know she likes art and painting."

"She loves to paint."

Andrew smiled. "Great. It's taken care of."

"Don't buy anything too expensive."

"Allie, I don't have any money."

"Good. I mean, I'm sorry you don't have any money. It's part of being a graduate student. I'm just asking that you don't splurge."

"Don't worry about it. I'm not going to spend a dime..."

"Good."

"...more than I have to."

"Andrew!"

"No, I'm serious. And please don't put me in that choke hold again! Tell me when you decide where the party is going to be. I want to hitch a ride."

"Yeah, absolutely." She tossed the cigarettes and matches into the trashcan. "Sorry again, about the whole choke hold thing." She pulled her smart phone from her back pocket and pretended to open an app.

"No, problem. See ya'."

"Bye." Allie waved.

Several steps later he disappeared along the dark sidewalk.

Allie stretched her thin neck to make sure Andrew was gone. She rummaged through the trashcan for the cigarettes and matches, found them and lit the first one she pulled from the pack.

She took a long drag and exhaled through her nostrils. It felt good. She smiled and sat back on the step.

"Enough!" She crushed the cigarette with her foot. Her muscles felt relaxed from her shoulders to her thighs.

It's time to get down to business. Allie picked up her phone and dialed Jess' number.

After the fifth ring, Jess Bergman answered.

"Hello. This is Jess."

"Mrs. Bergman, it's Allie Parsons."

"Well, I thought you might call. I had a sneaking suspicion that you'd look at that report again."

"Just finished some heavy reading. I want to see your pictures."

"Excellent! You won't regret this. Tomorrow?"

"That will work. I'll come to your house as soon as Chrystal gets home from school."

"Perfect, bring her along. This little visit just might change your life."

CHAPTER TWENTY FIVE
PRESENT DAY

The next morning Allie raced through the morgue doors at exactly 6:00 AM. She made her way to the autopsy suite and sliced into a 70 year-old female who suffered an unexplained death in the Intensive Care Unit.

A little before 7:00, Byron cruised into the dissection and, holding a mug of steaming coffee, nodded at Allie as she removed an undiagnosed abscess and cancer-ridden kidney.

"I found the cause of death." Allie held up the lumpy, pus-filled kidney and thick, yellow purulent goo dripped like raw honey from the cortex.

"Atta girl!" Byron raised his mug in a salute and disappeared from the door.

Throughout the day, Allie continued to grind away. She had a bite of bagel for lunch and took no breaks. The thought of visiting Jess Bergman and viewing the pictures of James Smith made her slightly queasy and killed her appetite. She tried to take her mind off of it by burying herself in work.

"Have you heard anything from Dr. Mann?" She glanced over her mask to Byron.

He finished slicing a brain into thin sections during an unsuccessful search for a tumor, then tossed his bloody gloves into the trash. "No, Ma'am. He's left the morgue to us."

Allie hid her disappointment and continued with the autopsy. There was more pus behind the spleen and the horrendous stench made her feel even sicker.

Since she had been first to arrive at the morgue, Allie felt a little less guilty about leaving early.

At 3:00, with work still to be done, Byron stood aghast as Allie breezed past.

She ignored him. This is for Chrystal and Luke. And the others.

Driving to Chrystal's bus stop, Allie decided that tomorrow she would again, be the earliest at work. That resolution helped her feel a little better about skipping out of the morgue. She saw Chrystal step off the bus as her Honda came to a halt.

"How was school?".

"It was fine." Chrystal heaved her backpack across the blue passenger seat so that it crushed the six Styrofoam cups that were stained brown from Allie's instant coffee. Having been there for so long, the cups were as much a part of the car as the cloth seats. "Mr. Morgan told me that I'm an incredible math student and I need to be an engineer."

"Oh, my Gosh! That's wonderful, Honey."

"No. Not, wonderful!" Chrystal pulled the stained seatbelt across her shoulder. "I want to be a fashion designer. Grandmother says I could be really good." A loud squeak eeked from the worn car door as she pulled it shut.

"But you always get 'A's in math." Allie steered the Honda out of the parking lot and onto Dale Mabry Highway. "Engineering's really good for math brains."

"I get A's in everything. But I want to design clothes. I want to be the future of fashion."

"Honey, I like what you've drawn. But you're so good at math."

"It's my style, Mother. I'm trying to find something that says, 'Chrystal'."

"Well, Sweetie. I believe in you. Just, please, keep up with your math while you're rocking the fashion world."

"Look, here's what I drew after school." Chrystal turned and reached behind her. She pulled a sketchbook from her bulky backpack and flipped to the middle.

Slowing to a stop at the intersection of Dale Mabry and Kennedy, Allie glanced down for a quick peek at the angular figures sketched in pencil. "Chrystal, that is really good. I'm impressed. It looks like something from Paris."

"Actually, more Milan." Chrystal closed her sketchpad. "I've got so much homework. Are we going to have spaghetti again?"

"Maybe." Allie opened her mouth, but didn't speak. She hesitated as she accelerated from the stoplight and then, after a deep breath, turned towards Chrystal. "Sweetie, have you seen anyone hanging around that seems to be looking at you or me? Driving a black Mercedes?"

"Mom, that's creepy. Why do you keep asking questions like that?"

"Have you seen an older man with a dark beard?"

"Okay, quit being weird. Why are you asking?"

"Nothing?"

"No, I haven't."

"Forget it. It's something all parents are supposed to ask."

"Are you serious?"

"Just forget it."

"Mom, it's hard to forget a question like that."

"But you're immensely talented and smart so I know you can. Are you up for a little drive?"

"I'm hungry. I want to eat."

"First, we have to meet someone."

"Mom. I'm so hungry and I'm really tired. Can't you just take me back to the dorm?"

"It's not a, a...I don't have time, Chrystal. It won't take long. It's a lady that used to work for your grandmother."

"Oh." Chrystal cocked her head towards Allie. She returned the notepad to her backpack. "Worked with Grandmother? What's her name? Is she a designer? Or is she a reporter?"

"I don't know what Mrs. Bergman did. But she needs help, so she called me. Her name is Jess Bergman. Or Jess Howell."

"Weird. Never heard of her." Chrystal sat up straight and placed her hands politely in her lap. "Where does she live?"

"What difference does that make?"

"It means everything, Mother."

"In Davis Islands."

"Oh my G--"

"Chrystal."

"Oh, awesome. What's the address? Please, Mom. The address!"

"It's on my phone, Loony."

Chrystal grabbed her mother's phone from the grooves abutting the gear shift. She scrolled through the contacts and gasped. "That's the same road Carly lives on. Are you kidding me? This is great!"

"So, you're okay if we drive over and see Mrs. Bergman tonight?"

"Mom! I can't wait. That's such a nice neighborhood! It's tres chic."

"So happy to hear that." Allie smiled. "I guess your homework can be on hold for a while?"

Chrystal looked around the interior of the Honda. "We have to clean this car. It's disgusting."

"It's not so bad." Allie watched Chrystal stack napkins, paper cups and odd pieces of paper at her feet.

"It's awful. We've got to clean it out."

"She won't care. Her husband just passed away. She's had a big loss. She just wants some advice. She won't be looking in my car."

"You don't know that! Besides, we can't take that chance. Can you pull over at a gas station so I can throw all this away?"

"Are you serious?"

"Of course, I'm serious. I don't want her to think I'm some slob. You have no idea of what we're getting ourselves into."

"What?"

"Trust me, you don't have a clue. But it'll be fine. I'll take care of it."

"Whatever. If it makes you happy, we'll do some cleaning."

Allie found a gas station and coasted through the parking lot, stopping a few feet from a trashcan. Chrystal hopped out of the car with a bundle of trash and dumped it in the can. As the lid flipped shut, she darted back to the car and wiped the dashboard and seat with a catsup-stained napkin.

While Allie was helping to dispose of a few tissues, she noticed a headline in the Tampa newspaper. "I'll be back in a second, Honey." Allie wandered over to the rack, deposited 75¢ and pulled the top copy out.

'Millionaire Murdered. Body Found in Bay.'

The article went on to recount the story of the Bergman murder, omitting the detail of the broken window and the vase. In the last paragraph, Jess and Franz Bergman's philanthropic work was covered.

"What are you doing, Mom?"

"Just reading something." Allie tossed the paper in the trash. She didn't want to scare Chrystal.

"Well, I'm done." Chrystal wrinkled her nose. "I guess that's the best it's going to look."

"Personally, I think it's great, Chrystal. This is the cleanest this car has been in years."

"That's a sad statement, Mom."

"You're right." Allie drew a deep breath and surveyed the interior of the car. "But this Honda has been loyal and reliable. We should be thankful for it. Hey, this little excursion will be fun. Maybe there'll be some rare art or fashion or something. You know, bring it on."

"Yeah." Chrystal looked over the car again. "You're right. Let the adventure begin!"

They crossed the bridge next to Tampa General Hospital and drove past Mercedes and BMWs towards the large houses that loomed in the distance. "This is it. This is the street Carly lives on."

As they passed each grand house, Chrystal read the addresses and commented on the neat lawns, columns, winding driveways and

Spanish architecture that characterized the palatial homes along Tampa Bay.

"Mom, I'm not exaggerating when I say these homes are bigger than our whole dorm building."

"Much bigger than our graduate student housing. Like a neighborhood of Spanish castles."

As they drove further towards the end of the island, Allie slowed the car. They approached an airport with lush, green grass surrounding a tarmac runway.

Behind the resort sized estates, majestic sailboats bobbed and listed on the glistening water of Tampa Bay. Their masts swayed across the purple horizon painted by the setting south Florida sun.

"Impressive. You know if you kept sailing west, you'd land in Texas."

"I can't imagine living here. I'd live in the garage. I'd live in the part of the garage that has the greasy spots."

"Chrystal, they put their pants on one leg at a time."

"Mom...cliché's. You promised you wouldn't lecture me in cliché's."

"Sorry."

"That's the address. The one on the right. Okay, turn here!"

"Which driveway?"

"That one with the palm trees. Slow down."

"That one? There's a gate."

"Yeah, but it's open. She knows we're coming. Now pull up the driveway. Oh, coconuts!"

"What's wrong?"

"Coconut trees all the way to the house. It's beautiful."

CHAPTER TWENTY SIX
PRESENT DAY

The tree-lined driveway led towards an ornate Spanish Colonial style house with stucco walls, red clay tiled roof and an arched entrance. A massive, wooden front door was secured with thick cast iron hinges.

As they parked near a tile fountain in the front yard, the dark door swung open and a thin woman in her late 30's walked from beneath the portico. She had short black hair, a delicate face with a narrow nose and a defined chin accented with a dimple. She stood motionless for a moment then descended the stairs to the driveway.

Her tired, green eyes disappeared behind black lenses as she put on her designer sunglasses. Two dimples appeared in her cheeks when she smiled.

"You must be Mrs. Bergman." Allie opened the squeaky driver's door and stepped out.

"Good to finally meet you, Allie. Please call me Jess." Jess Bergman spoke in a cultured British accent. "Thank you so much for coming."

Chrystal checked her makeup in the rearview mirror and opened the door. When she stepped out of the car, she towered over her mother and Jess.

"And you must be Chrystal. You are absolutely gorgeous! I love your blouse. That's the way the designer wanted it to look. I believe I met him in fact. Versace? Am I right?"

"It's from H&M, I think."

"Well done! It looks lovely on you!"

"Thank you, Mrs. Bergman. I love your home."

"You have a beautiful home, Mrs. Bergman." Allie reached out to shake Jess Bergman's hand and glanced around the grounds.

"Thank you. Yes, it came together well. Franz was very happy with the results. That's saying something, because he was a perfectionist. Some may say he was crazy, but I say he was a genius."

"Well, it's really amazing."

"Come in, please. Let's get away from these mosquitoes. Do they bother you, Allie?"

"They don't seem to like me."

"I'm glad to hear that, because they're pecking me to death!"

For a moment, the hair on the back of Allie's neck stood up and her tattoo seemed to burn. Instinctively, she looked up and caught a glimpse of a silhouette retreating from a second story window.

"Your son must be shy." Allie's eyes lingered on the empty window.

Jess stopped and looked back at Allie.

"Pardon?"

"I saw someone looking out the window, but he left when he caught me watching."

"Yes, shy." Jess coughed. "This has been hard on him."

Allie and Chrystal followed Jess as she ascended the steps and stopped on the landing. Opening the door, Jess stumbled on the 'Welcome' mat and caught herself on the iron doorknob.

"Excuse me, I must be exhausted. This tragedy with Franz is so daunting. I'm apologizing in advance if I'm not a gracious host."

"Don't worry about us, I understand how difficult this can be." Allie placed her hand on her chest as she spoke.

"We're fine, Mrs. Bergman. We're very sorry about your loss."

Jess took a deep breath and smoothed her shirt. "Well. Thank you. That means a lot.

I'm going to get through this." She leaned her shoulder into the door and it eased open. "Franz insisted on having this heavy door put in. It reminded him of Barcelona, where with his pale, bald head...uh, he always had one of those floppy hats on."

She stepped inside and motioned for Allie and Chrystal to follow. "Whew. I think it could hold out an armed assault. I'm afraid James Smith came in through the back."

When they entered the spacious foyer, Allie saw rustic, wrought iron rails adorning the numerous balconies and two stairwells. The sparsely decorated walls were smeared with a bright white plaster that was smooth at first but swept into waves and wrinkles between antique cornices and brilliant oil paintings.

Ornate sconces mounted in alcoves provided most of the light. A few hidden lights along the floor illuminated the remainder of the room.

An immense brick fireplace, five feet across, was carved into the opposite wall. In it, a large black, cast iron pot hung from a thick, black bar.

"This is like something from St. Augustine." Chrystal blushed. "It's just so amazing! It's like something in Europe."

"That's what he was going for." Jess sat down on a stool in front of a green granite bar. "I just need to compose myself. I apologize again, Ladies." She breathed heavily. "As I was saying, Franz wanted old world, and that's what St. Augustine is. He was fascinated by Florida's history, and he adored Spain."

"I would love to go to Europe." Chrystal gazed in wonder at the balconies and sconces that emerged from the old world walls. "This is an incredible house."

"One day you will go to Europe, Chrystal, and before you do, you must come and ask my advice. I'll set you up with the most fabulous guides and share the local secrets!"

"That would be wonderful!"

"It will change your life. I promise. Can I get you two anything to drink?"

"We're fine, thank you." Allie shook her head.

"Well, you won't mind if I have a glass of wine. That and a Xanax and I can actually fall asleep." Jess poured a glass, took a long sip, then placed the glass on the bar and sighed. "It's from a good year for Chardonnay, as Franz liked to say. Chrystal?"

"I don't care for any wine, Mrs. Bergman."

Jess chuckled. "So be it. Would it be okay if my son Isaac showed you around the house? Being an artist, I think you'd appreciate some of the architectural touches. Isaac's shy, but ask questions and make him talk. It'll be good for him."

Chrystal glanced at Allie. "Is that alright, Mom?"

"Sure. You don't get to see a house like this every day."

"Isaac?" Jess turned her neck and called towards the stairs. "Come down, Sweetheart. Chrystal wants a tour of the house." She faced Chrystal. "He's going to be very shy around you, Chrystal. He's 11, but you know boys. They don't mature as fast as girls. And unfortunately, like his father, he's always much quieter around pretty girls. But please, bring him out of his shell. This has been hard on him. I'll even cover a babysitting fee."

"No! We'll have fun. And I'd really like to see your home."

A few seconds later, the tapping of soft footsteps could be heard on the stairs. A pale boy with short hair as black as Jess' and parted on the side, descended the steps. He wore pressed khaki shorts cinched at the waist by a belt embroidered with whales, and a blue oxford cloth button-down shirt. His bare feet were crisscrossed with thready, blue veins.

When he reached the first floor, Isaac stood still and stared silently at Jess.

"Isaac, Honey, come over and meet the Parsons. This is Dr. Parsons and her daughter, Chrystal."

Isaac didn't move, but bit his lip and lowered his eyes. "Sweetie, give Chrystal the grand tour. Show her the whole place. Be pleasant, Isaac. Talk to her. Be a proper host."

"Fine, Mother. This way." He held his arms rigidly at his sides. "Upstairs is where I play a lot. That's also where Daddy lives."

"Thank you, Honey, I'm so proud of you, Sweetheart."

Chrystal looked towards her mother and gave a slight shrug of her shoulders. "Good job, Isaac. You're going to give a great tour."

Though stiff and awkward, Isaac walked very quickly up the stairs and Chrystal had to lengthen her already long stride to keep up with him.

When the children were out of sight, Jess gave an exaggerated sigh. Her lips drooped as she turned her gaze from the top of the stairs back towards Allie. "It's hard to keep it together in front of Isaac. But, of course, I have to. As you just heard, sometimes he talks as if Franz is still alive."

"I understand. I'm very sorry for what you're going through. I realize there's not a lot that can be said to help. When I lost...is there anything you need, Mrs. Bergman?"

"Where do I start? I'd like you to look over everything and tell me what you think. Let me know if I'm missing something. I'm going to be blunt here, if you're okay with that."

"I'm fine with that."

"According to the police, everyone is a suspect. That includes me. They told me not to leave town, so I'm living with my young son in the house where my husband was murdered. I don't believe they have the slightest clue who killed Franz...and I'm terrified that the murderer is coming back for me!"

Before Allie could respond, Jess continued talking.

"James Smith is Toro. That's why I'm scared. He's still out there! I'm telling you this because you ought to know. And all of Tampa should know. For everyone's safety."

Jess took another sip of wine and looked straight into Allie's eyes.

Allie pursed her lips and took a deep breath. "The police should be looking into anybody you think is suspicious."

"You're so very composed. No fear on your face. I'm very scared, and the more scared I am, the more wine I drink."

"So, what did the police tell you?"

"Detective Festoon laughed when I told him my suspicions. Then he gave my arm an inappropriate rub, and said, 'nothing to worry about sugar plum'."

"He can be a pill." Allie nodded.

"That is a very polite understatement. Something you're mother would never do. She would have gone for the throat, if I'd thrown her that bait."

"Well, I've learned. I listen now, instead of bite. I was told that's a good way to stay out of trouble."

"But you don't seem very worried about the possibility that Toro killed my husband. Either that, or you're a very cool character, indeed. Perhaps it's both."

"It's just I've gone through years of ups and downs with the investigation and the task force."

As Allie spoke, Jess sipped and nodded.

"There was always a strong suspect that faded into nothing and everyone I talked to had an idea about who it was. Some people claimed to hear guys confess, but always, after the facts were checked, there was nothing. I decided I was not going to let my emotions get dragged too high or low by the investigation."

"So, no solid suspect was found?"

"Not until Stan Kozlowski. The police shot him and that was supposed to be the end of the story. I try not to get caught up in the past."

"Good strategy. But I've decided if anybody breaks into this house, I'll be ready. I had the security system upgraded. There are cameras everywhere. And..." She took another sip of wine. "I learned to shoot a gun."

"You trained to shoot?"

"Yes and now I'm pretty good with a Glock. I've put in cameras, motion detectors, lasers and direct alarms to the police."

"It sounds like you've got everything covered."

"I don't know about that, but my room is directly across from Isaac's, and I'll kill any intruder."

"How long will you be on high alert?"

"As long as it takes. That's how strongly I feel about James Smith. As long as I think Isaac could be in danger, I'm going to protect him.

I'd like for you to walk through and tell me what you think. Tell me what does and doesn't make sense."

"I'm not a cop."

"But you're smart. You're a survivor. You defeated a man who, by all accounts, was powerful enough to knock down doors. I know this because it's in the Toro commission's report. You know at least a few things about the muscular beast that killed Franz. Just walk around the house. Then I'll show you our picture of him."

Allie sighed. "Okay. I'll tell you what I think. But I can't promise anything. First..." Allie took a deep breath and opened her hands. "Where did they find Franz?"

CHAPTER TWENTY SEVEN
PRESENT DAY

Jess took a gulp of Chardonnay, which finished most of the glass. "Thank you, Dear. It was out there." She pointed outside towards the large double-decker dock and stainless steel boatlifts. She inhaled deeply. "When I returned from New York, I walked in lugging my suitcase and complaining about how heavy that door is."

As she spoke, her eyes grew moist. She dabbed them with the corner of a monogrammed linen handkerchief. "Sounds silly, now, really. Complaining about the door, of all things. But I called his name, dropped the suitcase near the sofa and walked into the kitchen. He wasn't there. I called his phone. He didn't answer. Very peculiar. Particularly, because he knew we were returning. I searched for him for about an hour. And then I noticed the tiny specks of blood."

Jess jutted her jaw and wiped her eyes. "Right there!" She pointed towards a back door.

As Jess spoke, Allie stepped around her towards the door. She stooped and studied the hardwood floor.

"Here, by the door?"

"Yes."

"How much blood?"

"Some."

"You said you saw specks?"

"Specks, spots, drops, molecules. I'm not a scientist. I don't know how to describe it. But I know I saw blood. So, I called the police."

"And then?"

"What do you mean?"

"What happened after that?"

"The police showed up, asked a lot of inane questions and an hour later they found his body, bound to an anchor in the bay."

"And you are absolutely sure that was your husband?"

"Yes, I'm."

"How can you be certain?"

"Because, it looked like him."

"In what way? His face was unrecognizable. He was decomposing."

"You're being impertinent!" Jess crossed her arms and turned away from Allie.

"I didn't mean to be insensitive. I'm trying to cover all the details and you said you wanted to be blunt."

"You're right. Let me think. The police didn't cover this." Jess shook her head and waved her hand dismissively. "Give me a second. He never had hair and that was the same. Strangely, his body still looked the same... the way he carried himself. I had no hesitation. It was Franz."

"We have to build from the ground up."

"You're more skilled than you admit."

"I'm just trying to collect a story that makes sense. Festoon should have already gone over some of this with you."

"Well, he hasn't. But thank you for the warning, Dear."

"That figures. What else?"

"I'm really exhausted. I don't know of anything else to tell you."

Allie stood in the center of the kitchen and turned. "Festoon said that there was a broken window in the back and a vase stolen?"

"Yes. The police saw the glass fragments lying on the rug. I didn't notice anything out of place when I came home at first. Later, they had me look through the house and I noticed the vase was missing. The vase is some meaningless thing Franz picked up in Berlin."

Jess sighed and played with the stem of her wine glass. "I can't believe he's gone. People are so cruel. So horrible."

"Yes, they can be." Allie nodded and continued to study the room. "Did Franz know anyone who would want to hurt him? I mean anyone besides James Smith?"

Jess stepped back and resumed her seat at the bar. "I can say 'yes' but I can't tell you how many. When you're as rich as he was, you're bound to tread on some toes. He got on the wrong side of some Russians in the nineties."

Allie nodded.

"Certainly, a few businessmen from Berlin lost money to Franz. A sheik from Saudi had issues. There was a banker in Hong Kong who felt wronged. But you must understand, these are just things I overheard him talking about. He never shared any details with me."

Allie nodded again. "I understand. You have a child. He's your world. You want to protect him. It must have been difficult for you to hear about those conflicts."

"It's not the way I would have liked things. I didn't ask to live my life with a little boy when there were those sorts of dangers beyond these walls, but Franz was my husband. I loved him. And I did my best to support him."

"That covers it for me. Anything else you want to tell me?"

Jess raised her palms and shook her head. "No. I just wanted to see if something jumped out at you. I'm certain it was James. I think he murdered Franz in cold blood and then stole that vase to make it appear to be a robbery. And the police are completely fooled." Jess poured another glass of wine and took a sip. "Did the autopsy reveal anything?"

Allie sighed and sat down at the bar next to Jess Bergman. "This is all kind of new to me. But nothing appeared surprising to Dr. Mann. There's not a single detail we uncovered that would bust the case wide open."

"Allie, there must have been something. I've heard Dr. Mann is the master of the autopsy. Was there nothing to help find my husband's killer? And you haven't finalized the dictation."

"I do think we're looking for someone who your husband knew well. I doubt it would be a Russian hitman or something like that. And I don't think robbery was the motive."

"I agree, but just out of interest, why?"

"It doesn't make sense for the mob to kill someone and then disguise it as a botched robbery." Allie rubbed her cheek and glanced towards the window. "A hired hit is a way of warning 'don't do this again', to all the other people they're in business with."

"What do you mean?"

"Well. They bomb. They knock you off in public restaurants. Or, you disappear without a trace, though everyone knows what's happened."

As Allie spoke, Jess listened and sipped her wine.

Allie stood and began to pace around the kitchen. She rubbed her chin. "Also, they wouldn't need to mutilate the body with stab wounds."

"Why don't you think somebody just broke in to steal something, they got caught by Franz, so they murdered him?

"Simple." Allie stopped pacing and turned towards Jess. "For one thing, if your husband surprised a burglar, the guy wouldn't go after him with a knife after he was dead. And this is an incredible place full of expensive things. I can see thousands of dollars worth of electronics, silver and art that could be taken in seconds. A burglar would grab those things especially if he'd killed someone."

Jess smiled and nodded. "Thank you, Allie. That's exactly what I thought myself. It was James Smith. I'm going to keep my gun for a while."

"You have to make yourself feel safe."

"And a .40 caliber Glock handgun, makes me feel safe. You fought off Toro. But Franz couldn't. I know I couldn't. Toro beat down doors and tore through a mobile home."

"I'm aware of that, but Toro is dead."

"If you say so."

"Okay, let's look at your pictures." Allie placed her hands on her hips.

"Brilliant. Let's see James Smith. The man Franz..." Jess blinked back tears and took a deep breath. "The man my dear, departed husband knew was Toro."

CHAPTER TWENTY EIGHT
PRESENT DAY

Jess reached for the computer tablet on the bar. "It will take a second to open the file." She tapped the screen with her manicured red fingernail. "Here are the pictures of James Smith. They were taken from surveillance cameras mounted around the house. He didn't allow his photo to be taken knowingly. As you'll see, he's a big man."

Allie extended her hand towards the computer. She felt her throat tighten and she hesitated.

"It won't hurt to look at them." Allie's hand trembled.

"Of course not, Dear. They're only images. Pixels." Jess touched the screen and handed the computer to Allie. "Just scroll through. Take your time."

Allie grasped the computer with her anxious hands and stared at the grainy, black and white photo.

Her pupils dilated and her dark eyebrows rose. She exhaled through pursed lips.

The picture was enlarged to the point of being indistinct. The athletic male figure was walking past a pool and glancing over his shoulder. His blurry face stared intently at Allie from the photo.

The image chilled Allie to the core. The hair on her arms stood erect as did the fine follicles of black hair that lined the back of her neck. The man had the well-publicized bushy, black beard and full black hair. Unfortunately, his facial features were indistinct.

Yet, there was something about his posture, stature and build, along with the hair and beard, which made Allie gasp. She exhaled and studied the image from several angles as she moved the computer back and forth.

"It bothers you, I can tell." Jess clasped her icy, thin fingers on Allie's arm. "That's why I felt it was so important for you to look at these pictures."

Allie took a deep breath. "Yeah, there's something there. It's hard to tell for sure. I can't put my finger on it, but something about the picture seems familiar."

"So, you think he's Toro? The Bull?" Jess released her grip and took another sip of wine. "You recognize him."

"No. I certainly couldn't say that just based on this picture. There's something that feels familiar about him, but I couldn't ID him without any doubt. It's been nine years."

"You have goose bumps. Is it cold in here? Or is something else disturbing you?"

"No, I'm fine." Allie studied the other pictures. They were of worse quality and added nothing. She turned back to the first one and examined it more closely.

She considered the images before handing the computer back. Allie sighed. "It's definitely a strong possibility. I really wish I could say 'no'. I really want to."

"You look uneasy. Your skin is clammy. I can tell you're distressed." Jess' eyes followed Allie's every move.

"It's a little chilly in here, yeah, just a little. If the police can find a better picture of him, then maybe we'd know for sure. There has to be something better out there."

"Of course. Thank you for looking at those photos. Take a deep breath, Love." Jess leaned back and sighed. "Is there anything else that you need to ask me?"

"I don't think so. I've got a lot to consider. It's getting late. We really need to go."

"I understand. These pictures may be the passage out of this unending fear. So please, consider them."

"I will."

"Excellent, Allie. Now..."

"I do have one question."

Jess looked surprised and leaned towards Allie.

"What did you mean when you talked about Dr. Mann and the Toro commission?"

"Are you asking about the DNA?" Jess sat back in her chair.

"Yes. I'm just wondering what you meant when we talked on the phone."

"You read the report again?"

"I did."

"So then you know all the DNA from the suspects was explained away by Dr. Mann as caulk or dough or whatever, under those girls' fingernails when the police at first thought it was flesh. Flesh from Toro."

"Maybe it was caulk, or paint."

"Come on, Allie!" Jess scoffed. "Really, every time there was a substance found under the fingernails that police thought was tissue, Dr. Mann stated that it was some innocent substance. Please!"

"Okay. If that's true, then why would he do that?"

"I don't know. I can't explain his motivation. I'm just saying it doesn't make sense that not a single strand of DNA was found on those crime scenes after the police were sure they'd located samples."

Allie paused and shrugged her shoulders. "I don't know. Chrystal has the brains in the family."

"She's a lovely girl. She takes after you."

"Oh, thank you." Allie blushed. "She's so different. Chrystal is as straight and narrow as you can possibly imagine. Chrystal has planned her entire life out, she wants to design fashion and be a journalist and live in New York."

"That's spectacular!" Jess clapped her hands. "Good for her. She must take after your Mother, as well."

"You're dead on." Allie glanced towards the stairs. "Chrystal lived with my mother for a while when she was very young. She still visits her a couple of times a year. Up to midtown Manhattan and then back to graduate student housing and me. But," Allie extended her hand, "we have to go."

Jess leaned back in her chair, stared at the ceiling and ignored Allie's gesture. "As difficult as she is to get along with, Bea loves Chrystal very much. I'm guessing that you're trying to figure out how you're going to make Chrystal content in Tampa when she's seen all New York has to offer."

"You're right." Allie withdrew her hand and looked towards the stairs again, the last place she'd seen Chrystal. "That is a huge challenge. Until she leaves home, she's stuck with the simple things.

"She's 13 now?"

"Almost 13. We're trying to figure out what to do for her birthday. She's not thrilled with the options we've got."

"When's her birthday?"

"Saturday." Allie took a step towards the stairs.

"Well, the answer is obvious. You'll have it here!" Jess Bergman threw up both arms and her face glowed.

Allie stopped cold.

CHAPTER TWENTY NINE
PRESENT DAY

Allie cackled. "At your house? Absolutely not! The university pool is perfect."

"Please!" Jess clasped her hands together and leaned towards Allie. "I would love to have Chrystal and her friends over."

"We couldn't impose." Allie moved towards the stairs. "Chrystal! Time to leave, Honey!"

"Impose! It would be my way of thanking you for helping me. You answered all my questions." Jess rested her hand on Allie's forearm.

Allie took a step backwards. "Thank you very much. I'll get back to you." Allie turned to face the stairs. "Chrystal! Time to go! Get down here, now!" Allie yelled as she craned her neck towards the stairs.

"Do that, please." Jess looked to the top of the stairs. "I hear them now."

There was a tramp of energetic feet and, before she reached the last step, Chrystal jumped to the floor and bounded towards her mother. Isaac bounced behind Chrystal.

"Oh, my gosh, Mom! You should see their house. It's so cool and beautiful. Isaac showed me their pool from his window."

"It's beautiful!" Isaac jumped and clapped.

"Mrs. Bergman, I love the slate around the pool!"

"I hear you're about to have a birthday party. Would you like to have it here?" Jess clasped her hands together and smiled ear to ear.

"No!" Allie raised her hand to make her point, but no one seemed to notice.

"Oh, my gosh, I would love to, Mrs. Bergman! It would be a dream."

"Chrystal, we'll talk about it later."

"It's just down the street from Carly, Mom." Chrystal excitedly turned and looked at Allie. "She could practically walk here! I'm serious. It's that close."

"I don't think so."

"She could, Mom."

"I'm not talking about Carly walking here, I'm saying it may be a bit of an inconvenience for Mrs. Bergman."

"It's not, Allie. I would absolutely love for Chrystal to have her party here." As she spoke, Jess and Chrystal joined hands and leaned towards each other.

"Please, Mom! Please."

Small tears began to form in Chrystal's eyes and Allie rolled hers. She took a deep breath. "Chrystal, I... I hate to say this, but, this was very recently a crime scene, and—"

"Mom—"

"Do not interrupt me young lady. I think we should defer because of decorum and I'm part of this investigation, and... et cetera."

"But Festoon told me he's done with it. If it makes you feel better, we can stay off the dock. We'll use the area around the pool."

"But the university pool is a better choice."

"The university pool again! We'll share my party with five year olds and the six year old with social issues. Thank you so much, Mother!"

After the words left her mouth, Chrystal lowered her head into her hands. "I'm sorry, Mom! I was out of line. Please don't get mad at me."

"Really, Chrystal? Okay, let's think about this."

"Mom, It would be so easy."

Allie took a deep breath. Chrystal and Jess turned their heads in unison and looked at her.

Allie sighed. "It's no longer an active crime scene, that's true...It would be easy...It would be straightforward and you would be happy." Allie felt pressured. Having the party here would solve the current problem. "Okay. Low key. Nothing fancy. Just a quick, very small party."

"Wonderful! I'll start planning for Saturday."

"Yay! A party!" Isaac jumped and clapped with even more enthusiasm.

Chrystal ran and gave Allie a tight hug. "Thank you! You're the best! This is the happiest day of my life!"

Allie squeezed Chrystal. "I'll bring the food and decorations. And a cake. I'll bake the cake. Chrystal, you can only invite a few friends."

Allie tried to feel enthusiastic about her daughter's party, but two facts sapped the energy from her.

First, Dr. Mann had warned her, and now she had visited a crime scene without his permission. In addition, though he had not specifically forbidden having a party at the scene of a murder, she was fairly certain this also violated his rules.

"Are you okay, Mom?"

"Yeah, Honey. Let's thank Mrs. Bergman and get back home."

And then there was fact number two. As Jess embraced her in a suffocating hug, Allie realized she was only hours away from an awkward dinner with the father of her children. A man she hadn't seen since before Chrystal was born.

CHAPTER THIRTY
PRESENT DAY

On their ninth circle around Davis Islands, the occupants of the small Ford Focus observed what they'd been waiting for. Accompanied by her tall gawky daughter, the short dark woman with the huge scar on her face fled the mansion and scurried to her rusting car. The mother and daughter argued and didn't notice the Ford lurking in the distance.

A few seconds later, their beat-up Honda bounced over the curb at the end of the Bergman's driveway and disappeared in a cloud of exhaust down the road.

"For a girl with a glass eye, she drives fast." The acne scarred man laughed.

"They didn't look happy, Rick." His female companion dropped her binoculars on the back seat.

"Yeah, but look where she came from. You wouldn't be happy, either!"

The Ford slowed by the Bergman's driveway and the young woman hopped out with a black backpack slung across her shoulder. The man, tan with short bleached blonde hair, gave a quick thumbs up and drove off leaving Erin Warrant alone by the still-open gate. She slunk up the driveway, sticking close to the thickly landscaped azaleas, ferns and palmettos. Walking on her tiptoes, she advanced on the Bergman home in silence, her hair billowing over her shoulders. Erin stuck to the path she and her boyfriend had mapped out.

As Erin made her way to the house she fumed over her experience with the Bergmans. She felt Jess ran the house like she was the Queen of the Universe and that monstrous husband never spoke and gave her the creeps. Erin was also pissed that Rick wouldn't let her quit because access to that house of horrors might pay off someday.

It better pay off or he can find another partner! That witch deserves to be robbed, firing me hours after her husband turns up dead.

Erin had to admit that Rick's plan to return to the house to beg for her job and cut security system wires bordered on pure genius. She knew she wouldn't get her job back, but she could get a whole lot more.

It makes sense. If something comes up missing anytime soon, then they'll have to blame it on whoever broke in and killed him. I won't even be on their radar.

Erin could now walk up the unmonitored corridor to the garage. She had made herself a ghost to the motion detectors and cameras of the security system.

Using her copied garage key, she opened the door and slipped inside. It was pitch black but Erin knew the area very well. She maneuvered past the Range Rover without hesitating. Just in front would be the stairs leading to the house. Less than 20 seconds after entering the garage, she quietly pushed open the door near the kitchen.

In the distance she heard Jess' loud voice rising and falling. She could tell her former employer had been drinking and was somewhere on the vast second floor. That would leave the first floor wide open.

Erin felt her adrenaline surge. It was almost as good as the cocaine she favored. She missed the old days and the rush of coke.

She replayed Rick's instructions. Go for the gold and silver. Leave the electronics.

Erin knew the Bergman's had a lot of both that they had collected from all over the world. She had seen some in the form of exotic foreign statues and idols, but she didn't mind. Rick had told her it could all be melted down and sold to the highest bidder.

Erin stole another glance in the direction of the kitchen and then made a direct dash towards a cabinet near the TV. On the top shelf was a small solid gold elephant from India. She snatched it and turned like a gazelle towards the sterling silver in the dining room.

Within seconds, she'd swiped as many silver spoons, forks and knives from the armoire as she could fit in her backpack.

Now, she wanted to score the holy grail of the Bergmans' treasure trove.

Erin remembered Jess opening the safe to show a golden bull statue to her friends. She remembered Jess gloating about how rare and priceless the statue was. And she remembered how a hush fell on the group when they realized Erin was present. But most importantly, Erin remembered the combination to the safe. 13-17-18.

Swift and silent, Erin floated across the floor and found the sturdy safe hidden behind a wooden panel. Her eyes darted left and right, then she extended her trembling fingers towards the door of the safe.

Erin's arm shook and her lips quivered as she turned the dial and felt the firm clicks of the lock in the tips of her sweaty fingers. Her breath came rapidly in short gasps and she could feel cool perspiration forming under her arms.

Jess' voice grew louder and Erin retreated and ducked behind the couch. Several seconds later the voice died away and her own fast breathing was all Erin could hear. She stood up and peeked over the couch.

The hidden panel covering the safe stood wide open.

Erin rolled her eyes and huffed at her stupidity. A bead of sweat drifted from her hair to her eyebrow and she swept it away with a swipe of her dewy palm.

Erin swallowed the acid that had risen in her throat and once again crept to the safe. She bit her lower lip as she turned the dial.

She heard a satisfying click and the door popped open.

Even in the dark safe, the statue shone.

It was crude and reminded Erin of something she had seen in a museum on a school fieldtrip. The bull was only five inches high and five inches long, but when Erin tried to lift it, she was barely able to pull it towards her. As the idol reached the edge of the safe, it toppled over, but Erin strained her muscles and eased it to the ground.

She grunted, hoisted the bull to her hip and carried it like a tiny toddler. It was cold against her arms and Erin clutched her new gold baby, shuffling awkwardly towards the backpack. When she released it, the statue landed with a thump and a rattled against the silver.

With another grunt, Erin strained her arms and lifted the backpack to the level of her knees. She could feel the stressed fabric stretch. Using both hands to haul the backpack, Erin moved towards the garage, her heavy bundle swaying like a pendulum.

Despite the hefty, unwieldy load swinging her from side to side, Erin managed to careen towards the stairs leading into the garage. She stumbled down them and was stopped by the bumper of an unexpected car.

Erin dropped her pack, pulled her phone out of her pocket and texted Rick to come pick her up.

"Okay, I'm almost out of here."

She checked her phone to see if Rick had responded. "I wish I'd grabbed Jess' Xanax. That would be worth its weight in gold now."

She put the phone back in her pocket and tried to lift the backpack, but it was too heavy for her tired, thin arms, so she dropped it to the floor and dragged it. She moved along the front of the new car and then took a sharp right turn. She was so close.

Halfway down the side of the car the garage lights turned on.

Before Erin could respond, they flicked off again. Ghosts of the fluorescent fixtures floated in front of her.

She heard footsteps approaching.

Erin tried to drag the backpack, but it wouldn't budge, as if glued to the ground. Erin's heart raced and cold sweat ran down her back. After two frantic tugs, she abandoned Rick's plan, released the bag and retreated rapidly towards the door.

Rick'll have to get over losin' the gold. I'm gettin' the hell out of here!

She bumped into a car after a couple of steps. Now completely disoriented, she turned and stepped to her right and hit yet another car.

Her eyes darted back and forth, but she couldn't get her bearings in the dark.

"Erin."

She shrieked when she heard his voice. Petrified, she fled, tripped over the backpack, and with her feet flying through the air, fell head-first into a car. Her forehead smacked the door handle and she saw a bright light. Then, Erin Warrant fell to the floor, unconscious.

CHAPTER THIRTY ONE
PRESENT DAY

Chrystal peeked over the top of her Florida History textbook. "You put on make up. Why?"

"I can wear make up if I want." Allie shrugged and headed to the dorm door.

"I thought you're just going out with an old friend?"

"Yeah. Nothing else. I'm allowed to wear make up with friends, you know."

"You don't have to be so defensive."

"I'm not being defensive. I'm just defending my right to wear make up anytime I want."

"Jeez. Calm down."

"I'm calm."

"You usually don't wear makeup like that." Chrystal took a sip of her iced tea. "Your skirt is cute. I like it."

"Thank you, Honey." Allie smoothed her hair and gave her blouse a passing glance. "I'll be home soon. Lock the door."

She slipped out of the dorm before Chrystal could analyze anything else.

Allie drove to the Columbia Restaurant in a maelstrom of competing emotions. For some reason, she found herself interested in what Duncan might say after all these years. But she had to stand strong and couldn't be led astray by him...not after all she'd accomplished.

Allie remembered being escorted to an elegant, candle lit table at this same restaurant 25 years ago. The magical memories of sparkling crystal glasses, pearl white table linens, gleaming silverware and the spicy aroma of exotic food she experienced as a five year old, still glowed in her mind.

From what Allie could recall, her mother and father sat across from her, laughed and enjoyed a glass of golden wine while she rolled delicious dough balls out of the warm, fresh bread.

To Allie, the Columbia represented Sunday dinner at its best, and it hadn't changed in all these years.

When she arrived at the restaurant, Allie found Duncan already seated at their table. He looked exactly the same as last time she saw him, right down to his perfect tan and sun-kissed blonde hair.

Duncan rose and smiled broadly, flashing his camera-perfect smile. "Allie, It's so good to see you!"

"It's been a while." Allie joined Duncan at the table and sat without really registering Duncan's small talk. Think of something intelligent to say, Allie.

But words failed her, so Allie sipped her water and she stared at the ornate tile on the walls and floor and the numerous candles mounted around framed photos from the 50's. She felt comforted by the familiarity of the environment.

All of a sudden Duncan stopped midsentence and stood. "Hola, Marco! Good to see you, my friend!" Duncan grasped the man's hand. "Marco, I'd like you to meet Dr. Allie Parsons."

"My pleasure, Dr. Parsons." Marco smiled and shook Allie's hand.

"Marco runs the best restaurant in the world. He never fails to serve the most amazing food. Is Javier in the kitchen tonight, Marco?"

"Of course, Mr. Maxwell. I told him you're here."

"Well, warn him to watch out because I'm going to sneak in there and find out how he cooks those platanos maduros."

"I'll tell him, Mr. Maxwell. While you're waiting for your meals, may I suggest a bottle of 2002 Burgundy Chardonnay? It's an excellent vintage and, of course, it's on the house."

Duncan leaned towards Allie as he sat down. "I remember you like Chardonnay, Allie. Is that okay? Or we can stick to tea. I don't mind."

"Wine is fine." She took another awkward sip of water.

"Apparently it's a good year, and it's free, so let's give it a try. We can't lose, right?" He turned back towards Marco. "Okay, my friend, we'll enjoy the wine."

"It's our pleasure. Please, enjoy."

"Great guy." Duncan slid his seat forward and rested his elbows on the table.

As Duncan leaned towards Allie, a current of warm air from the candle carried a hint of his cologne across the table, where it caressed her nose. He hadn't changed fragrances since she first met him at her mother's Gasparilla party years ago, and just as before, Allie's arms grew goosebumps.

CHAPTER THIRTY TWO
17 YEARS AGO

Every year, sometime between February and March, the pirate Jose Gaspar invades Tampa from the Bay in a recreated pirate ship built in the fifties. After the successful invasion, the conquered mayor presents Gaspar with the key to the city. A triumphant, raucous, rambunctious parade through the crowded streets then ensues. The event is an excuse to party, connect and conduct business of all types.

Most of the men at her mother's party seemed uncomfortable talking to Allie. As she answered their questions about high school, they listened politely, but constantly looked down, glanced over her shoulder and squeezed their wine glasses with white knuckles.

Even after sneaking two glasses of Rose`, Allie was still bored. Then Duncan tapped her shoulder, and everything changed.

He gripped her with his gaze. She was mesmerized.

He flashed a sly grin. "Allie, Shouldn't you be doing something more exciting than hanging out at your mom's Gasparilla party?"

"Like what, Duncan? Do you have something in mind?"

"A beautiful girl ought to take advantage of what's happening outside these walls, especially on a night like this. There's a lot going on and if you don't escape soon you're going to miss it."

"I'm trying to break out of here, but Mother is all over me."

"Just go. I'll cover for you. Find your friends. Tampa's lit up, there are bands playing and you're too young to be stuck here." Duncan looked around the crowd, smiled and waved.

"I'm too young? I'm 18 and you're not much older."

Duncan leaned towards her and lowered his voice. "That's what happens when you get out of law school. All of sudden, you've got these obligations." He grinned, lifted his glass and finished the last swallow of his wine. "But you do this stuff, then you do the things you'd rather do. So get out of here and do your other things."

Allie felt a little tipsy and lost herself in his eyes. "I don't have anywhere to go. Do you have any suggestions, Duncan?"

"As a matter of fact, I do." He looked around and leaned closer. "When my obligations here are done, I'll show you the best Gasparilla party in Tampa. Is Francesca around?"

Allie nodded.

"Call her. Tell her to get over here. I'll pick you up at 10 pm. It will be the best night of your life, I promise. If it's not, I'll take you out every night until I give you the best night of your life."

"For as long as it takes? I don't believe you."

"You really hurt me, Allie. Okay, I have to share a secret. Some people draw or write poetry. I'm like the Picasso of parties or the Einstein of the good time. And, I'm a lawyer, so I can't make idle promises and not follow through."

"Why not? It seems to be the way everyone else does things."

"Because you'd sue and I really don't want to lose that much money."

"It would be complicated since, you're mother's lawyer, you'd be suing yourself. Did they cover those kinds of cases at the University of Miami, counselor?"

"I slept through that class. But I promised your mother I'd never lose a case for her and she pays me well to keep that promise, so I guess I'd be up the creek. I would lose everything. Definitely. I'd be obligated to take every dime I own."

"But you'd get 75% back in fees."

"Touche`. Still, it's a pride thing. I hate to lose. So. Is it a deal?" He held out his hand and they shook.

"Deal."

"Good. See you at 10, Allie Cat."

Early the next morning, after listening to the bands and dancing at the parties and sipping real champagne, Allie decided that she had, indeed, experienced the best night of her life.

But Allie lied and told Duncan she'd been to better parties. Furthermore, she was going to hold him to his promise or she'd sue.

Duncan smiled and stroked her cheek with his finger.

CHAPTER THIRTY THREE
PRESENT DAY

"**Y**ou're smiling, Allie. What are you thinking about?"
Duncan's question snapped her back from her thoughts.

"Oh..." She dabbed her lips with her napkin. "Nothing. Actually, I was wondering--"

"Why I wanted to see you?"

"Yes."

Duncan took a deep breath and looked at the ceiling for a moment before staring into her eyes. "Well, a couple of reasons. First, I want to apologize for the way I behaved in the past. I was young, but that's no excuse, I know." Duncan bit his lower lip and his eyes moistened.

Allie grabbed a small piece of bread and nibbled it nervously. "You weren't that young, Duncan."

"You're right. I should've known better. But as you said, I wasn't much older than you. In my defense, you told me you were 18."

"I...was... flirting!" Allie leaned towards him and tried to keep her voice low. "You were a lot older than me. You were my mom's lawyer!"

Duncan raised his eyebrows and stuck out his jaw. "You're right." After another deep breath, he leaned back in his chair. "I was a bad influence."

"All the drugs, Duncan! You could snort coke, or smoke dope or drink the lights out and then..." A waiter appeared and refilled her water. Allie smiled, grabbed another piece of bread and picked at it until he moved to the next table.

"And then, you'd get up and go to work like it was nothing. A few hours later you'd be at it again. I couldn't. I was heading slowly downhill before I met you. You gave me a giant shove over the edge. My life fell apart. I lost so much."

"I know. You lost everything."

"No. I lost a lot, but not everything. I thank God every night for what he left me. I still have the most precious thing in my life."

"How is your daughter?"

"She's beautiful and brilliant. She's a wonderful miracle. Our situation, without you, turned out for the best. So don't think about changing anything."

"I understand."

For several seconds they sat silently, occasionally shuffling their feet or rearranging the silverware.

Allie took a deep breath, followed by a gulp of water. "How are your boys?"

"Doing very well. They live with me since Meg and I divorced. They're good kids."

"You got custody?"

"Yes, of course." Duncan sipped his water.

"I thought the court always sided with the mother."

"Sometimes being a lawyer has its perks. Are you nervous?"

"No." Allie shook her head. "Why do you ask?"

"You're making little balls out of the bread."

"Oh, sorry." Allie dropped the bread onto the plate. "I used to do that when I was little."

Marco brought the wine and presented it to Duncan. After pouring two glasses, he bowed and disappeared amongst the crowd towards the front of the restaurant.

"I've never had less than stellar food or service here."

"It doesn't hurt that your family used to own everything around here. They did very well with cigars."

"True. I can't complain. I've been lucky." Duncan folded his hands on the table. "But I want to get to the other reason I invited you here tonight. Congratulations on your graduation and your new prestigious appointment. I'm so proud of you, Allie Florence Parsons." Duncan raised his glass. "To your achievements and a limitless future. Cheers."

"Thank you." Allie raised her glass and tapped Duncan's. She took a small sip and sat her glass on the table.

"While we're on that subject, Duncan, did you have anything to do with helping me finance my education?"

Duncan shook his head and held his lips tightly together as he swallowed his wine. "I'm not sure what you mean. I haven't had anything to do with paying for your education. Do you need help, though? I'd be happy to help."

Allie believed him. Though a skilled liar, Duncan generally elaborated more than necessary when being dishonest. He bent the truth with long sentences and twisted logic until it became too complicated to determine what he had truly said.

"No. I'm fine, thank you."

The food arrived, but Allie ate very little. Duncan talked about his sons, his latest famous client, and the difficulty of finding a true craftsman to finish the stonework on the addition to his house.

Midway through the black beans and rice, Allie dropped her napkin on the table and stood. "I'm sorry, Duncan. I have to go."

"I understand. Are you okay?"

"I'm actually very well." She reached for her purse.

"Good. Allie, let's get together some time. Just catch up."

"I don't think so, Duncan." She pulled out two $20 bills and left them on the table. "That should cover me."

"No. Take it back, Allie. I invited you. I insist."

"No, Duncan."

"Allie. Please, let me pay for this. Use that to buy your daughter something special."

Allie stared at his eyes and sighed. "Okay. Thank you. But we're done. I want to make that clear."

Duncan stood up and nodded. "Well, it was good to see you." He extended his hand and smiled. "Good luck, Allie."

Allie nodded and shook his hand. "Even though you didn't ask, I forgive you. And I have a confession. I lied. It was the best night of my life. If I'd told the truth, maybe you'd have left me alone and none of the rest would have happened."

Duncan stuck his hands in his pockets. "I would have kept after you, Allie Cat. Sometimes, even now--"

"Goodbye, Duncan." Allie turned and walked towards the door.

CHAPTER THIRTY FOUR
PRESENT DAY

At 5:00 AM, a chime from the alarm clock app stirred Allie from a deep sleep. Caught between her dreams and the harsh early morning reality, she rolled off the couch, landing on her knees with a painful jolt that shook her swollen eyelids and battered her sore back. An old quilt covered her shoulders in soft cotton.

Her grandmother had made the quilt on a foot-powered Singer sewing machine many years ago, and even though Allie didn't know what most of the squares represented, it still felt soft and warm on her neck.

Allie stumbled across the coarse carpet and colorful rugs that Chrystal had rescued from a thrift store. Just outside Chrystal's door, Allie cleared her throat.

"Get up, Sweetheart."

Allie heard only silence, then a soft moan. "I'm up, Mom."

Allie microwaved a cup of coffee and stared at the glossy white cinder block walls.

In the quiet predawn, she mused about dinner with Duncan and how well she'd handled herself. If she met him again, it would be in some place more casual.

Allie admonished herself. There would be no 'next time'!

She put Duncan out of her mind and considered the note on her car, speculating what Mann would say about it. He should have returned yesterday and be back behind his desk early this morning.

Allie sipped her bitter black coffee. What about James Smith?

What about that horrible photo made her gasp?

A few stray strands of black hair hung in front of her tired eyes and she brushed them away so that they blended with the others.

Allie took another swallow and her stomach burned. Either the wretched microwaved coffee or her continuous anxiety could be the cause.

Allie looked at the glaring red numbers on the microwave. "It's almost time to leave!"

"Coming, Mom."

Allie placed turkey bacon and egg whites in the microwave. As she listened to the food popping on the plate that turned in the small oven, her thoughts drifted back to the letter.

After a horrible night dreaming of intruders and ways to fight them, Allie faced another day completely exhausted. She rubbed her eyes when she heard her daughter's slippers rubbing across the floor. As Chrystal entered the kitchen, Allie handed off the cooling mug of coffee and headed to the bedroom for a shower.

With several seconds to spare, Allie dropped Chrystal at the bus stop. "See you this afternoon, Honey."

Chrystal lugged her heavy backpack towards the bus, then turned and waved. "I had a great time last night, Mom. I love you. Thanks for the birthday party."

Forcing a weary smile, Allie waved and tried to appear cheerful. She lowered her arm and watched Chrystal board ahead of the other bus riders. They played games on their phones and talked excitedly among themselves as they slowly trickled through the doors behind her. None of them appeared to notice Chrystal as she found an empty seat near the front.

"Doesn't she have any friends?"

Then it occurred to Allie.

Everyday she dropped Chrystal at the bus stop. Everyday Carly's mother drove Carly and her Davis Islands friends to school. Chrystal didn't ride in the cool, leather lined interior of the Thomas' SUV where her friends bonded and made plans to coordinate their outfits for parties or arranged to study at the newest café or gossiped about the cutest guys at school.

Allie lingered until the bus pulled away. As far as she could tell, no one spied from the white sand and palmettos of the vacant lot across the street and nothing suspicious lurked beyond the sidewalk. The recently opened stores occupying the brick buildings bordering the sidewalk bustled with early-risers, but the people moving in and out of the shops appeared to be minding their own business.

When the bulky yellow bus rounded a corner and slipped out of sight, Allie started her Honda and stared at her glove box. Just behind that small door was the ominous letter.

After a moment of hesitation, she pulled the latch and stuck her hand inside the tiny compartment. She needed to read it again.

Her fingers found nothing except worn felt and plastic. Her blood pressure rose and her heart raced. Allie probed frantically around the glove box.

Still, there was nothing.

Near panic, Allie leaned across the passenger's seat and squinted, peering into the small, black space. She twisted her hand and dug into the deep, dark, empty hole.

The note was gone!

Chrystal! The realization took her breath away. Oh, my gosh.

Her daughter had thoroughly cleaned the car in an effort to impress Jess Bergman. The note must have been tossed out and was now probably a tiny speck in a mountainous Hillsborough County landfill.

Breathing hard, Allie closed the glove box with a gentle shove and leaned back on the tattered cloth of the driver's seat.

She checked her watch. Allie knew the stakes. Right now, she risked being late to her highly coveted job--one that even impressed Duncan Maxwell.

Stay calm. There's a solution to this problem. I just have to find it.

CHAPTER THIRTY FIVE
PRESENT DAY

Allie pulled her purse to her chest and started a zig-zag path between the cars to the morgue's front door. The empty parking lot felt threatening, and combined with the haunting, eerily familiar image of James Smith, Allie found herself on the verge of panic. Her fingers tightly gripped the can of mace in her purse.

Allie unlocked and pushed the heavy glass door. As it opened, she escaped the warm, humid air. By the time she stepped onto the elevator, her arms felt cool and dry.

After a chugging noise and a chime, the elevator doors quietly slid open at the 5th floor. Allie made her way across the soft carpet.

As she walked past Dr. Mann's office towards the break room, Allie spotted Mann hunched over his desk, running his fingers through his gray hair. Too early. I need more coffee.

A closet sized space containing an old coffee maker and an ancient snack machine with pull knobs served as the break room for the entire floor. Allie poured herself a half cup of very dark coffee from the brown stained pot and then retreated back down the hall. She hesitated and took a breath, then knocked on Mann's door.

"Come in." He cleared his throat.

The knob clicked and the hinges squeaked as she pushed the office door open.

"Welcome back. How was your trip?" Allie tried to sound cheerful.

"It was fine, but now I'm far behind."

"I'll do what I can to help you catch up." Allie suffered a small swallow of the cold coffee. "Well, that'll wake you up. Do you have the good coffee in your lunch bag?" She glanced over at his red insulated cooler.

Mann looked up from his papers. "You're here early."

She raised her coffee mug. "Hard to sleep when there are things to take care of."

"I don't try to sleep anymore." Mann lowered his papers to the desk. "We need to close the Bergman case. His widow wants the body back for cremation." He put his reading glasses on the papers, leaned back in the chair and crossed his hairy arms tightly. "Why is your dictation on Bergman not here for me to sign as I directed? Doctor, you've had more than enough time to complete it."

Allie drew in a deep breath and pulled the cup close to her chin. "Hard to say. Maybe I'll go back over the body again?"

"My instructions to you were very clear. Crystal, in fact."

"Where?" Allie looked over her shoulder.

Mann appeared perplexed. "Where what?"

"You said 'Chrystal.'" Allie turned back towards him. "That's my daughter's name. I thought you saw her."

"No." Mann shook his head. "I said 'crystal' as in 'crystal clear'."

"Oh!" Allie laughed and tossed her head. "My gosh, that's funny."

Mann glared at her. "Why are you laughing, Dr. Parsons?"

"Oh, because I thought you saw Chrystal, but you meant...and then I..." She took a deep breath and assumed a serious expression. "You're absolutely right. It's not funny at all."

"So why haven't you finished the dictation?" Mann rocked back and forth in his chair.

"There's something that bothers me about the case."

"What?"

"I don't know."

"Dr. Parsons, I need that dictation. Don't make me complete it myself."

"I'll work extra hours, Dr. Mann."

"Good." Mann picked up a file from his desk and flipped through it. "I expect nothing less. It's regrettable this conference was held so soon after you joined our staff because I really felt with your less than laudable qualifications I must keep a close eye on you."

"I'll get it done. I really will." Allie took another sip of her cold coffee, but it now tasted very bitter. She grimaced and lowered the cup.

"You may leave." Mann leaned forward, replaced his glasses on his nose and picked up another file.

Allie nodded. "Okay." She turned towards the door and then hesitated. She glanced at Mann.

He appeared engrossed in a thick folder embossed with the State of Florida seal and didn't seem to notice her lingering.

"Just a question, Dr. Mann. Did you get my voice mail or emails?"

"No, my battery died and I didn't have a charger." He answered without looking up. "I'll check my emails later. I don't like this new technology. I really need to meet face to face or talk via phone. What did you want?"

"Oh, well, I wanted to know what your note meant."

"What note?"

"You know, the note you left on my car. 'Glad to see you have recovered. Looking forward to our next encounter. Bully for you. I'll be in touch. Take care of our friend Franz'. Something like that."

"What are you talking about?" Mann sat up. He cocked his head to the side and glared at her. "I'm confused. I didn't deposit a note on your car."

"I hoped you left it. Remember, you said you might leave me notes." She exhaled through pursed lips. "But I worry. After what he said...the way he looked the night he attacked me."

"What do you mean?"

"Never mind. Forget I mentioned it."

Dr. Mann leaned back in his seat, whipped his reading glasses away from his nose and stared up at her. "No. Not possible. Not this Toro fellow." Despite his calm demeanor his eyes shifted nervously. "Really, that's preposterous. It has to be some kind of joke."

"Why?"

"Why? Because he's gone, for crying out loud! That was the conclusion of the task force I was part of."

"How can they be sure?"

"Because the evidence was reviewed and that's the most logical conclusion."

"I'm sorry, Dr. Mann, I read the transcript and it seems the findings were not as firm as you make them out to be."

"If you were part of the commission, Dr. Parsons, you would realize that the consensus of the members was that Toro was definitely dead."

"Because of Stan Kozlowski?"

Dr. Mann nodded. "Yes. A known psychopath. Carpet fibers found at two of the crime scenes."

"One, actually, Dr. Mann. Sara Larson's."

Mann hesitated then shook his head. "It's been a while since I looked at the case. But he knew intimate details of some of the murders and was called 'Bull' by several friends. He was a large, violent man who liked to carve animals with his hunting knife. And, last but not least, he told friends he committed the murders."

"It's unfortunate the police shot him. So we can never really be sure."

"Yes, it is. He knew Renee Rowan. He spent time with her."

"We all ran in the same circles, Dr. Mann. And, I bet there hasn't been a single big man that hasn't been called Bull or Toro or something like that at some point in his life."

"Did you ever meet him at your bars or night clubs?"

"No. I..." Allie started to speak and then cast a puzzled glance at Dr. Mann. "I only saw him in the police line up, but he didn't look like the guy who attacked me. They both had beards, but their eyes looked different."

"I see." Mann scowled so that his lips were pulled over to right side of his face. "Show me the note and I'll see if it matches the ones he sent to the Tampa police and FBI. The script is quite distinctive. Almost calligraphy."

"It's gone."

"Gone?"

"My daughter cleaned our car out and threw it away."

"That's unfortunate, if not utterly foolish. Looking at it might have answered your questions."

"I understand. I was hoping that, like Detective Festoon said, maybe you wrote it and I misinterpreted the meaning."

"You realize that without physical evidence, there's really not much that can be done."

"I know that."

"Look, Dr. Parsons, I'll check to see if anything else has developed with regards to Toro. But I'm absolutely convinced that he's gone."

"I appreciate that." Allie placed her coffee on a bookshelf and rubbed her lips. "Before I leave, can I talk to you about something else?"

"Certainly." Mann pushed the papers aside and looked up at her. "I can spare a few moments in my overscheduled day. What is it? Hmm? Speak up."

"James Smith."

"James Smith?" Mann's eyebrows furrowed and he raised his chin. "What about James Smith? It's a very common name."

"He was mentioned in the report of the Toro commission. They wrote him off. But is it possible--"

"I'm going to stop you right there." Mann raised his hand. "James Smith was no more than a clever thief. So clever, in fact, that he managed to entangle himself in our investigation and waste our time. But it came to nothing."

"Did I ever see him in a lineup? In person?"

Mann sat back in his seat and took a deep breath. "Well, to be honest Dr. Parsons, he never was that strong a suspect."

Allie took a deep breath. "I need to let you know I saw a picture of him yesterday, and I can't say he wasn't the man who attacked me."

"You can't say?"

"He might have been. It was a very bad picture. But it might have been. He was familiar."

"Familiar?"

"He gave me chills. That sounds silly, I know. But it's the truth."

Mann shook his head and turned his seat to the side. "After all these years. Tell me, Doctor." He rubbed his thick gray hair and smirked. "Was this a picture you found on the internet? Say, you typed in a search for James Smith on your computer?"

"No."

"Well, then. How did you come across this photo after all these years. Because Dr. Parsons, the police showed you hundreds, perhaps thousands, of pictures back then, and you did not identify a single one of them. Nothing."

"Someone showed it to me."

"Someone. Might I ask whom?"

"You could ask."

"And..."

"I'd be reluctant to tell you."

"Well then, without a picture and without a note, I have absolutely nothing to go on."

Allie puffed out her cheeks. "I understand. I was contacted by Jess Bergman yesterday--"

"Jess Bergman? Franz Bergman's wife?" Dr. Mann suddenly leaned towards her.

"Yes, but hear me out--"

"Hear you out! What are you doing talking to a witness? You're a resident! Remember what I told you in our interview a few months ago? Remember my rules for your behavior here?"

"I know, Dr. Mann, but she thinks James Smith killed her husband...and he's Toro."

"Dr. Parsons, do you also remember what Detective Festoon said about the possibility of your presence on this investigation invalidating it?" Dr. Mann's face turned red and tiny drops of saliva flew from his mouth.

"I do, but....she has a picture!"

"And do you remember I spoke up for you?"

"I do, and I'm very thankful for that."

"Do you remember I backed your good name when he personally attacked you and I warned you never to embarrass this department again?"

"Yes, sir. I do."

"So, clearly you have an excellent memory. Use it and remember to stay away from Mrs. Bergman. Do you hear me? Do not give anyone a chance to say that we botched this. I demand your obedience!"

"But Dr. Mann--"

"Shh, Dr. Parsons." Mann raised his finger. "Now, you will listen to me very carefully, Young Lady. There are very few ways that you can be made to leave medicine. Physicians are, for the most part, forgiving of their colleagues and attempt to keep doctors in practice. However, committing a felony will get you thrown out in any state. Interfering with a police investigation is a felony. And I don't want to see you out of medicine and back...well... back at another job. Stay away from Jess Bergman!"

"So, you don't think I should worry about James Smith?"

"James Smith had nothing to do with Toro! I know that to be fact! I'll bet my life on it!"

"I should tell Pug about the photo of James Smith. He doesn't know about that."

"You can, but it will reflect poorly on your choices."

"I'm sorry, Dr. Mann. My choices?"

"The fact that you've inappropriately inserted yourself into this investigation. Look, Parsons, what's happened is that over time, you've seen so many pictures of similar faces that they've blended together. What you should do is allow the police to investigate. Concentrate on doing your job. So far you haven't disappointed me too much. Let's keep it that way."

"Yes, Sir."

"Anything else?"

"No, Sir."

"Actually, there is, Dr. Parsons."

"What's that?"

"You'll have that dictation on my desk by noon."

CHAPTER THIRTY SIX
PRESENT DAY

Allie faced an overwhelming number of tasks delegated by Dr. Mann. With Byron's help, she completed two routine autopsies involving hospital deaths. During these exams, Dr. Mann checked to make sure they were progressing appropriately. Allie then reviewed slides of surgical tissue samples and completed several dictations.

With great reluctance, she finalized the Bergman dictation and presented it to Dr. Mann by 11:30. He signed it without saying a word and flipped it back to her. She felt antsy, and found it difficult to concentrate.

Throughout the day, Allie pondered her predicament. But sometime between carving out the spleen of an ICU patient who bled to death with a low platelet count and reviewing the bone marrow slide of a leukemia patient, she reached a conclusion.

After promising Chrystal that she could have her party at Jess Bergman's home, Allie couldn't change her mind now. She wouldn't pull out and leave her daughter hanging.

She suffered through hours of internal debate, but Allie convinced herself that an innocent birthday party without discussion of the Bergman's case, would be harmless. Dr. Mann would never have to know.

For better or worse, she'd reached a decision. It'll be fine.

By the time cars began pulling out of the morgue parking lot, she had nearly convinced herself the party was a good idea. If only her nausea would go away, she could be reasonably happy with her decision.

What could possibly go wrong?

At 7:00 PM, she decided to call it a day and packed her books. As Allie passed Dr. Mann's office she waved and caught a glimpse of a grimace. Without hesitation, Mann stuck a small pill under his tongue and reached for his phone.

"Are you alright?" She leaned into his doorway.

He replaced the earpiece on the receiver. "I'm fine, Dr. Parsons. You startled me. I thought I heard you leave." Mann placed his hand over his heart. "I have some uncomplicated angina from time to time. A nitroglycerin clears it up."

"You're pale and diaphoretic. I can stay around if you need me."

Mann wiped beads of sweat from his forehead. "It's easing up now. Typical of my heart disease. Two coronary arteries 70% blocked with collateral revascularization. No need to operate, but a strong need for medicines. It's part of growing old."

"I shouldn't call 911, then?"

He picked up the phone again and held it against his neck. "I'm fine. I have this a few times a week. Don't start CPR, yet. I'll see you Monday."

"Okay, then." She lingered in the doorway. "I'll see you Monday."

Allie drifted down the hall to the elevators and pushed the down button. While waiting for a 'whirr' and a 'chime' she looked out towards the Tampa suburbs.

Dr. Mann had looked so pale and sweaty.

The elevator arrived with a 'ding' and the door opened. She hesitated and stepped away.

I'm just going to make sure he's not having a heart attack. He's an absolute jerk, but if he died of an MI and I hadn't done anything, well...

The elevator doors closed with a thud and she tiptoed back towards his door, not wanting to interrupt him.

"No, I don't think she knows...We talked about this...She received a note...Remember what I hold."

Allie gasped.

"Just a moment."

Allie shot like a bullet around the corner and pressed her back tight against the wall. She held her breath as footsteps seemed to approach, pause and turn away. She heard the door to his office slam shut. After that, only mumbles.

She made her way to the stairs without making a sound. She opened the door and squeezed through, pulling it closed with the softest 'click'. On tiptoes, she descended the five flights and reached the lobby.

By the time she arrived at her Honda, sweat covered her body and her hands trembled. She checked her rearview mirror as she backed out and someone darted beside her.

The smiling, moon face of Pug Festoon greeted her. He motioned for her to roll down her window.

CHAPTER THIRTY SEVEN
PRESENT DAY

"**P**ug, don't sneak up on me like that!"

"Had to catch you before you disappeared. You can be underground for weeks."

"I've discovered when I go underground these days my daughter gets lonely. What do you want?"

"I recently came into possession of some confidential pictures and I want you to tell me what you think."

Before Allie could reply, Pug pulled two blurry photos from an envelope. They were the same pictures Jess showed Allie, now enlarged beyond any reasonable quality.

"Seen this man before? Take your time."

Allie stared at the photos. Despite the bad image, something about the eyes, nose, mouth and hair sent shivers down her spine. She felt as if she were back in his grasp.

"They're awful pictures, but I'm pretty sure that's the guy who tried to kill me."

He pulled the photographs away from her and slipped them into the envelope. "You seem awfully calm."

"They're photos, Pug. Not the real thing."

"Not the real thing, Allie. But we know his real name. James Smith. He disappeared before we could put him in a line up. I can't say where we got these, but it's a reliable source." Pug smiled and bounced on

170

his toes. "Yes, ma'am, we got him this time. We're gonna run him to ground and tree him like a possum."

"Which is it?"

"Hmm? What do you mean?"

"I mean are you going to trap him in a tree or are you going to pin him to the ground? Because you just gave two different possibilities."

"What we're going to do is cuff him and throw his butt in jail! What problem do you have with that?"

Allie closed her eyes and sighed. "I'm sorry. I shouldn't be sarcastic. I've been under a lot of stress. Thank you. Please catch that guy. I'll be your best friend forever, Pug."

"In that case, I'll be calling you later, Good Buddy."

"That note left on my car? Could it be from him?"

"When we apprehend our man, we'll ask him if he wrote you a note. Where is it by the way? I'll take a look at it."

"I threw it away."

"Why did you do that? What were you thinking?"

"It was a mistake. Just catch this guy. The thought of him being out there doesn't make me happy."

"But it's different now. Not like nine years ago. We have good leads on where he might be. He's got no support system. We've got pictures."

"Terrible pictures."

"Okay. Then we've got you to point him out. This guy is practically caught. We'll get him."

"Dr. Mann doesn't think James..." Allie remembered Mann's warning about interfering with the case.

"He doesn't think what?"

"Nothing." Allie put the Honda in reverse. "Just catch James Smith soon."

CHAPTER THIRTY EIGHT
PRESENT DAY

Allie arrived at her graduate student housing cradling three, bulging bags of groceries. After fumbling with her keys and using her hip to swing the door open, Allie sprinted the short distance to the kitchen as the plastic began to tear. She dropped the bags on the counter just as the heaviest one split.

Only one egg broke.

"Crap!" She scooped up the egg and dropped it in the trash. "Chrystal! Lock and bolt the door!"

"I'm on the phone with Carly! In the shared bedroom!"

"I'm fixing your cake!" While Allie washed her hands in the tiny sink, she heard the door swing open. Allie glanced around the corner and saw Chrystal stick her head out.

"Why? Why are you baking my cake?"

"Because you need a birthday cake for your candles. Bolt the door, please."

"Why didn't you buy one that was already made? Have you ever made a cake?" Chrystal stepped towards the door and bolted it shut.

"Baked cakes are expensive, and of course I can make a cake. I drew blood from a 28-week preemie. I did a lumbar puncture on a 500 pound guy. I can bake a cake, Chrystal."

"What's a lumbar puncture?"

"Spinal tap."

"Gross, Mom!" Chrystal disappeared back into the shared bedroom.

Allie fished the instant cake mix out of the grocery bag and studied the back of the box.

"Now. How do you bake a cake?"

As Allie stirred the thick batter in the bowl with her right hand, she clicked the remote with her left and turned on the TV. The local news was half way over and she was informed that the weather for the next seven days would consist of sun, heat and rain.

"No kidding." Allie poured the batter into a cake pan. "Welcome to Tampa."

In the next story, Allie was shocked to see footage of Jess Bergman's house. The reporter, her old acquaintance Phillip Spears, revealed that police were hot on the trail of a potential suspect in the murder of millionaire philanthropist, Franz Bergman.

He added that sources that could not be named, felt the suspect may be related to the Toro case, though there were no definitive ties. Spears concluded his report and in a solemn voice, sent it back to the anchors.

Allie sighed and turned the TV off.

One hour later, the cake was done.

After slathering on canned icing, Allie crossed her arms and scowled. She studied her creation. It's lumpy, and a little lopsided.

Allie stepped forward and pushed from the side until the top layer slid even with the bottom. Better. Anyway, I bet it tastes good.

It took another hour to assemble a tray of assorted small sandwiches on a red plastic platter. Written on the plate was 'Happy Birthday!'

That should do it. She wiped her hands clean. Now, I'm completely prepared for tomorrow. She eyed the food again and nodded in satisfaction.

What could possibly go wrong?

CHAPTER THIRTY NINE
PRESENT DAY

Erin Warrant couldn't guess how long she'd been tied up. She'd awakened hours ago, though it may have been yesterday. No light penetrated the dungeon-like room. Her hands were bound behind her back, her feet tied at the ankle. Erin's head and neck ached where she struck the car in the garage.

At first Erin had quietly tried to free herself, twisting her wrists and angling her ankles one way then another. After what seemed like eons, she resorted to more primitive tactics.

Erin screamed, "Help!" repeatedly, but the tape over her mouth muffled her words so that they were no louder than the moaning of the merciless machine that accompanied her in the dark room. For a while, she felt certain Rick would find her.

She remembered texting him just before she heard the voice.

It was definitely his voice. The voice of the dead.

After many hours of squirming against the heavy tape that held her, Erin abandoned all hope that Rick would come to her rescue. She figured he had probably run off to alleviate all his anxiety with his favorite combination of Smirnoff and Oxycontin.

After some time, it dawned on Erin that she was on her own and she resumed her struggle with renewed energy. Her wrists grew slippery from the perspiration and she felt them slide against each other more than before. Maybe this could work. She took a deep breath and squirmed harder.

In the midst of her twisting and bending, she heard a loud squeak. The door to the room opened, permitting a tiny shaft of golden light.

"Help me!" She wailed towards the light, but the tape across her mouth stifled her words, changing them into more of a plaintive whine. "Help me!"

"What was that?"

She heard his deep, haunting voice then the door closed with a solid 'thump'.

"I can't tell what you're saying." He yanked the tape from Erin's mouth.

Erin's eyes opened wide with pain and terror. "You're dead!"

"No. I'm right here, Erin. I've lived for more years than you can imagine. I'll never die."

"You...just died!" Her eyes grew even wider.

"No. You're dead. You just don't know it yet. There's your casket in front of you. No longer occupied and ready to accept a new tenant."

"Why?"

"Thou shalt not steal, Erin. You must be punished."

Erin saw a large knife appear in the darkness. It glowed an eerie orange, a reflection of the indicator light from the merciless machine.

Before she could scream, the orange blade flashed towards her chest.

CHAPTER FORTY
PRESENT DAY

Saturday turned out to be a typical, torrid, tropical Tampa day. Making it even hotter was the heat produced by the massive crowd packed around Jess Bergman's pool. All 15 of Chrystal's invitees, six boys and nine girls, had shown. However, many more kids ran around the pool than had been invited.

In addition, Jess had included five friends of her own. Allie's little cake and single tray of sub sandwiches couldn't feed everyone.

When Allie and Chrystal arrived at Jess' house, they saw trays and trays of beautifully arranged sandwiches, drinks, hors d'oeuvres, and desserts displayed on decorated tables surrounding the pool.

Despite Allie's vow to provide the food, Jess had hired a caterer.

"No need for a fish and loaves miracle, I guess." Allie looked at her tray of sandwiches with embarrassment.

"I had to supply additional food, Allie. I invited some friends. It wouldn't be fair to ask you to feed them. And I expected Chrystal would need to invite more friends. It's so difficult to limit a wonderful party to such a small number." Jess motioned to the revelers.

Allie had to admit the caterer had done an amazing job. The cold fruit tray held marvelous carved melons that formed a leaping dolphin amidst a sea of kiwis. A tray held several pink and orange cream sandwiches Allie had never eaten before, but they tasted coolly delicious.

As they mingled and laughed, the mob of kids carried colorful tropical drinks with umbrellas and fruit spears bobbing across the top of the cups. Combined with the sunglasses, designer bathing suits and cocky talk, Allie felt this was as close as she would get to a Hollywood party.

As Allie served iced drinks and tiny square sandwiches to the energetic guests who flitted across Jess' backyard, a thin layer of warm perspiration enveloped her arms and shoulders.

Allie picked up yet another discarded dirty, plate, wiped her salty, damp face with a napkin and tossed both into an overflowing trashcan that had been placed in a shady corner under the cabana.

She felt like an unlucky lobster dropped into a big, boiling pot.

Beneath the fan of the cabana, the temperatures were tolerable, but once she left the shade, Allie felt her already dark skin burning under the full brunt of the south Florida sun.

For the first time in a decade, she played waitress and though she tried to serve Chrystal's guests as they shouted above the loud Indie music, she couldn't help but hear the refreshing blue water of Jess' pool calling her. She could not resist.

Allie had to jump in.

She peeled off her tank top, entered the shallow end and sank into the pool. A wonderful sensation engulfed her chest and back as the chilly water rose to her neck. The tension in her shoulders drained and she felt rejuvenated as she floated in the cool pool.

Allie's content eyes opened and she saw Chrystal glower as her mother's tattoos were exposed.

"It's only a cross, Chrystal." Allie climbed out of the water.

A quick dunk was all she wanted. Her tank top went back over the bikini top and the cross was covered.

Well, nearly covered. Her cotton shirt stuck to the wet muscles of her tan abdomen. Allie pulled the flimsy fabric away from her skin and she quickly covered herself with an abandoned towel.

"Allie?"

She sighed. Rowdy followed her around like a lost puppy.

"It's Ms. Parsons, Rowdy. You have to call me, Ms. Parsons. I'm not Allie to you. You have to understand this."

"Yeah. Can I help you clean up some of this trash?" He had to shout over the loud music.

"I've got it, Rowdy. Thanks for the offer." She rolled her eyes as she turned away and resumed cleaning.

"I'm here for you, if you need me!" Rowdy turned and was swallowed up by a passing group of boys.

She rolled her eyes again and looked up to see Andrew Wong approaching her.

"Looks like you've found a friend." Andrew ran his hand through his long, black hair. He was wearing a blue, flowered shirt, baggy shorts and flip flops.

"He's exhausting. This whole thing is exhausting. I want it all to go away. I can't believe I've dug a hole this deep, Andrew."

"Do you need any help?"

"Actually, that would be really great. I could use it. Because if you can't come through, plan B is over there." Allie smirked and motioned with her head towards the pool. "It'll be Rowdy and me."

Rowdy looked up from the cool pool, whipped the water from his black hair with a rapid twist of his handsome head and gave them two thumbs up.

"I can see that. He's a great catch, Allie. He's worth more than me right now. I think he's the one that drove up in the golf cart. I can't afford a golf cart."

"But, being a rocket scientist, I'm sure you could build a pretty cool one from our left overs."

"I could and it would be very fast."

Allie smiled. "I'd pay to see that." She sighed and looked towards the pool. "Seriously. I really could use some help and I'm not just talking about dealing with Rowdy and his friends. I have to keep this place clean. Just help me get all the trash."

"It looks like whoever owns this house could probably pay somebody big-time to bag all this up."

"Andrew, this is my party. My party and my call! It happens to be located at the Bergman house, but its my party and I'm taking care of all the arrangements, including the clean up. So, start tossing trash in the can." Allie paused and threw up her hands. "Not the low-key party I was counting on. Not at all."

"I see that. Good point. I hope this pays for the ride over here." Andrew picked up a plate and tossed it in the trashcan.

"More than pays for it."

"Hey, what's going on, you two?" From out of nowhere Jess appeared in high heels and a form fitting black one-piece bathing suit. Her thick brunette hair touched just above her shoulders. "Stellar party, Allie. Amazing. I'm having a fabulous time. You should be so proud."

Her voice slurred slightly. Clearly, there was more than passion fruit in her 'Party Juice'.

Before she could answer, Jess slid her right arm securely around Allie's shoulder and pulled her tight. "My goodness, you're fit, Young Lady. You must still dance in secret. I can see why this handsome young man and all Chrystal's boys here are so interested."

Allie leaned back. "Uh. No...he and I are good friends."

"I'm so sorry." Jess cocked her head and brought her glass towards her lips. "Honestly, I just meant to say that you're in great shape. No sin in that. Right, Young Man. I'm Jess, by the way. It's a pleasure." She extended her hand to Andrew.

"Andrew. Andrew Wong."

"Andrew Wrong?"

"Possibly. But, no. Simply Wong."

"It's Wong." Allie winced under the pressure from Jess' squeeze on her shoulder. "No 'R'."

Jess smiled sweetly. "With such a handsome man, a Wong could make a right."

"An excellent pun." Andrew managed a laughed.

"Thank you." Jess countered with a sly smile and batted her eyelashes. "I thought you'd appreciate that. So, tell me. What do you do, Andrew Wong?"

"I'm in aeronautical engineering."

"Fascinating. What company do you work for?"

"None."

"Oh." Jess leaned away and turned her chin downward as if disillusioned. "So shocking and disappointing. That won't last for long, surely. Please tell me no."

"I hope to work for one or start something soon."

"He's a genius." Allie slipped away from Jess' grip.

"Absolutely Allie! I can see that. Look," Jess squinted and appeared to lose herself in deep concentration. "Mr. Wong. I've met so many men who've gone from rags to riches because of their brains. My late husband for example." She gave a half-hearted smile and pointed towards the Bay. "Despite tragedies, life goes on unmercifully."

"So we beat on, boats against the current..."

"Well spoken. A poet and a scientist. Careful, or you just might sweep me off my feet. Well, enjoy yourself, Andrew." She tipped her sparkling glass towards him. "Any friend of Allie's is a friend of mine. I knew her mother so well that she and Chrystal are practically family. If you need any introductions in aeronautical engineering or IT, please let me know. I would be more than happy to share them and other things with you."

"Thank you, Jess."

"Anytime, Andrew." Jess tipped her glass towards Allie and winked. "Stellar party."

"Thank you for letting us borrow your home--"

Jess smiled and took the last sip of wine, placed her glass on the table and dove into the clear, sparkling water of the pool. She barely made a splash and somehow her high heels were left stationary on the terrace beside the pool. Moments later she emerged on the other side next to her friends.

"Weird." Andrew shook his head.

"Yeah. And, well done with the <u>The Great Gatsby</u> quote."

"I'm glad you liked it. I think she liked it, too."

"She thought you made it up."

"Great. It makes me look brilliant."

"What do you think of her, Mr. Wrong? I mean Wong."

"You have to admit, that was an excellent pun. I've only heard it, maybe 10 times in my life. But she seems really nice. She rubbed her toes against my calf before she dove in the pool. You probably didn't catch that. I like that personal touch. And that was my own pun. Personal touch. Against my calf."

"She rubbed your calf with her toes?"

"It was definitely a rub."

"I didn't need to know that. Jess seems to have her eyes on you."

"And they're pretty eyes."

"Yes, indeedy." Allie returned to collecting cups.

"But she is kind of hot."

"Especially for a widow. But we're all hot. It's got to be a hundred degrees out here."

"What happened to her husband?"

"Somebody blew his brains out and dumped him just off their dock." Allie turned to look at the house. "Killed him while she was out of town."

"When?"

"Less than two weeks ago." Allie covered her mouth. "I shouldn't have said that. Forget I said that."

"Seriously? Ouch!" Andrew turned his gaze back towards Jess and the pool. She was still talking with the ladies on the steps. "Wow. She moves on quickly, doesn't she? Then, why are you having Chrystal's party here? I mean, it's a little creepy."

Allie picked up a used cup and crushed it. "Because Andrew, I love my daughter and this is what she wanted and I couldn't give it to her if I didn't have the party here."

"If it makes you feel any better, very few people can provide this for their kids."

"Maybe it does." She flipped a handful of napkins into a trashcan.

"Did this guy's body come through your morgue?"

"Can't talk about it."

"Seriously? He did?" Andrew's jaw dropped.

"I can't talk about it."

"Are you like on some investigation here? Is this some undercover job? Oh, I heard about this on TV! This is where that guy was killed? Is that really why we're here?"

"Zip it, Andrew!" Allie crossed towards him. In a flash they stood toe to toe. Her jaw stuck out and her eyes narrowed into slits.

"Got it, Allie. If you're on some undercover thing, I'm done asking questions."

"Thank you. I have to be discrete. Get in and get out."

"You're absolutely right."

"Well, anyway, this is not going at all like I was hoping. " Allie scowled when she saw boys doing cannon balls in the pool. The girls crowded together and giggled.

"Andrew, if Dr. Mann finds out about this, I'm in big trouble. So we need to get out."

"Now?"

"Very soon. Let's get things moving."

CHAPTER FORTY ONE
PRESENT DAY

Allie took a deep breath and faced the crowd. "Hey everybody!" Chlorinated water splashed from the pool and stung Allies eyes.

"Awesome! Bro, did you see that! Dude!" A group of kids ran to the edge of the pool to see who had made the incredible dive.

Allie cleared her throat. "Can I have your attention, please? Guys! I'm Chrystal's Mom and this is very important!"

Between the pool, cabana and bay, the crowd undulated like an amoeba Allie had once studied under a microscope.

I know I didn't invite this many people!

Only a few kids noticed her attempts to attract attention. Fortunately, one of them was Rowdy and he was standing next to Chrystal.

"Rowdy, get those guys behind you to turn around. Thanks. Okay, let's go ahead and open presents and cut the cakes!"

"Mom!"

"We're going to move into the cabana."

"Mom!"

"What, Chrystal?"

"Cake then presents!"

"Yes, I know."

"You said it the other way around."

"I don't know what I said, but do it in whatever order you want to because it's your birthday. It's not a big deal."

"Aaagh!"

"Okay. Let's light the cakes, open the presents and all go home!"

"Just one cake, Mom. I just want to light Jess' cake. Please, just Jess' cake." Chrystal managed a half smile and raised her eyebrows. In a soft voice she whispered above the drone of the crowd, "Please!"

"I spent a lot of time on that cake and we are going to use it. It is a perfectly fine homemade cake. So, where is it? Chrystal, where is it?"

Before she could answer, someone yelled and Chrystal turned away from Allie. Rowdy leaped from the diving board and performed a flip into the pool. Chrystal giggled and covered her mouth.

"Has anyone seen my cake? I refuse to waste it. It was right here with the matches..." Allie glanced down. "Which also appear to be missing."

"I saw Chrystal pick it up a few minutes ago." Andrew strolled over to Allie, looked over her shoulder and pointed behind her. "I think she slipped into the garage."

"The garage? Why would she go into the garage with my cake?"

"Not sure. But I'm guessing it has something to do with one of the caterers saying there was a refrigerator in there. Don't worry. It's fine. Every thing will be okay. The kids will love Jess' cake"

"I want to find my cake. I don't care how fancy Jess' is."

"It really is fancy. It should be on magazine cover. Dolphins and stuff."

"Everyone in this frickin neighborhood can see it's a stellar cake! But I'm going to get mine back, because I put a lot of time and money into that thing. Even if it does look homemade. I'll eat it myself if no one else wants it."

"Allie, calm down. Listen, I'm on your side. I'll go find it in the garage."

"No. I'll find it. Just move everyone to the cabana. I'll be back in a few minutes."

"Fine. I've got this." Andrew turned towards the crowd of kids, waved his arms and let out a shrill whistle. "Okay, everybody! Squeeze under the roof! Keep moving! Pack it into the cabana."

As the crowd eased away from the pool and followed Andrew's gesticulations towards the shelter, Allie walked in the opposite direction towards the garage. When she reached the door, she looked both ways then turned the handle and jerked.

The door swung open with a squeak. There were no windows along the bare gray walls and a solitary fluorescent light in the ceiling provided a weak, bluish glow.

Allie stepped inside and pulled the door shut. She found herself in a large five-car garage with a Porsche, matching Land Rovers and a Jaguar parked on an immaculate floor. Allie could see a stainless steel refrigerator along the opposite wall between two doors. Together, the lights and refrigerator generated a hum that sounded like a hive of angry bees.

I'm proud of that cake! She squeezed past the Porsche. It may not be the prettiest, but I'll make Chrystal appreciate it. I put a lot of work into that thing. I bet it tastes great.

Allie maneuvered carefully, afraid she would trip over something and tumble into one of the expensive vehicles.

The lights went out. She stood in complete darkness.

Allie desperately turned, looking for any illumination.

She couldn't see anything and found the infernal buzzing completely disorienting. Her feel for the location of the refrigerator, became less certain. She heard the squeak of a door and what sounded like footsteps.

"Allie?"

CHAPTER FORTY TWO
PRESENT DAY

"Who's there!" Allie stamped her foot.

She couldn't be sure she had heard anything at all. It might have been her own breath. The sound had been a rumble as much as a word.

Somewhere to her right, near where she'd entered the garage, came the sound of quiet shuffling. Maybe scurrying mice. It was hard to say.

"Anybody there?" Her voice trembled and her heart rate quickened. "Please, turn on the light! I'm in here!"

"Allie."

Allie squatted and lifted her arms up to nose level like a boxer.

She stood poised for battle in the silence and complete darkness: only the sound of her breathing and the hum of the refrigerator could be heard.

"Who is it? Don't push me, because... I'll punch you. I'm warning you. I'm not playing games here!"

She felt a light touch on her shoulder and she whipped around and shot her fist forward.

Her jab struck nothing and her fist disappeared into empty blackness. She pulled it back, returned to her boxing stance and listened. Allie couldn't be certain she had been touched by anything more than a draft, but she stood her ground, ready to punch again. After another second she definitely heard feet on the floor behind her, so she spun and faced the opposite direction.

Aaagh! I left my phone at the pool! "This isn't funny! Whoever you are, I'll get you for this!"

A soft sound like shoes sliding across sand startled her. Allie whipped around and kicked with her right leg at the attack she anticipated would be coming from the back.

Her foot found only empty air and she retreated to her boxing stance again and waited.

After bouncing on her toes for a moment, Allie's eyes adjusted to the dark. A faint reddish glow appeared in the distance. Carefully, with her left hand outstretched before her and her right fist poised to punch, Allie slid her feet towards the light.

A few shuffles later, her hand touched cold metal. Using the car as a guide, she glided along the side and then around the front. She eased forward until she neared the red glow.

"Allie."

This time she knew it was a voice.

"Who are you? Turn on the light!"

She heard heavy breathing, and at first thought it might be her own. But she couldn't be sure.

She turned back towards the red glow and found it reflecting off the floor, very close to her foot, coming from beneath a door. Carefully, she extended her hand and searched for the knob. When she finally felt the cool metal she grasped it firmly and twisted.

It was locked.

"Allie."

"Give me some light!"

Desperately she tried to turn the knob again without success and then shoved her shoulder into the door. It didn't budge.

"Allie."

The voice sounded as if it were only a few feet away.

In desperation, she took a step back, and using her hips for power, kicked the door as hard as she could. The frame exploded, the bolt gave way and the door flew open, crashing against the wall of the room.

The red glow was coming from a small indicator light on an electric plug, but it was enough to illuminate the room. Allie dashed in and turned around.

She saw no one behind her.

"Who are you?"

There was no answer.

Allie's breathing began to slow and she backed further into the space. It was a large utility room with tools and lawn equipment stacked on shelves that lined all four walls. Her eyes darted back and forth as she searched for something that could be used as a weapon.

Taking two steps back, she struck the corner of a large object. She jumped and turned around.

She saw a metal box, six feet long, three feet wide and about three feet high. It sat in the center of the room amid the red glow of the light, like a coffin surrounded by candles.

Allie experienced a strong urge to look inside. She checked behind her again, then slowly gripped the lid and lifted.

The darkness beneath the door appeared to be an abyss, as if it could extend for miles below the earth's surface. A rancid smell worse than spoiled milk overtook her and an arctic blast rose up, chilling Allie to the core.

The lights came on and Allie jumped, dropping the door with a solid 'thump'.

"What did you do to my door?"

Jess appeared out of nowhere and seemed horrified at the battered lock and splintered wood.

"Oh, thank goodness, Jess!" Allie cleared her throat and looked nervously around the room. "Thank goodness, you're here. I'm so sorry. I came in here to find my cake and someone turned the lights off and I got turned around and ended up in this room."

"How did you break my door? This room is locked!"

"I...well...I sort of kicked it in." Allie rubbed her cheek.

"Kicked it in?"

"Yes. Uhm. Well, I heard someone in here with me." Allie desperately searched for the right words. "He kept calling my name, but wouldn't answer me. It was so dark and the only light I saw came from under this door. So, I got a little flustered and kicked the door. I'll get it fixed for you."

"You...destroyed...my...door! What kind of person are you?"

"If I feel trapped, I lash out. But I'm so glad you turned on a light. I'll get it fixed, I promise."

"No. I'll take care of it." Jess peeled off a small piece of broken pine. "Please. Let's just go. Everyone is waiting in the cabana for you. Andrew won't let them start until you get back and he said you went into the garage. So, I came looking." Jess motioned for Allie to step out. "Really, Allie, you're so impetuous."

As Allie stepped into the garage, Jess closed the door, but with an annoying squeak, the door swung freely on it's ruptured hinges.

"Sorry." Allie cringed.

"Let's move on, shall we?"

Allie tried to smile and shrugged her shoulders. "Maybe a bungee cord for now? It's amazing how much you can fix with a bungee cord, plastic ties and duct tape."

"No bungee cords. No plastic ties. It's not the way I do things around here. So, let's fetch this special cake and get back to your daughter's birthday party."

Jess opened the refrigerator door and Allie spied the cake, which she'd wrapped in wrinkled aluminum foil. She leapt forward and cradled it in her arms.

"Okay. Got it."

"I can see it is special. It must be delicious." Jess raised her eyebrows.

"I thought the same thing. And that's a fancy freezer you have in your storage room. It's better than what we have in our lab."

"So glad you approve, Allie. Now, follow me and don't dawdle."

As they walked towards the door of the garage, Allie hoped Jess wouldn't notice her palm prints smeared on the windows of the cars. Near the exit, Jess' eyes drifted towards the Porsche and a large smudge.

Allie felt frantic and quickly spoke. "Jess, could there have been anyone in your garage?"

"Of course, Allie. The caterers are in and out of here." She turned her gaze away from the car and continued her brisk walk towards the exit. "Perhaps hiding back here to avoid work."

"I hope they would have helped me when I called for the light."

"Maybe they were afraid they'd be caught sleeping or getting away from the kids. The children are having such a good time." Jess waved her hand as she continued towards the exits. "Honestly, with the great party going on out there, we couldn't have heard you."

They reached the door and, as Jess held it open, Allie walked past her into the bright sunlight. Jess pulled the door firmly shut behind them. "Allie, listen carefully. You are my guest. If you need anything from inside the house, let me know. I'll get it for you personally.

"I'll...yeah, right. Jess, one more question."

"Yes, Dear." Jess marched past Allie towards the cabana.

"Is it possible James Smith could have been in your house. Could he be around here?"

Jess stiffened and swallowed. "I'm sure my security cameras would have picked it up. And with so many people around, I can't imagine he could pass through without being seen. Now, let's forget all that talk and enjoy Chrystal's party."

"Hearing my name like that was very bizarre."

Jess took a deep breath and turned around. Her smile faded and her eyelids narrowed. "Allie, Dear, we have delayed this party because of you. We were looking for you, calling for you, and you were gone. Absent. Please, for the next hour or so, be there for your daughter. Be a good parent."

Allie glanced down at her clenched fists. "Mrs. Bergman, you're in no position to say something like that. You have no idea about my relationship with Chrystal."

"I'm just making a suggestion based on what I've observed." Her smile returned and Jess performed a smooth, dance-like turn towards the cabana. "Darlings! I've found our lost lamb. We can continue with Chrystal's wonderful party."

CHAPTER FORTY THREE
PRESENT DAY

Allie lit the candles on both cakes. "Happy Birthday to you..." she began singing.

The crowd joined in, and an ebullient Chrystal floated forward like a ballerina and blew out the candles. Everyone cheered and Chrystal beamed. Allie managed a smile.

"Presents, my darlings!" Jess slipped a silk sarong around her waist and made her way to the cabana. "Bring those gifts from the table, please!" Her voice slurred more than before. "Chrystal, my beautiful darling, please sit here." Jess leaned back with her hand on her hip and cocked her head. "Rowdy, you're so handsome. You feed the presents to Chrystal."

Like an assembly line, the gifts were handed to Chrystal who accepted them with a gracious smile, tore away the paper as quickly but politely as she could and, with peals of laughter, digested what she'd been fed.

In short order she'd acquired two designer purses, two shirts, a pair of shorts, a gift card to a store called 'Belle's Closet' and another to a boutique named 'Pretty Chic', a phone cover, and a pair of roller blades from Rowdy.

"Now, my present." Jess reached behind a curtain of the cabana, and with both hands, lifted a large gift, wrapped with, sparkling silver paper.

"Oh, thank you so much, Jess." Chrystal tore away the paper and slid out a pearlescent, white box. "Wow!" As her hand drifted over her heart, Chrystal glanced at Jess who smiled and nodded.

Carefully, Chrystal lifted the lid of the box and gently pulled out the present. Inside she found a crystal Swarovski castle that sent shimmers of light throughout the cabana.

"Oh, Jess, it's beautiful!"

"It's crystal for Chrystal! Be careful with it, Darling, it's quite expensive. It's from Austria. It's my hope that one day you will live in such a place. Would you like that?"

"I would. Thank you so much for the party and the present!" She ran over and threw her arms around Jess' shoulders. "You're like my aunt."

"Aunt Jess. I like that. And you're welcome, Chrystal. Now back to the pool. There's not much sunlight left, but still plenty of fun for everyone."

"One more."

"What?" Jess spun around.

"One more present." Andrew entered the cabana carrying a thin square wrapped in bright, pink, tissue paper. "I forgot to put it on the pile. Here you go, Chrystal."

Jess smiled, refilled her wine and sat back in her seat.

"Thank you, Andrew." Chrystal blushed. She tore away the tissue paper.

"Wow!" Chrystal stood transfixed. Her eyes darted from top to bottom and all around the square. "It's so beautiful."

"What is it, Chrystal?" Allie craned her neck to see around Rowdy.

Chrystal turned the square around so that Allie could see a vivid oil painting of a canary in a tree overlooking a distant ribbon of river. The colors were vibrant and the small bird appeared prepared to launch off the canvas. The old wooden frame was painted a faded gold, and intricately carved.

"My grandmother painted it in China. I always wanted to find someone who appreciates art, and gift it to them."

"Andrew, I...thank you. It's so special."

"I've seen what you've collected from estate sales and the paintings you've done. I know this artwork will be happy with you."

"Wow. Thank you so much." Chrystal stood motionless admiring the painting for a moment. "Mom would you hold it for me. I want to keep it safe. Oh, the crystal castle, too."

"Sure, Sweetheart. Pass them over."

Jess smiled brightly and clapped her hands. "More pool! Enjoy yourselves everyone. Fireworks at dark."

The kids retreated to the pool with enthusiastic cheers and laughter. As Jess rejoined her coterie, Allie tossed her head back.

"Fireworks?" Allie grabbed her cheeks in her hands. "Seriously?"

"So it would seem. What a party."

"Just incredible. It's really the bomb, Andrew. I'm thrilled I agreed to this."

"Sarcasm?" Andrew raised his eyebrows.

"It's far beyond sarcasm. I don't think there's a word for it. And Chrystal can't keep that painting."

"Why not? I really want her to have it." Andrew looked hurt.

"Because it was your grandmother's, and it's too nice."

"My grandmother would have loved for Chrystal to own her canary. Besides, she sold so many of them in her art gallery. She was always giving them as gifts to friends."

"You're sure?"

"Please, let Chrystal keep it. It would mean a lot to me."

Allie sighed. "It's a wonderful gift. Really insightful. Thank you."

Andrew lowered his head and nodded. "It's all good, Allie. You've raised a great kid. I'm glad you guys are my friends."

"Fireworks? Where did that come from?"

"So much for your low profile party, huh?"

"Right. And you're going to think this is weird, Andrew."

"What?"

"Fireworks are dangerous. They get me really nervous."

"Really? They're safe in the right hands."

"My palms are sweating right now. Some people have a problem with clowns. I haven't been able to enjoy the 4th of July since I was six."

"You wouldn't do well with the Chinese New Year, then."

"Yeah, you're right. I'll be back in a second. Find Chrystal and start moving her towards the car."

"What?"

"We need to get out of here!"

"Yes, Sir!" Andrew gave a quick salute.

With a nod, Allie left Andrew and wove her way through the crowd in search of Jess. It may have been an illusion created by the long shadows cast in the dying sunlight, but it appeared to Allie that there were more guests now. Tiki torches burned and the dancing orange light made it even more difficult to distinguish faces.

Because of the darkness and huge crowd, it was difficult to locate Jess. Allie finally found her sitting next to the pool with several friends. An orange arc cast by the setting sun created a fiery backdrop for the black silhouettes of the scurrying pyrotechnicians. Finalizing their preparations, they flitted back and forth across the fresh mowed lawn and counted down to launch time.

Allie squatted and sat cross-legged beside Jess.

"Allie, glad you could join us. You remember Gloria and Cornelia from earlier."

"I do." Allie smiled and the ladies nodded, making the floppy rims of their hats dip across their large sunglasses. They sipped their wine in synchrony and turned back towards the bay and the setting sun.

"I have to thank you for having the party here."

"Of course! I've had so much fun, Allie. I've needed this."

"Of course you have, Mrs. Bergman. But, it's getting late. How are we going to get your backyard clean in the dark?"

"Oh, please! Don't worry about that! I'll have the same crew here in the morning that cleaned up early today. They descended on this place like a plague. They'll have it all pristine by tomorrow."

"You're very generous. But really, fireworks are dangerous and Chrystal doesn't need them."

"Forget it, Allie. They're already paid for and what a beautiful night and special occasion."

"Well, I wish we'd talked about this. What will I do for her 16th birthday after this party?"

"Chrystal will want to have it here, of course."

"We can't, I...I appreciate everything you've done for her, but this is way more than I bargained for. So, we're going to say, 'goodnight'."

"Oh, nonsense. I love doting on Chrystal. And I love helping out the medical profession. Such a dedicated people." Jess rested her hand on Allie's forearm. "I remember years ago when my husband had that thing." Jess motioned towards her belly button. "Oh...his appendix. That's it. He had to have his appendix removed and they took him right into the operating room at 1:00 in the morning. Can you imagine, Girls? All of the medical people just as fresh as daisies and so pleasant that early in the morning. Buzzing this way and that to care for him. I was so impressed!"

"You mean, he had an appendectomy?"

Jess blinked then opened her eyes wide. "But you're not a real doctor, are you, Allie? You take care of people that are already dead. A little late to be any real help, don't you think?" Jess giggled, as did the ladies around her. "But I still admire whatever it is you do, Dear."

"You're sure they took his appendix out?"

"Of course, I'm sure. Snip, snip."

"An appendectomy!" Allie nodded and placed her palm to her forehead. "Now, it's so obvious what was bothering me."

"Yes. Allie, why do you find this so interesting? People have this done every day from what they told me."

"You said his operation was a few years ago, so Franz would've had a visible scar and no appendix." Allie bit her lower lip and scratched her cheek. "But the autopsy..."

"Oh, I see..." Jess finished the last of her wine and turned away. "I must ask, as a very close friend of your mother, do you still find that you have feelings for this man, Toro? I know you once did. Years ago you invited him into your home...Is it still possible?"

Allie trembled with rage, stood up and smoothed her shorts. "No! Absolutely not!"

Jess glanced down at her wine glass, a hint of a smile on her lips. "He's never been caught. And he did allow you to live." She continued looking at the bay. "I suppose he might like you."

"This conversation is over! I think you've had too much to drink." Allie could feel the back of her neck burning.

"It's a simple question. Do you have feelings for someone or not. Nothing more."

"The answer is no. No! No!"

"Sounds definitive. If I were you, I'd concentrate on being careful."

"Thanks, for the sage advice. I'm going to find Chrystal and Andrew and hit the road. It's getting late and I need to be in the office tomorrow."

"You work on Sundays?"

"I do tomorrow. I need to review an autopsy."

Jess stood up and hugged Allie whose arms hung stiffly at her side. Jess gave her a small peck on the cheek. "Let's not be strangers. I'll drop a note sometime."

"A note?"

"Or a text. Au revoir, my darling."

Allie pivoted and stormed off, wanting to put an end to this nightmare. Could this day have possibly gone any worse?

CHAPTER FORTY FOUR
PRESENT DAY

As Allie hurried to the car, the first fireworks exploded overhead in a series of orange and blue cascading, glittering lights. Simultaneously, a large fight broke out among a group of guys on the lawn in front of her.

A pimply boy with a scraggly 3-haired beard fumbled an illicit mojito. He failed to catch it, and, as it spun towards the grass the green drink splashed Allie in the face.

"That's it!" Allie felt her cheeks grow hot. "I'm ending this farce!"

A six foot tall preppy jock banged her hip as the crowd shifted. Allie secured her grip on the fine Egyptian cotton of his polo shirt and jerked his head down to eye level.

"Hey you! Get in there and tell them to break it up or I'll personally settle this myself!" She shoved her 'Medical Examiner' badge inches from his face. "Understand? You have one chance before this is taken downtown." She released his shirt and he sprang away like a green blade of grass.

"Yes, ma'am!" He gulped. "Hey, guys! The cops are here! Cops! Cops!"

Using his thin, wiry arms to muscle his way through the crowd, the teenager broke beyond the innermost ring of young spectators and flew towards the two twisting bodies. With a hard shove, he pushed past the last line and ripped the two combatants apart.

"Cops, Dudes!"

By then, the crowd had caught on.

"Cops!"

There was a stampede of adolescents towards their luxury cars, occasional pickup trucks and one restored 1984 Land Cruiser parked in the driveway.

"Cops!"

Instantly, the crowd melted and flowed away. Within minutes, Allie stood alone, like a silent monument on an abandoned battlefield, with the echoes of retreating V8 engines fading in the background.

She turned, and in the bright lights of the fireworks finale, found Andrew emerging from the cabana 15 feet behind her.

"And that's..." Allie rubbed her hands together. "That's how it's done."

"I didn't know you're a cop." Andrew looked sincerely confused. "Are you really undercover?"

"Apparently, I must be a morgue cop. Whatever that is. Where's Chrystal?"

"She's by the pool with the other 13 year olds. So, you're undercover. Please tell me you're not packing heat."

"Uhm, no, I don't have a gun. I'll tell you more, later. Let's get Chrystal and beat it out of here."

They found Chrystal huddled near the presents with Carly and Rowdy. When she spied her mother, Chrystal ran over to her.

"Mom, don't make me leave! That fight wasn't my fault!"

"First, tell me why there are 'high schoolers' here throwing alcohol all over me? And why are they trying to kill each other?"

"They're some high school kids Helene invited. I don't know them."

"Helene?" Allie raised her hands, palms facing skyward in exasperation. "Helene?"

"Mom, calm down. I know what parents say about Helene. But she's nice. She's been helping us get ready for High School next year, so we know who to hang out with."

"I didn't know she had a bad reputation until now, because you've never told me anything about this chick. I've never heard of her!"

"She's Carly's friend."

"You never mentioned a high school friend of Carly's with a bad reputation. Say goodbye to Carly and Rowdy, because we're leaving."

"Mom..."

"Now, Chrystal!"

"I've got to thank Jess!"

"Yeah, Well, write Mrs. Bergman a note."

"Why can't I thank her myself?"

"It's a long story." Allie fished her phone from her pocket and searched her contacts. "Where did Andrew go?"

"Coming!" Andrew ran towards them with two large, brightly colored packages tucked under each arm. "I scored a couple fireworks from the crew. I can use them in my lab."

"No way! I told you how I feel. Those things are deadly!" Allie punched the 'call' button. "Not in my car!"

"Fine. I'll put them back by the shed. Can I borrow your car and come back later?"

"Shh!" Allie held up one hand and pressed her phone to her ear. "Dr. Mann. Sorry to bother you...Yeah, it's Allie. Don't cremate Bergman's body! Because..." She sighed. "Oh, really. Too bad. Well, listen, go back to sleep. Oh, great. I'll catch you in the morning, then. I've got to talk to you about a missing scar. We've overlooked something big. Just finishing my daughter's party. This is really important ...okay, bye."

As Allie slipped the phone in her pocket, a movement in her peripheral vision caught her attention. She looked up and observed a silhouette in the window on the second floor of the house. The hairs on her neck stood up.

"Let's get out of here."

Andrew followed Allie's gaze to the second floor and saw the figure disappear. "I agree. The fireworks can wait."

That night, Allie insisted she sleep with Chrystal. The two of them crammed into the twin bed and Allie's hand remained firmly wrapped around a can of mace.

As Chrystal slept, Allie stared at the ceiling and thought about how much her circumstances had changed over the year since she'd been invited to apply for the residency. At first, she'd felt so safe and optimistic as she discussed her great opportunity with her advisor, Dr. Regis.

But that sense of security now felt threatened. As she slipped off to sleep, Allie remembered the meeting when her mentor had first hinted of an incredible future.

CHAPTER FORTY FIVE
ONE YEAR AGO

Meetings with her advisor were always awkward. Invariably, Allie received a message that was an odd mixture of pep talk and admonition.

Typically, Dr. Regis would greet Allie at the door of her office and ease her arm over Allie's shoulder, creating a cool sound as the creases of their lab coats crossed. Then, Dr. Regis would guide Allie to the leather chair facing her desk.

While walking casually to her own seat, Dr. Regis would ask Allie how classes were going, was she enjoying herself and what was her daughter doing these days.

That day, Dr. Regis' dress, shoes and makeup were perfectly coordinated with her red hair. There was the slightest hint of a floral perfume as the smooth linen of her skirt slipped onto her seat.

"Allie, my goal is to be a role model for young female physicians and professionals." Regis coaxed her seat closer to her desk. "At times, I may be harder on you than others. But I only want to bring out your potential. Being a woman in medicine can be challenging, and I feel a responsibility to prepare you as much as possible."

"I appreciate that, Dr. Regis." Allie tried not to fidget.

"When I was in my Cardiology residency and fellowship I had to achieve far above my male colleagues, not only academically and clinically, but my reaction to stress was also examined more closely. As I'm sure you're finding out, it can be unnerving."

"I'm doing my best."

"Yes, you are. A single mom, later in life, just starting your career. You really are holding your own. But I feel like being near the middle of your class, you have a lot of room for improvement."

"I promise you. I'm working hard. Sometimes I don't have the time I need to study. My daughter--"

"Of course, you're doing exceptionally well for your circumstances. I have to say, when I look at the entire picture, I can't help but be impressed. But, I bet with a little self examination with an eye towards improvement, you could find it within yourself to dance right to the top..."

Allie felt conferences with Dr. Regis were like riding a catamaran on the Gulf of Mexico in midwinter. From the crest of the wave to the bottom within seconds, then a rapid rise to the top, followed by a vertiginous drop. For hours after their talks, Allie felt queasy, like she was seasick.

"You're doing great...but not good enough." The message never changed.

"What do you think?"

"I want to improve. I really do."

"I'm so glad to hear that!" With a nod, Regis stared at Allie as if waiting for her to elaborate.

"Yeah, uhm, definitely."

Regis looked disappointed. "Anyway, do you know why I called you in this afternoon?"

"I'm not exactly sure, Dr. Regis." Allie stared down at her hands. "I thought it might have something to do with my disagreement with the surgery resident. Uhm, his behavior towards me was inappropriate and I shared my opinion with him."

Regis cleared her throat and tilted her head. "No. I hadn't heard about a problem with a surgery resident. Who was it?"

"Evans."

"The general surgery chief resident?"

"That's him."

"I've heard stories about how he conducts himself. Is everything okay?"

Allie sunk slightly in her seat. "I guess so. I mean, if you didn't hear anything. I have no problem with him anymore. I assume he learned his lesson."

"Well, I'm glad to hear that...I guess." Regis shook her head. "No, I called you in because I received a bit of surprising news."

Allie sighed and rubbed her forehead.

"No, Allie. It's not anything bad. It's very good news."

Allie slid her fingers down to her cheeks. "What?"

"It's good news, Allie. I can't say it's an invitation, because that's just not done, but you received a vote of confidence from the Pathology department of this university. Do you know what that means?"

"Uhm, Yeah. Yes. Well, actually, no, I don't."

"Do you like Pathology, Allie?"

"I do. Great hours, limited call and liability...What's not to like? I've done reasonably well in my rotations. I had some trouble with almost passing out. Uhm, but I think I've worked through that."

"How about your test scores in Pathology?"

"They've been okay. Sometimes, good. Up and down. Sometimes, poor. Mostly okay I'd say." Ohmygosh I sound like Dr. Regis.

"Well, curiously, I received a prompt to encourage you to apply for the Pathology residency at this university. They want you to match here."

Allie suddenly sat up in her seat. "Are you serious?"

"Who was your attending physician when you rotated through their department?"

"It was Dr., Dr., uhm, Dr. Harvey, maybe?" Allie crossed her arms.

"So, you don't remember."

"No, no, I don't." She grimaced and shook her head.

"Be that as it may, they routinely encourage one or two top members of the class to apply here. Of course, they receive applicants from all over the world for their spots. So, well done! You must have impressed someone important."

"Thanks. That would be nice. Chrystal would love to stay near her friends in Tampa."

"Chrystal?"

"My daughter."

"Of course. Well, I encourage you to study your Pathology and try to rotate through their department a couple more times before submitting your match requests." Dr. Regis glanced at her Rolex. "Meet some attending physicians so that they know you. Their chairman is Dr. Silas. The medical examiner is Dr. Mann. He's world renown in his field. There's a position for a resident to spend the majority of his time studying Forensic Pathology. He's got a reputation for being brutally tough, but he's one of the best in the world."

"That sounds exciting and a little intimidating, but definitely worth trying for."

"Yes." Regis chuckled. She rubbed her chin and cleared her throat. "Anyway, that's reserved for the best of the best. At this point, you've surprised me by being on their radar. I would die from shock if Dr. Mann chose you. But study, meet people, show them how enthusiastic you are, and who knows? Miracles happen."

"I'll try."

"If you graduate from their prestigious Pathology program, Allie, it's instant success. You're virtually guaranteed to work anywhere you want for top dollar."

Allie shrugged her shoulders. "I'll go for it. I'll show them my best side."

Regis' lips curled into a soft smile. "Of course, you will. And on that note perhaps you can change your wardrobe. Have you thought about a prosthetic eye? I'm not saying you need it. You're a beautiful person inside and out, Allie. But the patch is a distraction."

CHAPTER FORTY SIX
PRESENT DAY

At 6:00 AM on Sunday, Allie dragged Chrystal out of bed and drove her to an adult sunrise prayer service, leaving her daughter in the care of Pastor Virgil. He seemed surprised to see Chrystal so early, but happy to provide sanctuary.

Allie thanked him and asked Virgil not to leave Chrystal by herself. She never wanted Chrystal to be left alone again.

Virgil seemed alarmed by Allie's angst, but nodded. "Sure, Honey."

Chrystal wasn't awake enough to protest much.

"Coffee." Chrystal groaned and took Allie's travel mug.

Allie gave Chrystal a quick kiss, turned and strode to her car. She wasted no time and whipped the Honda through the parking lot on her way to the interstate. A few heads turned and frowned indignantly as she squealed her tires.

At 7:00 AM Allie pulled into the empty morgue parking lot, walked briskly towards the imposing building and entered the vacant lobby. Fortunately, the elevators were operating. Accompanied by the soothing sounds of the 70's, she arrived at the coroner's office.

As she scooted past Mann's office, Allie threw a brief glance towards his desk, which mercifully, remained unoccupied. With a sigh of relief, Allie dashed past the door and started her computer. Several clicks of the mouse later, she'd performed an image search for Franz Bergman.

Multiple rows of photos materialized on her monitor. Allie's eyes darted across the colorful screen as she scanned the pictures.

Several were black and white publicity photos from meetings and speeches released by **Light Optics**, his former company. Based on her perfunctory perusal, Allie surmised Bergman had always been heavy-set and short with thinning hair. After his retirement from **Light Optics**, he became much more reclusive, as had his hair, both nearly disappearing. Photos of him over the last decade were almost nonexistent.

There were three candid pictures snapped by newspapers over the last nine years. He was with Jess in the first, alone in another while driving, and onboard his yacht in the last. In every picture his head was shaved and the picture was of poor quality—blurry, grainy and shot from a distance.

In each candid photo, he wore sunglasses. Sometimes Franz sported a very short, graying beard.

Allie found an article detailing **Light Optics'** legal conflict with a Saudi company. Another story described Bergman's battle with the Berlin businessmen that Jess had mentioned. Both had occurred many years ago. Hard to imagine someone could hold a grudge that long.

She searched for Jess Bergman and found several references to charities and parties in the Tampa area. Nothing of note.

Not yet satisfied, Allie reached towards the aluminum shelf behind her desk and grabbed the file that held a copy of Bergman's medical records. Breathlessly, she flipped through the papers until she found a 'History and Physical' obtained from his Internist.

Allie stood, immobilized. She was stunned.

There, under 'Past Surgical History' was listed 'APPENDECTOMY'.

For nearly a minute she stared at the plain page with the simple print and sighed. Her head tilted until her hair slid against her back and she was staring at the ceiling.

Just like Jess had said. Just like Allie now remembered from her first glance through Bergman's records at the initial autopsy. Though she was too late in recalling it, the appendectomy was what had been nagging her.

A chime from the elevator startled her and Allie heard Dr. Mann clear his throat. She listened to his footsteps and the sound of his briefcase landing with a thump on his desk.

Seconds later she heard his chair squeak. While Allie listened to Mann settle into his office, she chewed on her lower lip and rubbed her temples.

Here we go. Allie smoothed her plain white t-shirt and jeans and took a deep breath. She recited one of her favorite verses from Chronicles. *"Be strong and courageous, and do the work"*. After another sigh she took one step... and then another until she slowly built up speed and was walking with determination towards Mann's office. Moments later, she was in front of his door.

He was studying an open notebook and didn't look up.

"Dr. Mann--"

"So, Dr. Parsons, what's on your mind?" As he spoke his eyes remained focused on the thick stack of papers he shuffled beneath his hairy fingers. Mann's reading glasses were on the end of his nose and he tilted his head as he perused the papers. "What's this about a missing scar?"

"How was your Saturday off?"

"It was fine. I finished a paper on MRSA and mortality."

"That sounds interesting."

"I'm simply elated it's done. That's what I do. I finish my tasks. I start them and then I complete them. You should learn to do that. So, Dr. Parsons, I'm waiting to hear about your concern." He still didn't look up from his notebook.

"Well, here's the thing..." Allie swallowed and took a deep breath. "Bergman had an appendectomy and our body didn't. To put it simply." Allie breathed a sigh of relief. Now it was out there.

Mann appeared nonplussed. "Sit, please." He rotated and pointed to the upholstered chair in front of his desk. "Now, to your first point. What makes you think he had an appendectomy?"

Allie fought to remain calm and sat down. "It's listed on his medical records. Something was really bothering me about his autopsy, that's why I was having a hard time completing it. I just couldn't pinpoint what was stuck in my subconscious." She smiled and glanced up at his face.

Mann remained emotionless and stared intently at her.

"Anyway, I remembered. His history and physical from his internist listed an appendectomy, but there was no scar on our corpse."

Mann shook his head and gave a downcast smile. "Come now. Isn't it possible that there was a mistake in the 'H and P'?" Mann intertwined his fingers near his nose like a fleshy basket. "Did you find an actual Operative Note of the appendectomy dictated by the surgeon? Did you consider any of this?"

"No, I didn't."

"Don't worry. It was the internist's dictation mistake. Not ours. Doctors wait until the end of the day to do their dictations, confuse patients and commit small errors. Don't concern yourself with it." Mann smiled uncomfortably. "Dr. Parsons, I'm impressed to see you working so early on a weekend and catching that detail. Don't you have church?"

"Uhm." Allie felt herself blush. Dr. Mann's compliment had startled her and derailed her train of thought. "There are several services I can attend...Anyway, what was I saying?"

As Mann stared accusingly at her, Allie desperately attempted to reorganize her thoughts.

"I...I..."

"You...you... what, Dr. Parsons? I'm busy and I don't have time to waste on you. What is it?"

Allie felt her face grow hot as a sudden wave of anger flashed like a geyser from her gut. "Give me a chance to finish!"

She formed a tight fist and fought the urge to slam his desk with her knuckles. She caught herself just as her shoulder flinched.

Do not be quickly provoked in your spirit, for anger resides in the lap of fools...

In her mind she heard Virgil's voice as clearly as if he were in Mann's office and reading to her from Ecclesiastes. Over the years he'd quoted the verse in juvenile facilities, prison and when picking her up from school detention.

Allie froze and her arm stopped before it rose.

She took a deep breath and leaned away from Mann's desk, relaxing her taut bicep as she retreated. The anger ebbed and her face cooled.

"Speak now, Dr. Parsons or get something useful done in the lab."

"Well, when I made the incision, I'm absolutely certain I saw an appendix."

"You were quite flustered during that autopsy. Did you even comment on the appendix being present in your dictation? Are you willing to bet your future on it?"

Allie took another deep breath and made sure she was in control. "I did mention a normal appendix in my dictation. Resolving this is simple."

"In what way?"

"I confirmed the appendectomy with another source last night."

"What source?"

"A very reliable one."

Mann started to speak and then shook his head. "Parsons, listen to me. Even if Bergman did have an appendectomy, the laparoscopic scars are less than a centimeter. They could be easily overlooked, even by the most veteran pathologist, which you are clearly not. There was advanced decomposition, making finding postoperative changes that much harder. Don't concern yourself with this matter. We need to move on to the next case and that will soon be followed by another and then another."

"Dr. Mann." Allie spoke in a deliberate, measured tone, determined not to let her temper erupt again. "I don't want to argue, but I examined him thoroughly. I had just read about autopsies in my textbook and pardon my pun, I did it by the book. Except for his back, which you said you did. I'm sure I saw an appendix, and I know for a fact Bergman had an appendectomy."

"What source told you Bergman had an appendectomy."

Allie shifted her feet and looked at the ceiling. "They want to remain anonymous."

"But you know their name?"

"Yes."

"Then tell me. It's not your role to decide who remains anonymous and who doesn't. You are not a reporter or the police. You're a resident under my direction."

Allie sighed and locked her hands behind her head. "It was Jess Bergman!"

Mann closed his mouth and his eyes and lowered his head.

"I know you're going to be mad, Dr. Mann, but stay calm and follow me here. Take a deep breath and count to 10. Doing that helps me a lot.

He massaged his forehead in large, deep circles. "Parsons. You should have never spoken to her!" Mann's face turned crimson.

"Dr. Mann, please calm down."

"Never! Never! I told you not to speak to that woman again!"

"What's wrong with finding facts in a murder investigation? It helps to form a more complete report."

"Do not talk with her anymore!"

"Dr. Mann, I'm sorry, but you kept telling me to cover every detail!"

"Talking to a witness is for the police to do. You should not have talked to her!" Mann's German accent grew thicker with his escalating anger.

"I wouldn't have answered her call, but she worked with my mother so I felt I should help her out if I could."

"I don't care if she is your mother! Stay away from her."

"Pug and Westbrook told me she's not a suspect."

"That doesn't matter! Stay away from her! Do not talk to her. Do not text her. Do not email her. Do not send up smoke signals! If you have ESP, I demand you do not think about her! Is that clear, Dr. Parsons?" Now, two large veins bulged on Mann's forehead.

"Very clear, Sir. I won't talk with her again." Allie meant to keep that promise.

Mann sighed and bit his lower lip. His breath came in quick, short bursts and he placed his right hand on his chest. "We won't mention your conversation with her to the police. Hopefully, they'll never find about it, and this situation will just go away."

Allie decided not to spring the story of the birthday party. "But Dr. Mann, the bottom line is Bergman had an appendectomy and our cadaver did not."

"I have to disagree, Dr. Parsons. He probably had an appendectomy and you missed it. You simply overlooked the minute scars and with the decomposition so advanced and so much blood in the abdomen, it would be understandable if you mistook clot, scar tissue or rotting bowel for an appendix."

"I could have made a mistake, but I didn't."

"So, if you are going to adhere to your story, what are you suggesting?"

"That we just cremated somebody besides Bergman. Another body."

Mann shook his head and took a deep breath. "That is a serious accusation. And one based on a missing scar the size of a single fingernail."

"But also an intact appendix. I included it on my dictation. You signed it and it's now part of the public and legal record."

"His wife positively identified him!" Mann pounded his palm on the desk.

"She could be mistaken...with all the decomposition."

"You expect me to accept that you can identify a decomposed appendix—which you've never seen before—better than she can identify a decomposed man she lived with for 20 years?" Mann shook his finger at Allie. "I'll not call into question our findings based on what you've said. Everything else has fallen into place. Dr. Parson's, you will accept our findings." Mann gritted his teeth and nodded. "If you don't, we'll have to deal with your insubordination."

Allie's eyes widened, she slid back in her chair, holding up her hands. "Dr. Mann, if I could throw something out there before you make me sign off on this. I have a solution."

Mann turned towards his desk and absently spun a pen so that it turned like a roulette wheel on the polished wood surface. "What is it?"

"We can obtain a DNA sample from his son, Isaac."

Mann's eyes narrowed and his face turned deep red.

"Jess mentioned that she and Bergman had a son, Isaac." Allie spoke quickly. "We compare the child's DNA with the samples we've obtained from the body. That should give us a very clear answer. We can say, through DNA, if they're related."

"No, that's impossible. I told you..." Mann stopped and licked his lips. He leaned back in his chair and crossed his arms. "But this idea does have merit. This would satisfy the objections that you've stated, yes? "

"I would accept that our corpse is Bergman."

Mann leaned forward. "I'll arrange it. I'll explain it as a bit of red tape to satisfy the inquiries." He rubbed his hands together. "Anyway, I'll get it through. But the police and I'll handle this and I demand you stay out of it. Agreed?"

"Agreed." Feeling victorious, Allie stood. "I'll go now if there's nothing--"

"You may go!"

Allie swallowed. "Yeah...I'll a..."

"Dr. Parsons. I'm going to be perfectly frank. If you see that woman again, if you have any contact with Jess Bergman, I'll fire you. And I guarantee, you won't be able to find another job as a physician in Florida. Am I understood?"

Allie stopped in the doorway and nodded. "Yes, Sir."

"Or you can play my game and travel the world when you've earned it."

"I got it."

"Doctor, my way is much more entertaining and lucrative."

"I can't argue with that."

"Now, since you're here, you may as well get some work done."

CHAPTER FORTY SEVEN
PRESENT DAY

By late Sunday afternoon, Allie was eager to pick up Chrystal and get home. Chrystal's not going to be happy about being left at church all day. She threw open the glass door of the morgue and hurried towards her Honda.

"Allie? Hey, hold on!"

Allie stiffened and turned. She caught a glimpse of a tall, thin figure sprinting towards her from behind a palm tree.

"Hey, Allie! It's Phillip Spears...from college. Good to see you!"

Allie relaxed, then tensed. She wasn't being attacked. At least, not physically.

He hadn't changed much since the dinner on campus when he'd insisted on asking her about Toro. His thick, black hair was parted on the side and perfectly combed. He wore a tailored blue suit without a tie. Phillip had deep dimples in his cheeks and chin and his eyes flashed a deep emerald green.

"Hey, Phillip. It's been a while. I don't mean to be rude, but I'm in a hurry. I need to pick up my daughter. Maybe we can talk some other time." She shook his hand roughly and let go. "Sorry." She resumed her march towards the Honda.

"Hey, hey, Allie."

Allie groaned. "Aagh!" She picked up her pace, but the crunching footsteps on the asphalt continued to close in on her. Apparently,

Phillip had grown more aggressive over the years, commensurate with his professional success.

"I don't have time to talk about the Bergman case, Phillip."

"Allie, do you know who I am?"

"My daughter tells me you're the investigative reporter for WTSP. But that means nothing to me and I have nothing to say to anybody about the murder. Just read the newspaper. They have a very thorough article. Goodbye." She fumbled for her keys.

"Your daughter's right." Phillip caught up to Allie. "Chrystal isn't it? She must have just turned 13. So how was the party?"

"You've always had a lot of questions."

"And you have very few answers."

"It's amazing how some things never change." Allie reached her Honda and stuck the key in the lock.

"Just let me ask you a few questions."

"Fine!" Allie opened her squeaky door and tossed her purse into the passenger seat. "Ask as many as you want."

"Allie, thank you. I appreciate it."

"No problem." Allie started the car, slipped it into reverse and began to back out of the space.

"Whoa! I thought you were going to let me ask questions?"

"I didn't say I was going to listen."

"Oh, that's really cute." Phillip jogged beside the car. "Okay, regarding the new note from Toro, have any comment?"

The Honda stalled and stopped dead. "Who told you about that?"

"I've got my sources." He produced a cheeky grin. "So, you know. Did they show it to you?"

"I threw it away a week ago. Did the police find it?"

"Threw it away?" Phillip wrinkled his brow. "It just got delivered last night to the TV station. We gave it to the police."

"What? You got a note?"

"What are you talking about? Is there another note?"

"No comment." Allie struggled to start her car.

Phillip grabbed her door and stuck his head inside the window. Allie gripped the manual roller and turned it, cranking the window up.

"Bingo! Are you serious? So, there's a second note from Toro?"

"No comment, Phil."

"Allie, please give me an interview. You're a great story. Rags to riches. Survivor! Gutsy girl! Great headlines! You'd get so many fans and followers." He pulled out of the window and began to jog beside the car, keeping his hand on the door as the car picked up speed. "You can trust me, Allie! Please! We've known each other forever!"

"I'm not talking about any of that, Phillip. I left all that behind."

"Anything to say about the Bergman case? I'm working on that, too."

"Please let go of my car."

He ran faster and breathed heavily, but still held on. "This is a great story. Please, Allie! Give me a statement."

Allie braked and the car lurched to a sudden stop. "I do have one statement to make."

"What's that?" Phillip bent down and leaned towards the window.

With a quick strike of her right hand, Allie punched Phillip squarely in the face, knocking him off his feet. "Let go of my car!"

Phillip landed on his butt and grabbed his face.

Allie released the clutch and shot backwards towards the exit. "And you can quote me on that!"

CHAPTER FORTY EIGHT
PRESENT DAY

Because she happened to hit green at every traffic light and exceeded the posted speed limit most of the way, Allie reached the church a little before 5:00 PM. She leapt out of the car and ran inside.

Chrystal flew towards Allie as soon she entered through the old wooden door, nearly knocking her mom over.

"Mom! Really! What was that all about?" She threw both hands in the air.

Allie placed her hand on Chrystal's shoulder. "Hi, Virgil. Thanks for looking out for her today. We have to run, but I'll stop by next week. Say 'thank you' to Pastor Virgil, Chrystal."

Chrystal turned around and smiled. "Thank you, Pastor Virgil."

"Thanks for keeping me company, Chrystal."

Chrystal swung her gaze back towards Allie, tilted her head and stuck out her jaw. "Really! Sunday School at 7:00! And then leaving me all day! I've been to six, count them, six classes and meetings."

"You didn't complain when I dropped you off." Allie turned and walked down the hall with Chrystal at her side.

"I wasn't even awake until Mrs. Reynolds gave me a cup of coffee and I realized I was in the seniors' class."

"It's good for you."

"Why?"

"Any Sunday schooling is good, don't you think?"

"I learned about social security benefits, Mom!"

"Do we qualify for any?"

"I don't know, but I have a list of phone numbers to call so we can find out. Here." Chrystal pulled a piece of folded paper from her pocket. "Pastor Virgil didn't include emails, because no one, besides me and him, knows what those are."

"You're exaggerating."

Chrystal unfolded the paper and held it up. "Really. Look. No emails."

Allie glanced at the paper. "I'm sorry. I had to work today and I can't leave you alone. So what was I supposed to do?"

"Why can't you leave me by myself? I always sleep late when you have to go into work early."

"First of all, those days of lounging around on the couch have sailed. You're 13, so you need to get up at a reasonable time on the weekends."

"That makes no sense, but okay. Next time, if you leave me in the dorm, I promise I'll stay up and study. You go to work. I don't need to learn about Medicare with people who want me to meet their great-grandson. I don't need a babysitter. "

"I don't want you by yourself. After last night, I just couldn't leave you alone."

Allie reached the driver's door of the Honda and unlocked it. As she slid onto the rough seat, she surveyed the parking lot. The only people nearby were the elderly church members leaving the class-room building.

She leaned over and unlocked Chrystal's door. The hinges creaked as Chrystal opened it and sat down. Allie started the engine.

"Why can't I stay at the dorm by myself anymore? I thought, as kids get older, they're supposed to be given more privileges. Parents don't take privileges away unless their kids have done something wrong. I should be given a puppy, or something to take care of. That's how this parenting thing works, Mom."

"Were privileges and parenting covered in Sunday school today?"

"Yes, in the young couples class at 2:00. By the way, I flatly refuse to go to that class ever again. They kept using me as an example."

"Well, for your information, you can't have a puppy in graduate student housing."

"I don't want a puppy. I was just using that as my example of how my freedom should be expanding, not shrinking. Why can't I stay by myself?"

"It's complicated, but in a nutshell, I don't think it's safe right now."

"Does it have something to do with the party last night? Those guys fighting. That wasn't my fault, Mom. I don't know them."

"It has nothing to do with the fight. I know you weren't involved. Combine alcohol with teenage testosterone and there's bound to be problems. I know. I've been there."

"It was a great party, though. Carly loved it! She texted me after we got home. And Helene did, too. So did Rowdy."

"Chrystal, we're not going to see or talk to Mrs. Bergman anymore. I just got in real trouble about that."

"Why?"

"It's a police issue."

"What does that have to do with me not staying home alone?"

"There are bad people out there. They'll probably leave us alone, but I can't be sure."

"Are you saying Jess Bergman is a bad person?"

"I'm saying, possibly. Along with others."

"That sucks."

"Chrystal, please."

"That stinks."

"Yes, it does."

CHAPTER FORTY NINE
PRESENT DAY

Mother and daughter climbed the stairs to their apartment. Allie took stock of their surroundings, looking for anything out of the ordinary before placing her key in the lock.

"Finish your homework." Allie opened the door and wiggled the key out.

"It's done. I did it in afternoon Bible study." Chrystal scooted past Allie.

"Then get ahead."

"Can I read, instead?"

"As long as it's not trash."

"*Slaughterhouse Five*?"

Allie rolled her eyes. "Alright, but we're going to discuss what you've read."

Chrystal retreated to her room, mumbling something that sounded like 'sure we will.'

"I'm serious about discussing it!" Allie dropped her keys on a table.

Allie collapsed on the couch and her hands landed on her knees with a 'slap'. She gathered her bunched up quilt from the cushions and folded it neatly before flipping it on the back of the couch. She fluffed her pillow and slid it to the corner.

Allie had a million things on her mind, but no one to talk to. She pulled her phone from her back pocket.

After a second, she pulled up Andrew's number and hit 'Call'.

He answered on the first ring. "What's up?" Allie heard a grunt and heavy breathing.

"Are you being tortured?"

"I'm running. So, yes."

"Oh. How far?"

"It's about five miles."

"Yeah. Hey, do you have time to talk?"

"You mean about what the heck was going on at Jess' party last night? And how you got into the morgue police?"

"That's a good start."

"I'll be there in a few minutes. Could you have some cold water ready for me? 'Cause it is crazy hot and I'm wicked, sticky sweaty."

"I'll do it. Ice is going in the glass now."

Andrew arrived 10 minutes later with a drenched t-shirt and dripping hair.

Allie met him with a glass of ice water and a cold towel. "I've found the towel helps."

"You're a lifesaver." He wiped his face with the towel. "I'll sit on the floor. I don't want to saturate your couch with my sweat."

"I appreciate that, because it's also my bed. Chrystal already complains that it smells."

Andrew took a gulp of water. "So, what's on your mind?"

Allie sat on the couch and Andrew crossed his legs on the floor a few feet from her.

"Thanks, for going with me."

"Happy to! It was unforgettable. That woman is...different."

"Yes, she is. So. Here goes. First, someone left a note on my car the other day." Allie spoke in a hushed tone and looked towards Chrystal's door. "It said 'see you later' and something like 'Bully for you' and 'take care of my friend Franz'."

"What's that mean?"

"I'm not sure, but there's the possibility it's Toro or someone pretending to be him."

"Wow." Andrew pulled the glass away from his lips and placed it on the floor where beads of condensation pooled on the linoleum. "That's pretty sick. Did you tell the police?"

"Interestingly, Festoon was a few feet from my car when I found it. He thought it came from Dr. Mann. But it didn't. I asked him. Now, Festoon thinks it may be legit."

"Did it match the original notes?"

"Shhh." Allie motioned to Chrystal's bedroom with her head.

"Oh, right. Sorry."

"Chrystal threw it away before I could have it analyzed."

"She threw it away? Why did she do that?"

"It wasn't her fault. She was cleaning out my car. I should've taken it to the police immediately, but I waited and then it disappeared."

"Do you think it came from Toro? Those were some crazy times, Allie. This could be really serious."

"I don't know. But about the same time I get the note, Jess calls me with a sob story about her husband. So, I go over there to talk about the case and the next thing I know, Chrystal's having her party at their pool. Then, this afternoon I got ambushed by Phillip Spears."

"The Phillip Spears? The reporter? Amazing! He's famous."

"Shhh. Unfortunately, he's not real bright. Take my word for it. But anyway, he told me another note went to the police."

"What did it say?"

"He didn't tell me."

"So what did you do?"

"Well..." Allie bobbed her head, then covered her face. "I punched him in the nose."

"You did what?" Andrew fell back. "Oh, my gosh! You punched him?"

"I did. But he deserved it. Sort of."

"So, call the police about the note."

"They all know about my past and there's no way they'd tell me anything. I'm sure I have zero credibility."

"Because you were, uhm, an exotic dancer?"

"Actually, I was a stripper. There's nothing exotic about it. Plus, a few arrests along the way."

"Wow. You've changed."

"I have, but some people don't see it that way."

"What does your supervisor say?"

"I talked to him this morning and it didn't go very well."

"What do you mean?"

"He got pretty upset that I went over and saw Jess. He felt I was interfering in the investigation. He almost fired me. He accused me of insubordination."

"Wow. What did he think about Chrystal's birthday party?"

"I felt it was better not to mention the birthday."

"I see." Andrew nodded.

"But Bergman's body didn't show signs of an appendectomy, which his wife and the medical record said he had, so I'm worried we've misidentified the body. Anyway, the body's been cremated, so it's too late to confirm whether the victim had an appendectomy. I'm positive I saw an appendix."

"What's your boss' plan?"

"Shhh. I don't want Chrystal to hear. I finally got him to agree to compare the DNA of the victim with Bergman's son, Isaac, to see if they match."

"Well, that's promising."

"So, what do you think?"

"About all of that?"

"Yes."

"Come on, Allie!" Andrew chuckled and shook his head. "That's like asking my opinion of <u>War and Peace</u>. I know you invited me over for advice, but I don't know what to tell you. Except, I would call the police, and demand they tell you about that new note. You're the only survivor of Toro and your safety might depend on what it says."

"I know they won't tell me."

"It's about your safety and Chrystal's. That's my opinion."

Allie rubbed her eyes. "You're right. I actually thought I should confront Festoon."

"Exactly!" Andrew sat up and finished the water. "He has to tell you, Allie."

"Then I keep wondering, if Jess is lying about the body being her husband, why is she lying about it? What could she gain? Insurance, inheritance? Maybe she's just mistaken, though, you saw, she's definitely not in mourning."

"You're right. I didn't see a sad bone in that well-toned, body."

"Glad you noticed. And if it's not Bergman we cremated, who was it? No one else fitting that description is on the missing persons list... Westbrook told me his cell phone signal abruptly ended after his last call to Jess."

"Good analysis."

"And why would she throw all this stuff at me about James Smith being Toro and killing her husband, if it's not her husband in the first place? The pictures she showed me look like Toro. They're the best I've seen."

Andrew leaned back on the floor. "Do the notes have anything to do with Toro being back? That note you got and the one Spears gave to the police."

"Shhh, Andrew. Chrystal will hear."

The bedroom door burst open and Chrystal flew out. "Hey, Andrew. Thanks again for my painting." Chrystal put her hand on her hips. "Okay. I heard what you said. Is the guy who tried to kill you back? Is this why you hauled me off to church at the break of dawn and won't let me stay by myself ever again?"

Allie took a deep breath. "You weren't supposed to hear our conversation. Maybe, he's back. Probably not. There's no way to know."

"You can hear everything in this dorm room. You should call the police!"

"I'm going to talk with one of them, soon...today."

"Can we get a gun?"

"You shouldn't have a gun unless you're sure you're going to use it. Otherwise it becomes a weapon for the bad guy. And I'll never use a gun again."

"I'm sorry, guys, I have to go. I can see you two have a lot to discuss. And, I've got to get changed and mosey to the lab. Can I do anything for you?"

"No. Thanks, Andrew. You're right."

"Any time. It's always an adventure." Andrew sucked up the small amount of ice that remained and then left.

Chrystal waited until after Andrew shut the door and turned to Allie. "Mom, can you sleep with me again? Maybe until this kook is caught?"

"Of course, Sweetheart. It's been a while since you wanted me to sleep with me. It's like you're 12 again." Allie hugged her daughter.

"Yeah. So long ago."

Allie smiled, pulled Chrystal's head towards her, and kissed her on the forehead. "I love you, Sweetie."

"Love you, too. Wanna do some yoga so we can relax? It will also help your back."

Allie tousled Chrystal's hair. "After leaving you all day, I guess I owe you one."

CHAPTER FIFTY
PRESENT DAY

Allie called the police station, drenched in sweat following an hour of power yoga. Despite the calming effect of the 'mountain pose', 'downward dog' and 'warrior', she found no inner peace. In fact, she felt more anxious to speak to Pug about the note.

Since it was Sunday, Festoon wasn't in the office and the secretary wouldn't disclose his contact information. Allie hung up and bit her lower lip as she ran through her options.

She found an old number listed as 'Pug' in her contacts, but hadn't called it in years. After mulling it over, Allie decided she had nothing to lose.

Pug answered his phone on the third ring.

"Festoon. What can I do you for?"

"Pug. I just heard there was another note."

"Well, hello, Allie. Good to hear from you. I'm doing fine. Thanks for asking. I'm having a very relaxing Sunday. Did Westbrook give you this number?"

"No. It's amazing what you can find written on the bathroom wall in a holding cell. So, tell me about this note." She paced nervously in front of her couch.

"I guess the TV fellows got a hold of you. I figured they couldn't keep that juicy bit of information to themselves for long."

"When were you going to tell me?"

"It's Sunday. I'm off today. I'm watching the Bucs. They're winning, the beer is cold, and I'm enjoying myself."

"What did it say?"

"Listen. We've barely had a chance to look it. It makes no sense, and even if it's real, there's no threat. We're closing in on this guy and this time we'll nail him. Not like nine years ago."

Allie strolled to the window, peeked outside at the setting sun and checked the lock. "Why do you say that?"

"Because, Sweetheart, have you read the papers? Seen the news? We have his picture everywhere. Everybody and their mother are looking for this goon. He can't move without being seen."

"Pug, I identified him in that picture because at one point he was inches from my face and seconds from killing me. The image of his eyes is seared into my brain. But it's a terrible picture, so I'm not convinced the public can do much with it. Plus, he can shave." She turned away from the window and walked back towards the couch.

"Allie, I really think we'll catch him, and soon. Our source has given us information about his last location, his habits, this and that. We've got a lot of stuff."

"I have to say, Pug, I'm more than a little worried about all this."

"Allie, Allie. It could be somebody just messin' with you. But if it's him, I promise we've got him cornered. Yeah!"

"Are you that enthusiastic or did the Bucs just score?" Allie endured several more seconds of Pug's yells and celebration from the TV.

"What?"

"Commercial break, I guess. Now focus for the next 30 seconds. What if you're wrong?"

"I'm not."

"Easy for you to say. What did the note say exactly? And put your beer down. I can't understand you with all that gulping."

"I can't tell you that."

"Why not?"

"So that only the person who wrote it will know what was in it." Pug belched. Allie winced and pulled the phone away from her ear.

"Was I mentioned in the note?"

"No."

"Pug, you can't leave me and my daughter hanging. Some crazy person might be after us. What does the note say? Tell me!"

"I can't say, Allie."

"Fine!" She gritted her teeth. "If that's the way you want it. I'm going to have my Mother's lawyer call your department and he'll find out. And you've dealt enough with Duncan Maxwell to know it does not go well for you." Allie picked up the speed of her pacing.

"Allie, let's don't be rash."

"I survived Toro's attack as did my daughter. We have a right to know if there is any further threat to us. Do you want Maxwell to take my sob story to the press? Make you guys look like heartless cops? Help me out here, Pug."

She heard him sigh. "We can work something out, but you have to promise not to say a word to anyone. I'm going out on a limb here."

"You know me. The last thing I want to do is talk to the press unless you force me to. Tell me and then you can get back to your beer and the game."

"Alright. But it's really stupid, it says "To the Preacher's demon that gives me joy. Toro."

She hesitated. "That's it?" Allie stopped pacing, her jaw dropped and her heart raced.

"I'm telling you, there's nothing to it."

"But there's a lot to it. He's talking about me. And it's him."

"How can you say that? He never mentions your name."

"I'm Parsons. Like a preacher parson. And I have a tattoo that he was obsessed with. It's him."

"Allie, just calm down! We're on top of it. As soon as we catch Mr. Smith, we'll have you come down and see if you can ID him."

"Great. Thanks for looking out for me. He could be at large for months. Or years."

"Well, actually, we thought we had James Smith cornered in a little hotel this morning, but when we busted in he was gone."

"What did he look like on the hotel surveillance cameras?"

"Allie, it's a run down old place with black and white TVs and pay telephones. The only thing that keeps a record of the guests at this dump is a parrot in the lobby that repeats everything you say."

"So nothing?"

"Hang on, now. It looks like he left the murder weapons, the shot gun and this big ole hunting knife. We're trying to match up ballistics and blood, but I bet those were the ones. The guy who runs the place says he must have left right before we got there. He ran off without some of his clothes and cash and now we have them."

"Ran off? In other words, he got away!"

"We're going to catch him real soon. He can't get too far. And when we do, Honey, we'll call you and you can spend as much time staring at James Smith as you want. If he shows his face, we'll have cuffs around his wrists before he can sneeze. He's not in a position to leave notes or follow you around."

"Well that's good to hear, I guess." Allie took a deep breath and tried to convince herself. She felt her chest relax. "I'll tell my daughter. That should make her feel better. So, it should be any day now?"

"Any day, Allie. I want him bad, too."

CHAPTER FIFTY ONE
PRESENT DAY

The next morning, Allie heated Chrystal's breakfast atop a chipped microwaveable plate, and turned on WTSP. The egg whites popped and the aroma of turkey bacon filled the kitchen as the neon blues and greens from the 'First News' broadcast cascaded onto the white concrete blocks of their walls.

Following the traffic report, Phillip Spears announced that the police were closing in on a suspect in the Bergman murder. Spear's nose appeared to be slightly swollen but a talented makeup artist must have hidden the discoloration with a convincing layer of foundation.

The blurry photo of James Smith that Jess Bergman had shown Allie flashed on the screen. According to Spears, Smith was known to be in the area.

"If anyone comes into contact with this man, he should be considered armed and dangerous." The photo of Smith flashed on the screen above Spears right shoulder.

In a solemn but cautiously excited voice, Spears revealed to his viewers that James Smith might have been involved in the Toro murders. Two anonymous and threatening notes had recently been sent to law enforcement authorities and a private individual. These messages were also linked with James Smith.

He cut to an interview with Detective Festoon who seemed pleased to be on TV and managed to grin and flaunt his white teeth while also appearing serious. He reiterated that the police were 'running this man to ground.'

Spears added that Allie Parsons, the only survivor, had no comment.

"I did have a comment. I said, 'Let go of my car'."

The news then switched to a story on proposed regulation of Christmas lights on boats.

She pulled the eggs and bacon out of the microwave and placed the plate on the kitchen table. As the bacon continued to pop, she opened her laptop and clicked on the Tampa Tribune's website. A headline trumpeted a link between Bergman and Toro. Before Allie could click on it, she heard a squeaky voice.

"Did somebody say your name on TV?" Chrystal marched through the door and appeared very perky, particularly for an early Monday morning.

Allie shut her laptop. "It was nothing. I've got your egg whites and bacon ready."

"I'm a vegetarian. Do we have soy bacon?"

"What?" Allie slid her coffee cup across the table to her daughter. "When did this happen?"

"I was talking with Carly, and we decided to make the jump and do it. We're going Vegan!"

"Wonderful. I'm so happy to hear you guys are making some sort of stand." She rubbed her eyes and yawned.

"I know. It's really exciting, isn't it?"

"What, uhm, what can I get for supper tonight? Lettuce? What do you vegetarians eat anyway?"

"I'll make some cereal now. I'll do it myself, Mom. Don't get up. Do we have almond milk?"

"Thank you. I'll sit back down. We just have cow milk."

Chrystal carried her coffee and sipped it as she walked to the pantry and grabbed a box of cereal. After finding a bowl and spoon, she sat down again.

Allie smiled.

"What's so funny?"

"When you were three years old, you and Luke...well, anyway you guys used to say, 'I'll have cereal, a bowl and a spoon.'"

"So long ago."

"Yes. A long time ago. And you've grown up. So, what about supper?"

"Well..." She swallowed and let the cereal fall into the bowl. "Carly texted me last night and asked me to spend the night with her." Chrystal placed the box on the table and looked at Allie.

"Really. Spend the night. Tonight? It's a school night."

"Please, can I? I won't have much homework. Her mother will pick us up from school and she'll bring me home tomorrow after school."

"Honey. I understand why you're excited about this. Really, I do, but with everything going on, I'm not sure."

"Like what?"

"There are these notes and..." Allie turned her eyes towards the ceiling.

"Mom, like you said last night, that policeman told you they've practically caught the guy. I heard about it on TV, too. I read the internet. His name is James Smith. His picture is all over the place. The police said he can't sneeze without them knowing about him. Everything is safe now. I mean the guy is as good as caught."

"Okay, you're right. The police are all over him. We have to live our lives."

"It's like he's already in jail. So we're fine." Chrystal nodded and a smiled.

"I...listen, Chrystal. I've been through this before and I know we have to be careful. I'll believe he's off the streets when they tell me he's in jail. I'm glad she invited you. But it's a school night."

"I know. We had to promise Carly's mom that we we'd get our homework done before we could do anything fun. She's all over it."

"I just...okay. Please, get your work done and get some sleep. I don't want you taking a nap at school."

"We'll be fine." Chrystal's words emerged in rapid bursts. "It's all good...You can go out with Andrew...and do something."

"Andrew?"

"Yeah. I think he's really nice."

"He is nice, but I think I'll just study tonight, if that's okay with you."

"I think you should have some fun, but it's your life."

"Thank you for realizing that. I'll take your opinion into consideration."

"Okay."

Chrystal began to eat her cereal and Allie stood.

"I'm going to take a shower. Let's leave in 15 minutes."

"Okay."

After a couple of steps Allie heard Chrystal clear her throat.

"Mother."

"Yes, Honey."

"I had so much fun at the birthday party. I know it kind of got crazy, but thank you."

"Well, okay." Allie shrugged. "You're welcome. But next year we'll find something really good." She continued to the bedroom.

"I was hoping we could have it there. At Jess' house."

Allie stopped in her tracks and spun around. "Chrystal! We're not going to see Jess Bergman again and we're not going to have a party there. And it's not 'Jess'. It's Mrs. Bergman."

"Why?"

"Because she's an adult and she's not your teenaged friend."

"No, I mean why can't I have my party there next year."

"We've been over this!"

"It's because she's friends with grandmother." Chrystal's lower lip quivered. She crossed her arms and leaned back into her chair.

"No, it has nothing to do with your grandmother. I don't think Jess is a nice person and I think she's playing some kind of game with everyone she meets. It's not who I want you to be around."

"You don't like anybody that was friends with grandmother."

"That's not true."

"Prove it, then."

"I love your grandmother. She just happens to not care for me right now. But I pray that one day, that will change. It doesn't affect my feelings for her, though."

"I think Jess is a lot like grandmother."

"She is in some ways, I guess, but I don't think Jess is honest and Mom is very honest. Brutally honest, in fact. She's uses her honesty like a sledgehammer and batters people with it. I still have bruises."

"Okay." Chrystal leaned forward and dipped her spoon into her cereal.

"Okay, what?"

"Just okay." Chrystal chewed and stared absently at the bowl.

"Okay, then. We'll leave in 15 minutes."

"Can I spend the night with Carly?" She looked up at Allie with pleading eyes.

Allie sighed.

"I really think they've caught him. I really want to go, Mom. And I'll have some friends, finally."

"Okay. You can spend the night."

"Oh, thank you! You're the best!"

CHAPTER FIFTY TWO
PRESENT DAY

Over the next three days, the internet, radio and cable posted frequent updates on the relentless pursuit of James Smith. His now familiar picture flashed across screens wherever there was photo or video capability. Several national cable news networks camped out on location downtown across from the Hillsborough County Courthouse. Tampa tensed with anticipation of catching James Smith. Everyone agreed, he couldn't move without being apprehended.

Allie began to feel more comfortable with Chrystal being away from home. The police pressure must be driving the guy underground, making him harmless.

She felt calm when Dr. Mann summoned her into his office.

"Sit down, Dr. Parsons." Mann motioned towards the chair in front of his desk.

Allie sat. "Dr. Mann—"

"You were wrong, Parsons." He voice sounded calm, but his jaw was tense and there were dark circles under his eyes.

"Oh, no problem. I'll fix it. Whatever it is, Dr. Mann."

"The DNA from Bergman's body matched his son. Scientifically tested and officially registered. According to the paternity test, the body we cremated in our morgue was Bergman's. It matched his son, Isaac."

"Okay."

"It's official." Mann leaned back in his heavily cushioned chair and looked over his reading glasses. He licked the back of his bottom teeth and jutted out his jaw.

Allie sat stunned. Mann seemed to study her reaction to his news.

"By the way, it was a perfect match."

"Well. That... really surprises me. I was so sure, Dr. Mann, but I mean, great. That was quick."

"Well, what did you expect, Dr. Parsons?"

"Obviously, I have a lot to learn. I was only trying to follow the protocol I was taught. I apologize. I hope you understand. I was only trying to do what I thought was right."

Mann turned towards her and placed a paper on his desk. "Don't worry yourself. You're young, ambitious, and a bit naive. You challenge me. As a matter of fact, I'm reading one of your dictations now. It's promising, but full of errors and rife with inconsistencies. Somewhat like yourself."

"Dr. Mann, I'm trying..." She caught herself and took a deep breath. "I'm determined to be good at this."

"I know, Parsons. But only time will tell if you have what it takes to be successful here. Currently, you are an amateur. You try hard, but you're not where we need you to be. Here at the coroner's office we must operate at a much higher level."

"To be honest, I thought it would take more time to get the results back."

Mann shook his head. He appeared irritated. "What do you mean? More time? Why?"

"I thought the process would be slower. More than a few days. I mean, obviously this morgue is state of the art. Obtaining DNA from Isaac and then getting it tested? I thought it would take longer. But I'm glad to have this settled. I was wrong."

"Yes, you were."

"I just felt I had to pursue this point. I didn't note that he had a scar and I could have sworn that I saw an appendix. But I was wrong, and that is very hard for me to deal with."

"When you're young, the mind is keen to find all sorts of conspiracies and inconsistencies. But in the end, it all makes sense. Franz Bergman was murdered and his body has been cremated. We, indeed, performed the autopsy on Bergman. I'll show you the DNA report." Mann raised his head to peek through the bottom of his glasses. After a second he located a folder in a stack near his knee. "Here's the report. Read it and tell me what you think." He slid the paper across the desk towards her.

Allie recognized the State of Florida seal at the top of the page and blushed. "I was wrong. I'll let it drop."

"Are you quite satisfied?"

"Yes. I'm satisfied. You were right."

"Good. Now, continue your work. There's a lot to be done and you need to pick up the pace. You're behind."

Allie stood and sighed as Mann took the paper. More work, but at least Chrystal would be home tonight. That Chrystal's sleep over with Carly had stretched into two nights, angered Allie, but she didn't want to take Chrystal away from her friends. As she headed towards her office, Allie tried to make sense of it all; James Smith was practically in jail, and apparently, Bergman was dead, she told herself. It was all coming together.

Now, if I could only spend some quality time with Chrystal. Allie glanced down at her phone and broke into a broad smile when she saw the image of Chrystal dressed as a nun.

Allie remembered the night she took that photo. They had watched 'The Sound of Music,' sang, laughed, and worked on getting Allie ready for her interview with Dr. Mann.

Maybe tonight we can watch 'The Sound of Music' again.

Thinking about Chrystal marching around the sofa and singing at the top of her lungs made Allie chuckle. She tried to fight it, but tears welled in her eyes.

As she turned the corner, she nearly bumped into Byron. His head was down and he was reading a typed piece of paper.

"Don't worry. He makes everyone around here cry, eventually."

"He didn't make me..."

Byron disappeared around the corner before she could finish.

Allie spoke louder. "Even Dr. Mann would laugh if he saw Chrystal as a nun."

No one replied.

"It would loosen things up around here!"

Allie thought about that night again and snorted in amusement. Seconds later, she was laughing and this time, she didn't hold it back. What a wonderful night!

CHAPTER FIFTY THREE
SIX MONTHS AGO

Allie grabbed some drinks and joined Chrystal on the foldout couch. As they lay on the lumpy cushions and watched an old VHS tape of 'The Sound of Music,' Chrystal obsessed over Maria's dress and Allie endeavored to prevent popcorn from collecting in her bed. Allie gathered each crumb that fell on her sheets.

"Isn't this a great movie, Mom? I've loved it since I was five!"

"Yes, you have."

"She's wearing such elegant gloves. I'd wear gloves like that to school."

"You know, I'd wear gloves like that to the hospital. Just to see how loud people would laugh. You're so much like your grandmother."

"I know, but you and I'll always be best friends. I won't cut you off like grandmother."

"Yeah, I know that." Allie smiled, leaned towards her daughter and hugged her around her tiny waist. "Thank you for saying that. You're my best friend. You kill me when you dress up with that pillowcase over your head! You're so silly! Are you like that at school?"

"No."

"Aren't your friends silly?"

"Yeah, but I met this new girl today in my English class, Carly. She's real serious, but very cool."

"Sounds good."

"She's really cool. Her friends are cool. And she has this awesome car."

"She has a car?" Allie popped a handful of popcorn in her mouth.

"No, silly. Her mother owns the car. But it's really nice. Oh, my gosh, I love this part! Watch."

As Allie turned her attention to the movie, she noticed Chrystal's eyes never drifted from the screen. A piece of popcorn on the tips of Chrystal's fingers lingered at her daughter's lips. Allie could almost watch the entire movie in the reflection of Chrystal's eyes.

Allie's good eye, however, wandered to the outfit she'd decided to interview in. A solid gray suit hung from the back of a kitchen chair.

"Thanks for helping me choose my suit."

"Well, actually, it wasn't what I picked out for you. I liked the Italian one. This will do, though. It has a classic cut."

"I hope I get this job so one day so I can afford an Italian outfit like that."

"It'll be okay if you get it tailored." Chrystal dropped another piece of popcorn into her mouth. "You can't wear it to your interview untailored."

"I'll see what I can do. But I never learned to sew. Your great grandmother could sew anything. She made gorgeous quilts and dresses."

"What about grandmother?"

"She sews pretty well, but not like her mother."

"Get it tailored, Mom, please. It'll look really nice, then."

"Thanks, Sweetheart."

By the time the movie was over, Chrystal had closed her eyes.

As the credits were rolling, Allie quietly slipped out of bed and turned off the TV. Gently, she eased back onto the thin mattress and pulled a thick, old quilt over them.

"Momma."

"What, Sweetheart?"

"I dreamed about Luke last night. He's doing great. He's very happy. He wants you to be happy."

Allie started to ask about Luke, but she heard Chrystal's gentle snore. Allie turned over and shut her eyes.

Sometimes, the simplest nights could be perfect.

CHAPTER FIFTY FOUR
PRESENT DAY

Eager to set the tone for a fun evening together, Allie rummaged through the VHS movies that sat stacked in disorganized piles around the TV stand. The phone rang and Chrystal's picture appeared on the phone screen just as Allie came across the 'The Sound of Music'.

"Hey, Sweetheart! You ready to be picked up? I found our favorite movie!"

"Mom, I need to spend the night with Carly one more night. Please!"

"What? One more night?" Chrystal's request stunned Allie. She forgot about the movie and drifted towards the couch in a daze. When she collapsed onto the worn cushions, the Von Trapp singers fell from her fingers, bounced off her big toe and landed on the rug. Allie felt so numb she didn't notice the bruise forming along the distal bones of her foot.

"No, Chrystal. You need to come home. This is ridiculous. Come home, get some sleep, do your school work."

"Please, Mom! I'll be back tomorrow. I promise."

"Your homework, Chrystal..." Allie looked around the dark, empty room.

"It's done. I'm getting A's."

"Chrystal, I really think..."

"But I'm having such a great time, Mom! You should see their pool. Rowdy is hilarious. Carly and I are planning this great party. It is so cool. Please! One last night! Please!"

Allie frowned and took a deep breath. The last of the sun's light was fading away.

"Honey, I thought we'd watch 'The Sound of Music'. It'll be fun."

"Yeah, but...my friends. We've got things I really want to do."

"Chrystal..."

"Mom..."

Allie sighed. She could hear Chrystal do the same. Their breathing took the place of words as Allie waited.

After a few seconds Allie couldn't take the pressure.

"Okay, Honey. But listen..."Allie cleared her throat and swallowed. "Just.. just...have fun with your friends." Allie sighed, mustering as much enthusiasm as she could. "Be home by nine, little girl. Do you need...?"

"Good, thanks."

"Okay...I'll see you tomorrow. Oh, wait! Chrystal do you need fresh clothes?" But her daughter had already hung up.

Allie stared at the phone and the photo of Chrystal until it disappeared. She tossed her phone onto the couch and slumped onto the stiff cushions. In front of her loomed the TV and to her right, a full bowl of popcorn.

Allie sank deeper into the couch and plopped a single kernel at a time into her mouth as she watched to the news. The top stories concerned Bergman's killing and the pursuit of James Smith.

Is he Toro?

Frustrated, she grabbed the remote and punched the 'off' button. Allie shook her head and scooped up her Pathology book from the sofa. The next chapter discussed diseased states of the heart.

Fun times.

Allie thumbed through several pages of the textbook and did her best to concentrate on the very technical writing. After 20 minutes, it was clear the pathophysiology of aortic stenosis had no chance of interesting her tonight, so she closed the book and placed it on the floor beside 'The Sound of Music.' Allie pulled a worn blanket out of the closet, turned off the glaring overhead light and fell into an uneasy sleep.

CHAPTER FIFTY FIVE
PRESENT DAY

After only three total hours of sleep, Allie rolled out of bed at 5:00 AM and headed to the morgue. As Byron walked through the door, she was squeezing her hands into a pair of tight, rubber gloves.

"You're on your own today, Girl. I'm just going to make suggestions."

"I'm ready. Bring it on." She fought a yawn.

"I know you are."

Allie was getting faster and more efficient and two hours later they were well into the autopsy.

"I don't know what's wrong with Dr. Mann." Byron placed a fresh #7 blade on the scalpel handle. The bloody handle was held in the bloody, blue glove of his right hand.

As Allie discovered, this was a bloody case.

"I've worked with him for 25 years and I've never seen the man look this worried. Do you know what I'm saying?"

Allie nodded and moved her scalpel below the spleen.

"No, Allie. Cut there. Just below the diaphragm. To your right, Sweetie. That's it. Dr. Mann's got bags under his eyes and he keeps mumbling under his breath."

Byron stopped speaking as Allie struggled to slice the tough ligament. "Here you go, Allie. Try this one. This will get the job done." Byron handed Allie the new scalpel. "He shuffles around the halls like he's an old codger. There you go. Look at that bad boy cut through the tissue. Now, Sugar, to your left. There's the gastrosplenic ligament."

"I thought maybe he's just working too hard." Allie sliced a thin white band that secured the spleen to the greater curvature of the stomach. "Maybe all the yelling he does at me is wearing him out."

The victim, YR14-124, had lost the majority of her blood through a large tear, which had been ripped in the splenic artery during a high velocity impact between her Chevy Impala and a Ford Taurus. She died from hypovolemic shock en route to Tampa General and now the escaped blood lay like cold pudding beneath Allie's fingers.

"It must have been a hard hit." Allie finished freeing the spleen and held it aloft. It sagged like fresh beef between her hands. "This thing is split in two." The cold, soggy clots of YR's blood fell and plopped into her abdominal cavity with a wet splat.

"T-boned at 70 MPH. I wouldn't be surprised if her aorta is torn, too."

"Amazing how stupid people can be and how it can really mess up innocent people's lives." Allie dropped the wet spleen on the scales. "But anyway, I've just been thinking that Dr. Mann is really tired from all this work. And he has that heart problem, you know."

"Listen, Honey, his heart isn't the problem. His entire career has been hard work, but I've never seen him like this."

"You know him better than anyone."

"Yes, I do!" Byron smiled.

"Alright, finished with the abdominal cavity." Allie wiped the sweat from her forehead with her sleeve, completely exhausted. "I've really got to get some water, Byron. After that, open the chest. Then what?"

"You okay, Allie?"

"I don't know, Byron." She lowered her head. "My daughter's been gone a lot and I'm trying to keep up with her. It's hard."

"It's not going to interfere with our work here?"

"No! It's nothing. It's all good." Allie cleared her throat. "So what's next?"

"Collect DNA from John Doe 14-121."

"Oh, crap, I forgot about that." Allie slipped off her blood stained rubber gloves, shot them into the trash and then pulled down her blue paper mask. "I've never done a DNA collection."

"Simple as pie, Pumpkin. The hard part is the paper work."

"Really? Why?"

"Chain of custody, Sweetheart. Procedure and policy. You have to show at each step that nothing was substituted. And it's all part of the public record. It's the most important part of the DNA process, at least from our standpoint. Without it, we look like fools in court and nothing counts, no matter how hard you worked."

"Can you show me how to do it?"

"No problem, Sweetheart. Just give me a second." Byron flipped his gloves into the trash and walked towards a file cabinet near the computer. "Watch and learn."

Rapidly he rifled through several files with his long fingers. "Here we go." He grabbed a folder and closed the cabinet with a bang. "FC14-120, Allie. The last DNA we did. The paperwork for this simple sample is as thick as my forearm. Nowadays, it's on the computer. But we also keep a paper trail."

"Jeez. All that?"

"Yeah, Sweetheart. Chain of custody. Nothing else matters. It seems simple, but this stuff takes forever."

"Crazy." Allie took the stack of paper from Byron. "Look at all this." She scanned the first page and saw that FC's DNA had been submitted three weeks ago. The results were still pending.

"So, when will we get the outcome?"

"Can't say. Any day. It's tough to know."

"Well anyway, let's get started." She took a step towards the door and stopped.

Allie turned her head and looked at Byron. "I'm sorry. Did you say that was the last DNA sent out of here?"

"Yeah. It's easy to tell with the paperwork."

"What about Franz Bergman?"

"What?"

"Franz Bergman. The guy killed in that fancy house on the bay."

"What? Oh, oh, him. If you need to get DNA from Bergman, I'll show you how to do it. But you know he's been cremated. We'll have to get the DNA from the tissue samples you saved. It's a little different, but the paperwork is pretty much the same."

"And then it has to go through the process? All those forms?"

"Yeah, Sweetheart. It's always the same."

"Can you show me how to check on the computer? Maybe the actual papers are missing."

"I'll look, Allie, but I'm sure we didn't send anything out on him. But it's simple enough to check." Byron walked over to the computer and logged on. "Let's see..." He mumbled as he typed. "Bergman. Bergman. No data." He logged off and turned towards her. "Why do you ask?"

"Just wondering." Allie rubbed her eyes. "Is there any other place the papers could be if the sample was sent off? I thought I heard Dr. Mann say something about submitting a DNA sample on Bergman. I mean, I could be wrong. I was thinking I would talk to him about it if he hadn't sent one."

"Nope." Byron scratched his chin and shook his head. "A while back, Dr. Mann kept some DNA documents in the file cabinets in his office. But that's been some years. I don't think he'd do that again. And it really should be on the computer, though he forgets to enter the orders, so that's possible. He's really lost when it comes to computers."

"How many years ago?"

"For what?"

"Since Mann kept DNA paperwork in his office."

"Oh, it's been a long time, Allie."

"Nine years?"

"Yeah, probably." Byron's smile melted and his lips tightened. His eyes narrowed slightly. "Some things are best forgotten and left alone, Allie."

Allie bit her lower lip and ran her fingers through her hair. "Just asking, Byron. Show me how to do the DNA on John Doe and then we'll open this girl's chest. I don't know about you but I plan to work, work, work, Buddy."

Byron hesitated, then his smile slowly returned. "Atta' girl. I like your attitude."

An hour later Allie took a break for supper. As she nibbled her peanut butter and grape jelly sandwich she walked towards her desk and heard Byron talking.

"I understand. I'm keeping an eye on things."

As she passed his office, Allie saw Byron hang up the phone. She paused by the open door as Byron packed up his cooler and prepared to leave.

"Have a good weekend." Allie smiled and gave a quick wave.

Byron jumped and whipped his head towards her. "Oh, you scared me, Sweetheart! You too, Allie. I'll see you Monday."

"Dr. Mann was on me to get caught up, so I'll be here a little longer."

"How much longer do you think?"

"Oh, another hour maybe."

"Lock up then." Byron stepped out of his office and locked the door. "I'll see you."

Allie leaned against the wall and chewed her sandwich as the elevator doors closed.

She wandered towards the window and waited until Byron drive off in his old cream-colored Mercedes. When the car disappeared into the traffic at the stoplight, Allie took the last bite of her sandwich and wiped her fingers on her pants.

Now to get a look at that DNA report on Bergman...and just maybe I'll find the DNA reports from the Toro days.

CHAPTER FIFTY SIX
PRESENT DAY

Alone in the lab, Allie diligently searched every freezer for a container that could potentially store DNA samples. There were plenty of boxes and test tubes, but none labeled 'DNA' from nine years ago or anything that appeared to be connected to the Toro case. Although it was very unlikely she would find such a thing, she figured it was worth a try.

In the expansive morgue there appeared to be no end to the possible locations for such a sample. Allie realized that Dr. Mann and the State of Florida invested heavily in refrigerators and test tubes.

Allie spent an hour reaching into liquid nitrogen storage tanks, grabbing glass vials and attempting to read their faded hand written labels. Finally, the frustration of not finding anything useful defeated her and Allie decided to quit. There was no way she could possibly locate a sample from nine years ago among thousands of stored samples, nor would she win the lottery. She pulled her hands out of the last -20°freezer, thawed her fingers with her breath and turned towards the only promising place she hadn't searched.

Dr. Mann's office.

It was the location most likely to hold information about DNA from the Toro case. The DNA report on Bergman might also be filed away behind that door. The first time Mann offered her the report she declined to look at it. This time she would study it carefully.

Many years had passed since Allie had broken into a secured room. She was relieved to discover she still possessed the skill.

Five minutes after starting, Allie's forehead was damp with sweat, but as her fingers applied tremendous pressure to the credit card wedged into the small gap at the handle, the lock finally released and the door to Dr. Mann's office eased opened.

An eerie creak from the tight hinges made her jump. She took a deep breath and wiped her forehead. Her thumping heart began to slow.

Allie remembered the mantra she would repeat to herself when she was nervous and next to go on stage.

Concentrate. Breath normally. Relax. Allie took a deep breath. No shot of tequila or vodka, tonight. Those days are over.

The back of her neck cramped and she rubbed it vigorously, trying to loosen up her tense muscles. It felt as if the demon in her tattoo were jabbing her with his pitchfork.

After a few seconds, Allie's anxiety subsided and her muscles relaxed. She squeezed her head through the small opening and entered the dark office on her tiptoes.

Allie raised her eyebrows and turned her head. "Uhm, Hello?"

She rolled her eyes. Obviously, she was rusty.

Nice, Allie. If anyone was really in here, I guess they'd say, 'Oh, hey, Dr. Parsons. Great job with the breaking and entering.'"

She shook her head and took a step inside.

Two small blue and green dots glowed on Dr. Mann's computer. Otherwise the office was pitch black.

The hum of the air conditioner seemed unusually loud.

Allie closed the heavy door, but left a crack, and then crept deeper into the office. Straining her eyes at the shadows of papers, notebooks and texts, she retrieved her phone from the pocket of her lab coat and activated her flashlight app.

A soft, blue halo enveloped the room.

With the hazy glow of the phone, she could make out Mann's cluttered desk and the two file cabinets standing on either side of the large window that occupied most of the back wall. She slipped towards to the desk and glanced over the scattered papers. There were letters imploring Mann to review cases, a Forensic Pathology Journal's request for submissions and several bulletins from state regulatory agencies.

But the DNA results Mann waved at her were not there.

This is insane. I can't believe I'm doing this.

Allie gulped and turned to look at the door left ajar behind her. *I've come this far. Just a few more minutes, Doc. Let's get some answers.*

She took a deep breath and walked to the nearest file cabinet. Allie's ears were primed for the sound of footsteps falling in the hall.

She reached the file cabinet, and to her relief, it pulled open easily and quietly. She had worried it would be locked and she would have to break into it as well. She directed the glow from the phone towards the interior.

In the soft, blue light, Mann's records appeared very old. Each manila file had been labeled by hand and appeared wrinkled, battered and flimsy. A musty odor of dust and old paper drifted up to her nose.

She guessed Dr. Mann must have smoked a pipe or cigar at one time. Along with the staleness arose the pleasant aroma of fine Cuban tobacco-the kind Duncan loved so well.

Allie didn't know exactly what to look for, but she furiously flipped through the files and searched for any written word that looked interesting. She hoped to find a reference to DNA.

Many of the items appeared to be photocopied journal articles. Allie noticed one that examined laser use in human tissue exams.

She also found dictations from autopsies dating all the way back to July 4th, 1983. For a few seconds, Allie paused at that file. As her eyes tracked across the old type written pages, she read the autopsy report of a 28 year-old male who had been killed by botched fireworks while watching a show near the old Tampa Stadium.

I knew those things were dangerous! Allie closed the file and moved to another. *I'm telling Andrew about this.*

There was an insurmountable amount of material and at her slow, plodding pace, she knew she'd never get through it all. She felt overwhelmed.

I have to move faster!

Allie took a deep breath, opened the next drawer and searched its contents. Nothing of interest. She worked her way down all four drawers, still nothing of note.

She drew heavy breaths as she slid to the other file cabinet and rummaged through it. The second file cabinet contained more useless information than the first.

Several articles summarized scientific analyses of enzyme assays. She glanced through a table listing the toxic effects of over-the-counter medications and then tossed aside a bulletin on the ballistics of modern bullets.

Allie plowed through the multitude of dictations of John and Jane Does, long forgotten by the community. She found phone numbers scribbled on scrap paper and several thank you notes written by various politicians.

Frustrated, Allie shook her head and stepped back from the file cabinet. She could spend months looking through all the paperwork and still not get a foothold on the Toro or Bergman DNA paper trail.

Think, think, think! Mann just put that paper away, not too long ago. If he stuck it in the file cabinet, he wouldn't want to bend down. Not at his age. He would reach straight ahead, stick the paper in there and get back to work. Or he could have thrown it away!

Allie pursed her lips and stepped towards the cabinet. She extended her arm and grabbed the handle of the top drawer and tugged. As the drawer slid open, she studied the multitude of colorful folders that were exposed.

He would most likely stick it in the very front or the very back, so he could find it later.

On her tiptoes, she looked at the files in the front. Nothing.

She worked her way to the last file in the drawer.

There she spotted a folder. A hand printed label simply reading 'DNA' was labeled at the top. Allie had missed it when flipping through the files.

You have got to be kidding me!

She pulled the folder from the file cabinet and illuminated it with her phone. It was old, and wrinkled, and appeared to have at one time held a thick stack of papers. Currently, the stretched walls of the file held only one sheet and a separate envelope that was rather thick. Allie slid the paper out and looked at it, trying to discern the writing using the dim light of her phone.

It was the DNA report Mann had showed her with the familiar State of Florida logo.

"A regular Sherlock Holmes, I am." Allie spoke quietly in a cockney accent she picked up from watching *Mary Poppins* with Chrystal at least a thousand times.

When Mann showed her the official report from the university lab several days ago, Allie hadn't paid much attention to it. As she looked at it now, two things struck her.

First, the report was amazingly short and consisted of two solitary paragraphs.

Second, it only stated the DNA matched. There was no reference to parentage or inheritance.

Allie used her phone to take a picture of the report. Then she put it back in the folder.

As her finger found the bottom of the folder, she felt a small, thick, square piece of paper. When Allie pulled it into the light of her phone, she could tell it was a color Polaroid photograph that had lost it's reds and blues over the years. She brought it closer to her nose and squinted.

Three people stood side by side. They wore startled smiles as if they had collided in bumper cars. The petite woman wore jeans that rose above her hips and a necklace with small gold beads. Her hair was long, curled and layered. She smiled and extended her left arm around the waist of a stiff, tall bearded man with glasses. He had thick black hair, a very thin build and looked familiar. His arms hung awkwardly at his side.

After a few moments of examining the picture, Allie realized it was a much younger Dr. Mann.

Next to Mann's knee was a boy of about five. He was thin, had thick black hair and stood gawkily with his chin pulled into his chest.

That kid looks just like Isaac...but he can't be.

Even though the trio had on short sleeves, snow capped mountains dominated the background. They could have been somewhere in the Rockies in July.

Allie examined the old photo for a few more seconds and then snapped a picture of it.

Next, she removed the envelope and opened it. Out flopped several papers. As Allie squinted and studied them in the dim light of her phone, she realized they were pages from Franz Bergman's medical records.

These should have been on Bergman's chart. Why would he have these in his cabinet?

She heard the 'ping' of the elevator and jumped with a start.

"Crap!" She stuffed the old photo back in the file, and closed the drawer. Since she didn't have a chance to take a photo of the medical records, she decided to keep them.

She heard the first footsteps as the elevator slid open.

It amazed Allie how quickly someone could ascend undetected to this floor and reach the office. She hadn't appreciated how little time it took.

Allie whipped around and saw the office door still ajar. She sprang like a cat towards the door and pushed it, as the footsteps grew louder. The interloper stood just a few feet away.

As the edge of the door touched the frame, Allie froze.

If the lock engaged, there would be a loud click.

She had to stop it.

Just as Allie caught the knob and turned it so that it would close quietly, her phone chimed. Allie reached down to turn it off and saw that Chrystal had texted. "Will be back by 10."

"Dr. Mann?" Byron's familiar voice sounded distressed.

Allie let go of the door and tiptoed back towards Mann's desk.

"Allie? Who is it? Anyone here?"

CHAPTER FIFTY SEVEN
PRESENT DAY

Allie weighed her options. She could come clean and walk out of the office. Or she could hide.

She was caught in the middle.

"Who's there!"

Allie resolved to hide. She swung around the carved corner of the desk and scooted under the lap drawer.

An instant later, the hinges on the door squeaked and Byron stepped into Mann's office.

"I'm armed, Mister. I'll blow your head off."

Allie withdrew further under Mann's desk. She intended to take full advantage of her small size, pressing herself tightly against the mahogany frame.

Allie could hear Byron sliding his hand against the wall, feeling for the light switch. When the light came on, Allie's hideout under Mann's desk held the only shadow in the room.

Ironically, when the lights came on, Allie could sense Byron relaxing. He must think there's no place to hide.

"Hmmm."

From her tight quarters, with her chin pinned to her knees, she could see his shoes near Mann's chair. He turned. She heard him drumming on the desk.

"Hmm."

Just when Allie thought her heart would pound out of her chest, she heard him walk to the door and the lights went out. The door shut solidly and he turned the dead bolt with a key from the outside.

A few minutes later she could hear Byron pacing up and down the hall and whispering. Allie remained under the desk for a good 30 minutes, waiting for some sign that Byron had left.

If she didn't get out of here soon she wouldn't be at home when Chrystal arrived, but she was trapped. She pulled out her phone, took a deep breath and dialed the morgue.

Byron answered. "County Coroner's office, Byron speaking."

"Hey, Byron, it's Allie."

"Oh, hey Sweetheart. Why are you whispering?"

"Chrystal's asleep."

"Oh, I see."

"Could you check the autopsy suite and see if I left my orange jacket? I think I hung it up next to the scale."

"Orange jacket. Sure, Sugar. I'm going to put you on hold. Just give me a second."

Allie heard Byron's footsteps in the hall followed by the sound of the stair door slamming shut as he headed down to the autopsy lab.

Allie unlocked Mann's door, which sounded like the 'pop' of a gunshot when the bolt turned. As she opened the door, its hinges screeched.

Allie closed it and flashed to the elevator. She jabbed the button repeatedly and bounced on her toes for what seemed like hours, waiting for the elevator to arrive.

"Aagh!" She moaned and stabbed the 'down' button again. She waited.

And waited.

"Are you kidding me!"

Her heart galloped and her breathing came in rapid, shallow puffs. She could hear Byron's footsteps echoing in the stairwell, getting closer.

"Come on!"

With a loud 'ding' the elevator arrived. Allie jumped inside before the doors had fully opened and punched the 'ground floor' and 'close' buttons and waited.

The doors started to slide shut as Byron rounded the corner. With the doors an inch from closing, she saw his shadow shoot across the floor and just before they sealed, she caught a glimpse of his hand groping for the disappearing gap.

As the elevator descended, she could hear Byron beating on the doors. The loud banging faded away as she left the morgue behind.

The instant the elevator opened in the lobby, Allie high-tailed it through the front door. She dashed around the corner of the building and down the dark street.

As she reached her Honda, she heard Byron speaking on her phone.

"Hey, Allie."

She gulped for air.

"Anything wrong?"

"No. No. Just getting a little work out."

"Okay. Well, I can't find your jacket."

"Oh, yeah. Thanks for looking." Allie unlocked the door to her car as she spoke.

"Someone broke into the morgue tonight."

"Are you kidding? Did they take anything?" Allie started the car, shifted into second gear and drove past the morgue without thinking.

"I can't tell. They were in Dr. Mann's office. And I just missed them getting back on the elevator. I'm fixin' to call the police."

"Be careful, Byron."

"I will, Sweetheart. Hey, how'd you know I'd be here?"

"How'd I know?" Allie shook her head and manufactured her best casual laugh. "Because you're always working. I knew you'd come back tonight. It's that dedication that Dr. Mann loves about you."

"What are you doing now?"

"Oh. Just working out like I said."

"I thought I saw your car from my window..."

"It's a pretty common car. There's probably dozens of them around. Talk to you later, Byron."

"Allie, where--"

Allie hung up and tossed the phone onto the passenger seat. Her fingers were tightly glued to the steering wheel and she leaned forward as the Honda raced home.

When she pulled into the dorm parking lot, Allie took a deep breath and fell back into her seat. She stretched her neck to relax her stiff muscles. Once again the sharp pains erupted in her lower back and neck. She could feel cold sweat seeping into her shirt.

Allie reached over to grab her phone and her hand brushed against a stack of medical records. She cocked her head and yanked the documents from the envelope.

Why did Mann remove these from Bergman's chart?

The first page was a History and Physical for a Life Insurance Policy in Bergman's name from six years ago. Allie flipped the pages until she found 'Past Surgical History'. There was no mention of an appendectomy.

She flipped to the next page and gasped.

In her trembling hands, Allie held the operative note on Franz Bergman's appendectomy.

CHAPTER FIFTY EIGHT
PRESENT DAY

"I'm telling you, Andrew..." Allie sipped her Guinness Extra Stout Ale, while seated in a small pub not far from her dorm. "Actually, I just don't know." She had to yell to be heard above the loud music.

A thick, creamy, foam floating atop the brown beer, then slipped over the rim, and descended down the chilled glass. It finally formed a sticky film on the table.

"I don't know what's going on with Chrystal, but it's going to drive me crazy. She's coming home tonight, but she texted me that it wouldn't be until 10:00."

Andrew raised his voice so that Allie could understand him above the loud Irish punk music. "I wish I could help, but it's been a few years since I was a teenager, I'm not a girl and I've never understood girls. So, I'm no help. But I'll listen."

Allie grabbed a handful of greasy fries from the basket. "Where'd these things disappear to? A minute ago there was a ton of them."

"Here, take mine."

"Are you sure?" Allie had to talk at the top of her lungs to be heard.

"Yeah, I'm done."

"Oh, excellent!" Allie shook more salt on the basket. "I'm starving. They're really good."

"I can tell."

"I haven't had two beers in a looooong time, but these are really good, too."

"Glad you like them."

"They're Guinness?"

"Yeah."

"From Dublin?"

"Of, course."

"I want to go there some day. So does Chrystal. She's told me like a million times."

"Me, too. Let's all go."

Allie raised her glass. "It's settled then. All three of us, to Dublin. The home of James Joyce, Oscar Wilde and *Stam Broker*."

"To Dublin!" Andrew tapped Allie's glass.

They each took a swallow of beer and placed their glasses on the table.

"So, Chrystal's coming home tonight?"

"She most certainly is! She's been with Carly. Like, four nights in a row!"

"I'm sorry to hear that."

"Me too." Allie pointed behind Andrew. "Who are those people?"

Andrew turned his head and spotted three guys and a girl giving him a 'thumbs up' from a booth across the bar. "Oh. Those are my ex-friends from the aeronautical program. Don't pay attention to them. They're extreme nerds."

"Why are they smiling and why are they, like, clapping?"

"I don't know. They're so weird. There's no reason to even be looking at them."

"They keep looking over here. Anyway, we're out of french fries."

"Do you want another beer?"

Allie thought for a moment. "No. Just fries."

"Hey, man!" Andrew motioned to the bartender. "Can we get some more fries. Thanks, Bud."

He looked back at Allie. "I've got this."

"Thanks, Andrew. I appreciate it. You're a good friend, my friend."

"No, problem, Allie. I'm here to help."

"No, I'm serious. There are very few people you can consider friends in this world. I don't have many."

"That's the beer talking."

"No, it's not." Allie leaned across the table towards Andrew. "I think Dr. Mann lied when he said he had a DNA match on Bergman's body. And this is not his first DNA debacle, Andrew Wong. I think he may be hiding some from the Toro cases, but I don't know where. I've searched long and hard."

"Why do you think he lied about Bergman's DNA, Inspector Parsons?"

"Well, for one thing, there's no paper work. No chain of custody. And that sort of thing is important, apparently. Very important."

"I can only imagine."

"No you can't." Allie hiccupped. "I spent many hours tonight stuck in his office because I broke in and found some incriminating stuff. I had to evade getting caught and possible execution."

"Execution?"

"No, I meant persecution. But it was still very nerve wracking."

"Allie, I don't think I should be hearing this."

"Yes, you should, Andrew."

"Why?"

"Because there's something else."

"What's that?"

Allie pursed her lips and wiped her mouth with the back of her hand. "Nothing... I broke into Mann's office when he wasn't there and it was off limits."

"Allie, you really shouldn't be telling me this."

"Shhh!" She held her index fingers to his lips. "You're my friend and you won't say anything. Honest to God. I got into his office by using a credit card. I found Bergman's hidden medical records. And I found the DNA report was too short to be real. And it just said the DNA matched. Not a thing about paternity. That means--"

"I know what paternity means."

"Of course, you do. I really need to get a sample of Isaac's DNA, but I have no idea how. It's very disturbing. Plus, Chrystal has spent a lot of time with Carly. As you know."

"Why is that?"

"I don't know, Andrew."

"Can I speak candidly?"

"Yes. Please, lay it on the line." She nodded and assumed a serious expression.

"I think, that because you almost lost her...Allie, you're afraid to do anything that might keep Chrystal from being happy. If she has a chance to have friends or experience life beyond our dorm--"

"Graduate student housing."

"Graduate student housing, then you don't want to intervene. And I can only tell you this sort of thing because I've had a few beers."

"I believe your speech has a lot of merit. Possibly, you're right."

"Still friends?"

"Absolutely. I need friends right now. What do you think about the DNA?"

"I think you should tell the police about the DNA. What's his name? Festoon."

"He'll never believe me, Andrew." Allie shook her head. "He hates me. And Dr. Mann is a legend in his field. But I'm sure we didn't cremate Franz Bergman's body."

"Alright then, what can you do about it?"

"Simple,...I need to get DNA from his son, Isaac, and compare it with what we've got stored."

"Can you just ask Jess for the DNA?"

"What are you talking about? After that party? Come on! She's up to something, so she's going to say no. Plus, it would tip her off."

"We could follow Isaac around and grab a cup he drinks from."

"I thought about that, but it sounds creepy. Following a child around? I don't want to scare him. Show up at his school or fish his soda can out of the trash? Jess is bound to see me. Everybody thinks I'm weird enough as it is. "

"Well, just grab his cup at Jess' party."

Allie opened her mouth to speak, then squinted. "What party?"

"Her party. Saturday." Andrew grabbed a few fries. "The one at her house? You didn't get an invitation? Are you kiddin' me?"

"I take it you did, Mr. Wrong." Allie raised her glass and took a small swig.

"Yes. I did. I have no idea how she tracked me down. I assumed she asked you." Andrew stared at Allie and then turned his eyes down towards his glass. "I can't go. Don't ask me to do that."

"You should go. You'll have a great time."

Andrew laughed. "Oh, yeah. It's a black tie thing. No way."

"You can get Isaac's DNA for me."

"Are you serious? I don't even know what he looks like."

"He looks like the kid from the 'The Omen'. What was his name? Damian."

"Oh, that's nice, Allie." Andrew rolled his eyes.

"I'm not saying he's possessed. He seems like a great little boy. I'm just describing the way he looks."

"I just can't do that."

"Please, Andrew! At least try. What do you have to lose? I mean at the very least, you'll be at one of the fanciest parties you'll ever go to. You might meet someone who can help your career."

"I already told her no."

"Call her tonight and tell her circumstances have changed and you can go."

"Isn't that considered rude."

"This is important stuff. We don't have time for manners. And it never hurts to know the people that run in those circles. My mother told me that and she was right. Even if it kills me to admit it."

"Just... just let me think about it. I need some time."

"Great! I'll drive you over there."

"I haven't said yes."

"But you're a good friend and Chrystal and I are in desperate need of help. So, I know you'll do the right thing."

"Fine. I'll do it. What else was I going to do? Run calculations on the computer."

"See. It's a great idea."

"I don't know about a great idea, but here goes nothing. Of course, you win like you knew you would!" Andrew smirked and shrugged his shoulders. "So, you ready to head back?"

"Yeah." Allie pushed her half empty glass across the table. "Chrystal will be home soon and I should go into work early tomorrow. We're really busy."

"It seems like you're there early every morning and late getting home every day."

"Just trying to keep my boss off my back until I can figure out what's going on." Allie slid off of the stool and her feet landed on the sticky floor.

They split the bill and walked with their hands in their pockets through the crowd of the packed pub. As they passed the booth of grad students, Andrew waved. They waved back, ducked their heads and laughed.

"What losers!" Andrew shook his head with an embarrassed smile.

"They seem nice."

Andrew held the door open and they stepped outside into the humid evening. They walked past empty beer bottles and discarded, soggy fast food bags towards the sidewalk. Just before reaching the end of the parking lot, Allie noticed a compact car with a TV news logo splashed across its side.

"Oh, no. You gotta' be kiddin' me!"

"What are they doing here?"

"Just keep walking. Don't ask questions. Stay low." Allie picked up her pace and made for the sidewalk, but after a few steps, a cameraman and Phillip Spears cut them off.

"Allie!" Spears ran towards her. His thick, black hair bounced and his deep dimples framed his broad smile. "How you doing?"

"I'm fine." She continued to walk. "How's your nose?"

"Better."

"I think you look as handsome as ever. But you could pass for a war correspondent now."

"Seriously, Allie. This would be an awesome interview."

"Not interviewing, Phillip." Allie pushed past him.

"Who's your friend?"

"Andrew Wong. W-O-N-G." Andrew smiled.

"Do you work with Allie?" He pointed the microphone at Andrew.

"Only when she talks me into something."

"Allie. Please." Phillip sounded plaintive as he pulled the microphone away from Andrew and caught up to her. The bright lights from the camera flooded the sidewalk.

"Just give me a chance. I want to ask you a few questions about Toro and the Bergman case."

"No. That's it, Phillip. No! I'll spell it for you N-O."

"You realize there was another note sent to the police from someone claiming to be Toro. Didn't they tell you? What do you think of that? Why is James Smith still free and how are these notes getting out? The police aren't doing their job, are they? They're failing the citizens of Tampa, aren't they?"

"Leave me alone!" Allie walked faster.

"Just give me a chance! One quote and I'll quit following."

"No! Leave me alone. I'm warnin' you!"

"What do you think about the family of Erin Warrant saying that she worked for the Bergmans and now she's gone missing?"

"I don't know. Never heard of her. Ask the police."

"But you're working on the case."

"If you're not going to leave me alone, I guess I don't have another choice."

Spears covered his face. "Don't punch me!"

"I wouldn't do that again. But you won't leave me alone, so you know what that means."

Phillip scrunched his face. "No....wait."

Allie turned and, before he could elaborate, slammed the toe of her boot into his shin. He winced, groaned, and then crashed to the ground.

"Come on, Andrew. Let's get out of here."

Andrew's eyes bulged. "Allie, you can't just....Allie!"

She grabbed his arm and tugged him towards the sidewalk.

"Now I've got to track down Festoon or Westbrook and find out about this new note."

Andrew looked at Allie and then turned back towards Spears.

Allie continued to stare straight ahead. "He's right, why haven't they caught James Smith? Supposedly, he's been cornered for a week now. I'm letting my daughter wander around Tampa because they are within a hair of catching him."

"He must have very thick hair." Andrew stumbled as he struggled to keep up with her.

"He does! I remember that very well!"

CHAPTER FIFTY NINE
PRESENT DAY

While the news crew occupied themselves with Phillip Spears' injury, Allie and Andrew retreated along the dark sidewalk. When they arrived at the dorm, they found the parking lot empty and quiet. Andrew said goodnight as Allie unlocked her door and went inside. She clicked on the light, and after a quick check of the rooms, dialed Pug.

The operator connected her to his voice mail. Gritting her teeth in frustration, Allie hung up without leaving a message and called the station again, this time asking for Westbrook.

A few seconds later, she heard his deep voice. "What's up, Dr. Parsons?"

Allie pulled the phone tightly to her ear. "I need help, Detective! I want to find out about this new note and what you guys have uncovered. I've got reporters chasing me." As she spoke, she peeked over her shoulder and through the window. The parking lot remained quiet.

"I feel your pain. But, they're all over us too. Like sharks."

"And they're circling me!"

"Yeah, well." Westbrook took a deep breath. "Yeah, well--"

"The Tampa PD owes me this, Detective!"

Westbrook hesitated.

"There's another note! I know! You guys owe me."

Allie could hear Westbrook shuffling his feet. After a moment he spoke. "Alright. We can talk, but we have to meet face to face. I know a great place. We'll hash this out."

Allie agreed to meet Westbrook early the next morning at an old dive just off of I-75. She hoped she wouldn't be too late for work.

It was nearly 10:00 PM when Allie hung up. She paced and repeatedly peeked out the window. Chrystal should be home soon.

By 10:15, she still hadn't heard from Chrystal and Allie shook her head in frustration.

"Chrystal!"

She picked up her phone and started to text. Just as she typed 'Where', a black Mercedes pulled into the dimly lit parking lot. Chrystal jumped out, leaned towards the car and spoke to the driver. She waved then dashed towards the stairs, her backpack bouncing against her shoulders. Allie jerked the door open.

"Whose Mercedes is that?"

"It's Carly's dad's car. Jeez!"

"Sorry, I thought you'd be in their SUV." She tried to hug Chrystal, but her daughter slipped through her arms. "Welcome home, Honey."

"I'm so tired, Mom." Chrystal dragged her backpack towards the bedroom. "I need to go to bed. I've got to get up early tomorrow."

"Good to have you back!" Allie tried to embrace her daughter again, but Chrystal stiffened and pushed Allie away.

"Stop, Mom! I've got school. And I need to go to Carly's on Saturday. Her mother will pick me up."

Allie locked the front door. "What are you doing?"

"Carly and I are having that party at her house that I told you about."

Before Allie could respond, Chrystal disappeared into the bedroom. "Remember I told you about it? Her mom is picking me up at 8:00 so we can get ready."

"Don't you think you should take a break from Carly and get a little rest, Honey?" Allie raised her voice so she could be heard in the other room. "Do you want a snack or something?"

"Mom, I have to make sure we're prepared for the party. It's going to be great. A lot of people are coming."

"Well, okay." Allie took a deep breath. She stuck her head into the bedroom. "What about a snack?"

"I'm not hungry. Please close the door."

"Chrystal--"

"Mom, I'm really tired and I need some sleep."

"Fine, get some sleep." Allie stepped out of the room and shut the door.

"Chrystal, I have to leave early tomorrow. I've got a meeting in the morning. I'll need to drop you off at school at dawn."

"Whatever."

Allie gathered her blanket and pillow, and collapsed onto the couch. Despite being bone-tired, she couldn't sleep.

CHAPTER SIXTY
PRESENT DAY

Early the next morning, Allie stole out of her dorm wearing her darkest sunglasses and a grey hoody. Chrystal trailed behind, shuffling her feet and groaning. As they made a beeline towards her car, Allie thoroughly scanned the parking lot, but saw nothing unusual. Besides the two of them, only the crickets and birds seemed to be awake. Apparently, Phillip Spears must be nursing his shin and sleeping in.

"Why are you wearing that, Mom?" Chrystal closed the Honda's door and shut her eyes. "You look ridiculous. It's so hot already."

"I get cold."

"And the sun hasn't come up yet. How can you see with those glasses? It looks like you're hiding from someone."

"That's silly. But let me know if you see any reporters."

Chrystal's eyes widened and she turned towards Allie. "What... did... you... do?"

"Nothing...nothing."

Chrystal huffed and crossed her arms. "Please, tell me...is there anything going on?"

"Nothing. Go back to sleep."

Neither spoke for the remainder of the drive. Allie turned off the radio when she heard the first few notes of one of their favorite songs.

After dropping Chrystal off at school, Allie found the diner where Westbrook wanted to meet. It hadn't changed since her first and only visit when she was five.

The diner was a dive but brought back a rush of memories of when she was a kid and loved to finger paint and use a Polaroid camera to snap pictures of her dog and her father. The colors in the photos never appeared as bright as real life. Although none of her paintings or photos remained, she felt those media embodied her memories... and her pain.

Allie thought about when her therapist had asked her to relate a happy moment prior to age 10, and then she conjured mental images similar to her finger paintings and Polaroids. Next, Allie described smears of blue, brown and gray pigments which swept into detailed descriptions of a couple of kids on a swing.

She remembered smiling faces and people turning away. Pictures with no one in them and blank spaces with nothing to say.

Even though it had been a long time since she last visited the diner, she had fond memories of men sporting faded panama shirts and fedoras and the clack of dominoes being smacked down on the formica. She vividly remembered lively debates about Pete Rose and Iran. These mental images haunted her as she parked her Honda.

Then, Allie recalled wearing soft orange pajamas with a giraffe print. She paused and sighed. Her father had driven her here in his old turquoise Cadillac.

The diner occupied a squat building, that kind that was popular in the 50's, and as she and her father pulled into the parking lot, the heavy car slowed to a stop with a creak and groan. Allie remembered seeing a dozen or so patrons through the huge glass windows bending over their coffees and newspapers, and a waitress in an apron, angry that a phone was ringing. The memory had the symmetry and construct of Edward Hopper's 'Nighthawks' painting.

Her father had brought her here as a treat for finishing her first day of kindergarten. After she enjoyed chicken and dumplings, he ordered a big piece of chocolate pie, sliced from the beautiful meringue-topped one that she'd eyed under a clear dome on the counter.

"You have to be strong, Allie. Fight like I taught ya'. If Druden comes after ya', remember, you can beat her."

He had a faint Irish accent.

But his last words to her, outlived his presence. Allie never saw her father again and never figured out what 'Druden' meant.

Today, the booths with their tattered red, plastic seats and table-tops scarred from years of forks and knives carving gravy-covered Salisbury steaks, sat mostly empty. Elderly retirees who took advantage of the lull in traffic early on a Friday morning were scattered among the tables. They drank coffee and ate servings of cold cottage cheese with pineapple on lettuce.

Allie spotted Westbrook's tall thin frame sitting with his back along the wall and facing the window. He nodded and gripped his mug of coffee tighter as she approached.

"Thanks for meeting me, Detective Westbrook." She slid into a chair across from him. "Sorry about the short notice."

"Hello, Dr. Parsons. Sounds like you have a lot on your mind."

"I need to find out about this new note."

"Who told you we received it?"

"Phillip Spears. He wanted to get a comment from me about it."

"What did you say, then?"

"I kicked his shin in."

Westbrook sat back in his seat and wrinkled his brow.

"Hopefully, they'll bury that footage. Anyway, Festoon keeps telling me that James Smith is going to be caught. 'Any day..., any day, any day, he says!" She closed her eyes and rubbed her chin in frustration. "And he told me there's no way Smith can get a note into the postal system, but yet, there's another one. It's been a week since you guys almost caught him in that hotel!"

Westbrook massaged the top of his nose with his fingertips. "Okay, Dr. Parsons. Be calm. Here's the truth. Be calm--"

"I'm...running... out... of... time!"

"We've almost caught him a couple of times, Dr. Parsons. We've received a few anonymous calls and nearly nailed him in another hotel and then he slipped past us at a campsite. Based on what he left behind, we just missed him."

Allie glared at him with a blank expression.

Westbrook shook his head and took a sip of his steaming coffee. "He's a slippery guy. I can't explain how he gets those notes off. It's like he's a ghost. Maybe someone is tipping him off or helping him. But we'll catch him, Dr. Parsons. I promise. We've gotten a lot of phone calls from people who've seen him."

Allie gritted her teeth and looked out towards her car. It was exactly where her Father parked his Cadillac, years ago. "Detective, I'd feel much better if he were in jail and I could get a good look at him. It's wearing me out worrying about Chrystal and some monster that could put her through what I've experienced."

"I agree. We'll all feel better when he's behind bars. With this publicity barrage, we'll catch him."

Allie continued to stare at the parking lot.

"I promise."

After a moment Allie turned her gaze back towards her mug of coffee. "So, Detective…" Allie leaned back in her chair and licked her lips. "What did the note say?" She stared at her fingers for a moment and then looked him directly in the eyes.

"Dr. Parsons, you know I can't disclose that information."

Allie took a deep breath and shook her head. "I know you can."

Westbrook raised his chin so that he was looking at the ceiling. "Come on now…before you get worked up, hear me out. I can tell you, it's got us concerned. Any note that claims to be from Toro is going to put us on alert. But personally, I can't make heads or tails of it."

"So, there must be something to it. Is it anything like his last note?"

Westbrook took a sip of coffee and bobbed his head. "I'm not at liberty to say. I can't see any direct threat in this note. I really don't understand what it means."

"Just please tell me. I have to know if he's talking about me again."

"Again? Did someone tell you what the first note said?"

"I'm convinced he was talking about me."

"Who told you?"

"I'm not at liberty to say."

Westbrook shrugged his shoulders. "Okay. I'm not talking either. Anyway..." He took another sip of coffee. "This new note doesn't sound threatening."

"Glad to hear it. What did it say?"

"I can't tell you."

Allie mashed her lips tightly together and brought her fist down on the table. "Look Detective, I was almost killed by this guy and my son..." Allie rubbed her face. "My son died. My daughter...please listen. I deserve this information."

"I can't--"

"Detective, I'm getting desperate. And society is not ready for another desperate Allie Parsons. Believe me."

Westbrook looked at the dingy ceiling as if expecting guidance. "If I tell you, I'll lose my job. My wife will certainly fail to understand the circumstances of how I became unemployed and my kids will go hungry. I can't."

"I promise, I won't say a word. My lips are sealed."

"Doctor, you don't understand how much I have to lose."

"Believe it or not, Detective, I have just as much to lose. And remember, I've already lost more than anyone else working on this case!"

Westbrook stared into her determined eyes. He averted his gaze and lowered his head. "This is between you and me. I'm only saying this because you're so vested in this case. I'll deny I told you anything if anyone asks me. Do you understand?"

"I agree to those conditions. Please, tell me."

Westbrook took a deep breath. "Okay. Here it is...and I quote, 'My neglector and protector, the vessel that bore a boy'."

"What?"

"I know." Westbrook threw his hands up and pushed back in the booth. "It's really weird. We looked at it and were thinking, this is crazy talk."

"No. It's a poem."

"I don't know who the neglector and protector are. But we figure the vessel is some kind of ship. It brought a boy somewhere."

Allie scratched her cheek. "Really weird. Let's see, if you combine the notes, it comes out..." Allie looked up and wrinkled her forehead. "It says, uhm, 'To the preacher's demon that gives me joy, my neglector and protector, the vessel that bore a boy.' He's writing some kind of poem."

Westbrook took a deep breath, and folded his arms. "Dr. Parsons, I firmly believe we have this guy on the run. Okay, if he did write the notes, maybe he can come out of hiding long enough to mail them, but he can't be as organized as he once was. Even if it is him."

"In the time since Jess gave you those photos, he could have shaved his beard off and dyed his hair blonde or red or purple or whatever. How can you say he's not walking by here right now?"

"I can't rule that out, true, but on the other hand, he can't change his size. I strongly feel that we're right on top of this guy. But by all means, be careful. There's never any harm in looking out for yourself."

"Well, what else can I do? So, my neglector and protector, the vessel that bore a boy. Could he be talking about me in that line, too? Who knows?" Allie kneaded her tired eyes and groaned. "Oh, well. I don't know. But, anyway Detective, thanks for meeting me here. I'm sure Pug is tired of hearing from me."

"I told him about coming to talk with you this morning. He's got an appointment, but he might swing by."

"So, he does care about me."

"Well, he really loves the food here."

A thin, ginger waitress in her 20's strolled by the table to take Allie's order. The uniform, a pink dress with a hemline near the knee and belted at the waist, had not changed since Allie's visit with her father. Allie ordered a plain black coffee.

She waited until the waitress walked away. "Detective Westbrook, what do you think of this girl Erin Warrant? She worked for the Bergmans and her family said she's been missing."

"We're looking for Warrant, yes. But, the girl was trouble. She could be anywhere, including somewhere in the bottom of the Everglades. It's not the first time she's disappeared. Sometimes even normal people disappear for normal reasons and then show up in a normal way."

"I understand, Detective Westbrook. I don't know much about Erin Warrant, but I think I used to be a lot like her and it's hard for me just to say she might be at the bottom of the Everglades and walk away, like it's no big deal. Someone has to care about people like her. I've been there."

Her coffee arrived in a white mug permanently stained brown. After plopping it down on the table the waitress asked if Allie wanted anything else.

"Do you happen to have chocolate pie? Like under the glass?"

"Sold out, Hon."

"Thanks, never mind."

Without another word the waitress tore the bill from her pad and dropped it on the table.

The bell above the door rang and Allie turned to see a beaming Festoon ambling towards them.

"Hello, lady and gent!" He slid a chair over from a nearby table. His tight, navy blue knit shirt restrained his bulging belly, but the fat still managed to sag over his belt buckle, covering the badge attached there. The diner's front door closed and the bell made a brassy 'ping'.

Allie thought he'd put on some weight since Bergman's autopsy.

"Sorry I missed the first part of this conversation. What's up, Detective Westbrook?"

"Well, like I told you this morning, reporters confronted Dr. Parsons about this latest note. I informed her, like you said to do, there's nothing to worry about. We will catch this guy and we'll be done."

"Meaning there's not a dang thing to worry about, Allie. I don't care what the press says. They can go after my throat if they want to and scream for my blood all dang day, but I ain't worried, because I know we'll catch this guy." Festoon looked up and winked as the ginger waitress approached. "Hey, Darla, how's it going, Girl?"

"Much better now, Pug." The waitress smiled and rested her hand on Festoon's shoulder. "Pie in a mug and coffee, Pug?"

"Two creams, two sugars and a make it as hot as you look today, Honey."

Allie couldn't help but gag.

"We don't do it any other way, Sugar. Bag it up and back in two shakes."

Festoon watched as the waitress flitted around the corner. "She's a doll. Amazing gal. Raising a daughter all by herself. Can you imagine?"

"Wow! What people can't do these days!" Allie swirled a spoon in her coffee and looked away from Pug. "Honestly."

"They do whatever it takes to pay the bills." Festoon tapped the table in front of Allie. "We'll have this guy locked up for Bergman's murder before you know it. Then we'll throw away the key."

"I don't believe you."

"She's questioning my integrity, Hector." Pug raised his hand to his heart. "Can you believe that? Jess Bergman doesn't seem worried." Pug lowered his hands and leaned back. "I just left her house. Incredible lady. She's planning a big shindig. This huge crew came to set it up. You should've seen it all, Westbrook! She invited me. Too bad, I can't go. But I told her this whole thing would be settled soon and she's really grateful. Why can't you be grateful, Allie?"

"Isn't it a little weird she's having a party so soon after her husband got shot and stabbed to death in her house?" Allie bent towards Pug, stroked her chin and raised her eyebrows. "I'm just asking."

"Naw. It's that British stiff upper jaw thing."

"It's a stiff upper lip."

From behind Pug's shoulder, came a mug of steaming coffee and a piece of chocolate pie.

"Oh, my!" Pug smacked his lips and dropped the front legs of the chair onto the floor.

As the waitress placed the food on the table, Allie noticed that her lips formed a crooked smile which exposed awkwardly angled teeth.

"Chocolate pie, Pug." Her smile grew wider. "Just the way you like it."

"Oh, man!" He groaned out loud as he grabbed a fork.

Allie gasped. "Hey! You told me you were fresh out."

"Oh, sorry." The waitress straightened her tight skirt and leaned towards Festoon. "We always save a piece for Pug. He's been coming here forever."

"I came here when I was five."

"Well, if you turn as cute as him and wear a badge, I'll save you a piece, too. Anything else, Pug, Honey?"

"No, Darla. Absolutely delicious."

Allie shook her head as Darla walked away. "Unbelievable."

"I know. It's amazing pie. Want a bite, Allie?"

"I lost my appetite. What if I....I'm going to...What would you say if I...Uhm."

"Spit it out!"

"Please, don't speak until you swallow. I'm going to show you something that's going to change your minds about the whole Bergman case."

"I dontshtinkdatspossible."

"Shut up and listen. I'm going to show you information that'll explain why Jess Bergman doesn't mind throwing a party when her husband was supposedly just murdered in their house."

"What do you mean by 'supposedly'?"

"Be patient. You'll see."

"What does she mean by 'supposedly', Hector?" Pug turned towards his partner and raised his hands. "Did I miss something?"

"Nothing we covered. What information are you talking about, Dr. Parsons?"

"I really can't say, because you'll tell me I'm crazy."

"Hmm." Pug snorted as he took another bite of pie. "I'll tell you you're crazy right now, no matter what you say."

"Don't talk with your mouth full, Pug. It'll explain why Jess is going on with that party."

"I'll tell you why she's having the party, Allie."

"Why?"

"It's because that's what the British do. Take Henry the Eighth. Heard of him?"

"Of course."

"Had ten of his wives killed. Had their heads cut off." Pug drew his hand across his neck and leaned back in his seat. "Sucker didn't miss a beat. Just moved on with his life and married over and over again. Ate like there was no tomorrow and enjoyed what time he had left. He got fatter than me. It's just the way them people are."

Allie's jaw dropped open and she narrowed her eyes. "You're kidding, right?"

"Nope. Saw it on PBS. You should try educating yourself a little more, Allie."

"Okay. I've heard enough." Allie stood up and pushed her chair under the table. "I'll be in touch, but please let me know if you hear anything else."

"Sure thing." Westbrook chuckled.

She dropped two dollars on the table and turned to leave.

"Allie."

"What?"

"Is that all?" Pug motioned towards the money. "Have some heart. Darla's got a kid."

"I bought coffee. That's all. You ate the pie."

"Yeah, but mine's free."

Allie rubbed her eyes and groaned. "Oh, my gosh. Here's another dollar for the college fund."

"Dr. Parsons, take your dollar back." Westbrook handed the bill to Allie. "I'll leave a good tip."

"No, no, no. Please. I don't want to deprive the needy."

"Thanks, Allie. Glad to see there's some Christian charity in you, after all."

As Allie walked past the cashier, Darla looked up from her <u>People Magazine</u>.

"Hey!"

"I left the money on the table."

"That scar on your face. You're that girl."

"What girl?"

"The one in the video on You Tube."

"What video?"

"You're kicking that Spears guy. It's hilarious. Way to go!"

CHAPTER SIXTY ONE
PRESENT DAY

When Allie arrived at the morgue, she found her reception from Byron as cold as the refrigerated room holding their next case.

"Nice of you to stop by, Allie."

"I had a meeting. I'm not that late."

"Uh huh. Better get started. Dr. Mann was asking where you were."

"Sure thing, Buddy."

Byron gave her a long look, then turned away.

During her lunch break, Allie passed Mann's door and saw a maintenance worker changing the lock. Mann sat at his desk and didn't look up from his reading material as she walked down the hall. Allie observed only the top of his gray hair.

"Can't say how they got this thing open." The worker unscrewed the lock and talked over his shoulder to Dr. Mann. "Doesn't look picked or busted, but we'll put in a security bolt. They'll have to remove the hinges to break into your office."

Allie grabbed her sandwich and returned to the autopsy suite. With his constant, silent spying, being around Byron unnerved her, but that didn't compare to being ignored by Mann.

The day progressed with more sickening silence. If not for a mid-morning text from Chrystal informing her that Carly's mother would bring her home by 7:00, Allie wouldn't have communicated with a single person.

The absence of social interaction forced Allie to get her work done and, by 6:00, she sat in I-75 traffic, allowing her to arrive home 30 minutes before Chrystal.

Allie opened the door when she heard footsteps on the stairs. "Hi, Sweetie!"

"Remember, Mom, I'm going to be at the party all day tomorrow." Chrystal rushed past Allie.

As Allie pushed the door shut, she looked out and saw Carly's Escalade leave the parking lot.

"Carly's mother is going to pick me up early in the morning and then I'm spending the night there."

"I don't remember the spending the night part. Do you want pizza? How was school?"

"No, I'm a vegan, remember. And I told you about spending the night."

"No, you didn't. And we can get vegetarian pizza."

"But it's not vegan. And I did tell you about that. Please, Mom!" Chrystal softly stamped her foot. "Let me stay with her. I'll be home for church on Sunday. I promise. I'll just fix some cereal for supper."

Allie felt too fatigued to fight, so she let it go.

Chrystal poured herself a bowl of cereal before disappearing into the bedroom.

More silence!

The next morning Allie stood by the door and waved as Chrystal disappeared into the interior of Carly's car.

By late Saturday afternoon, the video of Allie kicking Phillip "Award winning investigative reporter for WTSP in Tampa" Spears, had gone viral. One of the headlines on Yahoo, read: 'Coroner Kicks Correspondent.'

"They're trying to make me look unstable, but I'm not a violent person." She and Andrew made good time through the sparse, weekend traffic towards Jess Bergman's house. "I only act like a lunatic when people won't leave me alone."

Andrew adjusted his bow tie in Allie's rearview mirror. "That video has like 100,000 hits in just over 24 hours. Some people would trade their kid for that kind of publicity."

"I just want to be left alone." Allie glanced over at Andrew. "By the way, you look very nice."

"Well, thanks. I had to beg some friends to let me borrow this thing from the theater department. It's apparently really fancy. It comes with a top hat, but I didn't bring that."

"That was a good decision. Too Dickensian."

"It came with a cane, too. Yes or no?"

"Don't use the cane. You'll look like Willie Wonka."

"My friend said it was used in the Spring production of 'Dr. Faustus'. I promised her I'd bring it back without a stain."

"You're definitely making a statement. We're almost there."

"Glad to hear I'm making a statement. So, Detective Westbrook didn't say much about that note?"

"He's convinced they're going to catch James Smith."

"What about that girl Spears mentioned. She worked for Bergman. Now missing. Coincidence?"

Allie shrugged her shoulders and looked into her rearview mirror to change lanes. "Westbrook says people vanish from Tampa all the time and she's someone who's disappeared in the past. Bad choices in life. That kind of thing. They're looking into it. I hope she's alright. I've been in her shoes before."

"It's probably nothing. My freshman roommate vanished for a couple of weeks. Turns out he met some girl at a party and they went to the Grand Canyon. It was kind of crazy, but it worked out for them. They're still married. He's a great guy." Andrew tapped the cane on the dashboard. "So...Chrystal's spending the night with Carly again?"

"Yeah. She's at Carly's house now. I'm glad she's got friends, I guess. I hardly see her. Carly's mom picks her up almost everyday from school."

"I imagine it's hard for her to meet girls her age in university housing."

"Yeah. But it's like these kids are so different. They live this high society life with a lot of money. She actually asked me if we could join the country club because Carly's a member!"

"You told me I should mix more with that crowd."

"Yes, I did. And so you are."

They crossed the bridge and drove past the airport. Turning the corner, Allie caught sight of cars parked along the road. The Bergman home stood illuminated nearly a quarter mile away, but the closer parking had already been taken. "I think we should stop here, so no one sees me. Sorry about the long walk."

"It's so far! I'll get my tux sweaty."

"Sorry, Andrew."

"You're right. Let's not take the chance." The car door squeaked as Andrew pushed it open. "I'll text or phone if I have questions."

"At some point, Isaac is bound to drink something. Just get his straw or cup and we'll beat it out of here. Thank you, so much, Andrew. You can't imagine how helpful this is." Allie put her hand on Andrew's and gave a heart-felt smile.

Andrew took a deep breath. "No problem, m'lady. Grab the kid's cup. Get out. Simple! And I get a chance to impress some bigwigs, to boot." He stepped out of the car, shrugged his shoulders and waved at Allie. "Here goes nothing!" Andrew walked quickly towards Jess' house and didn't look back.

He took the cane! Allie laughed out loud. He does look like Willie Wonka. He's insane.

CHAPTER SIXTY TWO
PRESENT DAY

Andrew disappeared around the corner of the Bergman's long drive-way. Allie fidgeted and looked at her phone every few seconds. She nibbled on a granola bar and finished the cold coffee in her Styrofoam cup. Although she resisted the urge to leave the car and pace, she shuffled her feet enough to walk five miles. She regretted not bringing a book or some work to take her mind off the wait.

Allie still had not heard from Andrew after an hour. So she decided to text him.

"How's it going?"

After 30 agonizing minutes, Andrew texted back. "He's been upstairs. Can't get there."

Allie texted back, "Go upstairs! :(" Do I have to think of everything? "LOL!"

"Oh, for crying out loud!" Allie moaned and threw her head back.

"Meeting some great people. I think I'm a hit :)"

She shot back, "Great! Get cup!!!!!"

Another 20 minutes passed and Allie thought she'd crawl out of her skin.

"Jess all over me. Can't get upstairs. Spilled wine on my tux. :o"

Really, Andrew! Please, focus! Allie now gnawed on her cuticles and little spots of blood appeared at the corners of her nailbeds.

A few minutes later he texted "Ready to leave. Can't get upstairs."

Are you kidding me? She texted, "STAY THERE!" She thought a moment then added, "Open the garage door."

"???" Andrew replied.

"Go to the garage and open the door!!! Just do it!"

Allie growled in frustration and threw on her sunglasses. She stepped out of her car, surveyed her surroundings and began marching towards Jess' house. Allie kept her head down and did her best not to look suspicious. She whistled happily, hoping that somehow, sunglasses and a nonchalant attitude would keep her anonymous. As luck would have it, no guests wandered among the parked and polished Mercedes and Jaguars she passed.

After a minute she could see Jess' house. The garage door was still down.

Allie muttered under her breath. "Andrew, please! Just hit the button and open the door."

At that moment she heard a creak. The door slid open about three feet and stopped.

Good enough! Allie glanced down at her jeans and white t-shirt. If anyone noticed her, she'd look like a party crasher. She caught sight of the caterer's van parked by the garage. Because Allie had attended many of her mother's parties and worked a few others as staff, she knew the basics of running a party. She had an idea.

Allie strolled over to the van and opened the rear door. A cursory scan of the interior revealed a beat-up beer keg, a case of wine and three Igloo coolers. Allie felt exposed leaning over the battered rear bumper, wasting valuable time, so she hopped inside and quietly closed the door. As her eyes adjusted to the dim interior light, Allie spied a simple white server's apron hanging on a hook near the front.

Perfect! Allie grabbed the apron and fastened it around her neck and waist. She maneuvered between the kegs and trash and opened the van's back door, looked around, then jumped down. She raced towards the garage and slipped under the door.

The familiar Land Rover and Porsche coupe parked in the garage reminded Allie of her horrifying earlier experience here. Those lights better not go out! Allie eyed them suspiciously.

She studied the path into the house. If the lights went out, she wanted to know how to navigate around the cars and shelves without bashing into anything. Even though she now had a light source from her phone, Allie needed the capability of dashing inside if she couldn't turn it on. I won't be vulnerable again!

This time, the lights remained lit as she made her way to the door leading from the garage to the house. With her heart pounding, she opened it and stepped inside.

The quiet of the garage yielded to the loud conversations and music of the booming party. A speedy peek around confirmed no one had seen her enter.

The spotless mudroom seemed to glow, with its bright, white stuccoed walls. A large chandelier with dangling cut crystals hung from the ceiling. Allie wondered why anyone would need a chandelier in a mudroom. A white marble bench ran the length of the wall to her right.

As Allie crept across the black and white tile towards the kitchen, she kept her eyes peeled for Jess or anyone else who might recognize her. When she reached the butler's pantry, she found a tray holding six glasses of red punch, ready to be served. Bingo!

Allie hoisted the tray on her right shoulder and lowered her face behind the glasses of punch. Busing tables, just like old times.

She peeked around the corner and saw several servers preparing plates of small sandwiches, cubed cheeses and drinks. The kitchen buzzed with people moving in and out. Beyond the kitchen Allie saw the dining room with its long cherry table and medieval murals on the wall.

The guests spoke loudly, most of their words being lost in the din. Allie heard 'marvelous, Jess', 'magnificent party' and 'I adore your home'.

Time to act! Allie carried the tray past the servers and headed to the dining room.

One of the servers shouted above the kitchen's chaos, "I've got another tray. Hurry!"

Allie answered in a deep voice, "Will do!" I don't know why I used that tone. I'm not pretending to be a man!

As Allie approached the dining room she heard Jess' distinctive accent. She turned the corner and ducked behind the tray.

Jess had her back to the stairs and leaned against the rail as she talked to Andrew. As Jess spoke, she waved her glass in a circle and tossed her head. A drop of wine hit Allie on the nose.

Allie wiped away the chardonnay and eased closer to the stairs. Andrew's eyes drifted over Jess' shoulder to Allie's face, where they lingered for a second. At first Allie thought he didn't recognized her.

Suddenly, Andrew's eyes grew large.

"What is it?" Jess started a slow, inquisitive turn.

"Jess!" Andrew coughed violently.

"What?" She turned back towards him.

"Uhh, how can I get rich?"

"What?" Jess laughed.

"I want to live like this everyday. Not just when I attend your spectacular parties. And may I say, this is an event for the ages."

Allie rolled her eyes and placed her foot on the first step.

"Oh, Andrew Wong! You're so delightful!" Jess caressed Andrew's arm. "Well, of course, the easiest way to make money is to marry into it."

"Indeed."

As they chatted, Allie scooted past Jess.

"Are there any potential Mrs. Wongs or Mrs. Rights?"

"If she's rich, it could only be right!" Andrew belted out a boisterous laugh.

Please, stop! I'm about to barf! Allie made her way to the top landing. She lowered the tray to her hips and gripped it with both hands. She could hear Jess' girlish giggle.

Where do I go now? Think, Allie!

She took a deep breath and studied the ornate oriental carpets and the many doors lining the long hall. If she opened the wrong door, she might well bump into someone she didn't want to meet. A guest could come wandering the halls any minute. In any case, she had to get moving.

A thick heavy door secured the first room on her left. Allie bent her knees and placed the tray on the floor then wiped her hands on her apron and tried to turn the broad, brass handle, only to find it locked.

No time to pick that one.

She squatted, lifted the tray of drinks and moved down the hall. The glasses rattled as Allie walked along the thick, antique carpet.

Allie found the next two doors also locked. She hoisted the heavy tray to her chest. Her back began to ache and the glasses clinked from being jostled.

Allie knew she didn't have much time.

After a few more steps, she noticed a door slightly ajar. Oh, thank goodness! She pushed the heavy wood with her hip and ducked inside. A feeling of relief calmed Allie's anxious nerves.

CHAPTER SIXTY THREE
PRESENT DAY

Allie entered an ornate study bordered by built-in cherry book-shelves that rose all the way to the high ceiling. A massive mahogany desk sat before a tall stained glass window and a ballroom-sized red and green Persian rug adorned the wide-planked pine floor. She placed the tray on the rug and closed the door behind her.

Think! Isaac is probably in his room, like Andrew said, but I have no idea where that is.

She rubbed her temples.

A grandfather clock ticked loudly in the corner, obscuring the soft hum of the downstairs party guests.

I've gotten myself in big trouble, but I know I can figure this thing out!

Her eyes darted around the room as she took in her surroundings.

Okay. There must be 10 rooms on this hall. Allie bit her index finger and shook her head. I can't search them all!

Hoping for some help from Andrew, Allie slipped her phone out of her pocket and the photo of Chrystal greeted her.

Of course! Chrystal knows where Isaac's room is!

Allie shot Chrystal a quick message. "Where is Isaac's room?" She pushed 'send' and held her breath.

Come on, Chrystal! Please respond. The picture of Chrystal stared silently at her.

Allie wandered around the room, waiting for Chrystal to reply. She stood behind the imposing desk and glanced at the numerous framed photos on the polished wooden surface.

Among the shots of Isaac and Jess, she noticed a faded color Polaroid snapshot encased in a tarnished, silver frame. In the photo, a frowning boy dressed in pressed khaki shorts and a short sleeved white shirt, stood next to a smiling soldier in his dress uniform. A US flag and what appeared to be a barracks comprised the background.

Allie glanced at the photo, then back at her phone. No message.

Please respond, Chrystal! Allie raised her phone to text again.

Before she could push a button, she froze. Allie turned her gaze back towards the picture.

You've got to be kidding me!

She snapped up the Polaroid and gasped. I think this is the same kid in Dr. Mann's photo!

Allie studied the boy's face. Intrigued, she turned the frame right and left and angled it up and down in an effort to absorb every detail. After a few seconds, she replaced it on the desk. She snapped a picture of it using her phone then clicked the photo collection icon. She scrolled through and found the picture from Mann's office and compared the two. The children looked uncannily similar.

Suddenly, her phone vibrated and Chrystal's text appeared.

"Why?"

She typed, "Just tell me where Isaac's room is. Very important. I'll explain later. Love U."

She looked back to the picture, but another message from Chrystal popped up.

"Next to the bathroom."

Allie shook her head. She typed, "If I'm on the stairs looking down the hall, where is the BR?"

"BR is last door."

"Can you see the pool from Isaac's room?"

"Yes."

"Love you."

Got it! Thank you, Sweetheart!

Allie slowly pushed the door open and the sounds of the party grew louder. She stuck her head into the hall and scanned both directions. Empty.

She dropped her phone on the tray of drinks and hoisted it to her waist.

Allie's phone buzzed. Chrystal had texted back '?' Allie ignored the message.

Isaac's room should be behind the next to last door on the other side of the hall. If Chrystal's wrong, I might be having a heart to heart chat with Jess real soon.

Allie shuffled down the hall. She stopped outside the door and brought the tray down to her waist, pinning it against the wall. She used her free right hand to grip the doorknob. Holding her breath, she nudged the door open. Allie grabbed the tray with both hands and pushed her way inside, barely making a sound.

Jackpot!

Isaac sat on his bed, playing with a muscular action figure. He tossed and turned the headless doll between his hands making machine gun sounds. He wore blue shorts and a white shirt with a tie; his jet-black hair lay smoothly combed and gelled.

"Did you remember to bring my food?" Isaac didn't look up at Allie as he spoke. His bottom lip puckered and his eyebrows angled down making him appear quite cross.

"Uhm, well, Isaac, I brought you something to drink, Honey. It's, uhm..." Allie put the tray on the light blue carpet and took a sip of the red punch from the nearest glass. "It's, it's..." Allie stuck her tongue out and coughed. "It's way to strong for you! But, I'll get you some water. How about that?"

"I'm hungry."

"I'm sure you are." Allie ducked through the connecting door to the bathroom, dumped the drink in the sink and filled the glass with water. In a flash, she was back in his room. "I think food is coming soon. So, drink this right now and then you'll get something to eat. Okay?"

Allie held out the cup and inched towards Isaac. "Here you go, Sweetie."

Isaac looked up at her. "You're like the witches my Daddy told me about."

"Just drink this and then you can eat."

Isaac dropped the headless action figure and reached for the glass. "I want a cookie. I don't like the other stuff."

"We'll get you a cookie, Honey. Now drink the water. Please, just drink it."

Isaac hesitated then took the glass from her hands. He stared directly into Allie's eyes as he took a small sip. His lips lingered on the rim for a moment.

Without breaking eye contact, he leaned over and placed the glass on the tray. "What's wrong with your eye?" He pointed to his own eye with his other hand.

"I can take that now." She reached for the glass. "I lost my eye because of a bad guy, Sweetie." She grasped the glass and held it tight.

"You're that lady. That witch! You're Chrystal's mom."

With a sharp jerk, Allie tore the glass from his fingers and shoved it into the apron pocket. "Good boy. Now, Sweetie, we'll get you some cookies." It occurred to Allie that she did sound like a wicked witch.

"You're bad! I'm telling my Daddy!"

"Wait! Daddy?"

"Daddy!"

"You're telling your Daddy? Where is he?"

"Daddy, that bad lady is here!" With surprising speed he slipped past her and dashed into the hall screaming, "Daddy!" The door slammed behind him.

Allie froze.

As Isaac sounded the alarm, she could see no place to hide.

She desperately ran through her options: under the bed, the closet, the bathroom. She'd surely be caught in any of those places. She turned around and spied her escape route.

"What choice do I have?"

Allie secured the glass in her apron, dashed to the window and quickly unlatched the locks.

Planting her hands firmly beneath the wooden frame, Allie pushed up using her shoulders and thighs. Her biceps bulged and her face turned red from the strain, but the window didn't budge.

She groaned. "It's painted shut."

"Isaac, Honey!" Allie heard a female voice call from the hall.

Mustering all her strength, Allie's muscles exploded and she sprang from a crouching to a standing position. Amid a spray of dried paint flakes and shards of wood, the window burst open.

She felt warm air envelop her arms and fill her lungs.

Allie knew that 20 feet loomed between prison and freedom. She sprang to the window ledge prepared to jump and hoped she'd see something to cushion her fall.

As she tipped forward and readied herself for the leap, Allie stopped. A small balcony hung just beyond the window. She breathed a sigh of relief.

Allie stood on the ledge and closed the window. She moved to the edge of the small balcony and stole a glance inside. There, on the tray between two glasses, lay her phone. "Allie Parsons! You idiot!"

She lifted the window, wedged through the tiny gap and frantically lunged towards the tray.

Allie aimed for her phone, but during her desperate plunge, she knocked over several glasses. She swiped across the tray and managed to prevent her phone from sinking into a pool of red punch.

She heard Jess shouting from the hall. "She's in here!"

Allie narrowed her eyes, clinched her teeth and turned towards the open window.

CHAPTER SIXTY FOUR
PRESENT DAY

"Allie Parsons is in Isaac's room! Hurry. That witch is looking for my Isaac."

"Chrystal's Mom came into my room!"

"She came in here, my Love?"

"She brought me water and said I would like the cookies!"

"Water? Look in the bathroom and under the bed. I'll check the closet. Don't let that little slut escape this time!"

"Where is she? I see. The window's been opened! She's out here... she's...no. She's not on the balcony. Hmm.... She must have made it into the hall. Check all the rooms."

Allie heard the window close then loud footsteps retreating from the bedroom.

Allie clung to the elegant but sturdy cast iron brace that supported Isaac's tiny balcony, sticking close to the wall. As the voices faded away, she looked down.

It appeared too high to simply let go and not expect a broken bone from crashing past the azalea shrubs and onto the manicured lawn below. From her precarious perch, Allie could see the sedate waves of Tampa Bay gently rocking the anchored boats near the Bergman's house.

Chrystal's right. Isaac has an amazing view from his room.

A wasp buzzed near her lip, but a gentle puff and wiggle of her nose sent him away.

Allie swung back and forth on the bar, considering her next move. The only thing worse than being cuffed for breaking and entering would be doing so with two broken tibias.

Under these circumstances, she could think of only one other option.

Grunting and sweating high above Jess' neat hedges, Allie plucked the glass from apron's pocket and slipped it under her T-shirt. With her right hand firmly gripping the warm iron bar, she removed the apron with her left. She flung the apron over the bar and pulled the hem through the neck-loop of the apron. The entire length of fabric only cut off about five feet of her distance to the ground. Hopefully, that would be enough to make her injuries non-crippling.

Quickly, she lowered herself, hand over hand, down the fraying fabric like she'd once seen a Cirque du Soleil acrobat do.

Just a foot from the end of the apron she could hear the fabric start to tear. This is going to hurt!

But only a single seam gave way. The material gradually separated, tearing lengthwise, and Allie continued her descent as each thread popped apart. Five feet above the shrubs, the apron separated with a loud, tearing sound and the back of her ankles slapped the stiff stems and leaves.

Except for a few scratches from the branches, it didn't hurt much. More importantly, she had the glass.

Kicking and flailing, Allie fought to free herself. After thrashing for a few seconds, she hit the ground running.

Allie's thighs churned and her arms pumped liked pistons. She bolted around the corner of the immense house. Grass flew from her shoes as Allie zipped past the mailbox, and fled down the road.

It's nice, that all those track hours are finally paying off!

When she arrived at the car she found Andrew leaning on the door.

"Where have you been?" Andrew threw up both arms.

"I was hanging from a second story window. Where have you been?"

"They're all over that house like rats, looking for you."

"How long you been here?" Allie unlocked the door and tried to catch her breath.

"I left as soon as Jess said you'd been in Isaac's room." Andrew grunted and swung the door open. "When they couldn't find you, I figured you'd be coming back here."

As Andrew slid in, Allie revved the engine, the tires squealed and the Honda shot backwards into a nearby driveway. She shifted into first gear, popped the clutch and accelerated away from Jess' house. Allie's sudden acceleration pressed Andrew back into his seat.

"Did you hear Isaac say he was going to get his Dad?"

"No, I didn't. Wow! This car has some power. Jess checked her phone and ditched me midsentence. She ran up the stairs. I didn't hear a thing."

"Well, Isaac said 'Daddy' three times. So, I think Franz Bergman is still alive. I think he's in that house. This DNA will prove that the body we cremated is not Isaac's father."

"I hope it's worth all this. I think I formed an ulcer. Can you get one during a two hour party?"

"I don't think so."

"Well, something burns in my stomach."

"It was probably that cheesy conversation you had with Jess. I almost puked all over myself."

"I'm getting pretty good at it. You're right, though, I need the practice."

"So, glad to hear it. Here, look at the pictures of the boys in the old photos on my phone. I took one picture in Mann's office and I found one in the study near Isaac's room. What do you think?"

Andrew took the phone from her and scrolled through Allie's pictures until he found the two she was talking about. He studied them carefully for a minute.

"I think they're the same boy."

Allie nodded as she whipped the Honda through another right turn. "I do, too. I can't prove it though."

"I can."

Allie frowned. "This is no time for jokes, Andrew. Is anyone following us?" She glanced in her rearview mirror.

He peeked over his shoulder. "I don't see anybody. No. Listen, I'm serious. My friend is working on a second generation software that recognizes and compares faces. They use something like it in Las Vegas casinos except this makes their software obsolete. Her's can even match adults with their childhood photos and can make a composite photo from several partial photos. It's pretty hi-tech stuff. Not like iPhoto or phone apps. She got funding from the TSA. She'd actually like to test it on something like this."

"Are you serious?" Allie shifted into 4th gear.

"Completely. It's really sophisticated and very sensitive. It's a lot better than the stuff you can buy commercially."

"Awesome. Please, give it a try."

"Okay. I'll email these to her. She was at the bar the other night when we were."

"Was she the one that kept smiling at us? You called her a nerd, then."

"She is a nerd, but Beth is brilliant."

"Good. I could use some brains on my side!" Allie flew past a slower car, barely missing its bumper.

"Hey!" Andrew turned to look in the back seat. "I forgot my stupid cane!" He rubbed his hand along the floorboard and then reached under his seat. Allie could hear him patting the floor. His eyes were wide and he was panting. "Can we go back?"

"Are you kidding me? I barely got out of there alive! I was dangling from the second story holding onto an apron!"

"Well, what am I going to do? I promised I'd get this back to them in one piece."

"Don't worry about it. I think I've got one around somewhere."

"You have a cane?"

"Yeah."

"Why do you have a cane?"

"Long story. But I'll look for it."

"Please do."

"I'll take care of it. But the first thing I'm going to do is get Isaac's DNA analyzed." Allie glanced in her rearview mirror again. "Then we'll all watch Dr. Mann try to dig himself out of a very deep hole."

CHAPTER SIXTY FIVE
PRESENT DAY

Allie expected to be awoken by reporters banging on her door early Sunday morning. Instead, she slept until 7:00 AM when the alarm on her phone jolted her from her uneasy slumber. Allie leapt off the cushions and crouched like a wrestler in front of the couch and scanned the room for assailants. After a few seconds, Allie regained her bearings and silenced the irritating alarm.

In anticipation of being met by a mob of journalists and possibly police, Allie had outlined simple answers to questions about Toro, Franz Bergman, the assault of Phillip Spears and breaking into Jess Bergman's house. However, as she gazed bleary-eyed through the dirty window, she saw nothing unusual in the quiet parking lot. There were two news vans parked on the other side of the street, but not nearly the army of reporters she'd feared.

Hopefully, everyone's lost interest in me.

Allie sat on the worn couch and watched the early morning news while she sipped coffee and waited for Chrystal to come home. The familiar video loops continued to show the same Toro picture without any new information. None of the networks mentioned her escape from Isaac's bedroom.

At 10:00 AM, Chrystal arrived exhausted and sunburned. Holding her daughter to her promise, Allie drove them to church where Pastor Virgil preached from Exodus, on the Golden Calf.

After church, they ate tossed salad for lunch and again for supper. Chrystal spent her time alone in the bedroom, finishing her homework. Allie prepared herself for work on Monday.

She intended to get Isaac's DNA to the genetics lab, ASAP.

But Monday didn't start well.

At first, it appeared that Mann and Byron were going to drown her in work. Byron labored through lunch, leaving her no time to slip out without being noticed and questioned about her intentions.

Anxiously, Allie struggled to think of an excuse to go to the main campus and to the genetics lab. It would be a challenge, she realized, to escape Byron's constant scrutiny.

Wherever Allie walked or worked, Byron followed close behind. When Allie left the bathroom, she found his face peeking at her from around the corner. As she washed her hands following the autopsy of a 25 year-old drowning victim, she could feel Byron staring at her from across the room. Even a quick trip to the coffee pot included her new chaperone.

Apparently, he had been assigned to keep his eyes on Allie at all times. She had no wiggle room at all. So, Isaac's glass remained in a bag in her desk.

Then, late in the afternoon Allie found her opportunity. Mann called and informed Byron that someone from the morgue must attend the Pathology Department meeting. Mann had another meeting and would be late. Since Byron hated meetings, Allie graciously volunteered to attend.

Especially since, coincidentally, the Pathology offices sat adjacent to the genetics lab.

Allie drove right past the Pathology department straight to the genetics lab. She dashed up the stairs and found the lab on the second floor of the Biology building.

She turned the handle and opened the door.

Allie peeked inside. "Hello?"

A man wearing safety goggles popped up from beneath the counter. His eyes bulged behind the thick glass.

As he stepped around the jumble of centrifuges, beakers and decanters, Allie read his ID badge: Joe Shoe, Laboratory Technician. Allie caught herself just before she accidently called him Joe 'Show'.

"Joe Shoe." Joe strode towards her and extended his hand. "Haven't seen you around here before."

Joe appeared to be in his early forties and explained that he had worked at the University as a lab tech for 20 years, an incredible length of time to be a lab tech. Joe seemed to take great pride in his long tenure. As he told Allie, Joe had seen professors come and go, but like the Rock of Gibralter, he remained the same.

"Hey, where do you live?" Joe removed his safety goggles and placed them on the cluttered lab bench.

"University graduate housing. About a mile from here."

"No way! I'm right there, too. I haven't seen you around." Joe dressed in the popular lab tech fashion of khaki shorts, t-shirt, white tennis shoes and long white lab coat. His clothes hung on his lanky frame. A shaggy five day-old beard did little to compensate for his thinning mousy hair. "We'll have to hang out sometime. Have a beer or five."

"That would be awesome. It might be a while, though, 'cause I'm super busy with work."

"Hey, no prob. I can tell you're probably one of those health nuts because you're in great shape. Green tea. I'll brew some mad green tea. Ya gotta like green tea!"

"Totally."

"Green tea and yoga are the bomb. We gotta' hang out sometime."

"Sounds awesome, Joe." Allie nodded and tried her best to smile. I really need to work on my interpersonal skills! "But right now I need you to find the DNA on this glass, and compare it with the DNA you ran for Dr. Mann last week." As she spoke, Allie held up the glass in a plain zip-lock bag.

"Oh, yeah. The identical samples."

"You know, Joe, I saw the results, but not the conclusion. So, the two samples he sent were identical DNA?"

"Absolutely. I showed that to Dr. Mann, too, Allie. I don't know why he wanted them run. I really didn't ask. Just do what I'm told. Know what I mean?" He winked.

"So, there wasn't a paternity question?"

"Nope. They matched up perfectly. Both came from the same person. Not a parent and a child."

"I'm right there with you. Always doing just what I'm told." Allie cringed at her own lie. "Anyway, can you do that for me?"

"What kind of amateur do you take me for? I've been here 20 years, Girl!"

"I heard you're the best."

"Great! Who'd you hear that from?"

"Oh,... just.... people around the morgue. I don't really remember. Anyway, here's the glass and the bag."

"So, you don't remember any exact names of people who said that about me?"

"No, I...no, I don't."

"Nobody?"

"I think, uhm, it might have been George." Allie glanced at the floor and rubbed her cheek.

"Oh great, man. Cool."

"Get what you can off of this." She lifted her arm so that the bag was dangling in front of his face. "And compare it to the sample Dr. Mann gave you. The identical sample."

He frowned. "It's not labeled."

"I know. It doesn't need one."

"It's got to have a label that matches the requisition form and autopsy report."

"Just run it anyway." Allie shook the bag.

"I can't."

"Why not?"

"Because, it's got to have a label that matches the requisition form or autopsy report."

"Joe, you said you always do what you're told, right?"

"It's my lot in life, it's not a lot, but--"

"Joe, I'm ordering you to do this!" Allie tapped her finger on the black lab bench and stared him down.

"I've been told by Dr. Mann and several cops, not to do that for anybody, except Dr. Mann."

"Well, now I'm telling you to do this."

"It's got to have a label that matches--"

"I understand the procedure, Joe, but these are special circumstances. And if I don't get this done then I won't finish my work and I can't have green tea with you." She lifted the bag higher and wiggled it.

Joe looked at the bag then slowly took it from Allie. He furrowed his brow, as if thinking hard. "Okay, here's what I'll do." He pulled an orange and white paper with a carbon back from a drawer and handed it to Allie. "Get this requisition signed by Dr. Mann and I'll go from there."

"I can do it. I'll sign it." She pulled a pen from her coat and signed her name.

"Hey, uhm, Allie, it's really got to be Dr. Mann." Joe pulled the form closer to his face and squinted.

"But..."

Suddenly, Joe's face lit up. "Wow! That's where I've seen you. You're Allie Parsons, the girl that got away from that killer. You kicked the crap out of Phil Spears. I love that video! It's everywhere."

"Great. That's me!" Allie turned her face away.

"Really great meeting you, Allie, but..."

"Don't make me kick you, too, Joe."

Joe frowned.

"I'm just kidding," She grinned and gave Joe a playful slap on the shoulder. "I have to have a really good reason to kick somebody these days."

Joe relaxed his shoulders. "Good to hear. Okay, Allie. Don't worry about it. You know... it'll be fine. I'll get it done."

"You will? Thanks. That's so great, Joe!" Allie sighed with relief and placed her hands on her hips. "How long will it take for the results?"

"I'll need to look. It's hard to say, Dr. Allie Parsons. Let me check on the computer and I'll tell you."

Joe sat at his desktop computer and typed his password. He leaned back in his chair and waited. "My password is named after the greatest band in the world. You know who they are, of course."

"No, I don't." Allie peeked over his shoulder at the monitor.

"Just guess, Allie."

"Alright, the Beatles?" Allie rolled her eyes.

"Good guess, but no, a swing and a miss. The Ramones! Come on. But I had to add a number so it's Ramones four, because there were four of them. And Ramones has to be capitalized."

"You probably shouldn't give out your password like that."

"I trust you, Al. You're in the Path departamento and work with the cops. Who am I going to trust if I can't trust the cops or their friends?"

"Good point, Joe."

"Soooo slooow!" He slapped his thighs like bongos and hummed a tune.

"Can you name this Ramones song?"

"No."

"What about this one?"

"Your screen's up."

"Okay, here we go!" He typed fast and ended with a dramatic flourish of his hand. "Wait for it, Allie. Wait for it. There it is. And the answer is, one week-o. Thank you for playing!" He looked back over his shoulder at her.

"Can it be done any faster?"

"They're pretty much done in the order of the requisition form."

"But this one doesn't have a requisition form, so I guess it can be done in the order you want. You're just doing what you're told, Joe."

"That's the story of my life, Allie."

"See you around the dorm, Joe."

Joe smiled ear to ear and a faint blush colored his face.

Allie turned and walked briskly to the door so that Joe wouldn't have time to second-guess the plan.

Allie dashed to her car and flew back to the morgue, thrilled with her success. As she pulled into her parking place, she realized she'd forgotten to attend the Pathology meeting. She checked her watch. Too late. It would end in one minute.

Allie, you are such a ditz.

She took a deep breath, straightened her shirt and strode inside the building with as confident a gait as she could muster.

"How was it?" Byron looked up from his computer as she passed his office.

"They're all the same." Allie feigned a yawn. Despite the surge of adrenaline, she tried to appear calm, if not bored. "You know, this and that. I refuse to get bogged down by useless meetings. Life's too short. Right?" Allie laughed. "So, obviously we need get cracking on some work, Buddy. The longer we talk, the further behind we get."

"Anything we need to know about?"

"Uhm." Allie wrinkled her forehead. "Nothing I can think of." She wiped sweat from her brow and attempted a smile. It turned out crooked and shaky.

"Okay, then, I'll let Dr. Mann know you didn't attend. Those things are very important to him."

Allie sighed. She had become a terrible liar and she suspected that after her recent behavior, Mann wouldn't give her time to improve.

CHAPTER SIXTY SIX
PRESENT DAY

Allie bolted upright in bed and wondered, for a split second, why Luke had an alarm clock in his room. And why is it ringing so loudly? She realized she'd been dreaming and fell back onto the couch.

It had been a week since she'd given the cup to Joe Shoe. Since then, she'd spent every night tossing and turning on the couch. When she should have been sleeping, she found herself staring at the ceiling in the predawn hours. When she should have been alert and focused at work, she'd doze off.

Allie had been preoccupied with James Smith and became anxious to use the pending DNA results to prove Bergman hadn't been murdered. At the very least, she hoped to confirm his body hadn't been cremated in the Hillsborough County morgue.

The possible repercussions of breaking into Jess' house weighed heavily on Allie's mind. However, she'd heard nothing about her little adventure from either Jess or the police. The silence seemed to support her suspicions that Jess had something to conceal.

But last night she did fall asleep and her dreams rebounded with a vengeance.

She now stared at the solid concrete block walls across from her sturdy couch. Still half asleep, Allie remembered dreaming about Luke and Chrystal as toddlers. At times they walked arm in arm, giggled and talked in gibberish called 'twin-speak'. They had scribbled vibrant chalk art on the sidewalk just before a strong evening storm.

When the storm came, the colors that had once seemed so permanent became no more than flowing streaks in the rivulets of rain. After the clouds moved east, only indistinct splotches remained.

In her dream, Luke became violently sick and Allie hugged him. He cried and she told him everything would be alright.

The alarm blared again and Allie realized she'd fallen back asleep.

Allie wished she could return to the dream and hold Luke again. But the reality of work drove the memories of her dream away.

She made her way to the kitchen and called to Chrystal to get up, but received no reply.

Allie opened the door to the shared bedroom to wake her.

"Can't I sleep a little later? Carly and I have been studying so hard. Harder than you can imagine." Strands of her long blonde hair hung over her shoulders and pillow. Chrystal squinted her puffy eyelids as a slender beam of light from the cracked door crossed her face.

"I made it through medical school, Chrystal, so, yes, I can imagine just how hard you're studying."

"This is really tough stuff, Mom." Chrystal pulled the pillow over her head.

"You have to go to school, Chrystal. And the bus picks you up at seven."

"Yeah, but Carly's Mom will swing by and get me at eight. Which will work out great." Chrystal pulled the pillow tighter. "Please, Mom. Can I sleep a little later and go to school with Carly? Please!"

"Can I talk to Carly's mom about this? You've been spending a lot of time with her and I've never met her mother."

"You met her two months ago."

"Chrystal, Honey. I was volunteering at your cheerleading camp and she told me they didn't need any more help and I could take the day off. That's the only time I've ever spoken to the woman."

"She's very busy. Please, Mom, I really need the sleep."

"Then maybe you should spend a little more time at home and a little less time socializing. I'm very busy, too. I have a full time job."

"Mom!" Chrystal jerked the pillow off her head and sat up. "You know I really love our dorm! Great place to spend the rest of my miserable life which I think I'm doomed to endure but--"

"Do not yell at me!"

"Well, I can't spend anymore time here at this dump, Mom, because Carly and I and Tiff, and Sara and Malinda and Helene--"

"Why are you still hanging out with Helene?" Allie crossed her arms. "Why does my 13 year old daughter spend time with a teenager who opens up her party to drunk high schoolers and has a bad reputation? This makes no sense to me at all!"

"Why didn't you tell me about that video of you?" Chrystal's eyes flared, her shoulders trembled and her clenched fists dented the mattress.

"Video? You... you saw a video?"

"You know what I'm talking about. Don't lie!"

"I'm not lying, Chrystal. I just asked you a question. And don't talk to me like that! Don't make me angry, young lady. And who's Tiff? I've never heard you say a word about her."

"It's the video of you kicking Phillip Spears. Mom, it's so embarrassing. Why did you have to kick him? Can't you just walk away?"

"Because he wouldn't leave me alone!" Allie threw up her arms in frustration. "But that was the wrong thing to do. I'm sorry someone got it on video."

"Mom, he's a TV news reporter. They travel with cameras! Of course they're going to have it on video, that's their job. What world do you live in that you wouldn't think they have cameras?"

"How did you find out about it?"

"It's all over the place. I got emailed 20 links to it. People think you're insane. And it was in front of a bar. Were you drinking again?"

"I had a beer!" Allie huffed. "Don't worry, the video will go away and people will completely forget about it."

"A few years from now."

"Fine. I'm not talking about this anymore. Just sleep in. I don't care! Bolt the door from the inside when I leave!" Allie slammed the door.

TORO!

Allie microwaved some bacon along with a cup of coffee and headed to her Honda. Her hands shook, spilling the hot coffee over the top of the white, styrofoam cup. Allie's temper boiled.

Carly's mom will pick Chrystal up and that entire privileged entourage will be chauffeured to school! And I'm the one who doesn't live in the real world!

When Allie arrived at the morgue, Mann's door was closed.

She knocked on Byron's door.

"Allie." He didn't look up from his newspaper. "Nice of you to make it. Just waiting for you to get here so we can start."

Allie refused to acknowledge his childish taunt. She turned and, as she headed to the autopsy suite, bobbed her head side to side. "Nice of you to make it, Allie!" she whispered in a mocking voice.

He had greeted her the same way every morning since she had missed the Department of Pathology meeting. Wait until Joe Shoe gets my DNA back. You won't be so snotty then, Byron.

At 10:00 Allie received a call from Andrew, but she couldn't answer it because she was elbow deep in an abdomen. On his fifth attempt to reach her, Allie slung her gloves into the trash and picked up the phone.

"Hey, you busy?" Andrew sounded excited.

"Just extracting a cirrhotic liver. It's like cutting out a rock. Why do you keep calling me?"

"That sounds exactly like the reason I'm in rocket science and not medicine. Did you find your cane?"

"You've been calling me over and over to ask that?"

"No. I want to talk to you about something else."

"Well, anyway I can't find my cane. I think I left it at a party somewhere."

"That makes two of us. But I got up with my friend, Beth, and we analyzed your pictures through her program."

"Great. Did you find anything?" As she spoke, Allie noticed Byron studying her out of the corner of his eyes. She turned away and drifted a little further down the hall.

"You were right about the pictures. Beth went through the progressions with the facial recognition steps and the faces are the same. The kids are identical."

"Wow!" Allie ran her hand through her hair. "You're sure? I need some good news. So, it's pretty accurate?"

"Yeah, impressively so."

"So, I wonder who the child was?"

"You're going to love me for this."

"What did you do, Andrew?"

"I had this hunch. I found several pictures of Franz Bergman on the internet. Like you said before, there weren't any good recent ones but I found a lot of adequate older ones which should work out better, actually. We merged them all and created a composite."

"And."

"Now I know what he looks like."

"Well, I have no idea how that helps. Maybe we can give Jess a portrait of her late husband. Only I'm pretty sure she sees him every day."

"A little patience, please. There's more to it than that."

"Like what."

"Are you ready?"

"Would you just tell me! I haven't gotten a lot of sleep and no one will talk to me around here and Chrystal is being... difficult and I'm stressed so I'm not in the mood to play games."

"Sorry. The child is probably Franz Bergman."

"Wait." Allie stopped in her tracks. Her jaw dropped. "Our Franz Bergman. Are you serious?"

"Yeah. I mean, matching children's pictures to their adult faces isn't as accurate as matching contemporary pictures. And the program had to match them off of a composite face, but it looks like the child is Franz Bergman. All of them even have a similar scar near their hairline."

Allie leaned against the wall, stunned. "So, Dr. Mann has a picture of himself with his arm around Franz Bergman as a boy?"

She turned her head and saw Byron, now in the hall, staring sternly at her. Allie realized she was talking too loudly. She strolled towards her office.

"And supposedly Franz Bergman's corpse came through the morgue, and I'm guessing, Mann never said anything to you about knowing him."

"Never. He showed no emotion. But recently, he's been out a lot. He looks like he doesn't feel well. And Byron acts like he wants to strangle me. Something is definitely wrong."

"Should you go to the police about this?"

"Okay. Well, let's think about it. They'd never buy this story coming from me. And really, it's no crime to be close to a murder victim. It's weird not to say anything about it, but being 'weird' isn't a crime either."

"Tell me about it. If that were the case I wouldn't have a single friend. Except you, of course."

"I think Chrystal would argue I'm in the weird group. Anyway, I have to jump all over this before they fire me. We'll research Dr. Mann's background and find out what we can about him."

"Good plan."

Allie pinched the bridge of her nose as her thoughts raced. "What's going on between him and Franz Bergman? Are they related or something else. And then hopefully, soon the DNA from Isaac will be ready and I can prove that body wasn't Bergman."

"Well, it'll be nerds to the rescue again. I've got some friends who can find things on the internet that are hidden to mere mortals."

"Can you get something to me by tonight?"

"Probably. I can't say how useful it will be."

"Try, Andrew. I have this sinking feeling I'm running out of time."

"Because Mann is going to fire you?"

"Yeah. Or maybe Jess is going to have me arrested for breaking into her house. Or worse."

CHAPTER SIXTY SEVEN
PRESENT DAY

A police car cruised in and sat several minutes in the dorm parking lot. Allie had the horrible fear that they were going to arrest her for breaking into Jess' house or Mann's office. The policeman didn't get out of the car and he pulled away just as she thought she might vomit. Even though the cop had left, her anxiety escalated.

The phone rang and Allie answered it as she fished around the drawer for her secret cigarette cache.

"Hey, whatcha' doing?"

"Just, uhm, nothing really, Andrew." She jerked the drawer so hard it crashed against it hinges. "Did you find something about Mann?"

"We're still working on it, but I dug up something else that's interesting."

"What's that?" In the back of the drawer, Allie located a pack of sugar-free, spearmint gum and folded three pieces in her mouth.

"Did you know that 14 years ago there were five murders in Lisbon, Portugal attributed to a single man? One witness who saw him leave the crime scene minutes after the last murder reported that he was as 'big as a bull.' Then a year later, there were three murders in Barcelona and one in Madrid. A note at one of the scenes said the women had been gored by 'El Toro'."

"Wow. You found all this online?"

"Yeah. It's available to anybody. You just have to know where to look and how to search. I started with 'Toro, Tampa' and followed dozens of links. Are you chewing gum?"

"Uh huh. Is it bothering you?"

"You're really smacking. You sound like some greaser babe from the 50's."

"I'm chewing a lot of it."

"Why?"

"Because my daughter's not here! Plus, I'm stressed about all this."

"When I get stressed I read a book or go for a run."

"Good for you." Allie threw the gum in the trash. "So, is that all?"

"No. There were three more murders in Buenos Aires. Again, a note left at one of the scenes was signed 'The Bull,' El Toro. That was about 10 years ago. None of the women survived. The only witness was the man in Portugal who happened to be passing by."

"And that would give Bull the chance to come here and start his spree nine years ago. If it's the same man."

"Exactly. But it also means this guy is experienced and is probably very good at this sort of thing."

"James Smith, maybe?"

"Possibly. Be careful, Allie."

"I know. I'm trying. I really am. But what you said got me wondering. What do you think of Jess' home?"

"It's beautiful. I plan to buy it from her and live there one day."

"Good luck with that. But the décor, the style. What's different about it?"

"It's very Spanish. Very old world. Uhm, like a Latin-American village, maybe?"

"Exactly. It's like something you might find in Spain or Argentina."

"Come on, you're not saying that..."

"It's weird. I know Franz Bergman isn't Toro. Everyone describes him as short and dumpy."

"And actually, that's what he looks like in his pictures."

"Interesting, though. It's a bizarre coincidence. It just got me thinking."

They talked for a few more minutes until Andrew excused himself for a conference call.

Allie thanked him and hung up. The silence of her dorm was oppressive. She wished Chrystal would spend more time at home. But tonight, just like every night recently, Chrystal shuffled in at 10 PM, mumbled a few words and disappeared into the bedroom.

Early the next morning, Chrystal slept and Allie left for work. Chrystal would catch a ride to school with Carly. With all the more serious issues looming, Allie decided that addressing Chrystal's behavior could wait.

Over the next several days, Allie ignored the calls of reporters who managed to obtain her cell phone number. But she found it increasingly difficult to avoid the newscasts, which as one station proclaimed in prime time, 'Exposed the Source of the Toro Notes'. Every store, lobby and restaurant had a TV broadcasting the now famous picture of James Smith, a file photo of Jess Bergman's house or the missing girl, Erin Warrant's most recent mug-shot.

Allie noticed a new tone in the reports. Instead of a hopeful optimism that James Smith would be caught, the reporters now described a growing frustration in Tampa at the lack of an arrest.

No one reported any good news. The police found no new leads.

Every web report, video or internet search brought disappointment.

A gloom enveloped Tampa.

Just like nine years ago.

Two days after her last discussion with Andrew, Allie's cell phone rang at work. She ducked into a corner of the autopsy suite to answer it.

Andrew breathlessly told her he'd found interesting information about Mann. "Can you meet me at your dorm in an hour? I've got some great stuff to show you."

Allie looked at the wall clock. 4:30; Byron will be irate. "Sure. See you in an hour." She hung up, flicked her gown into the trash, clicked off the lights and headed towards the elevators.

Allie saw Byron glare at her as she strode out of her office. She was too tired to care and didn't look back again. She heard him punching the buttons on his desk phone as the elevator closed. On her way home, news talk radio mentioned a sighting of James Smith. But once again, he'd slipped away. Allie turned her radio off. She'd rather hear no news than bad news.

Pulling into the dorm parking lot, she saw Andrew waiting at her front door. He appeared anxious. He shoved his hands deep into his pockets, shuffled his feet and glanced at his watch repeatedly.

Allie whipped her car into the nearest parking space and dashed up the stairs.

"Thank God, you're here!' She took a deep breath as she turned the key to her dorm door.

"I think you're actually happy to see me." Andrew ducked through the door with a half smile.

She turned on the lights and tossed her purse on the couch. "Can I get you something to drink?" Allie disappeared into the shared bedroom.

Andrew stood still and scratched his head. "No, I'm good. Really, I'm just thinking that..."

Allie reappeared, wearing a warm-up suit, and sat on the couch. She patted the cushion beside her. "Sit."

Andrew squinted and cocked his head. "That was really fast. Exactly, how did you--"

"Andrew, just tell me what you found. I've got to get this figured out." She patted the cushion again. "Sit!"

Andrew sat beside her on the couch. "Okay." He took a deep breath. "Okay, you ready?"

Allie raised her palms and rolled her eyes. "Just tell me."

"This is what we found out about Dr. Mann. First,--"

Allie cleared her throat. "Stop!" She bit her lower lip. "Before you go on, where did you find it? Is this illegal?"

"Excuse me." He shook his head and cranked his lips into what appeared to be a sneer. "What is that supposed to mean, Allie?"

Allie shrugged her shoulders. "Well." She cleared her throat. "Well...the information you're about to show me...is it basic stuff open to everyone like you used to find out about the Spanish murders?"

"Okay... you're manic. Truly manic. Honestly, I can't keep up with this pace."

Allie clasped her hands in front of her nose and pursed her lips. "Sorry. Just tell me where you found this stuff."

Andrew took a deep breath. "All this is from the Internet. Some open to the public and a few lesser known portals."

"Thanks. But please keep this legal."

"Aagh!" Andrew shook his hands. "Honestly! I'm just more than a little frustrated. Which country's laws do you wish to uphold? If you're talking about China's laws then everything we've done is illegal. I might as well not show you any of this. But, on the other hand, in some Eastern European countries, exploitation of western computers is encouraged. And don't even get me started on North Korea." He clicked the return key and turned towards her.

"I don't like the idea of anyone hacking onto someone's secure computer."

"We didn't break any American laws." Andrew picked up his computer from the table and placed it in his lap.

"Okay. You promise?"

"I promise. Your conscience can stay clear. Can I continue.... please?"

Allie nodded. "Yes."

"Great!" Andrew clicked on a link and leaned towards Allie. "Dr. Leopold Siegfried Mann was born in Munich in 1942. He lived and worked in Germany until he moved here in 1984."

"Was he married?"

"Yes. But I can't find her name."

"I thought you guys are Internet heroes?"

"My friends are. But listen, Miss Impatient, there's more. You can be really difficult sometimes. You're telling me to watch my methods and then you're getting snarky because I didn't get his wife's name."

"I wasn't snarky. I'm just tired. I haven't slept in days."

"Did you find your cane?"

"No. I told you, I probably left it at a party."

"Recently?"

"No, not recently. Why would I be taking a cane to a party these days?"

"Why would you be taking a cane to a party in the past?"

"I can't talk about it. Just, just tell me about Dr. Mann."

"So, I'm still out a cane. But anyway, Mann was a force in Forensic Pathology there."

"Where did he work?"

"At the University of Munich. I've got the years right here and his old contact numbers."

"Oh, that makes it simple. Let's call them and ask."

"What do you mean?"

"We should just phone them and ask about Dr. Mann and his wife. There has to be someone there who knew him."

"I guess we could do that. Or we could try and find out stuff about his wife by delving deeper into the computer at the University of Munich."

"Sounds like hacking."

"That is a very broad term with lots of negative connotations and it sounds as if you're being judgmental."

"Did your friends hack, Andrew?"

"You know hacking is such a nondescript word. It's like asking, 'Did you lie?' You know. What's the definition of lying anyway? There are so many shades of gray. More than you can count. The world is so much bigger than trying to count shades of gray. It's very immature."

"Thanks for the sermon, but I think we can call and find out his wife's name. That's all I'm saying. We don't have to break through password boundaries."

"There's social hacking and internet hacking. Choose your poison."

"If I talk to a person and I'm honest and then they give me the information I need, then I'm okay with that."

"Or you could break into an office. Maybe, just crash someone's party and then raid their child's room. Cause your friend to lose the cane he promised to return."

"Harsh. I'm trying to be a better person."

"But am I right?"

"Probably."

"Say it, Allie."

"Yes. You're right. It can't be worse than what I did. Are you satisfied?"

"Yep!"

"Congratulations. What's the number to the university?"

"I'll pull it up." Andrew scrolled down the computer screen until he found the number. "Here it is."

"So, let's lay out what we know and what we don't know, and see if we need any other information besides his wife's name. Then we call and ask. If we can't get anywhere, we can consider your way."

Over the next few hours, Allie and Andrew reviewed all the unsettling facts of the case. It just didn't add up to Allie, and she wanted answers.

Allie's phone buzzed. "Chrystal's on her way up. Can we put this on hold for a few minutes?" She gave Andrew a pleading look.

Andrew looked at his watch. "Sure, the offices in Munich aren't going to open for 4 more hours anyway."

Allie heard stomping feet on the stairs and the door burst open.

"Hey, Honey. Andrew's teaching me to do an in-depth internet search...for work purposes." Allie reached out to hug Chrystal.

"Hello, Mom." Chrystal skirted Allie's hug. "Hey, Andrew. You might want to start with the basics, like 'what is the internet?'" Chrystal ran a glass of water and headed to the bedroom.

"Going to bed already?" Allie's smile faltered.

"I need to study, in peace and quiet. See you tomorrow. Good night, Andrew." Chrystal shut the door with a thump.

Andrew cringed. "So...want to get something to eat and hammer out a plan?"

"Yeah. We need food and a plan."

CHAPTER SIXTY EIGHT
PRESENT DAY

At 2:00 AM on the dot, Allie picked up her phone and dialed the number that Andrew had found on the computer. Andrew drummed his fingers on the table and shifted in his seat.

With remarkable clarity, Allie heard the secretary answer on the first ring.

"Yes. Hello. Do you speak English? Of course. You speak English really well. How are you?" Allie spoke slowly and carefully pronounced each word. "I'm Dr. Parsons from America. I'm trying to find someone who worked with Dr. Leopold Mann. He was a Professor at your university in the 70's and possibly into the early 80's."

Allie paused for a second then frowned. "Is there anyone there that could help me?...I'm sorry to hear that... No one?"

As she desperately appealed to the listener on the phone, Andrew furiously typed on his computer.

"Well, thanks for your--"

Andrew jabbed Allie in the ribs and pointed to a name on his laptop screen.

"Uhm, is there a Professor Rhinehardt...Frankfurter...there?"

Allie turned towards Andrew and whispered, "That cannot possibly be his name!"

He nodded enthusiastically.

Allie cleared her throat. "Yes, that's right." She coughed and tried not to laugh. "It's Rhinehardt, sorry I've got this bad cough. It's

Rhinehardt Frank...I'm sorry, my partner is going to have to finish this..."

Allie handed the phone to a stunned Andrew and buried her face in the cushion as she convulsed in laughter.

"I'm Dr. Parson's personal assistant in the state of Florida. Do you have contact information for Dr. Rhinehardt Frankfurter?" He glanced at Allie as she stuck her face deeper into the pillow.

"Is there a phone number where we can reach Dr. Frankfurter? Oh." Andrew scribbled on a piece of scrap paper and stared disapprovingly at Allie, who pulled the cushion more tightly over her face. "Thank you so much for your help. I'm sorry Dr. Parsons is feeling so poorly. She's a little under the weather."

Andrew hung up and stared at Allie as she continued to laugh.

"What's wrong with you, Allie?"

"Oh, I'm so sorry." Allie rolled with laughter and plummeted from the couch to the floor. She landed on her back with a solid thud. "The name. It's got me going into convulsions. I'm so tired."

"Allie, get a hold of yourself!"

"I'm sorry. I'm laughing so hard, I can't breathe."

"Well, you are going to have to compose yourself and come back to Earth. Because we are going to have to call..."

"Do not say that name!"

"You mean Rhinehardt Frankfurter?"

Allie fell over and writhed in laughter, which soon turned to sobs.

"That's very immature." Andrew looked down his nose at Allie.

"I'm exhausted! That's what's wrong with me. I think I'm losing my mind!"

"Do you want me to call him?"

"It's okay. I'll call him myself. I mean, this is my problem. Not yours."

"So, call him."

"But the issue I have is...I think if I say that name, I'll lose it."

"That name being?"

"Stop, I'm commanding you, Andrew!" Allie bit her lower lip.

"Commanding me? Really?"

"Whatever. I'm demanding. I'm pleading. Please don't say his name. Stop. I think I'll pee my pants."

"You mean, Rhinehardt..."

"Stop! Okay. Here's the phone. You make the call."

"I thought you were such a tough girl."

"I'm not tough, I'm just me. But you make the call. I give up. Maybe tomorrow I'll be okay, but I can't now."

"That bad, huh?"

"Please, Andrew. You call him."

"Alright. But this is going to cost you."

"Just tell the truth as much as possible."

"You sound like my minister."

"Good."

Andrew dialed the phone and bobbed his head to the ringtone.

A few seconds later, Allie heard a voice.

"Is this Dr. Rhinehardt Frankfurter?" Andrew looked at Allie and nodded.

"Dr. Frankfurter." Andrew sat up and cleared his throat. "Hello, my name is Andrew Wong at the University of South Florida in the United States of America and the state of Florida. How are you today, Sir?"

Allie clenched her teeth and her eyes teared as she tried not to laugh.

"I'm calling about an old acquaintance of yours, Dr. Leopold Mann."

Andrew hesitated and listened. From what Allie could hear on the phone, Dr. Frankfurter also spoke very good English.

"Yes, he is here. Well, I'll get right to the point. We're planning a surprise for Dr. Mann, and would like to reach out to his wife. I was hoping you could help me locate her."

Andrew paused and nodded.

"Brigitte? Yes, that's her."

Allie took a deep breath and leaned closer towards Andrew.

"I didn't know that. Remarried. Oh, really?" Andrew signaled Allie with a thumbs-up.

Allie's eyes widened in anticipation.

"Wow, that could be near us." Andrew shot an even more enthusiastic thumbs up. "Awesome. I'll do that. What was that about his son, FRANZ, Sir?" Andrew's eyes bulged and honed in on Allie's.

Allie sat stunned, unable to accept the possibility of what she'd heard.

"Oh, okay. Really? Wow. That must have been hard on him." Andrew licked his upper lip. "Really? That's fascinating. How many?"

"How many what?" Allie searched the couch for something to write with. After a few seconds of frantic hunting, she finally found a pen under the pizza box. Allie grabbed it and held the pen so that it hovered tensely above a paper napkin.

Allie jotted down notes and felt she'd crawl out of her skin as Andrew chatted for 20 more minutes, thanked Dr. Frankfurter, and hung up.

"Really nice guy."

"Awesome, Andrew. I'll send him some strudel. What the heck did he say?"

"Okay. Where do I start? Dr. Mann was married to Brigitte who was an administrator at the University of Munich. Apparently, though a lovely lady, she didn't have the same interest in academics as Dr. Mann."

"I can totally understand that."

"They had one child, Franz--"

Allie gasped. "That cannot be a coincidence!"

"They went through an ugly divorce when Franz was about six. A few years later, Brigitte was back on her feet and married an American soldier stationed in Germany. It sounds like Dr. Mann remained married to his work and came to the United States. Dr. Frankfurter heard that Brigitte and the soldier moved to Florida years later when her husband was reassigned back in the states."

"So, she might still be in Florida?"

"Yes. Could be. Frankfurter didn't know her husband's name and lost contact with her after that."

"Anything else?"

"Yes, there is. He mentioned that Franz took the divorce hard. Dr. Mann told Frankfurter that he didn't communicate with his son because Franz never wanted to see him again. It really bothered Dr. Mann. Do you think it's possible that Dr. Mann didn't know your gunshot victim was his son?"

Allie shook her head and stared at the white wall. "I can't imagine that. Not recognizing your own son? He would at least have to remember the name. What about the other stuff you discussed? Was there anything else important?"

"Not really."

"You talked for almost 20 minutes about nothing? That's like a $60 call! I don't have that kind of money!"

"I told you, I've never done anything like this before!" Andrew threw his hands up. "So, I went with my gut. I was nice. Sue me!"

Allie opened her mouth to speak, then sat back on the sofa. "Okay, you're right. I'll only eat noodles for a month to pay for the call." Allie drew an 'X' over the notes she'd jotted on the napkin. "Back to the pertinent material. I can't see how Mann wouldn't recognize Franz Bergman, if he's his son. I assume the soldier who married his ex-wife, was named Bergman. If he happened to unknowingly do the autopsy on his long lost son, it would be like a 'Ripley's Believe It or Not' moment. I love that museum by the way."

"Me, too. We need to go some time."

"We'll do it, but right now, I think we should Google 'Brigitte Bergman' and see if she's still in Florida." Allie grabbed her laptop and started typing.

Andrew and Allie sat in near darkness as the blue light from the screen illuminated their faces.

"Well, there's no Brigitte Bergman, but there's a Brigitte B. McHenry near Camp Blanding." Andrew pointed to the 3rd name on the list.

"That's an Army base! My father took me camping near there once." Allie clicked on the name, and an age, phone number and address appeared.

"She's about the right age. Maybe the second husband didn't work out, either." Andrew touched the screen. "Want me to call her?"

"I'll do it. It might go over better if she hears a female voice." Allie felt fully rejuvenated and ready for action.

"Allie, I don't think hearing any voice at this time of night will go over well." Andrew rubbed his face then gave his head a vigorous shake. "I'm not used to keeping doctor's hours. Let me get a little sleep. I'll come back and you can call at a civilized time."

"Thanks, Andrew. I don't know what I'd do without you!"

CHAPTER SIXTY NINE
PRESENT DAY

Allie couldn't sleep a wink. When Andrew returned at 7:00, she greeted him with an energetic bounce.

"Are you ready to do this?" Allie held up her phone.

Andrew looked at his watch. "Don't you think we should wait until 8?"

"Chrystal will be up soon and I have to get to the morgue. If we wait until 8, Brigitte might leave her house. The worst thing that can happen is we wake her up."

"Okay, but be calm."

Before Andrew had a chance to sit, Allie entered the number and hit dial. She didn't have to wait long.

"Hello?" The woman who answered had a slight German accent. Allie smiled at Andrew, nodded and then placed her phone on speaker.

"Hi, I'm Dr. uhm, Dr..." Allie wrinkled her nose and glanced at Andrew. She covered the phone with her hand and whispered, "What do I say?"

"Just leave it at that."

Allie nodded and moved her hand. "I'm calling from the University of South Florida. I'm trying to reach Brigitte Bergman McHenry?"

"I'm Mrs. McHenry. What's this in reference to, Doctor?" Her voice was thin and slightly raspy.

"Mrs. Bergman, I'm sorry to call so early, but we're trying to gather information about your son...Franz Bergman?"

"You said you're Doctor who?"

"I'm Dr. Parsons."

Andrew waved his hands at her and shook his head.

"I'm attempting to find information about Franz Bergman. We are trying to put together a true history of him."

Allie heard Brigitte sigh and swallow hard. "Well, Dr. Parsons." Allie heard another deep breath. Her voice sounded husky. "You probably heard he was murdered a few weeks ago. He was...he was...brutally killed..." Brigitte's voice faded as she delivered the horrible news.

"I know. I'm very sorry for your loss, Mrs. McHenry. That's the case I'm working on now. We're trying to solve it." Allie did her best to sound professional, but realized a hint of sadness carried in her voice.

"Well." Brigitte cleared her throat. Because of her accent, Allie thought it sounded like 'vell'. "Thank you. I found out about it through the papers. I haven't seen him much in the last several years. He married an awful woman. She is controlling, manipulative and conniving. Have you met her?"

"A few times."

"She made Franz cut me out of his life. I've really never even seen my grandson."

"That must be rough. Do you hear from your grandson at all, Mrs. McHenry?"

"Well, they never let me visit him. He sends me a card for my birthday, but my cards to him are returned."

"That's got to be very difficult." Allie waited a moment, weighing her next words. "Mrs. McHenry, I understand Franz did not spend much time with his father. Is this true?" Allie felt her chest tighten and endured a suffocating sensation.

It seemed liked minutes before Brigitte answered.

"You have to understand. When Leopold and I divorced, Franz was devastated. He never wanted to see his father again."

"Leopold?" Allie hesitated and swallowed. "Leopold Mann?"

"Yes. You must have that information, Doctor. They were estranged."

"I'm sure that was hard on Franz."

Andrew reassured Allie with a broad smile and hand squeeze.

"Yes, it was. Yet...yet Franz turned out to be a good man and very smart." McHenry's voice grew stronger and gained momentum as she spoke. "You see, he loved books of all kinds and the theater and art. He absolutely adored children. And he was a good businessman. You know, he started his optics company at a young age and then sold it for a substantial sum, from what I understand. I can't grasp why anyone would want to kill him. And in such a brutal way." As Brigitte finished, her voice trailed away.

Allie nodded. "That's what we're looking into, Mrs. McHenry. I need to ask, do you have any pictures of Franz and Leopold? Any old letters or anything that could show something about their relationship?"

"Yes, of course."

Allie smiled and high fived Andrew.

"I have shoe boxes full of letters and pictures. But why do you want such things?"

"When you're working a homicide case, sometimes you find a connection in old records that may help solve it."

"I see. Well, if it would aid you in finding his killer, then I'll certainly provide what you need. I know Leopold works somewhere in that area and I have tried to contact him, but he won't return my calls or emails. He can be a very difficult person."

"You're not kidding..." Allie caught herself and cleared her throat. "I mean...sorry to hear that. But I think anything you can show us would be of immense help, Mrs. McHenry."

"I'll do what I can."

Allie nodded her head enthusiastically and Andrew whispered "Yes!" as he shook both fists victoriously above his head.

"Thank you so much for your help, Mrs. McHenry." Allie shrugged her shoulders and looked at Andrew who was closing his computer. "My partner and I need to meet with you and look at your pictures."

"Certainly. So, is that all, Dr. Parsons?"

"No..." Allie raised her hand. "One more thing. I'm not sure how to ask this, but has anyone tried to contact you saying he is Franz Bergman?"

"No!" Brigitte sounded horrified. "Why would anyone do such a thing?"

Allie stiffened and Andrew froze as he was putting away his computer.

"I didn't mean to scare you. It's just that...there are some disturbed people out there. I need to make sure you're aware. If anyone does contact you, please let me know."

"I can't imagine a human being doing such a thing. But I certainly will call you if they do."

"As I said, any pictures, letters, that sort of thing will be of immense help."

"I'll do my best, Dr. Parsons. Now, you're at the University of South Florida?"

"I'm in Tampa, but I can drive over to Camp Blanding on Friday with my partner if that's okay with you. We can be there around 10:00 AM."

"That would be fine. My husband passed away a few years ago and I don't drive much."

"We'll see you then. Thank you, Mrs. McHenry."

Allie extended her finger to end the call when Brigitte suddenly spoke. Her finger hovered above the phone.

"Since you're in Tampa and working on my son's murder, do you see my grandson, Isaac, at all? I have a card for him. If you could deliver it to him, I would be forever grateful."

"I'm not sure that's a good idea."

Andrew waved his hands and mouthed, 'No.'

"Why not? I'll call ahead and tell them to expect you, Dr. Parsons."

"Please, don't tell Jess I've spoken to you."

"Why not?"

Allie paused and frowned as she desperately tried to think of something to say. "Well, uhm...we'd rather not let people outside our investigative force know where the investigation is going."

"Is Jess a suspect?"

"I have to keep that information confidential."

Andrew covered his face with a pillow.

"It's on a need to know basis only, Mrs. McHenry." Allie cleared her throat. "For example, you need to know some things, like we'll be there Friday."

"I see."

For several seconds, no one spoke. Allie could hear Andrew groan from beneath the pillow.

"Okay, Mrs. McHenry." She squinted and gritted her teeth while rubbing her forehead. "I'll pick up Isaac's card and deliver it to him. If that helps you out, I'll be happy to do it. Jess may not want to talk to me, but I'll get that card to him."

"Are you two not on speaking terms?"

Allie shook her head and cleared her throat. "Once again, that's a need to know thing, Mrs. McHenry. It rears its ugly head a second time, unfortunately. But we have your home address near Camp Blanding and my partner and I'll be there Friday around 10:00."

"Okay..." Brigitte's voice trailed off. "Bye bye, Dr. Parsons."

Allie clicked off her phone and laid it on her lap. "Why do I have to keep talking when I should just be silent?"

Andrew pulled the pillow off his face. "That was crazy. I'm not sure how she took it. She probably thinks we're in some clandestine government agency. Why did you tell her your real name?"

"Because I'm a terrible liar and I thought I would come across as sincere if I told the truth. I think I saved it, though. I pulled it together at the end. But at least we can see how part of this tangled web is woven together."

"Well, maybe she thinks you're an honest goofball. Why did you ask if she had heard from someone claiming to be her son?"

"Because I thought he might try to get in touch with her. It was a long shot."

"Nice try!" Andrew threw the pillow at Allie.

"I'll do better when we see her on Friday." Allie scooped the pillow from the floor. "When we get the DNA back we're going to prove that Franz Bergman wasn't killed, and that Dr. Mann is his father. Maybe, then we can get some real answers about what's going on around here."

"I hope you're right." Andrew looked at his watch. "Well, I gotta run. I really don't want to be here when Chrystal gets up."

Allie threw the pillow at Andrew. "Coward!"

CHAPTER SEVENTY
PRESENT DAY

As Allie poured cereal into her daughter's favorite bowl, she heard the sound of shuffling feet. A few seconds later, Chrystal moved zombie-like through the doorway towards the refrigerator. The bright light from the bare bulb in the ceiling seemed to annoy Chrystal, who shielded her eyes.

"Hey, Sweetie." Allie's voice lilted like an actor in a children's show. "You look tired. How are you doing?"

"Tired." Chrystal pulled the refrigerator door. Her lids barely opened as she stared into the brightly lit but sparse interior.

"Sorry, to hear that, but I can see why, since you got in so late last night." Allie shrugged. "Hey, listen I have a great idea! Let's hit the beach Saturday. Just you and me, like we used to do. I'm going to be out of town most of Friday, but we can go to Clearwater or Sand Key on Saturday. Walk through the shops. It'll be a lot of fun."

"Mother, I'm really tired." Chrystal grabbed a milk carton, shut the door and shuffled towards the table. "And Carly has this great party planned for Saturday. It's part of the 'Spring to Graduation Dance'. I can't miss it. I'm going to help her set up."

"Sounds fun. I can meet you after you guys get it ready."

"It'll take all day. Carly really needs me to be there. She's having fights with her boyfriend."

Chrystal pulled her thick terry cloth robe tightly around her thin shoulders as she sat down. She tipped the carton and poured milk into her bowl of cereal.

"Oh. A dance. Really? Are you going with anyone?"

"Rowdy asked me. I don't really like him, but he'll do."

"Chrystal, you don't have to settle."

"I know. But I'm okay with it, now."

"You should never be okay with settling. Ever. Rowdy's an interesting boy, but--"

"Mother, I need a date for this dance and he's a decent one, and I want to go with him!"

"Okay. I definitely want to see you guys before you leave. It's your first date. I need to get pictures. We have to remember this milestone. I didn't realize you had a dance coming up. I can drop you guys off at the school and pick you up."

"You didn't ask."

"I didn't ask what, Honey?"

"You didn't ask if I had a dance."

"True." Allie took a gulp of coffee. "Of course, I don't ask about dances every day, but now I know to start inquiring every night if you have a prom tomorrow."

"You're being sarcastic and argumentative."

"Excellent vocabulary, young lady."

"We're all getting dressed at Carly's and then her mother is driving us to school."

"I see. That's very generous of Carly's mother. Do you want to get a new dress?"

"Grandmother mailed me one from New York."

"Oh, your Grandmother. I see. I'm sorry you never asked me about it. May I see it? What's it like? Is it pretty?"

"It's at Carly's. You can see it tomorrow."

"Okay. So, I'll drive over to Carly's to take pictures, then."

Chrystal took another bite of cereal. "If you want to, but be on time, because we need to get to the dance early."

"How about doing something on Sunday?"

"I'll see. I'm probably busy."

"What do you have to do?"

Chrystal stood up. "I've got to get ready for school. Sorry."

Allie watched Chrystal drop her spoon in her bowl and shuffle towards the bedroom. Already late for work, Allie sat down at the table and stared silently at the walls, lost in her thoughts as her daughter brushed past.

Allie thought her arguments with Chrystal sounded like past fights with her own mother. During many of those clashes with Bea, Allie remembered being high, drunk or planning to get that way as soon as possible. Her goal had been to escape the house and its rules, find some friends and deaden her anger and anxiety by inhaling, drinking or smoking some substance.

She was wrenched from her unhappy memories when she heard Chrystal's sandals shuffling on the rug, then smacking the linoleum floor that lay before the door. Allie raised her head and turned at the sound.

"See you tonight--" The slamming door interrupted her goodbye. After that, Allie heard only Chrystal's sandals, as her daughter ran outside and down the stairs.

"--Honey." Allie finished her sentence to the empty room.

Allie pursed her lips and leaned back in the chair. She rubbed her nose and scratched her ear and then nervously ran her fingers through her hair.

When she was a teenager, she had several hiding places in her bedroom for cigarettes and various illegal substances. Despite her mother's efforts, none of them were ever discovered, not even a hallucinogenic mushroom.

Let's face it, I've got cigarettes hidden in this place.

She turned towards the shared bedroom and rubbed her lips.

I couldn't...Chrystal wouldn't...

Allie faced the table again and sighed.

Chrystal does call it a shared bedroom, which makes that room as much mine as hers. Why should I feel guilty about looking through my own bedroom?

Allie gritted her teeth and sighed. Maybe I'm just hunting for something I lost. Like a button dropped off my jeans last year. Who's to say it's not under the mattress or hidden in a box in the closet? It could happen.

Allie shook her head and moaned. Aagh. She pounded the table with her fists, took another deep breath and stood up. She eased towards the bedroom.

Allie thought about a time many years ago when her mother burst into her room and began a frantic hunt for drugs. Allie had screamed, cursed and hissed.

Allie's search would be less dramatic.

She walked directly to the closet and opened the door. A sudden squeak of the hinges made her jump.

Allie paused to let her heart and breathing slow, then reached down and rummaged through two shoeboxes below, but found only sandals. A quick search of the drawers and cabinets revealed nothing but a button that may very well have come from Allie's jeans.

There you go. She held the button and looked around the room with satisfaction. I knew I was right. I wonder what else I've lost that I can find?

Feeling vindicated by discovering the button, she renewed her search of the shared bedroom with more determination. Allie opened all the drawers and hunted for secret doors and compartments. She removed the battery cover to the alarm clock and examined every location that could possibly serve as a hiding spot, including the back of the headboard of the bed.

The old copper pot that Chrystal bought at an estate sale and used as a vase, held only flowers. There was nothing taped behind a landscape scene Chrystal had painted.

Though happy to find nothing, Allie knew her daughter could be more devious and creative when it came to hiding contraband.

After nearly 30 minutes, only one other place remained.

The mattress.

CHAPTER SEVENTY ONE
PRESENT DAY

With great trepidation Allie lifted the mattress. She prayed it would yield nothing. However, when the mattress peeled away from the bedsprings, she felt a pang of panic.

Allie gasped.

Just under the mattress, hidden in the center near the foot of the bed, she saw a thin, brown box, about a foot long and a foot wide.

Clearly, Chrystal meant to keep this secret.

Allie sighed and the sound of her breath echoed off the white walls. Chrystal! She moaned and dropped the mattress. It landed with a soft thud. Come on, that was too easy!

For a second, Allie contemplated walking out of the room, as if she hadn't found anything. However, since she'd rationalized her way through a thorough search, she couldn't back down now that she'd uncovered Chrystal's secret stash. Allie had to get some answers and confront her daughter if necessary.

They needed to start healing. They needed to watch the 'Sound of Music' again.

Allie turned from the door and faced the bed. She lifted the mattress and pushed it above her head.

Like a mole, she burrowed beneath the mattress, and, while it rested on her shoulders, retrieved the box. She stood up as the heavy weight clanged onto the frame.

Allie shook her head and felt the static electricity generated by the mattress and box springs lift the hairs that ran along the back of her neck and across the tattoo. The sturdy brown box she held in her hands had been elaborately decorated with a design of intertwining gold vines along the borders.

She recognized it as a gift from her mother to Chrystal for her 10th birthday. The ornate box, crafted to last for decades, had once held elegant stationary.

Allie lifted the top of the box, afraid of what she might find. However, she was completely unprepared for what lay before her.

Inside, she discovered a painting done in rich, vibrant acrylics. Allie knew Chrystal's style and recognized this as a portrait of Bea. It resembled a photograph Chrystal kept on her nightstand.

Chrystal's painting demonstrated warmth in Bea that Allie hadn't felt in many years. The painted smile was softer than the one in the photo and her mother's eyes sparkled. The painting portrayed a kind soul, and Allie couldn't resist studying it silently.

Well done, Honey. She placed the painting gently on the mattress.

Allie found another portrait beneath Bea's and instantly recognized that face.

Jess Bergman.

Allie took a deep breath. Oh, my gosh!

Once again the painting captured a sense of warmth and affection, depicting Jess laughing and looking towards the sky. Chrystal had done an excellent job of illustrating Jess' exuberance and vitality. As she held the edges and deliberated over the painting, Allie half expected the head to turn towards her and sneer.

Wow! Allie positioned the painting next to her mother's portrait.

The last painting really caught Allie's attention.

At first, it appeared to be a hideous beast, like something out of an R-rated version of Dante's *Inferno*. Allie studied the muscular monster closely.

To her shock, Allie realized she was staring at the back of her own neck. The painting represented Chrystal's interpretation of the demon tattoo that Allie tried to cover with her hair. In addition to the tattoo, Chrystal had painted a stone wall surrounding her head.

Allie took a deep breath. She bit her lower lip and fought to hold back the tears.

Serves me right. She tried to hide it from me.

Allie wiped her eye and carefully replaced the paintings in the box. Then she lifted the mattress and slid it back to its hiding spot.

Chrystal conveyed no warmth or kindness in the painting of Allie. Her mother and Jess had faired far better. Allie wiped her eye again and walked towards the door.

Time for work... another place that offered no compassion.

CHAPTER SEVENTY TWO
PRESENT DAY

The potentially disastrous repercussions of arriving after 10:00 AM consumed Allie's thoughts.

If she got lucky, she might be able to save her job.

At least for another month, or so.

The piped-in orchestral arrangement of 'Copa Cobana' concluded its serenade as the elevator arrived at the fifth floor.

I dove off the Bergman's balcony without being seen... and no broken bones, either. I know I can do this.

The soothing elevator music faded and the doors opened with a harsh 'ping!' Allie hesitated before stepping off. She hoped somehow she could wind her way to her desk without Byron or Dr. Mann noticing her.

It appeared no one was around.

Allie sighed and stepped from the elevator into the cold, air-conditioned hall.

"Dr. Mann wants to see you!" Byron had pounced as soon as she exited the elevator.

"Oh, Byron!" Allie, jumped. "You scared me. Just give me a second. What's it about?" Allie raised her eyebrows and bit her lip, attempting to appear surprised at Byron's harsh reception.

"He wants to see you NOW, Allie."

"I heard you."

"RIGHT NOW!"

"Honestly, Byron. Chill!" Allie's cheeks flushed. "I'm walking over there now. Right now! Back off! Jeez. Cool your jets."

Allie crossed the hall with Byron close behind, and knocked on Dr. Mann's newly reinforced door.

"I'm not going to escape, Byron. You can cut me a little slack. Please."

"Come in!"

Allie opened the door. "You asked to see me, Dr. Mann?" She tightened the muscles in her jaw.

"Sit down, Dr. Parsons." Mann motioned towards the seat in front of his imposing desk. He raised his eyes from a thick medical chart and pulled his glasses away from his nose. "And please, be calm. You can be so reactionary, like a raw nerve in a petri dish."

"Comfy chair." Allie bounced a couple times and patted the chair arms.

"Dr. Parsons, I'm going to jump right in. I've had some bad reports about you."

Allie nodded. "I thought you might have. Obviously, there are areas I can improve in, but I think I've done an adequate job under the circumstances. I've worked hard, but there's a lot to learn, as you've pointed out, yourself." Allie took a deep breath and slumped further into the chair. She could feel the tendons strain in her neck.

"As usual, a poor presentation and additionally--"

"Next time give me time to prepare!"

"What?" Mann lifted his glasses.

Allie clasped her hands and brought them tightly to her chest. "If you'd given me time to respond to these charges I could have prepared something better for you to hear!"

Allie did her best to emulate one of the speeches Duncan had used successfully on her behalf.

Mann growled. "You have some nerve, Parsons! Saying such things to me!"

"I'm doing my best to show you I belong here. What are your concerns with my performance, Dr. Mann?"

Mann gave a derisive laugh and shook his head. "What concerns me are the facts! You've been leaving early, arriving late and taking personal calls when I'm gone. You said you would represent the department at a Pathology meeting and you failed to do so."

Allie opened her mouth to speak.

"Your name was not on the register, so apparently you took a few hours off. And you've been second guessing Bergman's case to outsiders instead of bringing your concerns to me."

"You're right."

"Of course, I am." Mann scratched his beard and smirked.

"I'm doing my best. If my best isn't good enough, it's because I've been under a lot of pressure."

"That's the life of a doctor, Parsons." Mann replaced his glasses and lifted his nose. "One I'm not sure you're equipped to handle, frankly."

"I'm talking about the pressure of dealing with all these anonymous notes."

Mann raised his eyes from the charts, stared at her and tilted his head. "I guess you're talking about the notes the police are investigating as possibly being from Toro.

"Yeah. I haven't gotten any other notes. Plus, my daughter has been away a lot."

"The notes are fake! Toro was killed! If you can't accept that...if you are going to obsess over forgeries, then I have no use for you! Listen to me, Parsons."

"Dr. Mann--"

"Listen, I say!"

Blown away by his booming voice, Allie leaned back and gripped the arms of the chair tightly.

"Do not yell at me, Dr. Mann!"

"Dr. Parsons. Listen to me. I can only give you so much time and it is rapidly running out."

"I realize that, Dr. Mann, but there's a lot going on here. You can't ignore that fact that there's evidence about--"

"Consider this your two week warning. If there's no change in two weeks, you're out of my morgue and probably out of the program. That means another resident will be appointed to this position. Molly is still expressing interest in being here. She was number one in your class, you know."

"I keep being informed of that. Thanks for letting me know our class ranks haven't changed since graduation."

"There's a strong possibility you'll lose your housing. I'm sure you understand the implications."

Allie's mind raced as she considered her options. "Two weeks?"

"Two weeks. I expect marked improvement. No taking time off. No personal phone calls. No talking or gossiping about old cases. Am I understood?"

Allie stared past Dr. Mann, through the large window and towards downtown Tampa. "Seems kind of sudden, Dr. Mann. Chrystal and I could lose our dorm? Sir, that's our home. We've lived there for years."

"You're getting a warning, Allie. I've fired other people on the spot. Byron feels you should be terminated, but I've decided to be lenient. You're lucky, young lady."

"Thank you." Allie took a deep breath. "By the way, how are you feeling? Byron and I are worried about you."

"Don't worry about me. Worry about yourself."

"I'll...I'll look after myself." Allie stood. "I don't suppose there's a good time to let you know this, so I'll tell you now. I need to have tomorrow morning off."

"Tomorrow off?" Mann tilted his head. "Why's that?"

Allie scratched the back of her neck. "Because I've got a previous personal appointment that I can't reschedule. I'm embarrassed to talk about it. But, I promise this will be the last one."

Dr. Mann rubbed his chin and glanced back down at his papers. "Just the morning?"

"I'll be back in the afternoon, about 3:00. And I'll work late into the evening. I just have to keep this appointment."

"What is it?"

"It's personal, something I really don't like to talk about. Sort of a female doctor sort of appointment, if you know what I mean, Sir." Allie lowered her gaze in embarrassment.

"Fine. Be back tomorrow afternoon and we'll start anew. You can go now."

"Dr. Mann, I promise, I'll be a solid investigator and become an excellent pathologist for this morgue." Allie eyed the top of Mann's head.

"I'm so glad to hear that, Dr. Parsons." He didn't look up, but casually turned a page from the large stack of papers in front of him. "Promise me you'll do as you're told."

"I'll make the most of my second chance."

Mann grunted and continued flipping through the papers.

Allie nodded, turned and walked quietly to the door. As her hand touched the cold handle, she heard Mann clear his throat.

"You didn't promise."

"Promise what?"

"To do as you're told. We've been over this before."

Allie hesitated in front of his door without turning around. "Yeah. You don't have to worry. I'll do my job, Dr. Mann. I'll work in the best interest of the citizens of Florida. The people living in that big city through your window."

"Two weeks, Allie. I expect to see marked improvement. That's all you have."

"Yes, Sir." Allie closed the door and strode down the hall towards the morgue.

Two weeks ought to be enough time for me to figure this out. Allie walked defiantly past Byron and towards her office. *Then we'll see whose head's on the chopping block, Mister!*

CHAPTER SEVENTY THREE
PRESENT DAY

At 7:11, Allie watched from a morgue window as Byron started his car. He backed out of his designated parking spot and Allie hurried down the stairs towards to the lobby. Halfway down, she texted Chrystal.

"Is salad okay?"

When Allie reached the front doors of the morgue, Chrystal replied. "Have to study with Carly for big math test."

"Salad?" Allie texted back.

"I'll eat here."

Allie sighed.

She started her Honda, dialed the genetics lab and waited. Despite the hour, she took a chance; lab techs kept odd hours.

After three rings, someone picked up.

"Genetics lab, Joe Shoe."

"Joe. Oh, my gosh."

"It's me, that's right. Uhm, who are you?"

"Allie! You're sure working late. It's lucky I caught you."

"Allie Parsons?"

"Yeah."

"Awesome! So what's up?"

"Well, just praying you'd still be there."

"Wow. It's awesome to hear that I'm the answer to your prayers! I've got some stuff to do, but then I'm free. I work late, then I sleep

FRANK C. SCHWALBE

late. Pretty much got the run of the place as long as the work gets done, if you know what I mean."

"Sounds like a great situation. But, how long before you get those DNA results, Joe?"

"You're not into small talk, I can tell."

"Not now, Joe. Right now, I'm not into that at all." Allie drummed her fingertips on the steering wheel.

"That's totally cool, Allie. I can respect that. So what's up?"

"When's the DNA going to be back?"

"The DNA?"

"The stuff I left you on the glass."

"Oh, yeah. That. Let me check. I'll put you on hold. Enjoy the sounds of the serene 'on hold' music."

Allie heard him lay the phone down on the counter and then the squeak of his tennis shoes. Out of habit, she checked the rearview mirror.

Allie could discern the sound of keyboard clicks and computer beeps, then Joe returned to the phone.

"Allie, you there?"

"Yeah. Thanks for getting me off hold."

"At a minimum, two to three weeks."

"Two to three weeks!" She raised her free hand and slapped the top of the steering wheel.

"Yeah. Maybe more. We're backlogged like you wouldn't believe."

"Listen, Joe. I...no... The morgue can't wait any longer than two weeks. Do you understand?"

"Allie. It's busy. I'm working as fast as I can. You gave me no paperwork. I'm trying to get through all the red tape and everything and get you a result as quickly as I can, and not lose the job I've had for 20 years."

"My daughter is depending on this, Joe. We need our dorm."

"Your daughter? Your dorm? What does that have to do with this?"

350

"Joe. Just... put a rush on it."

"What case is this? I've got no paperwork, nothing."

"It's a case that's very important to me, Joe. This needs to be completed real soon."

"So, what about your daughter?"

Allie shook her head and sighed in frustration. "Okay, listen. Forget I said anything about my daughter or my dorm. They're not relevant. Just...just get me the results."

"I'm trying my best for you, Allie. I'm not sure what you'll do with this when the results come back, because the documentation is so far out of whack. But I'm doing my best."

"Joe..." Allie took a deep breath. "Joe. I'm so sorry... you're right. I'm getting carried away."

"Really?"

"You know, I get really--"

"Ambitious."

"Yes." Allie glanced in her rear view mirror again.

"I can tell. You're one of those career types. Type A personality. Lean on people and get what you want."

"So true, Joe. You nailed it."

"Heading up that Academic ladder, Allie."

"As fast as I can."

"Careful. It's a long way to fall."

"I'm not scared of heights, so the sky's the limit." Allie rolled her eyes and cringed.

"I'll work on pushing those samples through. Can't promise what I'll be able to do, but you can count on Joe Shoe. Remember, though, when you're Chairman, I want you to reward those who helped you out."

"Try to get the results before two weeks."

"Are you pressuring me?"

"I am, because I know you can handle the heat."

"Then, I'm on it."

"Thanks. Bye." Allie ended the call and stared at her picture of Chrystal for several seconds. Hopefully, Chrystal wouldn't be out too late and Allie could manage to get some sleep.

She needed to be sharp when she met Brigitte McHenry in the morning.

CHAPTER SEVENTY FOUR
PRESENT DAY

"This is great scenery, Allie." Andrew stared through the passenger window of the Honda, his chin resting wearily on his hand. "Don't get me wrong, I love miles and miles of green and flat. Occasionally interrupted by something a little greener or flatter."

Andrew's head moved side to side as he gazed at the cows that grazed on the thick green grass on the many pastures they passed. "I'm really enjoying the ride, and the scintillating company, but this whole thing has got me stressed. I don't mind telling you."

Allie slowed the car to a crawl as they reached the city limits of the tiny town of Waldo, a notorious speed trap that got most of its revenue from unsuspecting motorists. So absorbed in looking for the local police and their radar guns, Allie didn't acknowledge Andrew's comments.

"I mean, Brigitte didn't really seem keen on having us visit. Especially after all that 'need to know' stuff you threw at her. I can find pictures of Mann and Bergman on line, I bet. Give me a chance to try. We don't even need to talk to this lady."

"It's going to be fine!" Allie braked upon seeing a blue police car that protruded from behind an abandoned barn. "And it's better than hacking."

"Is it, Allie? Is it, really?"

"You worry too much." As the front of the Honda passed the town limit sign, she roared the engine and accelerated up to 60 MPH. "I've got it covered. I have two weeks to produce the evidence to prove I'm right."

"What's Mann going to do? Fire you?"

"Yep."

"Ah, he wouldn't do that."

"Don't bet on it. He's already threatened it."

"Really?"

"We had a little talk."

"What did he say?"

"It was the usual final warning speech from a manager. I've got two weeks to straighten up, or else."

"Are you worried?"

"Not too much. What he doesn't realize is that I've had the same threats so many times before. At this point in my life, I'm pretty tough to intimidate. But I do need to get this done soon. I have to be back at work this afternoon so I'm not fired tomorrow. And, most importantly, I need to take pictures of Chrystal before her dance on Saturday."

"I do understand that. So, how much further?"

"Probably about an hour. You're sure to get a ticket if you speed here."

After 40 minutes of flying through the pine forests that surrounded Highways 301 and 16 and creeping through the small towns that dotted the highway, Allie finally found the small road she was searching for. She pulled off the pavement and bounced onto a rough, sandy lane shortly before 10:00 AM.

"That's it." She pointed towards a modest ranch home just off the road. It was a simple squat, cinder block house surrounded by tall pine trees. The forest extended for miles and the thin trunks seemed to form a log wall around Allie's car.

"She's out in the middle of nowhere." Andrew scanned the surroundings.

"You ain't kiddin'. Okay. We'll meet Brigitte, win her over with our charm, get some pictures or letters and get out."

"I'd like to emphasize the get out part."

Allie shifted the Honda into second gear and rocked along the dirt road to the house. Seconds later, she stopped near the door. "Let's do this."

They fist bumped and climbed out of the Honda.

As Allie stepped from the car, the front door swung open with a loud squeak. It was difficult to see inside the dark house, but lurking just inside the closed screen door appeared to be a thin, short woman with long, silver hair.

"Mrs. McHenry. Hi. I'm Dr. Parsons and this is--"

The woman pushed the screen open with what appeared to be a long pole. "Do not take another step!"

Allie recognized the voice as Brigitte, and on closer inspection, she could see the pole was actually a shotgun.

"What the..." Andrew stepped back.

"Get back in your car! I've called the police! You're not investigating Franz, Dr. Parsons. You had something to do with killing him! Get back in your vehicle now or I'll shoot!"

"Mrs. McHenry, please be calm." Allie raised her hand and took a step towards the house.

Brigitte pushed the gun out further. "I'll shoot you! I will! Get back in your car!"

"Allie, I think we should get out of here, pronto." Andrew cautiously backed behind the car door.

"Listen, Mrs. McHenry, I don't know who you've been talking to, but you've been misinformed. We're on your side. You have to believe me!"

Brigitte lowered the gun to wipe a long strand of gray hair from her eyes and then heaved it back to her shoulder. "I spoke with my family and they told me the whole truth. They're coming to visit with Isaac. I'll finally see my grandson! I was told to call the police when you show up. I've already done that."

"Allie, I feel pretty strongly we should leave." Andrew stood frozen behind the car door. "Let's get out of here and use the computer."

"Shhh. I've got this, Andrew." Allie clasped her hands together. "Mrs. McHenry, I think you could be in danger."

Brigitte raised the shotgun and fired it in the air. "That's on a need to know basis, Dr. Parsons."

She and Andrew jumped when the gun went off. Allie thought she felt the hot, pressurized air from the discharge. Pellets whistled above her like fireworks.

"Allie! We're going to die!"

They jumped in the car and slammed their doors simultaneously. Allie started the Honda.

"Is she nuts! My life flashed before my eyes! My grandfather called for me to join him and he's been dead for fifteen years! What just happened, Allie?" Andrew covered his nose with his trembling hands.

The Honda's engine revved and its tires squealed.

"I'm worried she told Jess about us, even though I warned her not to." Allie looked over her shoulder and backed down the road.

"That double crossing--"

"Yeah, well, my guess is that Jess told her she could see Isaac if she called the police and didn't show us any photos or letters or whatever. But no problem, I'll be getting back to work early, and you'll get a chance to use the internet to find photos of Bergman and Mann."

"Was that not my original idea?"

"Yes, it was. You were right."

"Thank you. She said she called the cops. Do you think she did?"

"We haven't broken any laws. Don't worry about it. I know how to handle the police."

"I can't afford a lawyer, Allie."

"Neither can I."

"I know some excellent law students. They'd give us a discount."

"It's all good. We'll get gas and then head home."

"I just need to calm down." Andrew leaned back in his seat and ran his hands through his long, black hair. He blinked, as if having trouble focusing. "I've never been shot at before. It's terrifying, but kind of exhilarating at the same time. I appreciate life so much more now." He turned his head and looked out the passenger window. "The trees are so green. I didn't realize there are so many shades of green." Andrew leaned towards the windshield. "And I didn't notice those violet flowers on the drive here. They're beautiful. Did you see the rabbit?"

"No, I didn't see the rabbit."

"He was eating. It was incredible."

Allie glanced in her rear view mirror and spotted blinding blue lights rapidly closing in on her car. The sound of sirens grew louder.

"I thought you said the police wouldn't be a problem?"

"I've got this. Don't worry."

"Were you speeding? You said you shouldn't speed."

"It's fine. Calm down." Allie slowed the car. "We haven't done anything wrong." She pulled into a gas station parking lot and coasted towards the air pump and stopped.

Allie unfastened her seatbelt and opened the door. "I'll tell them that she invited us to her house and then uninvited us and we left. End of story."

"I believe it. Hopefully, they will."

"I'll be back in a minute."

As Allie stepped out of the car, two more police cruisers pulled in beside the first, their tires crushing the white, dusty gravel. All of the officers jumped out and crouched behind the open car doors with their guns drawn.

"Police! Get down on the ground with your hands behind your head!"

"Allie. Uhm, Allie. Time to start talking!"

CHAPTER SEVENTY FIVE
PRESENT DAY

"Hey, what'd I do?" Allie approached the closest squad car. "We were invited to Mrs. McHenry's house."

"I'm not going to tell you again!" The policeman pointed his gun at her chest. "Get down on the ground, now!"

"Calm down, Officer. This is going too far." Allie kneeled down, then lay on her stomach. She folded her hands behind her head.

"You! Passenger! Step out of the vehicle with your hands above your head and lay on the ground!"

Andrew opened the door and stepped out.

"Slowly!"

"It's hard to move slow when you're shaking so fast. Allie, when do we come to the part where you take care of all this?" Andrew flattened himself on the ground.

"I don't know what they feed these cops around here, but they're way too aggressive."

"Stop talking!" The taller policeman seemed to be calling the shots.

Like a well-oiled machine, the officers rushed Allie and Andrew, pinned their arms behind their backs, frisked them, cuffed them then hauled them to their feet.

"What the.... what are you guys doing, you thugs?"

They were shoved towards different squad cars.

Allie resisted.

"Don't make me use my stick!" The shorter policeman pushed Allie hard.

"Don't make me shove it--"

"Allie, stop right there! I wouldn't say that."

"They're acting like gorillas!"

"They said you were a real wild thing, Doctor." The short policeman pushed her head down and shoved her into the backseat.

Allie landed on her side, but righted herself. "Who are they?"

"Tampa PD. Detective Festoon. Ever heard of him?"

"Do yourself a favor and don't listen to a thing he says. And what does he care if I drive to Camp Blanding? It's a free country."

"Not for you, right now. You're wanted for breaking and entering and theft." The tall cop slid into the driver's seat. His partner popped into the passenger's side, and the car rolled out of the dusty parking lot. The driver quickly recited her Miranda rights.

Suddenly, Allie felt the wind leave her chest. She tried, but she couldn't take a deep breath. "Breaking and entering? Really?"

"You got pale all of a sudden there, Doc. Have a look at this picture they sent us." The policeman sitting in the passenger seat held up a photo. Despite the poor quality, Allie closed her eyes when she saw the image of herself dressed in an apron hanging from Isaac's balcony. It must have come from the Bergman's security camera, and there was no doubt it was her face. Allie's good eye was angled up and her artificial one was looking straight ahead.

"You look like a fly caught in a spider's web, Doc."

"Put it away."

"Better put it away, Bob. They said she can get mean when she's angry."

The short cop hesitated, then placed the picture in an envelope and turned around. "Just wanted to let you know this is more than a courtesy ride back to Tampa." He dropped the envelope at his feet.

"How did you end up hanging like that?" The driver looked at Allie over his shoulder.

"Stupid crooks!" Bob laughed.

"Yeah, well, I'm here now, aren't I? If that was me, it means I got down without an injury. I bet it's more than you guys could do."

"So, you're admitting that's you in the picture?"

"No. For the people listening to this recording..." Allie looked at the ceiling of the squad car. "I'm not admitting to anything except I'm being charged unjustly with a felony."

"You're something else."

"Why are you holding Andrew? He didn't do anything wrong."

"I know. We're letting him go. It's you we want."

CHAPTER SEVENTY SIX
PRESENT DAY

Festoon left Allie to stew alone in the small interrogation room for nearly an hour. While on the hard, bare wooden chair, she squirmed and did everything within her power to keep from going crazy. She alternated between slumping, leaning forward and resting her elbows on the tiny, plastic table.

An annoying panel of a one-way mirror mounted on the wall in front of her, dominated the room. She knew cops sat on the other side of the mirror, spying on her, but she couldn't see them. Every now and again, Allie would look directly at the mirror, roll her eyes and shake her head.

Finally, the door flew open and Festoon waddled in with Westbrook.

"Knock, knock! I'm not interrupting anything, am I?"

Allie slumped back in the chair. "I want a lawyer. I'm not saying anything until I'm appointed a lawyer."

"I'm surprised your mother hasn't sent one of her vermin scurrying over here."

"I've got other sources."

"Allie Florence Parsons." Pug grinned and shook his head.

"Why do you have to use my full name when you're about to give me a hard time, Pug?"

"That's Detective Festoon, and I'm asking the questions here, Allie Florence Parsons. So, you just sit back and enjoy my company." He plopped down on the chair and smiled.

"I demand my lawyer. I'm not saying anything until I have my lawyer."

"You know, you're charged with breaking and entering into Jess Bergman's house?"

"Someone along the line mentioned that."

"And theft."

"What did I take?"

"They're missing a glass."

"A glass?"

"Yes, a crystal glass. Did you take it?"

"I've got plenty of glasses. Why would I want her's? What I do want, is my lawyer."

"Why were you in her house, Allie? Anything to do with that evidence you promised Westbrook and me in the diner? Hmm? Anything?"

Allie lowered her head and shook it. "Not talking."

"Why are you tormenting Jess Bergman? She just lost her husband. And then you approached her son?"

Allie sat up and shook her head. "Really! Lost her husband? Pug, look at her! She just threw a party, for crying out loud. Doesn't that raise any red flags around here?"

"People grieve in different ways. When my grandmother died I--"

"Please don't tell me you invited a couple hundred of your closest friends over and had a cocktail party."

"No, I went fishin' and people thought that was weird."

"He's alive Pug! Franz Bergman is alive!" Allie slammed her fists on the table. "Don't you get it! Don't any of you people get it! That wasn't his body we autopsied and cremated. It was somebody else."

"Why do you keep saying that?"

"Because his medical records don't match the autopsy results! Because his son kept calling for him!"

"His son?"

"Isaac."

"When was this?"

"I'm not saying anything else."

Westbrook leaned forward. "Dr. Parsons, please. Think about this. If he isn't Franz Bergman, why would Mrs. Bergman say he is? And then why would she insist James Smith killed him? What you're suggesting makes no sense, Dr. Parsons."

"I don't know why she's doing it but I'm sure she's lying about her husband's murder."

"Fine. But Dr. Mann, who I might add, unlike you, is immensely respected in his field, says it was Franz Bergman that was killed in the Bergman house." Festoon pointed his pudgy finger at Allie.

"Dr. Mann is lying."

"Incredible!" Festoon crossed his arms and leaned back in his chair. "Unbelievable. We may be adding a slander charge to our growing list. Care to explain?"

Allie started to speak, then shook her head.

"Hmm? I didn't catch that, Allie."

"It's because, when I told him about my concerns over the identification of the body, he sent a phony DNA test to prove it was Bergman, instead of performing a legitimate one."

"And that's it. And you can prove it?"

"Yes, I can prove it. It will take me a few more days. Only a few more days."

"I won't hold my breath."

"And there's something else."

"What?"

Allie sighed. "You won't believe me."

"What have you got to lose? You've dug a hole so deep you might as well keep on to Shanghai."

"Okay, fine. Franz Bergman is Mann's son and he never let anyone know."

"What?" Festoon laughed. "I think all those drugs you took finally fried your brain."

Allie crossed her arms and glared at Festoon. "It's true. I can prove it."

"How?" Festoon shook his head.

"Call Dr. Rhinehardt Frankfurter at the University of Munich and he'll tell you."

Pug and Westbrook burst into laughter.

"Oh, my gracious." Festoon wiped the tears from his eyes. "Westbrook, don't call Germany, call the psychiatrist. I just can't take this anymore. She's hearing voices. Dr. Frankfurter, really Allie? Does he work with Sammy Salami? Did they build Frankenstein?"

"It's true!" Allie leaned forward and shook her fists. "Listen to me! Ask Franz Bergman's mother! That's who we were going to see at Camp Blanding!"

"Stop, please. Actually, I'm starting to feel sorry for you."

"Don't feel sorry for me! It is true, Pug. It's for real. Franz Bergman is his son, Detective Westbrook." She turned towards the other officer. "Please, believe me. You're the brains around here. I've got evidence cooking! It will just take another week or two. Please, believe me!"

Pug and Westbrook stood up.

"Okay, here's what's going to happen. You're going to be booked, jailed and arraigned this afternoon. Bail will be set." Festoon placed his hands in his pockets.

"I know how this works." Allie stood. "I need to make a phone call."

"Alright, you can call your lawyer."

"No. I want to call my daughter." Allie wiped her eye. "I'm going to miss her dance."

CHAPTER SEVENTY SEVEN
PRESENT DAY

"**H**ey! I need to take a look at my phone real quick!" Allie yelled from behind the bars of her Orient Road Jail cell. She directed her shouts towards the tall, uniformed female guard standing only five feet away, but on the free side. Allie barely reached the large woman's chest.

"Whaddaya need your phone for?" The guard held her belt and looked down at Allie while rocking back and forth.

"They took it when they booked me, before I could write down my daughter's cell phone number."

"You don't know your own daughter's phone number?"

"I bet you don't know your daughter's phone number. We all just pull up the name and push a button."

"Seriously, I do... well, you know..." The policewoman squinted and scratched her cheek. "Huh. Imagine that. I don't remember it. Is she going to post bail for you?"

"No, I've just got to tell her I'm in a little jam...a big jam. Someone has to take care of her. She has a dance tomorrow and I need to take pictures. It's her first date. She's only 13."

The guard studied Allie for a second and took a deep breath. "It's been impounded, but let me see what I can do." She stared at Allie for another second and nodded. "I'll be back in a sec."

"Thank you, so much. I appreciate it."

Allie turned and walked back to the corner of the cell and sat down. Around her, also in bright orange jumpers, were three other female inmates. For the most part, they kept to themselves.

However, one of them, a tall woman whose sizable arms were barely contained in the jumpsuit, eyed Allie closely.

Allie stiffened her jaw and jabbed her finger in the woman's direction. "Don't mess with me!"

The lady turned around and stared at the white cinder block walls of the cell. Allie looked down and studied her fingernails.

Before long, the guard sauntered up to the bars and held up a phone. "This it, Pumpkin?"

Allie shot up and hurried towards her. "Thank you, so much. I want to make my phone call."

"Not with this you won't." The guard unlocked the door. "You're using the prison phone. I'll let you look at your contacts, but don't dial nobody. If you do, there'll be repercussions."

"Thank you." Allie stepped out and the door slammed shut behind her. "I won't call anyone with this phone. I just need to talk to Chrystal."

"Chrystal? I was going to name my daughter that. But I went with Diamond. You know, they look a lot alike, but a diamond is more precious."

As Allie walked down the hall with the guard trailing her, the sounds of their footsteps echoed off the walls.

"Diamond's a very pretty name."

"Thank you. The phone is on the wall on the right."

"I know."

"You've been incarcerated before?"

"It's been a long time, but it's coming back to me too easily."

"You seem like a nice girl. Why do you keep coming back here, then?"

"I don't know. Even when I try to do the right thing, I end up in the wrong place. It's like I'm cursed."

When Allie reached the prison phone she found Chrystal's number. After she dialed, Allie looked at the guard and smiled. The guard smiled back and continued to rock on her feet.

On the fourth ring she heard a voice answer. "Hello, dear Chrystal's phone." It was a woman's voice and she spoke with a familiar British accent.

"I'm looking for Chrystal!"

"She's in the pool. Can I give her a message?"

"Jess?"

"Yes, who is this?"

"This is Chrystal's mother, Jess! What are you doing with my daughter's phone?"

Jess cleared her throat. "Oh, Dr. Parsons. What a sincere surprise. I'm simply looking after her while you're incarcerated, that's all Dear. Surely, a caring mother would understand that."

"Listen very carefully. You put her on the phone right now!"

"She's enjoying herself, Allie. She's in the pool with her friends. She's having a fabulous time. I'm not going to spoil it by telling her you're incarcerated."

"Jess!"

"And she has a dance tomorrow."

"Shut up!"

"Your mother was right about you."

"Put her on the phone right now!"

"You know, Allie, when social services get's involved in your case, I might adopt her. She's a wonderful child."

"Jess!"

"Toodle-loo, Darling. I'll send you pictures of Chrystal with Rowdy. I understand he's selected an amazing corsage."

"Jess! Jess!"

Allie's desperate pleas received no reply and the phone went dead.

"Are you okay, Sweetheart?"

"She's taken my daughter! I've got to get out of here."

"Honey, it'll be okay. She's your daughter. She'll love you."

Allie's eye flooded with tears and she slumped to the floor. "You don't understand. I've got to get out of here and get my daughter. I can't catch my breath!"

Allie gasped, leaned against the wall and sobbed.

She felt a warm hand on her shoulder. "It's okay, Honey. It'll be alright. Have faith, Sweetheart. I'll be praying for you."

"I can't catch my breath! I think I might pass out."

"You're fine. Calm down." Her grip on Allie's shoulder tightened. "Take a deep breath."

Allie swallowed and gulped. "I've lost her."

"You haven't lost your daughter. Find your faith. Fight for her."

"I did a terrible thing nine years ago. And I don't think I'll ever be forgiven."

"Honey, did you ask the Lord for forgiveness?"

"I did." Allie held her face against her knees.

"Then it is so. Amen. Now, faith is confidence in what we hope for and assurance about what we do not see. That's what the Bible says in Hebrews."

"But, I have done--"

"Shush. Shhh. It doesn't matter what you did in the past."

With a gentle pull, the guard guided Allie to her feet. "Now get up and be strong."

Allie wiped her eye and sniffed. "Thank you."

"It's my duty. Are you okay to walk?"

"I'll be fine."

"Of course, you will. I have to take you back to that cell, you understand? But don't let it confine your spirit. You'll be appearing before Judge Frylon this afternoon. She's extremely tough, but you can prevail."

"I know about her. I understand."

"Okay, then. Be strong. When you get out of here, if you need a job, my brother owns a restaurant on Dale Mabry. His name is Solomon

Eubanks. He's always looking for good help. He's a good man and if you need a job, he'll take care of that."

"I'll keep that in mind, Officer Eubanks. At this point, I don't know what's going to happen to me."

A few feet from her cell, Allie stopped. "I need to make one more call. I have to talk with my friend. He'll get Chrystal."

"Do you know the number?"

"It's on my phone."

Officer Eubanks sighed and looked up at the ceiling for a second. "Okay. Just call from your cell phone. Don't tell anyone I did this."

"Thank you." Allie wiped her nose. She dialed and waited.

"Allie?"

"Andrew! Oh, thank goodness!"

"Allie! Are you alright?"

"I'm fine! Listen, you've got to get Chrystal! She's at Jess' house and Jess is going to keep her. Take my car and go pick her up. Get her out of there! If you have to call the police, do it."

"What's she doing there?"

"I don't know. It doesn't matter. Just do it!"

"I'm on it."

"Thank you. I'll see you soon. Bye."

"Bye."

Allie turned off her phone and handed it back to Eubanks.

When they reached the cell, the guard opened the door and Allie entered. The other inmates stared at her. One of the women moved towards Allie.

"If anyone messes with her or says one harsh word to that girl, I'll put you in solitary, right now!" Officer Eubanks slammed the door.

All their faces turned back towards the wall.

CHAPTER SEVENTY EIGHT
PRESENT DAY

In her bright orange jump suit, Allie marched in shackles before Judge Paula Frylon. Allie's hair hung wild and tangled, and dark bags sagged under her eyes.

Several news crews with cameras, and more observers than usual occupied the courtroom. Allie yawned and barely registered their presence. Her court appointed attorney stood silently beside her and read through a stack of papers.

Frylon recited the charges against Allie. "How do you plead?"

"Not guilty."

A murmur filled the courtroom and Allie could feel the cameras focus on the back of her head. Her tattoo burned. She heard clicks from the cameras. Her attorney didn't move his head but continued reading.

"So noted." The judge lowered her glasses and gazed down at Allie from her towering bench. In contrast to Allie, she appeared well put together, with perfectly coiffed graying hair and a freshly pressed, crisp white blouse under her pristine, black robes. "Based on the evidence, the fact that you're a doctor and you were working on the case of the victim's husband's homicide, I've--"

"He's not dead."

"Excuse me." Frylon, glared at Allie then turned her eyes towards the multitude of media and scowled. Her attorney whispered in her ear, but Allie ignored him.

"He's not dead. She's not a widow."

"I demand your silence. Based on the fact that you are a doctor, who should be trusted, but clearly are not trustworthy, and even now are bordering on contempt, and based on the fact that you have a prior history of charges--"

"I haven't been convicted on any of those charges."

"The court did not give you permission to speak. Do you want to be held in contempt of court?"

The attorney bent over to whisper again.

"No, ma'am."

"Then do not speak, unless I give you permission. Based on these facts, I set bail at $200,000." Frylon banged her gavel against her desk and pushed her papers aside. "Next."

A large male guard grabbed Allie by her upper arm and roughly maneuvered her towards the exit. Her lawyer folded the stack of papers and walked back to the defendant's table.

"$200,000?" Allie couldn't comprehend how a simple B&E could amount to this.

Before she reached the door, a voice erupted from the back of the courtroom.

"Your Honor, I'm Allie Parson's counsel. I wasn't given a chance to present my case."

Allie turned her head and caught a glimpse of Duncan walking confidently towards the judge's bench.

"With all due respect, Mr. Maxwell, proper protocol has been followed in the arraignment of Dr. Parsons."

"Yes, but she is my client and I was not informed of her incarceration. Therefore, she was represented without my legal counsel." In a flash Duncan flipped his briefcase so that it plopped onto the defendant's desk and then popped open.

Duncan smiled at the public defender. "Thanks, Bob. I'll take it from here." The public defender nodded, cleared his papers from the desk and walked towards the exit.

At that moment, Andrew dashed into the small courtroom and slid into the front row. He was out of breath as he collapsed onto the first chair. He wiped his brow, turned towards Allie, and winked.

"Chrystal's fine." He gave a thumbs up.

Duncan approached the judge. "Judge Frylon, despite formidable obstacles, Dr. Parsons has risen above her environment and compiled an admirable list of accomplishments." He slid one hand into his pocket and tilted slightly so that the long bangs of his blond hair barely covered one eyebrow. "She is an active member in her church and graduated from medical school. She has never been convicted of any crime. There is no credible evidence to show she is guilty of anything at all. When she has her day in court, I'll clearly demonstrate that she has been unfairly treated and has a strong case for a counter-suit for libel and false arrest."

For a few uncertain seconds, Judge Frylon sat silently. "You make a compelling argument." Paula Frylon spoke without conviction. "Bail is reduced to $50,000. Mr. Maxwell, please let the court see your calendar so we can schedule the trial." She banged her gavel again. "Next! It's late. It's Friday. We need to finish!"

Allie was led away before she could speak to Andrew or Duncan.

CHAPTER SEVENTY NINE
PRESENT DAY

Two hours after her court appearance, Allie sat on her bunk and stared at the bare, coarse, concrete walls of her cell. She mulled over several plans to free herself from this mess. Only one seemed to have any hope at all.

As Allie considered how to go about petitioning the governor for a pardon, Officer Eubanks appeared at the cell door. The imposing guard knocked on the jail bars and raised her prominent chin.

"How you doin', Honey?"

The echoes from the steel door died away along the long prison hall.

"Hanging in there I guess, Officer Eubanks. Thanks for asking."

"Mr. Maxwell and his assistant are here to see you. Okay, I have to ask you, Parsons. What did you do?"

Allie looked up. "What do you mean?

"Duncan Maxwell! You must have connections or more money than I gave you credit for. You know, he looks just the same as he does on TV. Why didn't he run for governor? I'm sure he would have won."

Allie stood up and rubbed her cheeks. "I don't know. These things just happen to me."

"You've got some heavy hitters looking after your butt. You just hang in there, Sugar."

"At this point, I just want to take care of my daughter."

"I hear that. It's not easy being a single parent, let me tell you."

Eubanks led Allie towards a familiar conference room with a bare wooden table and a trio of pale fluorescent lights flickering in the ceiling. Through a window in the door, she could see Duncan and Andrew sitting at the solitary table.

As soon as the door opened, Allie stumbled over and gave Andrew a hug. Duncan stood up and smiled. "Oh, thank you so much, Andrew! I appreciate this. You can't imagine. I'm sorry I dragged you into this mess."

"You've got 30 minutes." Officer Eubanks closed the heavy iron door.

"Hey, good to see you, too, Allie. You're looking, uhm, rough. Are you okay?"

"I'm fine. It's been a rough day."

"Allie, I found Mr. Maxwell. I remember you said something about your mother knowing him. You know he's the best, and that's what you need."

"I know."

"He jumped right in. He's all over your case."

"Just as I would expect. But right now I don't have any choice. So thanks, Mr. Maxwell."

"No problem, Dr. Parsons." Duncan straightened his jacket and politely shook her hand. "Good to see you. Not to worry. We'll get this taken care of."

He was wearing a blue wool, custom tailored Italian suit, with shiny, black leather Italian shoes. Despite not having a tie and sporting a two day-old beard, he appeared confident and professional. He reminded Allie of a male model from a perfume ad in one of Chrystal's fashion magazines.

"First thing's first, Dr. Parsons, your defense is pro bono. No fee. Now, the second thing. Bail."

"Okay, Mr. Maxwell." Allie pulled a chair from beneath the table and sat across from them. "That's a big thing to me. Honestly, I have no clue how to come up with $50,000. I'm thinking about appealing to the Governor for a pardon."

"I meant it's taken care of. Somebody posted bail. You're free."

Allie leaned back in her chair and swallowed.

"I suppose I should thank you?"

"No. Someone beat me to the punch. Apparently, there are still good people in the world."

"You're kidding. I'm shocked." She sighed and rubbed her eyes. "Uhm, So you don't know who bailed me out?"

"No. You've got some good friends, even if they prefer anonymity. But, really, bail is a non-issue since I'll get the charges dropped anyway. The good news is, because someone paid it today, it means you get out sooner."

Allie sat up and rubbed the back of her neck. She leaned forward and cupped her fingers over her trembling lips. "Free. I'm free. Wow! Whoever did this, thank you. I can't express how desperate I am to be out of here."

"I'm happy to hear that. Just be careful when you start tossing around the word 'desperate'." Duncan chuckled.

"I didn't do anything wrong and I want to be out of jail and hug my daughter. How's that, counselor?"

"Perfect. You may not have done anything wrong, but we definitely need to demonstrate you did nothing illegal. I like the sincerity. I've always loved...anyway." He hesitated, looked away from her towards his briefcase and unsnapped it. "Anyway, that's just what the court is looking for. A mother's pure love for her daughter. However, let's run through a few things so I can get started on your defense."

"Let's finish this so I can get home." She leaned back in her chair with a determined look on her face.

"Good plan. Most importantly, did you ask for a lawyer?"

"A few times. I remembered to hammer the police about that as much as I could."

"So, when they arrested you and questioned you, Allie, you did ask for one?"

"Yes. Several times."

"But the police didn't get you one?"

"No. I think they thought I was going to call one myself like I've done before."

"Doesn't matter, you didn't have a lawyer before being questioned even though you asked for one. That's the first point." Duncan placed reading glasses on the end of his nose and flipped through papers in his briefcase. "Point number two, at one time you were a guest in the house of Jess Bergman?"

"Uhm. Yes. She invited my daughter and me over several weeks ago and then not long after that she volunteered to host Chrystal's birthday party."

"Did she ever tell you not to come into the house?"

"No."

"Did you break any locks to get into the house the day of the party?"

"No. I broke one, at another party at her house a while back, but nothing at this party."

Duncan rubbed his chin. "Okay..." He pulled the glasses from his face and held them near his nose. "I'm sure that'll be an entertaining story for another day. But, the answer is, 'no'."

"Right. No."

"And Andrew, who was invited to this party, told me that he invited you." He nodded at Andrew.

"Yes...he asked me to take him to the party."

"I'll argue that therefore, you were his date." Duncan picked up a sheet of paper. "If Andrew invited a pizza delivery person to come in the party, the host, unless there were specific instructions, cannot then have the pizza person arrested for breaking and entering or trespassing. This is more of a party crashing crime, which is misdemeanor trespassing, but that's weak, too."

"I like it." Allie felt things were looking up.

"Now, there's the matter of a stolen glass."

"Yes."

"Where is it?"

"In a lab. But I can get it back."

"Good. Do that. We'll return it. It was an accident. Borrowed. Now returned. I don't think Mrs. Bergman will want to make a production about a glass. We'll make it so that it's not worth her time. If she wants to manufacture some kind of issue out of this, I'll get a court order to inspect the crime scene, take pictures, and interview her guests. She'll soon agree it's better to leave you alone."

"What about that picture they have of me hanging from the balcony?"

"Excellent point!" Duncan touched the frame of his eyeglasses to his lips. "Clearly, if you fell out of a window like that, it's unsafe. In reality, it's a miracle you weren't hurt. Perhaps if your back should start to ache, Mrs. Bergman could begin signing the checks for the doctors."

"I'm glad you're on my side." Allie tried not to smile.

"Me, too!" Duncan grinned. "And I'm glad young Andrew here thought to call me." He closed his briefcase.

"So, is Chrystal okay?"

"Yeah. I went over to Jess' with Mr. Maxwell right after you called and got her. She's at Mr. Maxwell's house. I couldn't think of any other place." Andrew shook his head.

"Dunc...Mr. Maxwell's?"

"It's fine, Allie. I hate to say it, but my house in Avila is a castle. She and my oldest son are hanging out together. I think they really hit it off."

"Okay. At least she's out of Jess' clutches. Let's just go get her as soon as we can. Did Jess give you a hard time?"

"Initially. What a piece of work she is. She threw out all this stuff about social services, but I set her straight real fast. Chrystal is your daughter and keeping her at that house against your will and without a court order is dangerously close to kidnapping. Jess soon saw the error in her judgment."

"What did Chrystal think about all this?" Allie's voice quivered.

Duncan hesitated. "Obviously, she came with us. But it doesn't matter what she wanted. You're her mother and she's a minor."

Allie swallowed. "Thank you both so much for doing that."

"No problem. Now, I was talking to Andrew and he gave me the short version of your morgue experience. What's this about Franz Bergman not being murdered? You were trying to get DNA from her son? Is this true, Allie?"

"I'll do my best to explain it. But only Andrew believes me."

"Well, now there are two of us that believe you. Let's get you out of here. We can talk as you're getting processed out. Who knows, I might be able to help you with the Franz Bergman case, too."

CHAPTER EIGHTY
PRESENT DAY

After dropping Andrew at his dorm room, Allie followed Duncan as he whipped through the Tampa traffic and zipped north towards his house. Her old Honda struggled to keep up with his red Ferrari, but Allie managed to keep Duncan in her sights. She could hear the hum of his V-12 engine as he accelerated and shifted gears. Just as she would catch up with him and trail his bumper by only a few feet, she'd hear the roar of his engine then seconds later he'd be nearly out of sight.

Allie felt like her Honda could maneuver well enough under most circumstances. But the Ferrari was a completely different beast.

Duncan slowed as he approached his neighborhood and Allie closed in on the chrome bumper. His vanity plate read 'MINOS'. The closer she crept, the louder the Ferrari seemed to rumble.

She focused on the horse insignia on the back of the Ferrari and inched towards it as the gate to the neighborhood opened. Once inside his posh domain, Duncan obeyed the speed limit and Allie had no trouble keeping up. It was an easy drive for a few more minutes until they stopped at another wrought-iron gate: this one guarded his driveway.

You've got to be kidding me! Allie sat in awe.

True to his word, Duncan's house resembled a castle.

Marble walls enclosed a manicured courtyard and ornate spires rose from the tops of the third story windows. Duncan's home appeared to be the masterpiece of old-world craftsmen. The inspiration for the blue slate roof must have originated from an historic French chateau. Allie expected to see rows of grapes lining distant hills and a small medieval village on the horizon.

Seven acres of property comprised the grounds, with shrubs trimmed so neatly that, more than plants, they appeared to be creatures from a Dr. Seuss book. Surrounding the house was an endless lawn that could have served as the world's largest putting green. And winding through the carpet-like grass and perfectly shaped bushes, was a bright white driveway that swept past a magnificent fountain towards the front door.

Mesmerized, Allie followed Duncan and parked her car near the columns of the grand entrance.

"Fun drive?" Duncan removed his sunglasses.

"I was at a disadvantage." Allie stepped out of her car and joined him in walking towards the front steps. Her eyes grew wide and her mouth fell slightly agape as they approached the house.

"You move your car pretty well." Duncan bent and unlocked the front door.

The door swung open, and as Allie's eye grew accustomed to the darker room, she found the interior more lavish than the exterior. Dark, hard wood paneling on the walls framed the polished marble floors and magnificent inlaid wood was displayed in the soaring ceiling. Her breaths grew deeper and the sound of the air leaving her lips echoed off the walls.

"Duncan. I'm in awe." She turned in a circle and looked at the ceiling. "I can't imagine taking care of all this."

"Neither can I." Duncan looked at the ceiling. "That's why I have a cadre of staff to man the castle, as my kids like to call it. There's no way we could do this ourselves. Uhm, so, I know you're eager to see Chrystal. My guess is that she's with my son in the game room. It's in the back, this way."

Allie followed Duncan to the rear of the house, their footsteps echoing along the hall. She couldn't help but gaze in wonder as she studied the endless paintings, vases and statues that adorned the walls and floors. Instinctively, Allie fell into a museum mentality and walked with her arms stiffly at her sides, fearing she would accidentally brush against a priceless object and send it crashing to the floor.

As Duncan predicted, they found Chrystal in the game room, watching a movie on the large flat screen TV.

"A movie room. Nice."

"No. We have a theater upstairs. This is just a game room."

"Oh." Allie pursed her lips and nodded. "Of course you do."

Chrystal stopped texting, turned around and looked at Allie. She slipped her phone into her pocket.

"Mom! You're okay!" Chrystal jumped up and ran over to Allie. The two hugged. "Oh, I'm so glad. Jess acted like you were never going to get out. But Mr. Maxwell told me you'd be fine. He said he wouldn't let you spend anymore time in jail."

"He got me out." Allie brushed the blond bangs from Chrystal's face. "And he got you out. It's so good to see you, Honey."

At that moment a tall, gangly boy of about 11 stood up from the floor and walked towards Allie. She inhaled slightly. He had features similar to Chrystal.

"Hi. I'm Luke." He extended his hand.

Allie took his hand and held it. "Your name is Luke?"

The boy looked confused and raised his eyebrows. "Yes, ma'am. Unless something has changed in the last few minutes." He laughed awkwardly, glanced at his father, then shrugged and gently slid his hand from Allie's.

"We've had a great time, Mom. Thanks for everything, Luke."

"My other boys are around here somewhere. Where the heck are they, Luke? Horace and Julian. Are they out at the pool?"

"Yeah, Dad. Wendy's with them."

"Wendy's our nanny, Allie. Great lady. Wonderful, positive influence on the boys. Come on out and meet them."

Allie turned towards Duncan. "Luke?"

"What's wrong?"

Allie cleared her throat and took a deep breath. "Uhm, Chrystal, give the Maxwells a thank you because we need to get out of here. We've got a lot to do."

"Right now, Mother?"

"Yes. Right now."

"Okay. Thank you, Luke. Thanks, Mr. Maxwell. I appreciate it."

"You can come over anytime, Chrystal. I can send the driver over if I can't pick you up myself.

"Thanks again, Duncan. Let me know if there's anything I need to do. We really need to go, Chrystal."

She turned and rushed for the door.

"Allie..." Duncan tried to keep up with her fast pace. "I'll be in touch. It's going to be fine. Don't worry. I'll look into the Bergman case for you and let you know what I find."

Duncan threw open the front door so she wouldn't crash into it and Allie flew out of the house, towards her Honda. Chrystal followed.

As Luke and Duncan waved, Allie and Chrystal buckled their seatbelts. Allie wasted no time starting the car and they screeched down the driveway.

"I like Luke, Mom. He's really nice. Are you crying? What's wrong?"

"No. No. I'm just a little emotional now, Sweetie. There's so much going on." Allie wiped her eye with her hand and sniffed.

"You're sure?"

"I'm fine. Uhm, so, just asking...do you find it odd that he's named Luke?" Allie didn't slow the car as she drove past Duncan's gate and onto the street.

"No. I mean, it's a common name."

"Just..."

"Just what?"

"Nothing." Allie shook her head.

"Okay." Chrystal smiled. "He's younger than me, but really funny. He's so much like me. And can you believe their house? They have a seven car garage and..."

"Chrystal, Honey, you are not to see him again."

Chrystal's jaw dropped. "What? Why?"

"For more reasons than there are hours in the day."

"Mom!" She threw her hands up.

"No! End of story." Allie sniffed and wiped her eye again.

Chrystal folded her arms and shook her head.

At first Allie thought her blurry vision resulted from the tears, but then after feeling an ache in her stomach, she realized she hadn't eaten since yesterday.

She decided to stop at the University Cafeteria and force herself to eat something. Allie grabbed a pizza and sat at an isolated table near a window. When she returned with her salad, Chrystal sat down and stared at the lettuce, poking at it with her fork.

They ate without speaking. Allie nibbled on a piece of pizza and Chrystal managed to take a few bites of lettuce. After an unbearable silence, Allie laid her crust on the plate and stared at her daughter.

"Is there anything you'd like to say?"

"No. Not really." Chrystal scooted a tomato around her plate.

Allie rested her chin on her hand. "Fine. I'll start. Are you going to the dance tomorrow?"

Chrystal shook her head. "Rowdy texted me at the Maxwell's and said he's not going to take me."

Allie sighed. "I'm sorry that my past has caught up with me again and that I was impetuous and got myself in trouble. I love you with all my heart, and I'll do whatever I can do to make this up to you. But I'm innocent and you have to understand that when you're right, you have to fight. And that's what I'm doing."

Chrystal placed a small piece of lettuce in her mouth and chewed it slowly.

"You've got something on your mind. What's up?"

"Well."

"Come on. Might as well get it out in the open. There's an awful lot to talk about."

Chrystal swallowed and looked down at her plate. "Okay. So. Why did you break into Jess' house?" Chrystal continued to stare at her salad. "Everyone thinks you're nuts. I know you're not, but they feel sorry for me. They say you must have some kind of brain damage from when you were attacked or from when you were on drugs or something. Jess says your brain is fried."

Allie's eyes narrowed at the mention of Jess. She took a deep breath. "First of all, I don't have brain damage. Second, I didn't break into her house. Mrs. Bergman and the police were way out of line arresting me. Third, don't let anyone feel sorry for you. Ever."

Chrystal sat silently and chewed another forkful of salad.

"Chrystal, do you understand?"

"Did you take one of Jess' glasses?"

Allie placed her hands around her mug and took a sip of her hot tea. "Well, I borrowed a glass from Mrs. Bergman. I'm going to return it. I mean, why would I break into her house to steal a glass?"

"I know, Mom." Chrystal exhaled. "That's what I thought. We've got plenty of them."

"Exactly."

Chrystal took another small bite of salad.

"Now, I have something I need to ask you."

Chrystal put her fork down and chewed her salad. She lifted her eyes towards Allie. "What?"

"How did you end up at Mrs. Bergman's house?"

Chrystal swallowed her lettuce and cleared her throat. "Well, uhm, Carly's mother and Jess are good friends, and Jess invited Carly and her mother over to swim while I was at Carly's house, so really I had to go."

"And some of these nights over the last few weeks, I'm guessing when you've been out late, and I've been waiting up for you, were you at Mrs. Bergman's?"

Chrystal lowered her head so that her nose was nearly in her salad. "I was, Mother. I'm sorry. Yes, I was with Aunt Jess."

"Do not call her that! Do not..." Allie raised her index finger, looked at the ceiling, took a deep breath and waited for her rage to subside. "Now, were you at Mrs. Bergman's party when I asked you where Isaac's room was?"

Though her nose was nearly touching her salad plate, Chrystal managed to squeeze her fork into her mouth. "Not exactly."

"Now, you sound a lot like me when I was your age. What's the whole truth?"

"Well." Chrystal took a deep breath. She paused for another second and swallowed her salad. "I was on her yacht. She told me Andrew was going to be at the party and I didn't want him to see me. She's really, really nice, Mom. We went out on Aunt...on Jess' yacht."

"And then you texted her I was in her house."

"You see--"

"Did you tell her I was inside the house?"

"Here's what happened--"

"Did you?"

"Let me answer, please. I thought it was weird you were asking all those questions. I didn't think I was telling on you or anything."

Allie rested her chin on her hand and leaned towards Chrystal. "What's done is done. But here's the deal. You're never to go over to Mrs. Bergman's house. And Chrystal, it is Mrs. Bergman. It's not Jess. And it is absolutely not Aunt Jess. She's not your pal and not by any stretch of the imagination is she your Aunt."

"She wants me to call her Jess."

"Well, you won't be calling her anything from now on, because you're never to have contact with her again. Understand?"

"Mother, please. Listen. Listen to reason. That's not fair."

"Of course, it is."

"Why? You won't let me see anyone!"

"Because! Chrystal, I'll explain this one more time and it will be the last. Mrs. Bergman is a very bad person and you are not to have contact with her. I understand she has great tastes and a lot of money, and that attracts you, but you will not see her again. Do you under-stand? This is my last warning."

"What if Carly goes over to Jess' house when I'm spending the night?"

"Then you call me and I'll come and pick you up. And if that becomes an issue then you are not to see Carly again. Clear? And it is Mrs. Bergman."

"What if you're in jail?"

"I won't be in jail again, but if I can't come and get you for some strange reason, then call Andrew."

"Mom! Jess..."

"Chrystal!"

"Mrs. Bergman is a very nice person. Mom, please. Please listen to me." Chrystal slumped back in her seat. Her eyes began to tear. "You two just had a misunderstanding. She's too much like grandmother for you, but she's a nice person."

"We're done talking about this, Chrystal." Allie leaned closer and placed her hand on her daughter's fingers. "I think she's very dangerous. As a matter of fact, I know she is. You're too young to recognize how evil and deceitful people can be."

Chrystal pulled her hand from beneath Allie's and looked away, but Allie grabbed her daughter's fingertips. "Listen to me, Chrystal. People will tell the most awful lies, just to get you to do something that you know deep down is wrong. They'll tell you exactly what you want to hear to win you over. I've been there. I learned the hard way. I don't want you to suffer through that lesson. Do you understand?"

"Yes." Chrystal averted her eyes.

"You're sure."

"Yes. I understand."

"Then that issue is settled and we're done talking about it." Allie pulled her hands away from Chrystal's and sat up.

Chrystal nodded and pushed her nearly untouched salad away.

"Good, here's what I think we should do." Allie smiled.

Chrystal's phone buzzed and she checked her message. She slipped her phone back into her pocket.

"What was that about?"

"Do you want to go to a movie?" Chrystal looked crestfallen.

"Sure, Honey. I think that would be fun. We haven't done that in a long time."

"Maybe they'll be gone by the time we get back."

"Who'll be gone?"

"Carly said our dorm is on TV. The reporters want to talk with you. There's been another note."

"Okay. Well, Honey, the two of us are going to go see a long, late movie. Tomorrow we'll visit Pug and find out about this note."

CHAPTER EIGHTY ONE
PRESENT DAY

Allie whipped her car into the first empty spot near the police headquarters at the corner of Franklin and Madison. She hopped out and eyed the imposing building. It appeared to be an endless wall of glass and blue panels adorned only by US and State of Florida flags. Large yellow letters above the doors spelled out 'Tampa Police', leaving no doubt who controlled this turf. Chrystal walked to the front of the Honda and together they made their way towards the intimidating building.

"Do you know where you're going, Mom?" Chrystal pulled her purse close to her body.

"All too well, Honey."

"You forgot your purse."

"Believe me, they'd never allow what's in my purse in there. Tried that and failed miserably."

"When was that?"

"Fortunately, a long time ago."

They passed through a metal detector and then two female guards searched them. After they gained access to the building, Allie approached the closest desk and smiled.

A gray haired woman in her early 60's typed on a desktop computer and didn't look up. "Can I help you?"

She sounded completely disinterested.

"Hi, Sylvia. I need to see Pug Festoon."

Sylvia looked up and Allie saw that her full cheeks and moon face had not changed over the last nine years. Sylvia removed her reading glasses, frowned and gave an exasperated huff. "I'm sorry, what's you're name?"

"It's Allie Parsons. Don't bother checking the appointments in your book, I don't have one."

Sylvia replaced her glasses. "Allie Parsons? I didn't recognize you! Look at you! My gosh, all grown up. It can't be!"

"I didn't think you'd remember me."

"Of course, I remember you! And who's this?"

"Sylvia, this is my daughter, Chrystal. Chrystal, Sylvia Watkins."

"Nice to meet you." Chrystal extended her hand.

"Allie, she's absolutely beautiful!" Sylvia shook Chrystal's hand. "Oh!" Sylvia fanned herself and snatched a tissue from the box next to her keyboard. "My gosh. You've turned out so well. Beneath that tough skin, I knew there was a lot of caring." Sylvia dabbed her eyes and tossed the tissue into the tiny plastic trashcan under her desk. "And you darling..." She turned to Chrystal. "You're just what I need to see in this sea of inhumane humanity."

"I have to confess, Sylvia--"

"You always had the best confessions, Dear."

Allie's face reddened and she tilted her head towards Chrystal who was staring at her mother with a wide-eyed, mystified gaze.

"Anyway, I must confess, I don't have an appointment with Festoon, but I really need to talk to him."

"And why's that, dear?"

"It's about these notes. I work in the coroner's office. I'm the medical resident."

"Well, bless my soul. Of course, you are. Detective Festoon has been passing that information around, in a sort of... Festoon... sort of way, as we like to say. But anyway, he just got back and is at his desk. Head on back."

"Thank you so much, Sylvia. I have another favor to ask."

"Anything, Honey."

"Do you still have the room for minors? Those that haven't been arrested, but maybe awaiting custody."

"It's still there."

Allie looked around at the angry people sitting in the waiting room. "Can Chrystal stay there until I'm done?"

"Of course. It has cable TV now. It's set on BBC America, to encourage the kids to read."

"Perfect. I'll be back soon, Sweetheart." Allie kissed her daughter on the cheek.

"Hey!" A heavily bearded man with a torn FSU t-shirt and cargo shorts stood and approached the desk. "I was here first. They can't go back!"

"Sit down! She's on official business!" Sylvia's commanding voice rumbled throughout the room and everyone fell silent.

"Now, Dear." Sylvia winked at Allie. "Detective Festoon will see you."

CHAPTER EIGHTY TWO
PRESENT DAY

As Allie closed the door separating the waiting room from the inner offices, the grumblings of the irate citizens gave way to the sounds of ringing phones and tapping on computer keyboards. She forged ahead, down an aisle that ran between two rows of desks, and zeroed in on Pug's unmistakable thick back. He sat hunched over a cluttered desk and held his phone to his ear with his right shoulder.

Festoon's booming voice filled the room. "I don't care! Just find him!"

"Hey, Pug. I need to know about this new note."

As Allie's words reached his elephant-like ears, Festoon whipped around in his swivel chair. He grabbed the phone and huffed, "I'll call you back, Westbrook."

"Well, Allie Parsons." Festoon slammed the phone down. "Look at you, coming in here to brighten my day."

"Just call me little Miss Sunshine, Pug." She stood several feet from his desk and crossed her arms.

"You're waltzing in here without warning. Sylvia always did like you." Festoon tilted back. "What brings you to our little neck of the woods?"

"A problem, that apparently, has us both worried. James Smith. I heard there was another note."

"Oh, that. Great! Already public knowledge." Pug cleared his throat and brought his thick fingers together in front of his chest.

He tapped the tips against each other and stared over her shoulder towards the far wall.

"Well?" Allie leaned forward a bit and cocked her head. "You seem a little less sure of the case right now."

"Why don't we take this conversation to the conference room?" He spoke in a whisper and made a furtive scan of the office before turning his gaze back to Allie. "It's a little quieter. We can talk."

"Lead the way, Detective."

Pug pushed himself from his chair. As he left his desk, he grabbed a thin folder and led Allie to a conference room that had a view of the city. She sat down in the closest of the six chairs surrounding a long table. After he closed the door, Festoon waddled around the table and parked himself across from her.

"I'm glad you made bail." He fought the chair closer to the table.

"Really?"

"I am, Allie. I'm a caring guy." Festoon fidgeted with the edges of the folder.

"Well, I don't appreciate the way you've treated me. And my lawyer, Duncan Maxwell, is highly motivated to make sure everyone knows that."

Festoon's cheeks sagged, so that his initial look of shock morphed into an appearance of exhaustion. "Just pile it on, Allie. The press is out for my blood, so Duncan Maxwell might as well finish me off."

"A lot of heat in the kitchen, I guess."

Pug shook his head and sighed. "I thought we'd have caught this guy by now. People are demanding to know why we haven't."

"That's what happens when you go on TV and become the face of the Tampa PD's quest for Toro. Hero to zero. The public needs one or the other."

"I've been giving interviews so people can know what's going on. It's my civic duty to keep the public informed. That's why I've been on TV so much."

"You seem to enjoy it."

"I like my job. So, sue me!" Festoon hesitated and shook his head. "Actually, please don't. Anyway. Here's the deal. I need your help."

"Me? A nearly convicted criminal? You're asking me for help?"

"Only charged, not convicted, I know. How do you keep coming up with Maxwell anyway? Over and over again, you walk out of here without a scrape on you."

"I've got great friends. Now, what's up with this note? Why are reporters parked in front of my dorm again?"

"That's what I need help with." Festoon opened the folder, pulled out a photocopy and slid it across the table to Allie. "It's a picture of the note that came in yesterday afternoon. I'm not sure what it means. I was hoping you had some ideas."

Allie looked at the paper and narrowed her eyes. "For each tolls a bell." She thought for a second after she read it. "That sounds like a threat."

"How can that be a threat?"

"It's from John Donne's 'Meditations'. The bell tolls for thee. It means death."

"Oh, yeah. I saw that movie."

Allie shook her head. "Let's see, if you put his whole message together, it's 'To the preacher's demon that gives me joy, my neglector and protector, the vessel that bore a boy, for each tolls a bell.'"

"I don't get it, Allie. I've pored over those things. No fingerprints, of course. We can't trace the paper. Mailed from Tampa."

"It sounds like it could be about me." She scratched her chin. "I'm the preacher, the Parson, with the tattoo. I don't know how I could be a neglector or protector. A vessel that bore a boy? I had a boy. But then, he says 'For each tolls a bell'. That's definitely a threat." Allie placed the photocopy on the desk. "Is that all you have?"

"That's all there is."

Allie massaged her temples. "I don't know. I don't get it."

"Great! I was hoping you'd have some ideas. Don't tell anyone about the note. You understand?"

"Unlike you, I have no desire to speak in front of the cameras. Give me some time to think about it. Hopefully, we've got a little while."

"I'm not so sure about that."

"Maybe we can figure it out before he does more damage."

"Too late." Festoon shook his head.

"Too late for what?" Allie looked up from the paper. "What do you mean?"

Festoon pulled two more sheets of paper from the folder and slid them towards her.

"What do my you mean by 'too late', Pug?"

"These accompanied the note."

A sense of dread overcame Allie. She looked at the pictures, gasped and held her hand over her mouth. "Oh, no!" Allie recoiled at the sight of the first photo. It showed a young woman with a vacant stare, pallid skin and blue lips. "Poor girl. Erin Warrant, I guess."

Festoon nodded. "If you think that pic is bad, get a load of the other one."

The next photo showed a hand that had been severed at the wrist. It was lying on a blue towel and a white ruler had been placed in front of it. A label adjacent to the hand gave the date, time and read 'Tampa PD'.

"He sent her hand?" Allie looked at Festoon.

"Yeah, along with the picture of her body. The fingerprints match the ones we have on file. On the palm of the hand is written 'poetic justice.' It's the same handwriting as the note."

"A thief?"

"What?"

"She must have been a thief. It's considered justice in some societies. Poor thing, she must have stolen something. It's awful." Allie slid the photos back to Pug. "We have to catch this guy."

"Did you ever know her? Do you recognize her?" Festoon returned the pictures to the folder.

"No." Allie shook her head. "It's...it's brutal."

"When this gets out, there'll be panic in the streets."

"Who last saw her alive?"

Pug leaned back in his chair and placed his hands behind his head. "Her sister saw her drive off with her boyfriend about three weeks ago. So, he was the last person we know of that saw her."

"I assume you questioned him. What did he say?"

"No, we didn't question him." Pug pulled his arms down and leaned forward.

Allie shook her head in utter disbelief. "Why not?"

"Because we found him dead of a narcotics overdose in his apartment. At the time, we suspected that he had something to do with her disappearance and that maybe the pressure had gotten to him. But obviously, this..." He lifted the folder. "This changes everything."

"Does her family know yet?"

"Her family consists of her deadbeat Daddy, who we will have to hunt down, and her sister. But to answer your question, no, they don't know, but we'll inform them this evening."

"You have to catch James Smith, Pug."

"I don't think I'll have time."

"What else are you doing? Are you too busy trying to get me locked up?"

"Allie, I've got a bull's eye branded on my back. I'm surprised you didn't see it when you walked in. The department has me lined up to take the fall. I don't have much time left on this assignment. I might be back to issuing traffic citations real soon."

"I'm sorry you're in that situation. But the most important thing is that we catch this guy."

"I know. But when it all falls apart, the first order of business is to assign blame, and I've received that assignment. And apparently, I'm going to be very good at that job. Too bad for me." He grabbed the folder.

"So, that's what made you desperate enough to ask me for help."

"Desperate times call for desperate measures, Honey."

"I'm not much help."

Festoon stood up and shook his head. "I thought I had him this time around."

Allie rubbed her eyes. "If I think of anything, I'll call you. I can't promise anything."

"Whatever you come up with, I'll plop it on a plate and call it dinner." Festoon gave a weak smile. "Anyway, I hope those boys from the press don't bother you too much."

"My daughter and I are going to lay low and keep away from the dorm."

"Good luck."

"Thanks." Allie walked to the door.

"Allie."

She stopped with her hand resting on the handle and turned towards him.

"That McHenry lady you visited near Camp Blanding...she was killed last night. Looks like attempted robbery. It appears the intruder got the shotgun away from her and used it to its full effect. Obviously, you have a solid alibi. That's one good thing about being in jail."

Allie crossed her arms. "Someone silenced her. She asked too many questions. And she wanted to see her grandson so badly. That's Franz Bergman's mother, you know."

"We're checking that out. But since he's dead, I'm pretty sure he's way down on their list of suspects. Probably somewhere near Jack the Ripper."

"That's not Bergman's body that we cremated."

Festoon stretched his arms. "Right. So, where's that evidence you promised Westbrook and me?"

"It's coming. Just a few more days."

"I used to believe in Santa Clause, Allie. But every time I got close, I found a fake beard and a lot of disappointment. So, I'm not holding my breath."

"And you know, Mrs. McHenry was Dr. Mann's ex-wife."

"Dr. Frankenstein told you that, as I remember."

"It's Frankfurter."

"Be that as it may, that case is out of my jurisdiction. The boys in Starke or at the FDLE may be interested, but I doubt it. It was a burglary gone bad. They cleaned out the house... everything they could carry." Festoon stared out the window at the busy city. "Let me know if you have any ideas about this note. We'll all be waiting."

Allie found Chrystal sitting alone in the children's room. A CGI cartoon of a cockney blue baboon and nine golden geese cavorting in a wondrous world of cotton candy played on the flat screen TV.

Chrystal looked simultaneously scared, relieved and annoyed, and bolted for the door the instant Allie arrived. Allie gave her a quick hug.

Allie ignored the angry faces that dissected her with their steely cold stares. "Sylvia, thanks for all your help."

"Allie, Honey, don't be a stranger. And you, Chrystal, are such a lovely young woman."

Chrystal responded with a nervous smile.

The pair walked silently through the building and to the car. When they reached the Honda, Chrystal ducked through the door and secured her seatbelt. "Really, how could you stand going to that police station when you were my age?"

"I was a little older than you are now."

"It's awful! It's horrible!"

"I made mistakes. And I had to grow up quickly."

"And I guess you knew everything was going to work out. Just like you know now? Please, tell me things are going to work out, Mom!"

"I didn't know that, then. It's a leap of faith, but I believe it's going to be fine now, one way or another. In Hebrews there's a verse that reads 'Never will I leave you; never will I forsake you.' So have faith."

Chrystal stared out of the window. "I hope you're right. I'm really scared now. It feels like everything is out of control. I wish I could see Grandmother."

Allie opened her mouth to speak and then closed it. "Everything will be fine." She hesitated. "Even if it's not the way we would have planned it."

CHAPTER EIGHTY THREE
PRESENT DAY

After a full day of avoiding their home, Andrew texted 'It's safe' and Allie and Chrystal returned to the dorm around 11 PM. According to Andrew, the last oversized news truck, with its prominent satellite dish perched on top, had returned to its stations an hour ago. Allie and Chrystal slipped into their dorm unobserved by cameras, lights and reporters.

Allie microwaved popcorn, brewed herbal tea and sat on the sofa beside Chrystal. After several urgent text exchanges between Chrystal and Carly, it became clear that Carly's mother would never again drive Chrystal Parsons to or from school.

Allie sipped her hot tea and let the steam envelop her eyes and sinuses as a flood of relief rushed through her. *At least I won't have to worry about her going to Jess' house anymore!* Instead of celebrating, Allie calmly consoled Chrystal. "I'll be happy to drive you to the bus stop or all the way to school, if you want me to."

"Thanks, Mom. I'll think about it." Chrystal stood and headed for the bedroom. "See you in the morning."

Allie lay back on the sofa and closed her eyes.

Sunday passed uneventfully. The press were still in bed when they left their dorm at dawn. After dark, Andrew texted 'All clear' and Allie and Chrystal slipped rapidly up their dorm stairs and bolted the door behind them.

However, Allie knew there was no way to avoid the troubles Monday was likely to bring.

When the alarm clock rang, Allie jumped off the couch and found Chrystal already up making breakfast. Chrystal appeared lost in thought; she ate very little cereal and spoke even less. Allie made sure not to smile when Chrystal took a piece of bacon from Allie's plate.

"What would you like for supper tonight, Honey?"

"I don't care. Just pick something."

"Spaghetti with tomato sauce? Then we could watch a scary movie."

"Sure. You can put meat in it. Is it time to go yet?"

"A few more minutes. You want some coffee?"

"No, thank you. Well, maybe half a cup. Could you put some milk in it, Mom?"

It felt good to have her daughter back.

A half an hour later, Allie watched Chrystal trudge towards the bus with her oversized backpack slung over a single shoulder. Before she stepped onboard, Chrystal turned and blew her mother a kiss. Allie smiled and returned the kiss as she watched Chrystal board.

Nothing else in the world mattered to Allie. She took a deep breath and pulled away from her parking space. She couldn't predict what kind of reception she'd receive at work, but for now, she felt whole.

When she pulled into the parking lot, Allie saw Byron pacing in front of the door to the morgue. He pushed his hands deep into his pockets. From the looks of things, Allie knew not to expect a warm welcome.

Okay, Allie. Walk tall and be strong. She checked her makeup in the rearview mirror and tensed her jaw. Here we go.

With a hard push, she threw the door open, stepped out, slammed the door shut and advanced on Byron. "Morning, Byron!" Her flat heels clicked off a fast rhythm on the asphalt as she approached. "How are you?"

Byron stood with his hands in his pockets and glared at Allie. As she came within a few feet, he freed his hands and crossed his arms.

"Sorry to tell you this, Allie, but you don't work here anymore." He stood like he'd just unloaded a bombshell and expected the fallout to hit him.

"Oh…" Allie tried to appear shocked. "Why's that? Dr. Mann said I have two weeks to get my act together."

"Dr. Mann and the Pathology chairman are going to meet with you at noon in her office. However, as of this moment, you need to leave the premises." Byron gave a curt nod as if to add emphasis to his announcement.

"Uhm, okay." Allie took a deep breath and raised her gaze from Byron's shoes to his eyes. "I've got personal effects I need to collect, Byron. Pictures. Papers."

"My instructions are to make sure you're off the property and know about the meeting at noon. Don't make me call the police."

Allie stepped back. "No. Don't do that. They've seen enough of me lately. Byron, it's been nice working with you. Thanks for teaching me." She extended her hand, but his arms remained fixed firmly across his chest.

"Okay." She pulled her hand away. "Well, bye." She turned and walked back to her car.

She was nearly to her car when she heard him clear his throat.

"Allie."

She turned and faced him.

Byron fidgeted with the beeper on his belt. "Take care of yourself. I think there are some bad people involved in all of this."

Allie hesitated and then nodded. She made her way to the Honda and opened the door.

As Allie returned her gaze towards the building, Byron disappeared inside.

There are some bad people involved, and I think your boss is one of them!

CHAPTER EIGHTY FOUR
PRESENT DAY

Allie rocketed through the asphalt parking lot and squealed the Honda's tires, leaving a thick trail of smoke and aerosolized rubber.

Allie thought Byron seemed distressed. Not so much about firing her, but about 'bad people'. His words haunted her and caused her anxiety to swell. She caught herself and shifted gears.

This mess is almost over. The DNA from Isaac will set things straight. She shifted into third gear and launched across the intersection, sending her car airborne. She lifted her phone from the console, found the number she wanted and dialed.

After a few rings, a male voice answered. "Genetics Lab."

"Can I speak to Joe Shoe?"

"That's me."

"Sorry, Joe. This is Allie. I'm driving in traffic and I'm a little distracted. I'm going to an important meeting with my department chair."

"Shouldn't be a distracted driver, Allie. It's as bad as DUI."

"You're right, Joe. So, I'll make this quick. Have you been able to get the results?"

"You're a lucky girl to be working with the miracle man."

"Who?"

"I'm talking about me. I got the results."

"And?" Her heart began to pound and she inadvertently pressed the accelerator.

"Congratulations!"

"Congratulations?" Allie's heart leapt.

"Yeah, congratulations!"

"I don't follow you. Why congratulations?" Allie used her left hand to make a screeching right turn.

"Just think about it."

"Joe! Honestly! I don't have time and I'm getting more distracted. You have to tell me what you mean."

The car behind her honked. "Cool your jets!"

"What?"

"Not you, Joe. What did it show?"

"It's a boy! The sample from the glass is the son of the autopsy you guys were doing. Do you get it now?"

"What!" Allie brushed her hair back with the hand that held her phone. "The DNA from the autopsy can't be the father of the DNA from the glass!" Allie had trouble catching her breath as she waited for his answer.

"Yes, it is. The DNA from the glass is definitely related to the DNA from that autopsy. It's a match. It's a boy. Great job, Allie."

Joe's words sounded as if they were spoken from far away.

"Allie? Are you there?"

"Thanks, Joe." She lowered the phone from her ear and stared off into the distance.

"Allie, how about green tea on Saturday?"

She hung up, stunned.

Franz Bergman is dead. And so is my future.

Allie drove aimlessly, not paying attention to her path or what lay in front of her. She didn't notice when she drove past the beach where she and Chrystal had spent many Saturday afternoons looking for sharks' teeth. When she passed the movie theater where Chrystal first saw the 'Sound of Music', Allie felt no pangs of nostalgia.

She had no memory of the trip when, after 30 minutes of driving, she rolled onto campus near the Pathology department.

Allie parked in the medical school lot near the Pathology office and sat in the car; her hands firmly gripped the wheel and silent tears rolled down her cheeks. She agonized over how she could've be so wrong. She'd been so sure.

Allie had to make one phone call before going in to face utter defeat. She wiped her tears and swallowed. She slid her phone from her pocket, dialed and waited anxiously.

Festoon answered on the third ring. "Yellow."

"Pug, I have to come clean."

"Allie? You got a cold?"

Her voice trembled. "I managed to get DNA from Franz Bergman's son, Isaac. I got it from his saliva."

"From his spit? How'd you do that?"

"That doesn't matter now. The point is, it matched our body. I was wrong. You and Westbrook were right. It was Franz Bergman's body."

"I've never heard you admit you were wrong before."

"I was wrong, Detective Festoon. I'm sorry. I'm about to answer for my actions in our chairman's office. I'm like you, I've got a bull's eye branded on my back."

"You kidding me? No more screaming at us about Bergman being alive?"

"No, I'm done. I never want to hear that name again. Please, find James Smith, so all those notes will go away."

"Hey, it's okay."

Allie couldn't respond.

"Like I told you, Allie, as long as they keep me here, I'll keep working on it. As long as I have a job. And Allie..."

"Yeah, Detective..."

"Allie, go get'em, girl. You...you're a survivor. No one beats Allie Parsons. I saw this PBS documentary once..."

"Thanks, Detective." Allie managed a small smile as she hung up the phone.

CHAPTER EIGHTY FIVE
PRESENT DAY

Allie took a few minutes to pull herself together. She rubbed the remainder of smeared mascara from her face and gritted her teeth.

Let's get this over with.

Allie stepped out of her car, straightened her skirt and marched towards the formidable concrete building. Have faith.

The clothes Allie wore to work seemed perfectly appropriate attire for an emergency meeting with the Chairman of the department. Her fitted black skirt fell just above her knee and her white silk blouse and dark grey jacket had been dry-cleaned. Luke's tiny gold crucifix hung around her neck. Although conservative, thanks to Chrystal, it appeared slightly stylish.

Allie made her way to the Chairman's office. She considered every possible mitigating factor that might convince the department to allow her to keep her job.

And roof over her family's head.

A few minutes later she found herself in a quiet office, seated in a thickly cushioned chair, across from the secretary. Allie shuffled her black leather ballet flats on the ornate Persian rug and rested her nervous hands in her lap. Periodically, the secretary would smile at Allie, then resume typing on her computer.

After an eternity, the door swung open and the Chairman appeared.

"Dr. Parsons. Please, do come in." She spoke in a soft, sad voice with the slightest hint of a British accent.

"Thank you, Dr. Silas."

Allie took a deep breath, stood up and walked towards the office. Dr. Silas waited for her to enter then closed the door. She motioned for Allie to sit in an empty chair in front of her large desk.

In the matching chair, sat Dr. Mann.

He remained impassive with his head down and hands folded in his lap. He didn't acknowledge Allie.

Framed diplomas, recognitions and awards covered the wall behind Dr. Silas' desk. Allie thought the small tributes occupying the entire wall, from ceiling to chair rail, looked like a self-made shrine.

Silas walked confidently behind her desk, smoothed her skirt and sat down. Allie thought she looked good for a woman in her mid-sixties. Her short gray hair swept away from her forehead and swung back under her ears. She wore a blue linen jacket, which matched her skirt.

Dr. Silas had always reminded Allie of Margaret Thatcher.

"Now..." Dr. Silas swallowed, raised her chin and touched her fingertips together as she rested her elbows on her desk. "It has come to my attention through Dr. Mann that you have run afoul of law enforcement in regards to a case that you're working on in the medical examiner's office. And you were recently arrested and imprisoned. Is this correct, Dr. Parsons?"

Allie opened her mouth to reply and then closed it. "In some ways, yes."

"In what ways?"

Allie shook her head and grimaced. "In a lot of ways."

"Please, elaborate."

Allie stood and took a deep breath. "He's absolutely right." She straightened her shoulders. "I was convinced we didn't correctly identify a patient, but now I believe Dr. Mann was right. I really do. And I was arrested and jailed but I won't be convicted. I promise."

For a moment, the group sat in silence.

"I'm not quite sure I follow that, but it's clear your conduct has fallen beneath the standard set by the department."

Allie took a deep breath. "I only did what I thought was right. I followed my heart. I apologize. I'll say that, though I was arrested, I have a good lawyer." Allie swallowed. "Anyway, I'm getting off track. What I'm trying to say is that I've been convicted of no crimes. Being arrested and convicted are two very different things, as I'm sure you're aware."

Allie looked at Dr. Silas. Her gaze met a blank stare.

"Okay, maybe you don't appreciate the distinction between being arrested and convicted. Anyway, I'm prepared to work towards finishing my residency with the Department of Pathology here at this university, and, uhm, that's about it. Thank you."

Allie sighed. She glanced at Mann and Silas, but they both stared back at her with vacant expressions so she flopped down in her seat.

"Well, I don't know how to put all that together." Silas folded her hands on her desk.

"Nancy..." Dr. Mann looked directly at Dr. Silas.

Allie could see the deep wrinkles that sagged below the dark circles under his eyes. He looked gaunt. "Nancy, please. We have to stop this nonsense."

"There's no nonsense in due process, Leo! We've been over this. Dr. Parsons, you didn't differentiate between what is proper procedure and behavior for a resident and what is not."

"I--"

"Stop! And your failure to differentiate continued despite multiple warnings from your attending physician."

"I agree." Allie allowed herself the slightest glimmer of hope.

"I'm happy to hear you agree, but at this point what you think is of no consequence." Dr. Silas took a deep breath and leaned forward. "So, Dr. Parsons, you have been dismissed from this department. As of now you are no longer a physician with us."

Allie thought she might vomit. She clenched her jaw and fought back the tears.

"And I do hate to say this. You'll never qualify for a medical license in Florida. Your career is done, I fear."

"Wait..." Allie leaned forward.

"I believe the University gives you three days grace before you must vacate your housing. Perhaps you should start making arrangements, to save face if nothing else."

Allie's mouth fell open, but words failed her.

"Dr. Parsons? Do you have something to say?"

Allie's mind went blank then the reality of the situation hit her. She began to focus her thoughts. "I think this is premature, Dr. Silas. I should be allowed to present my side of the story."

"You just did." Silas shook her head. "For what it was worth, anyway." She held up her hand as Allie leaned forward. "I'm not finished. Due to the generosity of Dr. Mann, a family medicine residency in Idaho will accept you into their program, if you agree to start on probation. At this point, I think it's your best choice. Dr. Mann used some contacts to get you this spot. He stuck his neck out for you."

"But I don't know anyone in Idaho. It's so far away."

"It's a lovely state. Beautiful mountains and lakes. You should consider yourself very lucky."

"I'm sure it's wonderful. But I just can't pick up and move to Idaho."

"There's nothing for you here, Allie. No positions."

Allie shook her head. "I did get one job offer in Tampa. It's in a diner off Dale Mabry."

"Well." Dr. Silas chuckled. "Good luck, Allie. It appears, as usual, you think you have it all figured out. I, however, have work to do. That's all. You may leave now."

Allie struck the chair arms with her palms. "I guess this has all been decided. My presence here wasn't necessary. Thank you, Dr. Silas." Allie stood. "I'm not too proud to work as a waitress."

Silas averted her eyes and her smile faded.

Allie straightened her shoulders. "And good luck to you both. God Bless you." She turned to walk out of the office, but then hesitated and faced the two of them again.

"Dr. Mann, I do want to explain why I did those--"

"This meeting is adjourned, Dr. Parsons!" Dr. Silas slapped her desk. "Find a place in Idaho or on Dale Mabry and make something of yourself."

Allie turned on her heels and left the office.

CHAPTER EIGHTY SIX
PRESENT DAY

Allie lay in wait near a newspaper stand at the front of the building, anticipating Mann's departure. After 15 minutes, she saw his stooped, gray form turn the corner.

"Dr. Mann, wait!"

Dr. Mann cowered, as if being ambushed, and retreated into the shadows of the building. After a moment, his face registered recognition, then anger. "Parsons! You...you startled me!" He leaned towards Allie.

His breath felt hot against her cheek.

Allie held up her hand, determined to speak her mind. "I'm not stalking you. I just want to say--"

"I must return to my lab. Now!" Mann's eyes darted around erratically. "Get far away from here. Go to Idaho. And luck be with you." He gave Allie a quick clap on the shoulder and hurried towards the door.

"Stop! Please! I have to tell you why..." Allie lurched forward and grabbed the sleeve of his worn cotton jacket, dragging him to a halt. "Please, I want to apologize. You were right. Now, I know we cremated Franz Bergman."

"Too little, too late, Parsons." Dr. Mann jerked his arm away from her grasp. "I have a morgue to run. Move away from here and restart your career." Mann resumed his march.

"I really thought the DNA I got from Isaac Bergman wouldn't match our corpse. But I just found out Isaac's DNA does match our cadaver. We cremated Jess Bergman's husband!" In her desperation, Allie's voice grew loud.

Dr. Mann stopped mid-stride as if lassoed. "Did I hear you correctly? You ran Isaac Bergman's DNA against our cadaver?"

"Yes. I got his DNA off of a glass he drank from."

"What did you say about the DNA?" Mann walked towards Allie.

"Well...the lab retrieved Isaac's DNA from the glass and it matched the DNA you submitted from our cadaver."

"Did Joe Shoe run the DNA?"

"Yes, it was his lab. And he said the DNA matched. Isaac and our cadaver are father and son."

"Impossible!" Mann's face faded from angry red to sickly white.

"I'm sorry Dr. Mann, why is this so surprising? It supports what you've said all along."

"It's impossible, though."

"Really? I... I'm very confused, Dr. Mann. I've just been kicked out of my residency over this. So how does Isaac's DNA matching our cadaver become impossible?"

Dr. Mann grabbed Allie's shoulders and shook her. "Get out of here, Parsons! Take your daughter and move away at once!" Mann eyes danced about in a feverish frenzy.

"I just want my daughter to be safe, Dr. Mann."

"That is why you need to get out of here, Parsons. Stay safe. Get far away. I have a lot of work to do." Mann pushed Allie aside. With surprising agility, he dashed through the doors.

Allie stood alone wondering if Mann had gone mad.

CHAPTER EIGHTY SEVEN
PRESENT DAY

Dr. Mann didn't slow as he pulled into traffic. Allie's mind raced, as well.

Based on Mann's alarmed reaction about her news of Isaac's DNA, something had changed. But what? Was he crazy or was there a rational explanation?

If he were sane, she needed somebody who could provide quick information on what Mann was babbling about.

The press?

The police?

Allie knew it wasn't the news guys.

She found Festoon's office number on her phone and dialed it. After several rings Sylvia answered.

"Detective Westbrook's office. May I help you?"

"Oh, Sylvia. This is Allie Parsons. I thought I dialed Pug."

"Allie, Honey. So good to hear you." She cleared her throat. "There've been some recent changes. Detective Festoon has been transferred and Detective Westbrook is now in his position."

"Pug lost his job?"

"Well, he's in limbo, pending reviews and procedural steps. How are you, Honey?"

"A little confused right now. That was sudden." Allie ran her hand through her hair. "Okay, well, I guess I'll call him on his cell phone, then."

"I'll connect you, Honey."

"Thank you."

After the first ring, Festoon answered.

"Yellow."

"Pug, it's Allie."

"Allie, I don't have time for you to spit on my grave. I'm not in the mood to talk right now. I'm trying to save my butt."

Allie shook her head. "Actually, I'm in the same boat as you."

"Then I should warn ya', I renamed this boat of mine, 'Titanic'. I'd jump ship if I were you."

"Too late."

"Done hit the iceberg, huh? I saw that on a PBS special. Nobody survived."

"Well, there were passengers that...never mind." Allie sighed. "Have there been anymore threats or notes or anything? Any more information? I'm trying to put this whole story together in my head and it's not making sense. Something doesn't feel right and I have this awful feeling that something big is about to happen."

"I can't help you, Allie. I haven't heard of any new breaks in the case. They've cut me off. I think they're going to make me a sacrifice. Like the ones in New Mexico back when Columbus was here."

"You saw a PBS special?"

"Yeah. You saw it?"

Allie ignored him and checked the time on her phone. She realized she had 45 minutes to make it to the bus stop to meet Chrystal. That gave her just 45 minutes to figure out a strategy for their future and how to present it to her daughter in the most positive light.

"I gotta go, Pug. I'm sorry about your job."

"I guess we're more alike than I ever thought we'd be. I hope things turn out okay for you, Allie."

"Thanks, I--"

"Oh, wait! I have an idea. Talk to your preacher. People say he's a crackpot, but he's a straight shooter. Back in the day of Toro, he said 'something big is coming,' like you just said. You sounded just like him."

Allie smiled. "That's actually really good advice, Pug. That's actually helpful."

"Why do you sound so surprised? I'm always giving good advice. For example, I told this one fellow who wanted to be a Marine Biologist that he should go into the Air Force instead. The perks are much --"

"I'm going to hang up before you ruin the moment. Bye."

Allie arrived just as the yellow school bus rounded the corner and stopped. Her best plan consisted of a general philosophy, more than distinct steps.

The theme revolved around being as honest as possible, since she was a horrible liar. Sincerity would have to work.

I'll just throw it out there. It's time for Chrystal to grow up a little.

A knot formed in Allie's stomach when Chrystal stepped off the bus. More than 'throwing it out there', Allie wanted to throw-up. But she forced herself to focus on her message as Chrystal approached the car.

Allie leaned over and pushed Chrystal's door open. "How was your day?"

Chrystal tossed her backpack into the Honda and plopped down on the seat. "Awful. Carly and Helene won't talk to me anymore. I officially have no friends. How was your day? Did you get in trouble?"

"Awful! I got in big trouble." Allie steered the car onto the street.

"Did they yell at you?"

"No, they acted remarkably calm."

"That's good." Chrystal pulled a book from her backpack.

"Very calm... when they fired me."

"Oh, my gosh!" Chrystal bolted up and turned to look at Allie. She looked aghast. "You were fired! You don't have a job?"

"Well, the good news is, they offered me another job."

"Thank goodness!" Chrystal sighed hard and dropped her shoulders. "I was so worried." She turned and slumped into the seat. "Is it a good job?"

"Well, that remains to be seen. It's in Idaho."

"Idaho?"

"It's still up in the air."

"Idaho, Mom? I don't want to move there!"

"I hear it's a great place, Honey. Mountains, lakes, clean air." Allie felt a tear form in her eye and sniffed hard to prevent it from falling.

"Where could you have possibly heard that?"

"The chairman told me."

"Fine. Go to Idaho with your books. I want to stay in Tampa with my friends."

"You said you don't have any friends." Allie wiped her eye.

"I exaggerated. But I'm certain I have no friends in Idaho."

"I want to stay here, too. Dr. Mann seemed a little conflicted when he walked out on me. So, it may be that we stay here, anyway."

"When he walked out on you?"

"Yeah. That's how it seemed to me. Like there's a remote possibility I could keep my job here."

"I don't know how to tell you this, but when your boss walks out on you, it's never good. It doesn't matter if he's conflicted or not. I know that and I've never had a job."

Allie swallowed and cleared her throat. "Okay, plan B. I have a job offer in Tampa."

"Doing what?"

"It's a good job."

"You're going to be a waitress."

"You say that like it's a bad thing."

"I say it like, we'll have to find an apartment we can afford to rent on a waitress' salary. Which isn't easy in this city."

"How do you know that?"

"Because you lecture me on that every time I want to find something with two bedrooms."

Allie sighed. "You're right. At this point it shouldn't surprise me, but you have a terrific grasp of the facts."

"If I can't stay here, I want to move in with grandmother."

"Chrystal, you can't!" Allie came to a stop at a red light.

"Why?" Chrystal sat up and dropped her book to her lap. "Tell me why? She has a very nice apartment in Manhattan. It's got great schools around it."

"That sounds just like your grandmother. She must have given you that speech."

"She did, but it makes sense."

"Chrystal, give me a chance to work this out."

"At least think about letting me move to New York. I'd love it there. This would actually be an excellent time since I don't have any friends here now."

Allie tossed her head back and groaned. "Alright," She struggled to maintain her composure. "I'll think about it. I need a little time to figure all this out."

Chrystal turned on the radio and spun through the dial. The only signal came from a station in New York that played hits from the 50's. When the sound turned to static, Chrystal turned it off.

"Can we go shopping? I don't want to buy anything, so don't worry. I just want to see if there's anything I might need if I move in with grandmother."

"Sure, Sweetheart." Allie felt relieved. "We can walk and talk. It'll give us a chance to let it all sink in."

"Yeah. We'll let it all sink in." Chrystal turned her head and stared out the window. "And then I'll be with Grandmother."

CHAPTER EIGHTY EIGHT
PRESENT DAY

Instead of walk and talk, Allie and Chrystal strolled in silence. Allie tried to engage Chrystal, but her daughter seemed lost in thought as she flipped through the hangers of designer dresses and blouses. Before long, Allie felt drained and abandoned her efforts at conversation.

Chrystal gave a deep sigh. "I'm ready to go."

The sun had begun to set as they exited University Mall. Allie still had no idea what to do for housing or work.

"That was fun." Allie tried to sound perky. She closed the car door and sighed. "Well, I enjoyed it. Did you, Sweetheart?"

"It was fine."

Allie looked at Chrystal whose eyes followed the words printed on the pages of a tattered book she held in her hands. A reading light perched atop the frayed pages of the thick novel illuminated her nose, lips and long eyelashes.

As Allie looked at the light, she remembered the happy Christmas morning when Santa had left the light and book for Chrystal. Then Allie felt an emotional tug, as if some comforting force had jerked her to get her attention. She experienced a strange sensation... almost a smell, like mint and pine...and felt as reassured and calm as when she would fell asleep in front of the red glow of her grandmother's hearth.

Allie felt rejuvenated.

She sat up and cleared her throat. "Chrystal, we need to see Virgil and then we'll get you settled."

Chrystal turned a page of her book. "Is he okay?"

"I think so."

"Why are we going over there tonight?"

"Because I promised Pastor Virgil I'd do something that I'm not sure I can do. And I could use his advice. And I have this feeling that right now we need to see him."

"What did you promise him that you can't do?"

"I'd rather not talk about it."

"You make me talk about everything."

"Well, I'm still your mother. And I can get away with saying that."

"Not fair, Mom."

"It's one of the few perks of the job, Sweetheart."

Chrystal turned another page of her book.

Allie pulled into a drive thru and ordered a milkshake. A few minutes later she pulled into Virgil's driveway and parked.

Chrystal jumped out and ran to ring the doorbell. Virgil called for them to come in.

The door was unlocked and the house was dark.

When she pushed the door open, Allie could see a blue glow cast by the TV onto the walls of the hall.

"I'm in the den. Watching TV." Virgil coughed.

"Virgil? You okay?" Allie flipped on the light.

"Fine, Honey. Just tired. Chrystal with you?"

"She's here."

"Well, come on back."

Chrystal and Allie made their way to the rear of the small house. The den was an enclosed back porch that seemed to sag slightly towards the backyard. Virgil lay nearly flat in a reclining chair.

"I brought you a milk shake."

"Oh, thank you, Allie. Just put it on that table. Chrystal, do you like Gunsmoke?"

"I've only smelled it once. But I like campfire smoke, if it's not blowing right on me."

"Oh!" Virgil chuckled then coughed. "Shows how old I'm. And how young you are. I guess you don't do puzzles anymore."

"Oh, my gosh. Chrystal has way out-grown those days, Virgil."

"I guess time flies when you're having fun...and in my case, when you're not having fun, too."

"I've got my book, Pastor Virgil. I'm fine."

"Hey, I've got a new cat. I bet you'd like her."

"Awesome. Where is she?" Chrystal craned her neck and looked around the room. "I love kitties."

"Do me a favor and find her for me, would ya'? She's somewhere in here. Just showed up on my front porch the other day and I think she's adopted me. I call her Goldie because she's got this thick gold coat."

Chrystal placed her book on a coral colored, crocheted tablecloth. "I love cats. They won't let us keep one in our dorm. But I'm moving to New York and I can have a kitten there, I think." She shuffled to the kitchen. "Goldie! Meow!"

Virgil pushed his chair to an upright position. "What's this about moving to New York? When are you doing that?"

Allie took a deep breath. "Well, she beat me to the punch. That's one of the reasons I came over."

"Turn down the volume on Marshall Dillon, there." He motioned to the TV. "New York? That's a big change."

Allie sat down on the couch and used the remote to mute the TV. "Virgil, how do I start?"

"Just lay it out there."

"I lost my job."

Virgil curled his hands across his stomach. "Did you flunk out?"

"You don't flunk out as a resident. I... I... In a nutshell, there's something funny going on in the morgue. I'm convinced my boss, Dr. Mann--"

"I was worried about him, you know."

"Yes. Anyway, I'm convinced Dr. Mann is covering up information about a case we were working on. I thought...mistakenly...that he had intentionally misidentified a patient. But I'm pretty sure he's the father of the victim and he never disclosed it."

"And?"

"And that's it."

"They fired you for thinking these things?"

"They fired me because I said these things."

"You got fired for expressing your opinion?" Virgil frowned and shook his baldhead. "I'm so fed up with people who condemn others for speaking their mind. They 'bout ran me out of town."

Allie nodded and cleared her throat. "Well, I also broke into a house to prove it. And I got arrested, but my lawyer says that the charges will be dropped."

"Allie." Virgil shook his head again. "Just like old times."

"In some ways, I guess."

"So, you and Chrystal are moving to New York to get another job?"

"No. The only job they will recommend me for is in Idaho."

"Idaho?"

"Yes." Allie sighed and her shoulders drooped. "It's so far away."

"I've been there before. It's nice."

"That's what they tell me. But Chrystal, the city girl, doesn't want to move there. She wants to move to New York with Mom."

"What do you think about that?"

"I don't know anymore, Virgil. I really don't know." Allie took a sip of Virgil's milkshake. "I always promised Chrystal that things would get better for us. For years, I've said wait one... two... three years, Chrystal, and things will be better. But now I've been fired. So, I really don't know what to tell her."

Virgil stared at the silent TV and pursed his lips. "I'm sorry to hear that."

"I know I promised you, Virgil. I promised you I'd stick this out."

"That doesn't matter, now. You have a strong conscience and you followed it. All you've told me supports what I've been saying for years. They want to call me crazy."

"What does this have to do with your premonitions?"

Virgil rubbed his chin and the blue light from the TV screen reflected off his eyes, making them glow in the dark room. "In my dreams and when I pray, I see catastrophic events. Toro is involved and there's a new breed of human. Not natural. Faster. Stronger. Somehow Dr. Mann is part of it. But I can't say how. I just can't put it all together."

"It sounds terrifying."

Chrystal walk in holding a small cat. "Found her! She's a sweetie, Pastor Virgil. She came right to me. Do you have any food for her?"

Virgil blinked slowly and shook his head, as if emerging from a trance. "Uhm...in the kitchen, Honey, under the sink."

"Thank you. How did she end up on your doorstep?"

"She had kittens across the road, but this mean cat I call Meany, moved in and drove her away. I felt sorry for her, so I let her in my house. Mean ol' Meany. He's a bad cat."

"I'm glad you let her in." Chrystal gently stroked the cat's ears. "She's purring... listen to her. Let's get some food, Goldie."

Chrystal meandered into the kitchen and Virgil sighed. "I'm glad someone else appreciates that cat as much as me. Sometimes I think I'm becoming one of those crazy people who lay around and their only friends--"

"So, Meanie stole Goldie's family?" Allie gesticulated with her hands.

Virgil tilted his head and looked at Allie. "Yes..." He narrowed his eyes. "That's what it seems like. You've got that look like you're thinking. You've done that since Bible School. You squint and stare off into space."

"You raised animals--goats, horses, pigs, cows. You could tell where the offspring came from? Who the dominant bull was, right? You've talked about this before. It was part of being a good farmer."

"That's true." Virgil nodded. "I grew up right around here. You can't tell where the pasture was, now. But you had to make sure your herd bull was doing his job. He had to be studdin'. Now, I have to tell you, I don't care much which cat sires another cat. That makes no difference to me."

"Were you ever surprised?"

"How do you mean?"

"Surprised, say, another bull got into your herd?"

"Well. Yeah. I remember this one time, a purebred Hereford bull got through a hole in our fence. He was a big bull. He cost Mr. Tucker a lot of money. Daddy had this mixed, kind of scrawny herd bull back then. That Hereford sired our calves that year and we had a good group. As a matter of fact, when we patched the fence and sent the Hereford back, we kept one of the calves as our new herd bull."

"What did you do with the scrawny bull?"

"Well, we had no use for him anymore. We sold him at auction in Okeechobee."

"Thank you! Chrystal and I have to go." Allie sprang to her feet.

"Why?"

"I can't say right now." Allie hugged Virgil. "Chrystal, put Goldie down! We have to leave."

Allie looked through the contacts on her phone and dialed.

"What's going on, Allie?"

"I'm not exactly sure, Virgil, but I think Dr. Mann may be in way over his head."

The phone rang once. Allie spoke into it, giving rapid-fire orders. "Andrew. I need you to create another composite picture using that software. I only want you to use the most recent pictures of Franz Bergman. Nothing older than nine years. Yeah, I know there's not many, but let's see what it looks like. Now, if not sooner. In her lab? Yeah, I know where it is. Meet you there in 30 minutes."

"What's this about, Allie?" Virgil pushed his recliner to a sitting position.

"Gotta' run, Virgil. I'll tell you later."

CHAPTER EIGHTY NINE
PRESENT DAY

Allie whipped around the cars that crept past Virgil's house and flew towards the interstate. She needed to reach the computer lab as soon as possible.

"Why did we have to leave so fast? And why are you driving like a maniac?" As Chrystal spoke, she used both thumbs to text and balanced her open paperback across the legs of her skinny jeans. Her head bobbed back and forth with each pothole as she read the replies on her bouncing phone.

"We're meeting Andrew. I need to look at a picture."

"Okay." Chrystal returned to texting and Allie veered right, onto Dale Mabry.

"Carly and Helene texted me that they're at the university library studying. Can I go there instead? It's right next door."

"I don't know, Chrystal. I thought they weren't your friends anymore."

"Please. I'll walk with you to the steps of the library. I'll go right in and then I'll meet you at the door when you're ready to leave. I want to say goodbye before I move to New York."

"I can't say that things are safe right now."

"Mom. Let's be honest. I'll be going to New York soon. I won't see them again, ever. Just give me a chance to say goodbye. I promise, we'll study. And there'll be hundreds of people around."

Allie sighed.

"Please. It'll just take a few minutes, then I'll walk away from them forever. I'll be in New York with Grandmother or with you. Probably both. We'll be a family."

"Fine. But do not leave the library!"

"They just want to ask me about some homework."

"Please be careful, Chrystal. You're not to be by yourself, even for a minute."

"I promise. I'll be careful."

"Alright. Before we get to campus, I need you to read those medical records at your feet."

"These?" Chrystal held up a folder full of papers. "All of them?"

"Yes, those. And no, not all of them. There should be a history and physical from a surgeon in there somewhere."

Chrystal rifled through the folder. "Here's a history and physical from a life insurance policy."

"Actually, that might have what I need. I didn't really look closely at it the other day. Do they have a height and weight listed for Bergman? It should be under a section called physical exam."

"Just a second...yeah, there is."

"What does it say?"

"Uhm, 192.5 cm and 138 kg. Wow! He's a huge guy."

"Yes he is, Honey. And that explains a lot about what's going on."

"If you say so." Chrystal slid the pages into the folder and resumed texting.

A few minutes later, Allie careened into the lot, parked the car and walked with Chrystal to the front of the library.

"Don't go anywhere until you hear from me."

"I won't. Have you called Grandmother about me staying with her?"

"Honey, I will. I haven't had time."

"Please, call her."

"I promise. As soon as I get a chance."

Chrystal waved and walked up the stairs to the library, which glowed with fluorescent light. When her daughter opened the immense glass door and went inside, Allie turned and made her way to the Engineering building nearby.

In contrast to the library, the Engineering building appeared completely dark and vacant. She put her face to a window and peeked inside, but could see only a few feet of dark hall and a red exit sign on the opposite end of the corridor.

Hmmm. Andrew should be here by now.

She grasped the door handle and pulled. To her surprise, it swung open.

"Andrew?"

Her voice echoed.

Great.

Allie checked her phone and closed the door.

She opened the door a second time. "Andrew?" No one answered.

Allie crossed her arms and tapped her right foot. Where is he? Inside? He's had plenty of time to get here. Maybe he's waiting for me.

Allie glanced at the bright lights from the library that shone through the tall windows and cascaded like white cotton sheets over the steps of the Engineering building. Through the glass façade of the library, Allie could see thousand of books stacked on endless shelves.

And in there somewhere, Chrystal studied with her friends. Allie didn't want her to be alone for long.

I'm going in. Allie took a deep breath and jerked the door open. Be calm. Keep your wits about you.

Allie headed in the direction of the lab. It should be halfway down the hall and on the right. Maybe, Andrew's there, waiting for me. Allie's heavy breathing drowned out the sound of her footsteps.

Why would he be waiting in the dark?

Using the light of her phone to guide her, Allie eased down the hall and walked past the first door. Her shoes squeaked on the slick linoleum and the sound of her breath now seemed deafening.

When she reached the fifth room on the right, Allie stopped and turned the knob. The door was open so she stepped in.

"Andrew?"

No answer.

Allie fumbled for the light switch to her right, and felt relieved to find it with her flailing fingers. The fluorescent light flickered on and Allie saw 10 desktop computers scattered around the room amidst a mess of notebooks and miscellaneous papers.

"Where are you?"

A dull hum emanated from the lights.

Allie sat in one of the chairs, pursed her lips and looked around the room. The humming seemed to grow louder.

Allie thought she'd crawl out of her skin. She needed to speak to someone. Anyone.

Since they'd just parted minutes ago, she couldn't call Chrystal. She didn't want to nag Andrew. Hopefully, he was on his way. After some thought, she decided to call her mother.

Allie took a deep breath and hit dial. She reached Bea's voicemail.

"Mom, it's Allie. I know it can take you a while to get back to me, but this is urgent. Please, call me back." She poised her finger to hang up. "It concerns Chrystal." She ended the call, then stuck the phone into her back pocket.

Allie heard a door slam, followed by loud footsteps scurrying down the hall. She stood and looked around for something to defend herself with.

"Andrew?"

The door handle turned.

Without thinking, Allie reached down, grabbed the first thing at hand and raised it above her head.

The door swung open.

"Aaagh!" Andrew ducked and raised his forearm in front of his face.

"What took you so long?" Allie lowered her arms.

"I had to get the passwords! What are you doing?" He shook his head, appearing very incensed.

"I'm defending myself!"

"Against what? And with a pencil sharpener?"

Allie lowered the object and looked at it. "I grabbed the first thing I could reach."

"Okay, put the pencil sharpener down, nice and gently on the desk, Psycho. We don't want anyone to get hurt."

"You're hilarious! Where were you, you jerk?"

"I was getting all the security codes. This isn't a user friendly system, for crying out loud."

"You could have told me about that."

"I didn't think 10 minutes would matter. Why do I argue with you? You're the only person I fight with like this."

"It was like 15 or 20 minutes." Allie took a deep breath. "And you obviously weren't raised in my family. Sorry. I shouldn't have yelled. And you're not a jerk."

"It's alright." Andrew turned on the rest of the lights. "I'm a little stressed."

"I'm wound a little tight tonight, too. Where's the composite?"

"Right behind you." Andrew pointed over Allie's shoulder. "Her desk is in the back."

Allie followed Andrew towards the back of the room and sat down at the last desk. He booted up the computer and waited while it whirred and purred and came to life. A few clicks later, he opened the face recognition program.

Allie leaned over his shoulder and squinted. Her chin nestled near his deltoid.

"Okay, Allie. There you can see the picture of Bergman when he was a boy. You recognize that. The circles on his face are the areas the computer matched. And now..." He moved the mouse and gave a forceful click. "This is the composite picture we made of Franz Bergman. From the young pictures."

Andrew pushed 'enter' and a large picture of a pudgy bald man's face filled the screen.

Allie carefully studied the image from several angles. "It's a little off, don't you think? I mean I'd recognize him but I think the single photo would do better."

"Yeah, I see what you mean. The program probably needs some of the kinks worked out."

"So, now, use only the photos that are less than ten years old."

"There aren't--"

"I know. I know." Allie slapped the desk. "There aren't many of them! But I just want to try something. I think a bull may have come in through a hole in the fence."

"What?"

"Let's just see."

"I have all the photos saved so I'll select for those less than ten years old and..." He hit return. "This will be interesting."

"How long will it take?"

"With so few to work with, it may be pretty quick. As a matter of fact, there he is. Oh...wow, he looks like a completely different man!" Andrew's mouth fell open as he stared at the screen.

As Allie leaned closer, a chill ran up her spine. "I don't believe it!"

CHAPTER NINETY
PRESENT DAY

Allie stood and started pacing. "He looks different, because he is different. That last composite you made using only recent photos is not Franz Bergman. But I know who he is."

"Who?"

"Print it out!"

"Okay. Give me a second."

As the printer churned out the photo, Allie ripped open several drawers and tossed around pens, paperclips, and pencils as she urgently searched for something.

"What are you looking for?"

"Found one!" She held up a black marker.

Allie walked to the printer and snatched up the paper as it fell off the tray. She turned and dropped it on the nearest table.

Without hesitation, she scribbled on the photo with the black marker.

"What are you doing?"

"Andrew..."

"Yes? What is it?"

"Congratulations, Andrew. You now know exactly what Toro looks like! You and I and one guy from Portugal are the only living people who've seen him."

She held up the photo, now complete with bushy black hair and beard. It trembled in her hands as she fought to remain calm.

"Franz Bergman? Toro? How?"

"No. Not Bergman. I was wrong. We did perform the autopsy on Franz Bergman. He was killed so the big bull from another pasture could take his place."

"What?"

"Never mind. Dr. Mann thought this guy, Toro, was Franz, because he'd been separated from his son since he was a child and Mann had no idea what Franz looked like." Allie walked towards Andrew, mesmerized by the photo. "But Franz had been murdered by Toro. And probably stuffed and frozen in a -70° freezer for nearly 10 years. I saw a huge deep freezer at the Bergman's house. I wondered why someone needed a laboratory quality freezer in their garage."

"So, you're saying Toro took Bergman's place?"

"Right. I'm guessing he had an affair with Jess and they murdered her husband, Franz Bergman. Later they sold his shares of the optics company and Toro retired into seclusion, a very rich man. He played the roll of Franz Bergman, though he had to be pretty much a hermit so no one would notice he wasn't Franz. I think that's why he stopped appearing in public so abruptly."

"And all this stuff about James Smith..."

"I bet James Smith hasn't been seen in a decade. Jess threw that story out there to get the police chasing a ghost. I bet she and Toro anonymously called in the sightings. Probably planted the guns and knives. Maybe, paid people to corroborate their story. Those pictures the police are showing the public are so bad no one is going to be able to recognize Toro."

"No one but you. You know what he looks like." Andrew shook his head.

"Exactly. I could ID him. Now you could and maybe that guy from Portugal."

"What about Dr. Mann?"

"I think Mann believed he was helping his long lost son, who had gotten himself into a jam. Maybe Mann was shamed into it. I'm not sure."

"And that leaves us with a serial killer on the loose."

"Yes, it does. And I need to get Chrystal right now. I'll text her."

Andrew raced after Allie, who'd made a beeline for the exit. She shoved the front door open and marched down the stairs heading for the library.

"What do we do, now?" Andrew's breathing came in rapid, shallow bursts and he wiped sweat from his forehead. "You're certain he's Toro, Allie?"

"I'd bet my life on it!" Allie labored to catch her breath and fought to maintain control. Despite the warm, gentle breeze, a chill shook her. "I'll get Chrystal and then we'll drive to the police station and explain this to Pug or Westbrook."

"He's probably living in Jess' house."

"It's his house. He built it. That's why Franz Bergman has had to keep such a low profile these recent years. That's why Isaac kept calling for his dad. He never really knew the real Franz. I'm guessing Toro's getting tired of all that."

"I bet Jess got paid a large sum of insurance money once Bergman was found dead."

"You're right. As if they weren't rich enough already? It's been an elaborate hoax with me in the middle of it. Even the police bought it."

"Why not just call the police now? Tell them to arrest Jess." Andrew jogged to keep up with Allie.

"They won't just arrest somebody based on hearsay. You'll have to show them how this composite image software works and then we'll have to show them these pictures and explain the whole story. Let's get Chrystal first."

They reached the library and Allie scanned the front of the building looking for her daughter. Allie texted Chrystal. "I'm here. Meet me outside."

Nervously, she tapped her foot on the library's steps, smoothed her hair and waited for her daughter's reply.

"How did you figure this out?" Andrew put both hands in his pockets and bounced on his toes.

"I was thinking about Bergman's DNA, Erin Warrant and that poem and how it could all fit. Then, I talked to an old farmer about livestock."

"I don't understand all this livestock stuff." Andrew looked out at the empty campus.

"You can't assume your herd bull is the only one around. Sometimes a dominant bull will sneak in. Then there's no place for the scrawny bull, so he get's made into hamburger."

"I'm sorry. I still don't get it. Erin Warrant, she's missing right?"

"She was. Now, she's Toro's latest victim." Allie held up her phone, hoping she'd see a new message. Nothing.

Seconds later, her phone rang. Allie whipped it to her ear. "Chrystal! Where are you? I've been waiting!"

"Hello, Allie. This is your mother, Bea Parsons. I'm returning your call."

"Oh, Mom! I'm sorry. I'm a little surprised. I thought you were Chrystal. Thanks for calling me back."

"You said in your message that there's an issue involving Chrystal?"

"Yes."

"Why are you breathing heavily?"

Allie cleared her throat. "Sorry. We've got a lot going on right now, Mother. Yes. I want to know if she can live with you for a while?"

"Of course, she can. I'd be delighted to have her."

Allie noticed a hint of enthusiasm in her mother's voice. "There's a lot to explain. But, basically, Toro is back. And they want to transfer me to Idaho. Chrystal doesn't want to go, and I think she'd be safer with you. At least until things settle down."

"Allie, are you alright?"

"I'll be fine. But I think Chrystal needs to get away. And she wants to get away." Allie continued to look for Chrystal through the library doors and windows.

"Well, things must be getting desperate down there if you're sending her to me. But she'll always have a place with me. When can she come? I'll purchase the airline ticket for her this evening. Are you both safe?"

"I'm pretty sure we are...anyway, I think I know who Toro is. Well, as a matter of fact, this will shock you, it's the husband of a lady you used to work with, Jess Bergman."

"Who?"

"Jess Bergman. Oh, I'm sorry. She told me you would have known her as Jess Howell."

"I've never heard that name, Allie."

"No?" Allie scanned the front of the library again.

"Allie?"

"Sorry, Mother. Jess worked with you in Tampa? She knows all about you. Petite, pretty, short black hair in a bob. British. In her 30's."

"I remember everyone I've ever worked with. But I don't recall that name or description."

Allie took a deep breath. "Well, that's interesting."

"It does sound like a reporter who interviewed me several weeks ago. All she wanted to know about was my time in Tampa and my family. I told her that was none of her business and ended the interview. She was an impertinent, arrogant little thing."

"Okay, Mom, I've got to go." Allie hung up before her mother could reply.

Andrew stepped towards Allie. "So, what's up?"

"I feel like a fly in the middle of the web. The spider's coming, but I can't see him."

"That doesn't sound like a good feeling."

"I actually want to puke."

Allie's phone buzzed and she looked down to see Chrystal's face pop up. "It's Chrystal, finally!"

Andrew took a deep breath. "What a relief!"

Allie tilted her head as she read the text.

"Make Wong leave, NOW! We're watching you. BTW, I like your white t-shirt."

"Make... Wong... leave?" Allie spoke in a whisper. Her shirt white t-shirt grew damp with sweat.

"What did she say?"

"Nothing, really. Uhm...Andrew...do you see Chrystal?"

Andrew gave the area a final sweep. "Nope. I don't see her."

"Then, go home."

"What?"

"Leave now, Andrew."

"Allie, are you okay?"

"Just...just please, go right now."

"Well, okay." Andrew shrugged and licked his lips.

"Go! Now!"

"But, Allie, we have so much--"

Allie stretched out her arm and pointed to the parking lot. "I don't need your help!"

"Okay...I'll call you soon." Andrew hesitated and backed away. "But get in touch if you need help."

As soon as Andrew turned the corner, Allie's phone buzzed, announcing another text. Chrystal's glowing face greeted her.

"Go to your dorm now! Turn on your computer. We're watching you."

Allie gasped. She rotated in a circle and her eye frantically darted over every bush, tree and wall, checking for anyone who looked suspicious.

Nothing.

The rest of the world remained oblivious to her nightmare.

Allie texted: "Who is this?"

"You know."

She texted: "Chrystal?"

"I love you mommy!! Please don't let me die!!!!!"

CHAPTER NINETY ONE
PRESENT DAY

Allie sprang into action and sprinted to her car. As adrenaline coursed through her veins, she inhaled deeper and ran even faster. She arrived at the old Honda feeling light-headed and nauseated, slid behind the familiar steering wheel and gripped it with sweaty palms.

I can do this.

She turned the key, and the vintage engine roared, giving Allie a boost of confidence.

We're going to finish this thing. One way or another.

She punched the clutch, shifted from first up to third gear and steered the car through the small lanes of the university, finally screeching to a stop in the parking lot of her graduate student housing.

Her Honda careened across the concrete curb of the handicap spot and landed on the sidewalk. As her head bounced against the window, Allie turned the car off and threw the driver's door open.

In a flash, she dashed up the stairs, lunged towards her door and shoved the stubby key into the lock.

Allie burst though the door. "Chrystal! Are you here?" She only heard the hum of the refrigerator.

She grabbed her laptop from the wobbly table by the TV then waited.

Minutes passed, but nothing appeared on her screen.

Breathing heavily, she leaned towards her laptop. Suddenly, her phone buzzed. Allie jumped and checked to see who had texted. Not now, Duncan! But Allie read the message, anyway.

Duncan's text read: "Found some disturbing stuff about Jess. Don't think there is a J. Smith. Possible danger. Call me ASAP."

Allie remembered the warning from earlier and returned her phone to her pocket.

Three agonizing minutes later, her computer beeped and a request for a Skype session appeared. To her horror, the request came from Dr. Mann. Allie accepted without hesitation.

When Dr. Mann appeared on the screen, he seemed to have aged since earlier in the day. The bags under his eyes sagged much more than usual. He wore a garish orange shirt and strands of hair hung over his droopy, red eyes.

"Dr. Parsons?"

"Where's Chrystal, Dr. Mann! What did you do with her?"

"Who?"

"My daughter!"

He hesitated as if thinking, then nodded. "Ah, yes. I don't know. But I'm sorry for all the suffering I've caused you, Parsons." The flickering, jerking picture accentuated his nervous appearance.

"What are you talking about, Dr. Mann? I'm trying to find Chrystal. They said I could find her here."

"Here? On the computer?" Mann shook his head. "Byron convinced me that I could talk with you in this way...but we're running out of time."

"I got a text that there would be information."

"I don't know what you mean. But I do have some things I want to tell you. As you surmised, I'm Franz Bergman's father."

"Where is Chrystal, Dr. Mann?" Allie frantically gripped both sides of her computer screen.

"I'm trying to help you. Please, be patient. I divorced my wife when Franz was very young. We were in Germany."

"I know all this, Dr. Mann!"

Mann stopped and stared above the camera and nodded. "My poor son was beaten by his stepfather. And his mother allowed it. But I knew nothing of this. If I had known he had been abused in that way, I would have dropped everything and intervened. Do you believe me, Parsons?"

"Where's Chrystal?"

"Do you believe me?"

"Yes, I do!"

"Then, nine years ago, we had the Toro murders. You know about those as well as I."

"Of course! Where's Chrystal?"

"My long lost son..." Mann swallowed. "My long lost son, who I left to an abusive guardian, came to me for help. He was the murderer. But he was ashamed and lost and deeply, deeply regretted committing those heinous acts."

Mann cleared his throat, paused and looked away from the computer.

"We're running out of time, Dr. Mann!"

He took a deep breath. "We...we had an emotional reunion and I realized that he is a truly incredible man. Extremely strong and brilliant. Far beyond any human I've ever seen."

"Please get to the point, Dr. Mann!"

"I was partially responsible for his bad behavior because I abandoned him when he needed me most. It was clear he'd seen the error of his ways. He knew right from wrong. I could help him change, but I had to make sure he stayed free. I owed him that. Don't you think? After all those years when I wasn't there for him."

"But, Dr. Mann, he is not Franz!"

"I realize it's hard to accept. But he is Franz. He showed me pictures of the two of us from long ago."

"Those are not pictures of the man that has been talking to you!"

"After we reunited, we reminisced. It felt good to have my son back, after all those lonely years. I see myself in him. He has my genes.

He shouldn't be a sadistic killer. Logically, it's because I left him. Therefore and therefore? Parsons, fill in the blanks."

"I have no idea what you are talking about. I only want to get my daughter back. Where is Chrystal, Dr. Mann?"

"I don't know where your daughter is! Very well, I'll answer my own question. Listen carefully. It's important that I get through all this so we can set it straight. Do you understand? Because I'm running out of time to fix this."

"I don't know what you're talking about."

"Of course you don't. You've never lost a child and then had the chance to get him back. You'd do anything. So I decided to raise him myself, even though he was now an adult. I could give him a second chance. It was a difficult decision, but I decided to bury the DNA results in the Toro cases to provide Franz with a new lease on life. We became very close, Dr. Parsons."

"Where is Chrystal, Dr. Mann?"

"Patience, Dr. Parsons. I believe I was successful in rehabilitating Franz. As a matter of fact, I found out recently it was he that paid for your medical school training. It was he that insisted I hire you as my pupil. He told me that he had wronged you in the past and needed to find closure."

As Allie listened to Mann's lecture she suppressed the urge to scream. Her face turned red and the veins in her neck bulged, but she maintained her silence.

"I was against it, since you were not qualified in the least, but he was adamant and I felt I needed to help out in his charity. He bailed you out of jail. See, Parsons, he has changed. Franz wants to correct the wrongs he perpetrated against you."

"Where...is...Chrystal?"

"In trying to protect me from a blackmailer, he killed again. Do you want to know how this happened?"

"How, Dr. Mann?"

"Everything was going so well. Franz was married. He had a son. My dear grandson, Isaac. Then, right as you joined our lab, Franz called me in horrible distress. James Smith, the one you continued to ask questions about, somehow found out about Franz's past and my suppression of the evidence. James threatened to release the information about me and Franz and the entire Toro affair and expose us all. Despite Franz having reformed, he would be prosecuted for a crime that was as much my fault as his. And my career would be ruined. So--"

"There is no James Smith!"

"So, in an absolute rage, Franz killed James Smith and threw him in the bay. Franz did not plan it. It just happened because of the threat. Franz is so strong and physically gifted, that James did not stand a chance. Franz is superhuman."

"Call the police! Tell them what's going on so they can get Chrystal!"

"Of course, you're right, Dr. Parsons. I should have gone to the police several weeks ago. But I was convinced that this was only a setback because of the rage of being blackmailed. He loved me! He respected me and he was protecting me from being blackmailed, too. Such a powerful being... loving me. My son..." Mann shook his head and looked down at his desk.

"Dr. Mann, get to the point!" Allie trembled as she raised her hands in frustration.

"Dr. Parsons, it's hard to blame a son for trying to protect his father and it's not as if he had become a serial killer again. I told him very sternly that I would tolerate no more of this malignant behavior." Mann shook his head and appeared to emerge from the trance of his deep thought.

"Dr. Mann!"

Mann jabbed his index finger on the table. "I let him know that I would help him one last time if he, Jess and Isaac disappeared. They must go to a place where they would have a final chance to escape his past. Go where no one could blackmail him and he could continue on the good path he had started. He chose Ireland."

"So, you planned to pass that body off as Franz Bergman? Can't you see, it was Franz! It was your son!" Allie leaned closer to her screen.

"But something has happened to him. He's writing notes and taunting the police. I talk with him and he won't listen to me. Something dark and evil has taken control of my only son, Allie!"

"He's not your son!"

"Everything would have been fine, Allie, if you had just remembered what I told you in our first meeting. I keep asking you if you remember my instructions, but you behave as if you don't. Do you remember our first meeting, Allie?"

"I do, Dr. Mann."

CHAPTER NINETY TWO
SIX MONTHS AGO

Allie sat alone before the Chief Medical Examiner's intricately carved mahogany desk. In the 30 minutes since Dr. Mann's assistant had shown her in, Allie had studied every diploma and certificate that adorned the walls.

Allie ran her finger along the edge of his desk and sighed. Maybe he's changed his mind.

"Parsons!"

Allie whipped around to find the source of the booming voice.

A serious and stern looking man, with lively bright blue eyes, bounded towards her, extending his hand. "I'm Dr. Leopold Mann."

Although he appeared to be well into his 70's, he exuded the energy of a doctor in his 40's. His bright white hair sprang in all directions from his scalp and reminded Allie of exploding fireworks.

"Please, don't get up." He walked past her and sat behind his desk. "This won't take long. Now first, I assume you want to join this department. Completing this program successfully is certain to launch a fruitful career."

"It would be the answer to my prayers."

"Hmm. Parsons, I don't mess around. I make a decision, act, then move on." As he spoke Mann searched through the drawers of his desk. He opened and closed each in rapid succession. "If you choose to apply here for your residency, we will consider it. However, I'm not sure you'll qualify to work with me in the medical examiners office."

"I understand." Allie scratched her head and took a deep breath. "I'll work on my grades."

"You must."

"I'll do my best."

"I hope that's good enough." Mann stood. "I wanted to talk with you face to face. You'll find out about our decision on match day, of course."

Allie sensed the meeting had been adjourned and stood, also. "Thanks for your time. I'll put you guys at the top for my match."

"Do what you must." Mann reached down for an insulated red satchel that lay near his feet.

"Can't forget your lunch."

"Ah, well, this is much more than lunch. It's the first thing Byron will look for when I'm gone." Mann cradled the bag and turned to a bookshelf.

"Must be a great sandwich!" Allie tried to smile, but her nervous lips formed a crooked crescent.

Mann touched each volume on the shelf, one after the other. "If you beat the odds and join our program, there are several rules you must follow. Ah, found it." He pulled a small book from the shelf.

"I'll do anything, Dr. Mann."

He turned towards Allie holding a small textbook entitled *Understanding Abnormal Behavior*. For the first time since entering the office, Mann stood still and looked Allie squarely in the eyes. "First, you must follow my directions without fail. Second, you are never to discuss our cases with anyone on the outside. Third, if anyone outside this office ever inquires about our cases, direct them to me. Finally, and most importantly, do not question my authority. I can be very hard to work for, but I can also help those that do well under my tutelage. Do you understand?"

"Yes, Dr. Mann."

"Good."

"This would be the answer to my prayers, Sir."

"You already said that!" Mann turned back to the bookshelf. "You may leave now."

CHAPTER NINETY THREE
PRESENT DAY

Allie's phone buzzed and snapped her back from her thoughts. Duncan texted: "Where are you? Call me ASAP!"

Allie put her phone away. "We have to speed this up, Dr. Mann. I'm going to do the talking, now."

"I'm not going to let you talk to me like this!"

"You have no choice!" Allie slammed her fist on the table. "You did your best to make the evidence show that the body in our morgue was that of Franz Bergman, even when the facts didn't support it and you, yourself thought it was James Smith."

"Yes!"

"But you underestimated me, and I managed to throw a wrench into the gears."

"You're right. We...Franz, Jess and I... disagreed on the details and logistics of Franz's disappearance. She wanted to make it appear James Smith was Toro. I felt she was complicating matters. I thought Toro should remain Koslovski, as determined by me and the Toro commission. I told her to stay away from you."

"I assume those pictures she showed me in her home were the real Toro."

"I don't know what pictures she showed you. Everything had begun to slip out of my control by then. I don't know why she insisted on contacting you after I told her not to."

"It's very simple, Dr. Mann."

"What could you possibly mean?"

Allie ignored Mann's question. "The DNA I got from Isaac proves the murder victim is his father. How is that possible if Franz is still alive, as you believe?"

"I spoke to Franz this afternoon and we concluded that your DNA sample must have been contaminated."

"If you believe that, then you've been manipulated by an evil man who has killed on three continents!" Allie slammed her fist again. "Look at the facts. Franz is the father of Isaac. The DNA of the body we cremated matches Isaac's DNA, therefore that body can't be James Smith! There was no blackmail. Toro murdered your son nine years ago. He kept Franz' body frozen and then threw it in the bay. It looked like a recent murder because he'd been so well preserved in that industrial grade freezer. And now Toro has my daughter!"

"I know my son! We reminisced! He had pictures."

"All stolen from your real son, years ago. Do you realize your ex-wife was recently murdered? She's the vessel that bore a boy. Just like in the notes. And why does Jess continue to contact me?"

"I think she's trying to learn about you. She's jealous."

"Dr. Mann, I'm the preacher with the tattoo."

"That's all speculation."

"Toro is moving quickly. He's eliminating all those potentially damaging loose ends in his past. I'm one of them. Franz's mother was one of them."

"I confess, I'm concerned about that, too, Parsons. That's why I want you to get far away. I can no longer be assured that he won't kill again. With all these notes and odd behavior, it's like it was before."

"But Dr. Mann, you're a loose end, too. You're the 'neglector and protector'. And the bell is tolling. This is all laid out in the notes he's been sending the police."

"I don't know if you're right, but I possess the DNA from his first murders. And I'm ready to turn it over to the police, if necessary. Even if it means ruining my career."

"Toro's coming for you."

"He may. He's so unpredictable now. If anything happens to me..." Mann pulled three vials from his insulated red bag. "These are to be sent to the police with an explanation. I've told Franz if he betrays me, he'll be turned over to the authorities."

"That's why you carry that bag with you all the time? That's the lost Toro DNA? That's your leverage against him?"

"It is. And he can't escape it. Sometimes you need a whip to tame a bull. And this is my whip."

"Dr. Mann, I received a text message saying someone would be contacting me on my computer. Does Franz know you're talking to me tonight?"

Mann's eyes darted around. "Yes, I told him I would contact you after we discussed Isaac's DNA."

"He's coming for you, Dr. Mann. You need to get out of there!"

"You're wrong! It's not me he wants."

A loud thump on the computer speaker startled Allie. Mann jerked his head up and his eyes opened wide.

Mann stepped back from the camera. "My boy! No! No! Stay back! Remember--"

A split second later, Allie heard two loud bangs and a flash of orange light momentarily bleached the screen.

Clouds of gray smoke hovered over Mann's desk. She heard Byron moan in the background.

Allie stood transfixed, staring at her computer screen.

A heavily bearded beast, with long black hair that fell well below his ears, appeared. His cobalt blue eyes locked on Allie's as he slid across the screen.

Toro gave a sinister smile. "Let the pain begin!"

CHAPTER NINETY FOUR
PRESENT DAY

"Where is my daughter, you monster?" Allie's rage boiled inside her.

"She's with me. I realized that the only way to acquire you, would be to use your daughter as bait."

"Do not hurt her! This is between you and me!"

Allie heard a soft groan off screen, somewhere behind Toro.

Toro looked down and to his right. "Un momentito." He ducked away.

Allie heard a loud grunt and a short time later Toro's face reappeared on the screen. Fine drops of arterial-red blood, speckled his cheeks.

"Papa. Difficult to the end." Toro sneered and held up the vials that Mann had shown Allie. "I found these. Such a tiny whip."

"Where...is...Chrystal?"

"Here's how you're going to see her. When I say 'run,' you'll fly downstairs as if your daughter's life depends on it. My wife is waiting for you in a black Mercedes sedan. You'll have exactly 10 seconds to reach her."

"Don't hurt her!"

"I don't want to kill Chrystal, but I do want to kill you. I'll release your daughter if you sacrifice yourself for her."

Allie tensed her lips.

"What's your decision?"

"You're going to pay for this! We beat you before!"

Toro took a step back and growled. "If you want to see Chrystal, you'll get into my Mercedes, whore!"

"I'll do whatever it takes." Allie balled both hands into fists. "But you're gonna pay."

Toro bellowed. "Here are the rules, harlot. Do not call anyone. Do not contact a single person or Chrystal will die."

"I won't. Just let her go."

"And, Allie..." He leaned close to the screen. "Run!"

Allie bolted through the door and lunged down the stairs. She slipped, caught herself on the rail, and then vaulted onto the sidewalk. After an agile landing on her tiptoes, she bounded around the corner of the building and darted towards the parking lot. She wanted to call someone for help, but she dared not deviate from Toro's instructions.

She found the black Mercedes lurking in the parking lot like a dark demon. Allie skidded to a halt beside the left headlight, her running shoes nearly touching the tire. Through the misty windshield, Allie saw Jess.

Jess waved and flashed her perfect white smile, as if simply meeting Allie for dinner and drinks. With no apparent urgency, Jess leaned over and pushed the passenger door open.

Allie stood frozen in front of the Mercedes, her eyes wide and her jaw clenched.

"What are you doing? Get in, you imbecile! You only have a few more seconds!"

Jess' words jolted Allie into action and she grabbed the doorframe and swung herself inside, sliding across the smooth leather seat.

Allie breathed heavily and turned towards Jess. Sweat dripped from her hairline and crossed the bridge of her nose.

"Well, close the door, Silly."

Like a robot, Allie turned towards the door and slammed it shut. She couldn't catch her breath.

"Jess, please, think of Chrystal."

"I have no sympathy for you. Your mother gave you all the advantages. And you threw it all away. I gave you a chance and you tossed it back in my face. I had nothing when I was born. Raised in working class Whitechapel. I had to struggle for every scrap."

Jess whipped the Mercedes around a corner and sent Allie's head bouncing against the passenger window. The car screeched to a stop.

Allie's head swam.

Jess shifted the car into park. "Let me see your hands! Together in front of you!"

"Jess, please."

"If you want to see Chrystal alive, you'll put your hands in front of you. Otherwise, I'll call my husband. Or if we haven't met him in 15 minutes, you're both dead."

Allie moved her hands in front of her.

"That's a good girl." Jess grabbed a roll of duct tape lying near her right hip. She wound the tape around Allie's wrists several times, binding them tightly together.

"Now, you'll see your daughter for a short time."

"Please, don't hurt her, Jess. She admires you so much."

"I don't think you've noticed, but she's an amazing young woman. So beautiful and intelligent. Athletic and artistic, too. She needs a mother that can give her the best in life." Jess smiled wistfully and shifted the Mercedes into drive. "When you asked her for directions to Isaac's room, Chrystal called me and told me you were on the second floor. That's how I was able to find you so quickly. Betrayed by your own daughter. That must hurt."

"Don't let him harm her, Jess!"

"If she survives all this, Allie, I'll take care of her. I'll raise her as my daughter. I expect it may take a while before she thinks of me not as 'Aunt Jess', but as her mother. But it will happen. Eventually, her memories of you will fade."

A few minutes later they arrived at the Bergman's house.

Jess turned off the car and leaned towards Allie. "Sorry, Love." She tilted her head and pouted.

Before Allie could say a word, Jess pressed duct tape over her mouth.

CHAPTER NINETY FIVE
PRESENT DAY

The extensive landscape lighting and the floodlights of the state of the art security system had been extinguished. The thick tropical foliage completely blocked even the faintest beams from the moon and stars above. Not a single bulb shone in the house, leaving the windows inky black. Allie found herself swallowed in pitch darkness.

Jess hurried around the front of the car and opened the passenger door using a small flashlight to guide her. For a moment, Allie didn't know what to do.

She felt a firm grip on her elbow and Jess ushered her out of the car. Barely able to maintain her balance, Allie stumbled towards the front steps.

"Come on, you clumsy girl. I can't believe you were ever a dancer of any sort."

Jess shoved her in the lower back and sent Allie crashing into the front door. Jess twisted the knob and opened it.

"Move it!"

Jess pointed her flashlight at the dark floor. Allie followed the bouncing beam of light as it flashed around corners, crisscrossed the walls and zigzagged up the stairs. The light finally settled on the door across from Isaac's room.

"You recognize this, don't you? You were up here harassing my son. Don't think you can get your dirty hands on him tonight, because he's on the yacht and away from harm. There's only the four of us here. And there'll be less than that when we're through."

Jess opened the door and shoved Allie into the dark office.

Allie couldn't see anything inside the room and she tripped on a thick rug. A split second later, her back slammed against a wall, followed by 'thump' as the back of her head smacked the thick plaster.

Allie bounced forward and landed on her knees. Her head spun and ears rang from the blow.

"Welcome, Allie."

She recognized Toro's baritone voice.

"So, no one would heed your alarm?"

His voice had the gravelly sound of a heavy cardboard box being dragged over pavement. Allie recognized 'Seigfried's Funeral March' playing in the background. She supposed he considered it a clever and symbolic touch.

"This must be a frustrating conundrum. Like the Princess Cassandra, your prophecy is correct, but no one will heed it."

Despite the disorienting blow to her head, Allie managed to stand. Although she couldn't see his face, she lifted her chin. "Uhm, mm, mm!"

"What are you raving about? Jess, light the candles!"

Allie heard the shuffle of feet on the carpet. A small flame appeared. It glimmered in the darkness, alone.

One by one, small flames began to ignite. In short order, the solitary flicker expanded to include a row of candles along one wall. The small points of light grew more numerous, reaching the summit of a bookshelf. Minute flickers appeared on the far side of the room. They surrounded Allie at the level of her feet, then her hips and head before finally reaching the ceiling.

The light cast by the scores of candles threw eerie shadows across Toro's face.

"The conflagration grows from a solitary flame into a luminous multitude. Just like our forces." The candles flickered as he drew in a deep breath; the flames seemed to be drawn towards his mammoth chest. "No primitive human can possibly understand what I mean, but they shall know Druden."

Toro exhaled as he approached Allie. His narrowed eyes reflected the red and orange candle light.

She gasped as he reached for her and grasped her jaw with his massive hand. He lifted Allie up by her neck and pinned her against the wall. As he leaned forward, his lips drew close to her forehead and Allie shut her eyes. Jess emitted a malevolent hiss, but Toro raised his hand, silencing his wife.

He released Allie and stepped back. She dropped from his hand to the floor, thankful that, even though her legs felt weak, she swayed but stayed on her feet.

Raising his arms as if in exultation, Toro surveyed the candles and slowly turned. "How mystical." He inhaled deeply and closed his eyes. "I revel in the aroma of burning organic matter. It's rapturous."

"MMM!"

As the shadows gyrated across his face, Toro opened his eyes and stared down at her. He drew his lips tight and his jaw quivered. Allie recognized the anger and hate that inhabited his soul. Despite her fear, she refused to turn away. She fixed her eyes on his, and challenged his gaze.

"MMM! MMMM!" Saliva pooled in the back of Allie's throat.

Toro ripped the duct tape from her lips and Allie tasted the saltiness of her own blood.

Toro reared back and his lips formed a heinous smirk.

Allie swallowed and gasped for breath but kept her eyes locked on him as her chest heaved. "Where's....where's Chrystal?"

"She's safe, for now."

"Let me see my daughter! Or I will--"

"She's worthless, Allie, but Jess likes her. She lacks your genes."

"Let me see her!"

Toro raised his chin and the flames from the candles flashed in his eyes. "Haul that lamentable creature in here. Ahora!"

Jess murmured something and ducked into the shadows. Allie heard the door open.

Toro touched Allie's scar. "You survived even though I had the knife. I outweigh you by almost two hundred pounds. I ambushed you." He ran his finger down her cheek. "But you turned the tables on me. No one has ever come close to doing what you did." His voice softened. "Do you know what you are? Do you have any idea? You are the passage between two worlds."

Allie spat blood. "If anything happens to her, I'll--"

"What?" He grabbed her cheeks tightly in his huge hands. "What will you do?"

"Please, let me see her."

Toro snarled and let go of Allie's face. "She's with that thief. I kept Erin in that deep freezer, too."

The door opened with a squeak and Chrystal staggered into the candle lit room. Allie could see her silhouette as she fell to the floor. Jess followed and shut the door.

"Ah, there she is." Toro snickered. "So skinny and gaunt. The runt of the litter!"

"Shut up!" Allie jumped and lunged at Toro.

With a forceful flick of his wrist, Toro sent Allie stumbling backwards into the wall then she slid to the floor. He sauntered towards Chrystal and towered above her. Chrystal cowered and covered her face.

"I saw a diseased goat like her in Italy. We had to put it out of its misery. I can't believe this piteous being is your offspring. What possible value can she have?"

"Shut up!" Allie struggled to stand and then lunged at him again.

In a flash, Toro descended on Allie and grabbed her throat. He squeezed causing Allie's eyes to bulge.

"My father used to yell at me!" Toro clenched his teeth and his face turned red as the large veins in his neck and head bulged. "When we went camping in the Alps he would berate me. As he taught me how to fight with a knife and collapse bodies with arrows, he would castigate me. I know now that might makes right. And I'm the mightiest of all!"

As he roared, Toro's spit sprinkled Allie's eyes. His cheeks inflated and sank with each heavy breath. His furious mouth frothed.

"Do you understand?" Toro's face loomed mere inches from hers and he squeezed her throat even more tightly.

"Let..." Allie fought to suck in some oxygen. "...her ...go."

"I'll--"

Suddenly, a chime sounded.

Allie and Toro both froze.

He released Allie's throat and stepped back. She fell over and gasped for air. His gaze drifted down to her jeans.

Allie wheezed. "It's my phone."

The interruption seemed to snap Toro out of his rage. He rubbed his hair and turned towards Jess. "You idiot! You were supposed to take that!"

"I'm sorry." Jess dashed forward and fawned. "Please forgive me, my Love."

Allie heard soft footsteps approaching and then saw the shadow of Jess's head. Jess retrieved the phone from Allie's front pocket.

"I have it, my Beloved. They hung up."

"Take it and destroy it."

"How do you want me to--"

The phone chimed again.

Allie smiled.

Toro turned towards her. "You find your situation amusing?"

"It's Andrew."

"Wong? What about him?"

"We have an agreement." Allie's voice cracked but she concentrated on staying calm. A tear slid down her cheek. "Since you started sending those notes, we have this agreement that if I don't answer after three calls, he'll send the cops to find me. They'll hone in on the app I have on my phone. They can find me anywhere. You might as well let us go and make a run for it. You've only got a few minutes."

"That's a clever, but apocryphal tale."

"By the third call." Allie nodded. "And they're guaranteed to arrive within minutes. The commercials are all over television for that service. You have to have seen them. But you probably don't watch much TV."

Toro stared accusingly at Jess. Allie's phone rang again.

"Third call. You're toast." Allie shrugged her shoulders and raised her eyebrows. "Yeah. That's the third ring. They're coming right now. You might have enough time to get away."

Toro ripped the phone from Jess' hand. He stepped towards Chrystal and held the large Bowie knife to her throat.

"Recognize this blade? Yes, of course you do, Amiga. Answer the phone and tell Mr. Wong that every thing is fine. Then hang up. Anything more and this scrawny runt dies. Understand? I slice her open without a problem. Just like I did with Erin Warrant."

Allie nodded.

"Jess, hold it up to her ear."

Jess took the phone back and clicked. She lifted it to Allie's face.

Allie tilted her head towards the phone and cleared her throat.

"Andrew. Hey, there...my main man. What's hanging...Dude?"

Her voice sounded hoarse and she cleared her throat again.

"Oh, yeah. I know. That third ring thing. Kind of scary for you, I guess. But we're fine. Fine as wine."

Allie glanced across the room illuminated by the dancing light of the candles and saw the shimmering blade move closer to Chrystal's throat.

"Andrew, I've got to go! We're fine." Think, Allie, think. "Listen, I have no idea where your stupid cane is! Look for it where you lost it! I've got to go!"

Jess pulled the phone away and used her thumb to press "End Call." Instantly, the phone rang again and Jess looked at the caller ID. "Duncan Maxwell?"

Allie nodded. "He's got the same app."

Toro grabbed the phone from his wife's hand. "Let's get down to business." He dropped Allie's phone in the water of a nearby vase. "No more signals. Now, It's only us."

CHAPTER NINETY SIX
PRESENT DAY

"Allie? Allie!" Andrew paced in front of his dorm door. He pressed the phone to his ear and waited for her to answer. "Come on!" He redialed Allie's number repeatedly and each time his call went straight to voice mail. "Allie! Come on!! Oh, come on!!!"

Okay, what do I do here? He collapsed onto his couch. As he fretted, Andrew tussled his long, black hair with his hand. Something's going on. Oh, Lord, please just help me figure this out.

In the precious few seconds he had spoken to her, Allie had called him 'Dude'--which was a first-- and said he should search for his cane where he'd lost it.

What could that possibly mean? It wasn't a proper answer to his question. Andrew felt his stomach tie into a knot. It was a horrifying thought, but he knew Allie had sent him a clue.

Then he felt his body go numb as the meaning of her secret message dawned on him.

He'd lost his cane in Jess' house. Allie must be somewhere in that monstrous mansion. And since she'd disappeared in such a rush, Allie must be in deep trouble.

Andrew closed his laptop. He hesitated and shuffled his feet.

How can I help Allie? As he wavered, Andrew remembered something his grandmother had once said, 'It's do or die.'

We need a cop, NOW! He straightened his back and rubbed his face. Allie would go for it. She wouldn't hesitate. She wouldn't just sit here and worry about things.

Do or die!

Andrew leapt to his feet, whipped open the door to his apartment and headed straight for the fire alarm that lay behind a pane of glass a few yards away. Without thinking he smashed the glass with the base of his palm and jerked the alarm with his bleeding fingers.

That's what Allie would do!

As the alarm blared, Andrew beat it down the stairs and sprinted into the parking lot. He dialed 911 on his cell phone.

A very calm voice answered. "Hillsborough County 911, what is your emergency?"

"My friend has been kidnapped and she's in Davis Islands." Andrew paced and held his bloody hand above his head.

"Okay, sir. What's the address?"

"I don't know. It's Davis Islands." Andrew tried to catch his breath.

"Stay calm. I'm here to help. Can you tell me an intersection or major landmark?"

"It's Jess Bergman's house... there was a murder there. Near the airport, on the bay side. Looks like a Spanish mission. My friend has been kidnapped!"

"Murder? Is someone dead?"

"I don't know!"

"Does your friend have a pulse?"

"I don't know." Andrew ran to the front of the dorm.

"Check to see if she has a pulse and if she's breathing. Are you trained?"

"Trained for what?"

"Where is the body?"

"I don't know!"

"Sir, I need you to calm down. It's hard for me to understand you with your heavy breathing. I want to help. Do you need fire, police or medical assistance? I need your location."

TORO!

"What..." Andrew felt his world spinning out of control. He drifted backwards into the street, scratching his head as the sirens grew louder. He tried to think of a plan as he waited for help to arrive.

Andrew turned just in time to see a white car from WTSP slam to a stop as it hit his knee. The passenger door opened and Phillip Spears jumped out.

"Are you okay? Are you drunk? You could've been killed!"

Andrew spoke into his phone. "Never mind, help has arrived!" He punched the end call button. Andrew rubbed his knee and steadied himself. "Hey, I've seen you before."

"Yeah, I'm Phillip Spears." Spears flashed his award-winning smile. "Are you sure you're not hurt? You ran into the road."

"Allie Parsons broke your nose!" Andrew pointed at Spears.

"Yes, she's..." Phillip rubbed his chin. "Difficult."

"You can finally get what you want! You can have an exclusive with Allie." Andrew could barely contain his excitement.

Phillip looked skeptical, but took a step closer. "And how do you propose I do that? She won't talk to me."

"I'll tell you in a second. Get in the car."

"What?"

"Just get in the car, you idiot!

"Why?"

"Because I'm about to give you the most exclusive interview you've ever had."

"Where?" Spears reached in his pocket and pulled out a pen and notepad.

Andrew lunged towards the car, pushed Spears in and hopped into the passenger seat. Spears landed supine between Andrew and the driver on the center console.

"Jess Bergman's house!" Andrew spoke over Spears to the driver. "On Davis Islands. Can you get us there?"

"Are we being carjacked?" The young driver had a scraggly beard and wore a thin white t-shirt, stained brown with the coffee

461

splattered from a Styrofoam cup he had been holding. "You spilled coffee all over me, Man!"

"Phillip, you and your news crew will be the first on the scene if you get me to Jess Bergman's house. I'm serious! This isn't a hoax."

Phillip clawed his way to an upright position. "Let's go! First on the scene? I'll get a bonus."

"We've got to roll, NOW! It's do or die."

"Go man!" Spears pounded the dashboard.

Spears slid back as the driver peeled out of the parking lot. "Davis Islands! Colt, Dude, head in that direction. I'll look at 'previous destinations' in the GPS. It'll be there. Now, what's the story?"

"Spears, call the police and give them the address. Allie's going to need them. Go faster! We're running out of time."

Andrew's head snapped back as the car rocketed onto the interstate.

CHAPTER NINETY SEVEN
PRESENT DAY

After he destroyed Allie's phone, Toro paced on the antique Persian rug that lay between Allie and Chrystal. He appeared distracted and paused several times as if listening for a sound in the driveway or yard. The orange glow from the dozens of candles cast black shadows across his face, causing them to cavort across his nose, lips and cheeks like a coven of dancing demons.

"Andrew and Duncan know where I am. If you don't want to deal with the police again, you should leave now."

Toro remained mute and absently stroked his cheek with the side of his shimmering, sharp knife as he walked back and forth. After another minute of silence, Allie decided to pursue an alternate strategy. She had to buy more time.

"Where is James Smith, anyway?" She gulped and forced herself to look Toro in the eye.

He snorted and turned his right ear towards the window. "James Smith is long gone."

"That's what I thought." Allie stole a quick glance at Chrystal. She gave a confident nod. Her daughter nodded and swallowed.

"You think you're so clever. Brava!" He stepped away from the window. "Leopold Siegfried Mann, the brilliant Dr. Mann, actually believed the victim you two autopsied was James Smith."

"You're right. You had him fooled." Allie added a husky laugh in an attempt to appear amused. "The great Dr. Mann. Not so great, really, was he? So, how did you meet Franz Bergman, anyway?"

"I met Franz in a hotel bar in New York. After a few drinks, he told me that his father was the chief medical examiner in Tampa but that he hadn't seen him since he was six. He boasted about his wealth and his beautiful wife."

"If you're in the killing business, it's good to know the M.E."

"I thought well beyond that. What if I could possess Franz's money, his wife... his life? I relished the thought of killing a man so utterly."

"You captivated my heart. When I heard your glorious proposal, I could never have gone back to that boring old lump." Jess cooed in the dark.

"So, I took Franz's life. His mortal life and his material life. I took it all. Instantly, I became wealthier. It's true what they say. The rich do get richer." Toro walked to the window, again. "I knew Papa Leo would protect me."

"Because he thought you were his son?"

"Well, really, I was his son. He abandoned Franz. Why not adopt me?"

"And you kept Franz on ice?"

"Yes. Frozen Franz we called him." He peered outside. "That freezer preserved him very well. I had this idea that I could keep a body deeply frozen and then produce it when I had a need and an alibi."

Allie heard a faint siren in the distance. She felt a surge of hope, took a deep breath and waited. Toro turned his head side to side as if he were gauging distance and direction.

Allie's optimism faded as the sound slowly died away. Apparently, the squad car or ambulance must be racing to someone else's rescue.

Toro snorted and exhaled. "Because of the freezer, Mann had no idea his son's murder was the first I committed in Florida."

"And you took Franz's identity?" Despite the disappointment of the siren, Allie focused on keeping Toro talking.

"Yes. Leo wanted to reform me and held onto my DNA from the crime scenes as a threat. What a shock it would have been to the police if anyone had been allowed to sequence it!"

"What do you mean?"

"I had to be weak and pathetic Franz. Since I couldn't be seen by anyone who knew him, I built this beautiful house to be my prison."

"You murdered Erin Warrant."

"I did. She attempted to steal my most treasured possession."

"What was it?"

"An idol that Druden gave me. It's very precious. Now that it's time for my kind to rise, I have to destroy my past here and move on. So, we unfroze Franz, claimed a vulgar amount of insurance money, and tonight, after we tie up the last of the loose ends, we're going to sail off into a magnificent future."

"I guess I surprised you when I found the freezer."

"When I saw you enter that garage, I already knew your skill and intelligence are superior. But, that was when I accepted that Druden was right and you must die. I couldn't kill you because everyone knew you were inside. Instead, I had Jess get you out."

"Did you ever get the door fixed?"

He turned away from the window, towards Jess. "No." Allie heard Jess shuffle her feet in the dark.

"You planned to hold us down there tonight, but the door won't close, will it? There's a gap in the insulation and the room isn't sound-proof. You couldn't risk someone entering the garage and seeing or hearing you."

"This room will serve the purpose. The windows are covered, the door is solid and the walls are thick. I designed them that way."

"Why did you send the letters?"

"It pushed you to visit our house and look at the photos. And I enjoyed it. You may not know this, Allie, but I've killed all over the world."

"Portugal, Argentina and Spain. There's a witness in Lisbon."

"Beauty and brains." Toro strolled from the window and leaned towards Allie. His hot breath seared her cheeks. "You keep talking, but time is up. Your final gambit is a bust. No one is coming to save you."

"Why did you pay for my medical school tuition?"

"You got away from me nine years ago. No one has ever done that. I mistakenly believed you could be useful if you were educated. But you threw our gifts away like they were trash. Druden demands your death."

"Just let us go. I won't say anything."

"It's too late, Allie. Druden demands your blood."

"Druden? You keep saying that. My father said that name, too. Tell me about Druden!"

"She's omnipotent."

"Who is she? What are you?"

"It no longer concerns you."

"When we met, you said something about Methuselah."

Toro stepped away then abruptly turned. His shoulders stooped and his lips curled to reveal his large teeth. "You people think the stories of Methuselah are a myth! You have no idea what's coming! There are ancient people..."

At the height of his rage, Toro took a deep breath and seemed to relax.

"I hear a car." Chrystal wiggled in the candlelight.

"Shut up!"

"You're going to try and pin this on Dr. Mann. Like a cover up or something." Allie felt a sudden rush of adrenaline. "Right?"

"They'll think the eminent Dr. Mann was protecting James Smith. And since the police killed Toro, the case will be closed. Now..." He held up the knife. "Your time is up."

TORO!

The doorbell chimed and Toro's eyes glared. A knock on the front door echoed in the hall.

"No!" Toro growled.

Allie thought she might not be heard, but took a chance anyway. "Help!"

As she yelled, the doorbell erupted continuously like a machine gun and someone pounded on the front door.

Toro snatched the old strip of duct tape from the floor and slapped it over Allie's mouth.

"Jessibel!" Toro's eyes bulged and his face turned red. "Answer the door and send our visitors away! I want to do this my way!"

CHAPTER NINETY EIGHT
PRESENT DAY

"So, why do you think Allie's here?" Phillip Spears used his cell phone as a mirror to check his hair.

Andrew's fists ached and the lacerations on his fingers began to bleed again, but he kept pounding on the door and ringing the bell. "Because, she told me over the phone to search for my cane where I lost it, and I lost my cane at a party here."

"But why didn't she just say she was in this house?"

Andrew stopped knocking and looked at Spears, raising his bloody hands in disbelief. "Because she must be here against her will!"

"I don't get the connection."

"You're not a real reporter, are you?" Andrew resumed pounding on the door.

"Yes, I am. I've won seven awards for investigative journalism."

Andrew shook his head. "Jess, let me in! I know Allie's in there! Let me in!"

He listened, but heard only the chirping of crickets and the croaking of frogs.

"There's got to be another way." Andrew took a step back from the house and looked up and down the walls.

Just as he was about to walk towards the door, he heard the sound of tires on the driveway. Andrew turned and saw a police cruiser pulling in quietly behind the news car.

"Oh, thank goodness!" Andrew walked towards the police car. "Finally some real help."

A policeman stepped out of the car, his hand resting nervously on the holster on his hip. His fingers drummed on the gun handle.

"Good evening, Gentlemen. What seems to be the problem?"

"My friend, Allie Parsons, is being held against her will in that house!"

"Who?"

"That doesn't matter! She's been kidnapped!"

"I know that name." The cop furrowed his brow.

"You might have run across her she's--"

"Yeah! Allie Parsons. She was just arrested for breaking and entering this home. Right? Is that the lady you're talking about?"

"Yeah." Andrew nodded and pointed towards the door. "But the charges were dropped. So, we need to get her out."

"Sir, did you see her taken into this house against her will?"

"No, she told me she's in there."

"Actually, she told him to look for his lost cane in there." Phillip appeared eager to contribute to the discussion.

"Gentlemen, what does that have to do with her being in this house?"

"Honestly, I don't get the connection, either." Spears looked confused.

"Uhm..." Andrew tried to think of something to say. "She told me she was being held at gunpoint by Toro! Officer, Sir, we have to get in there!"

"She did?" Spears now looked completely dumfounded. "Because that's not what you told me."

"Shut up, Phillip!"

"I'm just trying to get the facts straight. That's why I'm award winning."

At that moment, an intercom speaker buzzed. "Can I help you?" Jess' voice sounded calm and collected.

Andrew dashed to the door and stuck his mouth next to the speaker. "Let her go, Jess!"

The policeman stayed close to Andrew's back. "Yes, Ma'am. This is Officer Mitchell of the Tampa PD. These gentlemen seem to think that someone is being held here against their will. Are you okay, Ma'am?"

"I'm a tired of their incessant banging on my door. It's keeping my son and husband up. But otherwise, we're all fine. These men are trespassing."

"Her husband is supposed to be dead!" Andrew turned to the cop. "She's lying!"

Mitchell raised his eyebrows. "Why is her husband supposed to be dead?"

"Because they cremated his body!" Andrew shook his fists and gritted his teeth.

"Okay. Now, I can see a story building here." Spears bit his lower lip and jotted something on his notepad. "I can see it coming together."

"Her husband is Franz Bergman!" Andrew kicked the heavy door in frustration. "Let me in!"

"I'm sorry, Sir." Officer Mitchell grabbed Andrew by his shoulders and pulled him back. "I can't allow you to do that."

"This is going to be a great story." Spears nodded excitedly.

"Allie's in real trouble and she's in that house!" Andrew kept kicking.

"I understand you're frustrated, but at this point I can't determine that anyone is in danger, and I can't allow you to harass a private home owner on her own property. I'm going to ask you to leave the premises."

"I need to get in that house!"

"I can start the process of getting a warrant. But, unless there is some clear danger such as a fire or something like that, I cannot allow you to remain on the property."

"Fire!" Andrew had a brilliant idea.

"Fire? Where?" Phillip looked around.

"I gotta' go!" Andrew ripped his shoulder away from Mitchell's grasp and disappeared into the dark before the policeman could unholster his gun.

CHAPTER NINETY NINE
PRESENT DAY

Jess stepped back into the room and shut the door. "They'll be gone soon. The police officer ordered them to leave. Phillip Spears is standing there like a buffoon and Wong ran away."

"Ironic. Don't you think, Allie?" Toro stuck his nose in the air. "The police have chased away the rescuers."

Toro held the knife against Allie's face. The blade felt icy against her hot cheek.

"As far as the world knows, the phantasm that is James Smith killed Brigitte Bergman, Erin Warrant and Leo Mann, and eventually the police will find you dead." He ripped the tape from her mouth. "That realization should have ended any hope you're clinging to."

"I'm at peace. You can't silence the truth."

"Maybe you should lose your other eye, first." Toro brandished the knife over Allie's right eye.

"You don't frighten me at all. My soul is in God's hands." Allie squared her shoulders, facing Toro head-on.

"How about pain, then? Or how about the fact I took your son, and now I'm going to take your daughter. I'll either take her life or destroy her connection to you."

"It's okay, Chrystal." Allie looked towards her daughter. "Just trust in God. It'll be okay, Sweetheart."

"Trust in me! I'm the one who controls your fate!" Toro dug the blade into Allie's cheek.

Allie heard an ear piercing whistle and saw a flash of brilliant red and blue light and felt intense heat against her face, all in the same instant. At first she accepted that Toro had blinded her with his knife, but then Allie saw shadows against a backdrop of bursting lights. A thunderous explosion knocked her backward and left her head pounding.

"No!" Toro raised both of his massive arms in rage.

Two gunshots echoed in Allie's ears as she crashed to the floor. In slow motion, spectral images jerked in front of her like old black and white cartoons.

Allie heard a dull scream somewhere near the wall.

After another bright flash, she couldn't see anything except pure darkness with sporadic bursts of colorful light.

Seconds later, she saw a streak of orange and yellow fire shooting down the hall, followed by another deafening explosion. The windows shattered and shards of glass flashed through the room. Gunpowder-scented smoke billowed around her and Allie coughed as a thick, sulfur haze stung her eyes and throat.

Toro had vanished. Flames shot from the room across the hall through the splintered door. Blistering hot air from the blaze battered Allie.

As her eyes adjusted to the dark, Allie found Toro's knife on the floor and she grabbed it using her feet. Leaning forward, she brought the duct tape that bound her wrists against the razor sharp blade and sliced it.

She stood up and ran to where Chrystal had been standing.

Her daughter lay on the ground moaning. Next to her, Jess' lifeless eyes stared at the ceiling and blood dripped from her mouth and chest.

Allie could hear the flames clawing at the heavy wood of the house.

"Chrystal!" Allie held out her hand to her daughter. She raised her voice to be heard over the roar. "We've got to go!"

Chrystal turned over and opened her eyes. "Mom?"

Allie used the knife to slash the tape from her daughter's wrists and ankles. She helped Chrystal to her feet and they made their way out of the dark room and towards the stairs.

Allie could see the path to freedom at the end of the corridor.

Toro bounded into the hallway and towered over them; his shadow extinguished all the light and his immense body left no room for escape.

"I've still got to take care of you two. Druden demands it."

"You've failed and I've got to get out of here. You're blocking our way."

Toro pulled a pistol from behind his back. He aimed at Allie's chest and a small red dot of light appeared over her heart.

Allie draped her arms around Chrystal's shaking shoulders and pulled her close. "I took you for a knife-man, Bull. That gun puts one of us at a huge disadvantage."

"Too bad for you. I win!"

"No. You lose!"

Allie's foot whipped around and knocked the gun from his hand. Toro's eyes opened wide as she planted the same foot squarely in his chest and launched him down the stairs. He landed a foot beyond the last step, crashing onto the mahogany floors.

"Let's get out of here, Sweetheart!" Allie took Chrystal's hand. The flames roared and the ceiling crashed to the floor behind them.

"How did you learn to do that, Mom?"

"I don't know." Allie strained to see through the dense smoke and blinding flames. "I've always been able to fight. I can't tell if there's a way out through the fire at the bottom of the stairs. Can you see anything?"

"I just see fire everywhere. We can't get out!" Chrystal covered her mouth and coughed.

"There's always the window. I've done that before."

"Is anybody in here?" Allie could barely hear the voice above the din from the splintering wood and howling fire, but the beam of light from his flashlight cut through the smoke.

"We're coming down the stairs! Is it clear?" Allie coughed violently. "My daughter is hurt!"

"It's clear at the bottom! Get down here, now! The fire's closing in!"

"Let's go, Honey." Allie embraced Chrystal and they barreled down the stairs.

Allie hit the floor and rolled. She heard the thump of running footsteps and a policeman appeared through the smoke and flames. "I'm Officer Mitchell. We've got to get you all out of here! This place is an inferno. That stupid pyromaniac shot fireworks through the windows. Is anybody else here?" Mitchell guided Allie and Chrystal to a window.

"Jess Bergman is dead on the second floor. Toro shot her. I just kicked him down the stairs. I don't know where he is now."

"That must have been him running for the back door. You're Allie Parsons?"

"Yes, and this is Chrystal Parsons."

"They kidnapped you?" He motioned to the window frame. "Careful, there's still shards of glass in this window."

"Yes." Allie eased through the shattered window frame. "Toro and Jess Bergman kidnapped us both."

"Careful. Careful!" Mitchell helped them through the broken window. "I guess that guy was right. I didn't believe him."

The fresh air felt like cool pool water on a hot day to Allie. Chrystal took a deep breath and collapsed. Mitchell cradled her limp body and carried her to his squad car.

Andrew sat handcuffed in the backseat of the cruiser.

"Are you okay?" Mitchell gave Chrystal a gentle shake.

Allie felt Chrystal's wrist for a pulse and checked her breathing. Chrystal opened her eyes.

"She's okay. I assume an ambulance is coming."

Just as Allie spoke, she heard sirens.

Chrystal smiled.

CHAPTER ONE HUNDRED
PRESENT DAY

"So, you remembered those fireworks. The ones I wouldn't let you carry in my car?" Allie adjusted the framed picture of Chrystal that sat on her large new desk in Dr. Mann's former office.

"Yeah, sorry about the close call." Andrew sat on the edge of her desk looking out at the Tampa skyline. "Honestly, I didn't know what else to do. And you're right, those things are dangerous." He turned to look at Allie.

"But I've never been so happy to see a fireworks show in my life!" Allie ran her fingers along the sutures in her right cheek.

"I bet! I aimed as best I could at the windows guessing the trajectories, but those rockets have a mind of their own once they're launched. That policeman freaked out, but he said a fire was a reason to enter the house, so I had to come up with a fire, fast."

"Quick thinking. At that point, anything would have been less dangerous than the situation we were in."

"How's Chrystal?"

Allie felt her phone vibrate. She checked the message and saw Duncan's name. "Oh, uhm." She put the phone back in her pocket. "She's recovering. It's more emotional than physical. She's learned how deep evil can extend. You have to fight it. When you stop fighting it, you've lost."

"She's not going to New York, then?"

"Mom and I talked and..." Allie took a deep breath. "We've reached an accord. Chrystal will spend the last two weeks of July with her."

Andrew pursed his lips and nodded. "It's a start."

"Like a New Year's day egg."

"What?"

Allie laughed and shook her head. "It's something Pug used to say."

"How's he doing?"

"He called me and apologized...sort of, anyway. He said..." Allie squinted and clenched her teeth. "He said his Meemaw told him his brains were as good as his wings."

"Meaning...?" Andrew furrowed his brow.

"It took me a second, too. I think he's implying he has neither."

"Oh!" Andrew nodded. "I get it."

"But I think his department is bumping him back up the ladder since Toro was knocked off the continent."

"Did you speak up for him?"

"I'd never admit that."

"A good word from you looks like it might carry some weight. You're doing well at the morgue." Andrew motioned with his arms spread wide.

"Dr. Mann's old office." Allie rolled her eyes and sighed. "With some new furniture. Hard to believe, right? It's a relief to be back in the program."

"They reinstated you pretty quickly." Andrew crossed his arms and nodded towards her posh space. "And in style."

"I think Dr. Silas is afraid I'm going to sue. I just got a call from her secretary."

Allie paused, glanced around, then leaned towards him and whispered. "I think they're going to give me a research fellowship. It means some extra income."

"Wow!" Andrew smiled. "Are you going to sue?"

"Of course not." Allie shrugged and tried to suppress a grin.

"Are you sure? Because Mr. Maxwell would really go after them."

"No. That's crazy. But..."

"But they don't need to know."

"Exactly."

"So, Toro is gone. They never caught him, though."

"Nope." Allie lifted her mug from the large desk and sipped her coffee. "Jess' body came through here but they're still looking for Bull. I saw the images of him taken from surveillance cameras running away from the house towards a neighbor's dock. And the neighbor's boat was stolen."

"What about Isaac?"

"They never found the yacht. My guess is that Bull reached Isaac using the stolen boat they sailed away."

"He's still rich. You can hide for a long time if you have enough money."

"I'm hoping he disappears far away with that Druden person, whoever that is. They can organize their uprising somewhere else."

"I hope so, too! So, anyway, I've got to head out, but--" Andrew stood up and leaned towards the door.

"Uhm, Andrew." Allie cleared her throat and looked down at her hands. She took a deep breath and sat back in Dr. Mann's large, leather chair.

"Before you go, thanks. Uhm." She swallowed. "Yeah, anyway, I owe you big time. You've done so much for me. Actually, you've been wonderful to both of us, Chrystal and I. Actually, so I was wondering--"

Andrew closed his eyes and raised both hands. "Stop! I'm your friend, Allie. We're buds."

"But, Andrew--" She rubbed her cheeks and bowed her head.

"I've got to run back to my lab. How about dinner tonight? We'll call it even."

She exhaled and pulled her hands from her face. "I'll be back in my room by 6:00. Will that do?"

"Can Chrystal come?"

"I think so...actually, yeah, of course. She can take a break from her homework."

"Alright!" Andrew beamed. "See you, Allie."

She waved and watched as he bounced down the hall towards the elevator. If she left the morgue by 5 o'clock, she'd still have time to stop by Virgil's house and check on him. Either the break from chemo or the news of Toro's defeat had energized Virgil, because for the past week he was back to his old self.

As soon Andrew stepped out of sight, Allie plucked the phone from her pocket and scrolled through her messages. Duncan wanted to meet for dinner on Saturday.

It might be okay. She waited a moment then texted back "Maybe". She paused again and added, "Have you heard of someone called Druden?"

A few seconds later, his text appeared.

"I need to talk to you. Druden=an Irish demon. Also something else. Marco will save us a table. Can you meet me?"

Marco. She closed her eyes. Allie shook her head and stared at the recently framed snapshot of Chrystal.

Well, one more trip to the Columbia wouldn't hurt.

Allie sighed and typed, "Yes."

She was still smiling when Dr. Silas' secretary buzzed in on the intercom.

"Dr. Parsons?"

"Yes." Allie pulled a file from her desk and opened it.

"When I got here this morning I found something for you."

"I love presents!" Allie flipped through the first few pages of the file.

"Me, too. But this is a message. Very small and handwritten."

Allie froze. "Don't tell me..."

"It's a note."

ACKNOWLEDGMENTS

I am indebted to the many friends, co-workers and family, who were instrumental in the completion of this book. Many thanks to the staff of **Carolinas Medical Center-NorthEast** in Concord, NC and **Carolinas Medical Center- University** in Charlotte. I am inspired every day by each of you, from the women and men in Environmental Services who cheerfully wish me a good day, to the nursing staff who place the well-being and health of their patients above all else. With this team, I feel confident that **CMC-NE** and **CMC-University** provide the best care anywhere.

Thanks to Diane Black, RN, Cheryl Smith, RN, Bobbie Wilkerson, RN and Natalie Browning, RN. Not only are these ladies wonderful nurses and dedicated professionals, but they are also exceptional book critics and bibliophiles. They logged countless hours reading a very rough manuscript and provided invaluable insight and suggestions. And thanks to Ryan Struble of Elon College who has a keen eye for editing. Thanks to Pam Heaton for all she has done and thanks to my publicist, Cindy Campbell.

Thanks to Kay Craven for sharing her immense knowledge of literature and offering many ideas on how this book could be improved. She is an exceptional teacher and I learned so much from her. I am grateful to Jen Fromke for generously sharing tips and lessons learned from experience and providing pearls of wisdom about the craft of writing. Check out her short story 'Special Delivery' and her novel A Familiar Shore which will be rereleased with her new novel.

I am indebted to Martin and Norma Downing who introduced me to Lee Troup, my very knowledgeable and wonderfully skilled editor. I am very fortunate to have had the opportunity to work with him and Anita and to benefit from their experiences and talent. Any grammatical errors or misspellings are mine. Sadly, Lee passed away before he could see this novel published, and I'm forever indebted for all he taught me.

My sister, Elisabeth Ball, was vital to this process and I appreciate her patience and the hours she spent reviewing this work. I hope to return the favor someday.

Thanks to my children Emily and Mary Grace who endured years of serving as a long-suffering audience and sounding board.

Finally, I want to thank my wife, Marcie. I hope one day, I will develop enough skill as a writer to convey how much she means to me and to adequately express my admiration of her courage, her intelligence, her kindness, her honesty and her love of life, learning and literature.

Made in the USA
Charleston, SC
17 June 2015